WOLF AT THE GATES

A GRIPPING STORY OF LOYALTY, SACRIFICE, AND THE
BATTLE FOR ROME

THE SERTORIUS SCROLLS
BOOK SEVEN

VINCENT B. DAVIS II

For Mila.

Thank you for making me laugh even on the hardest days. I doubt I'll ever be able to write a character as funny as you. You bring so much joy to our family. I am so grateful that I get to love you like my own. Don't forget us when you grow up and become famous!

THE SERTORIUS SCROLLS
READING ORDER

Although this book can be read and enjoyed on its own, The Sertorius Scrolls series is intended to be read in chronological order:

A NOTE TO THE READER

To help immerse you in the world of Ancient Rome, *Wolf at the Gates* uses the Roman dating system, occasional Latin terms, and authentic historical names. A full glossary, a list and guide for all characters, and an explanation on the Roman calendar are available at the end of this book.

For more companion materials to enhance your reading experience, as well as downloadable full-color maps, Roman family trees, and more, please visit www.vincentbdavisii.com or scan the QR code below.

INTRODUCTION

I write this from my winter quarters fortifications outside Saguntum. It's been ten long years since Sulla marched his troops against Rome, as I last recounted, and the Republic hasn't experienced a day of peace since then.

Yet, while I prepare my troops for the snows to melt and battles to return, I have been in the strangest company. These past few days, I've shared wine and broke bread with several sailors who've returned from a voyage to the west.

They are pirates by trade, but one wouldn't believe that to see them now. For pirates—like soldiers—plunder and destroy. Yet rather than trinkets and jewels, these men returned from their voyage with nothing but smiles on their faces and stories to tell.

They speak of an island they discovered. What began as an expedition of conquest, resulted in finding a treasure they couldn't have imagined.

With wine on their lips and a glimmer in their eyes, they recollected what they discovered on the "Blessed Isles" as they described them.

A gentle breeze drifts through constantly, carrying with it moderate, nourishing rains. Each morning, a soft dew settles over the earth, leaving the fields lush and fertile. They tell me the soil is so bountiful, the island's people eat their fill without toil. Even a middling farmer like me, they say, could reap a generous harvest. Most remarkably, they swear no blood has ever soaked this land nor iron scarred it.

The winters are moderate, requiring no animal furs or wool cloaks. Each season comes and goes as temperately as the last, with barely a perceivable shift to indicate the passage of time.

It's as if life stands still in the Blessed Isles, they tell me. Despite the lack of cities or forums, senate houses or theaters, the locals gather daily for wine and song, and to share their harvest. None bring swords or daggers to their congregations. They have no reason to distrust the intentions of their fellows. The inhabitants were never taught to fear one another.

The sailors illustrated their point by telling how the locals greeted them. Reeking of the sea, with weapons drawn at the ready, they descended onto the Blessed Isles as pirates but were welcomed as guests. When they tearfully departed, they were merely sailors.

They all agreed—swore even—that this was the Elysian Fields celebrated in the legends of Homer.

I'm skeptical by nature; life made me that way. A land without warfare is more difficult for a Roman to comprehend than flying horses or a snake-haired woman who turns men into stone. But in the quiet moments I find in camp, I imagine it.

I have ships. I could take those closest to me and sail there, leaving war and bloodshed behind me.

When first the thought occurred to me, I thrust it away at once. If such a place really existed, I refused to tarnish it. I wouldn't expose these isles to the bloodshed that ever stains my hands no matter what lengths I take to wash them. But, perhaps with enough time, the Blessed Isles could even cleanse me. Perhaps I could bury my sword deep in that fruitful soil and never draw it again. Perhaps I could learn to trust my fellow man and stop looking over my shoulder and sleeping with a dagger under my pillow.

And then, after a lifetime of toil and strife, I would be at peace.

But this would mean abandoning my people, not only those who serve me here in Hispania but those who remain loyal to me in Rome. It means abandoning even those who detest me and my efforts but suffer under the yoke of tyranny regardless.

It means abandoning Rome herself, the Rome of my fathers.

I cannot go.

So, I will fight on. In another life I may have called the Blessed Isles my home, but in this one I will continue serving Rome until I have restored the Republic or give my life in the effort.

Now I return to the story at hand, as Sulla's forces stormed Rome, so that I may explain how I ended up here: drinking wine with sailors and dreaming about a life of peace I'll never know.

Quintus Sertorius
676 Ab Urbe Condita

PART I: FUGITIVUS

"This was the beginning in Rome of civil bloodshed, and of the license of the sword. From this time on, right was crushed by might, the most powerful now took precedence in the state, the disputes of citizens which were once healed by amicable agreements were now settled by arms, and wars were now begun not for good cause but for what profit there was in them."
— Velleius Paterculus, Roman History Book II, 3.3

SCROLL I

Quintus Sertorius—The Kalends of Sextilis, 666 Ab Urb
Condita

The canopy of trees above me was a living mosaic. Sunlight
pierced through in scattered rays, painting the forest floor with
shifting patches of light and shadow.

The rustle of green and golden leaves concealed the sound of
my movement. A layer of fallen needles muffled my footfall
even further. My prey remained unaware of my presence,
though I couldn't afford to move much closer.

My belly grumbled. I'd eaten nothing but bread harder than
my shield since I set off on this hunt two days before.

I hoped Barca fared better. We split up to increase our odds of
success, but it was easy to get lost in these woodlands. I wasn't
certain where we were, as we stayed off the roads to avoid
passing armies, but it was somewhere in the wilds near Reata.

I reached back to my quiver and pulled out an arrow. The
feathers brushed away dirt from my fingers as I notched it.

The buck moved gracefully, each of its steps deliberate and
careful as it approached the small stream. White smoke billowed

from his nose with each soft snort. The muscles in his body rippled beneath his tawny brown coat. Yet, despite this beast's imposing nature, I envied his calmness.

He stamped the riverbank to test its integrity before dipping his muzzle to drink.

I pulled my bowstring taut. The buck's ears twitched as he picked up the sound of forest, but he hadn't heard me, or he'd have disappeared already.

He was at least two hundred paces away. Not a hard shot, at least by my father's measure, but I wasn't the hunter I once was. My depth perception changed when I lost my eye over a decade prior. I could easily miss the shot if I didn't measure my breathing properly. And I couldn't afford to miss.

Since we fled Rome, we'd been staying near a small town in the heart of Italy. I ushered my wife, daughter, and mother from the city before Sulla's victory was complete. We helped many others escape as well, but soon we separated and went our own way. Barca, the once-famous gladiator and now-famous *lanista*, traveled with us, along with three of his gladiators. We had nearly a dozen mouths to feed. Perhaps the locals would have helped, but they had their own troubles, and I wanted to remain anonymous.

One could never know what Sulla would do now that the city was his, but nothing to my benefit. For years he'd tried to bribe me to support him. When that failed, he threatened me. In the end, he enlisted my son, Gavius, to serve in his legions. He expected me to play my role while he held the power of life and death over my son, and he was almost right. But when he marched on Rome, I had no choice but to resist him. And I would have fought to my death . . . until I saw Gavius. I watched my son slay Romans in the forum. And it broke me.

Now Rome belonged to Sulla.

I couldn't reveal my identity to anyone. And I couldn't miss this shot. I had to return with my prize or hunger would do Sulla's work for him.

I wished I didn't need to kill this deer. Nature was better with him in it. But my wife and daughter were far more precious than any stag. I would spare nothing for them.

With my breathing slowed, I began my count. On my next exhale, I would release the arrow, and the buck would feed us for days. My heart slowed; I centered my breath.

The buck cried out. One sharp screech of protest. The beast collapsed into the creek. The thud reverberated throughout the forest. But I still held onto my arrow.

I eased the tension on my bowstring and slunk back against an ancient pine for cover.

Perhaps I'd simply crossed paths with Barca, though I didn't know how. This was untamed land, and I hadn't expected to see anything but my prey.

I peeked around the tree and spotted four men emerging from the shadows, moving swiftly toward the buck.

"Not a bad shot, Opimius," one of them said.

"Not bad? I could be shooting in tournaments you know. Look, I got him right in the neck."

"Even a blind Vestal Virgin could make that shot with this favorable wind. Do it again, and I'll buy you a jug of garum."

We were in Samnite territory, yet these men spoke Latin rather than Oscan. They weren't locals. They were Roman, and their accents indicated they hailed from one of the more opulent hills like the Palatine or the Caelian.

What would bring them here of all places?

"One more shot for garum, and if I hit two more, you'll let me bed Aemilia. Do we have a deal?"

One of them threw a punch at the other and they laughed.

"Let's move. Sun's going to set soon. I'm ready for a hot bath and some wine."

"As you wish. But I killed the deer, so you carry."

"Me? Why? Should be Caelius."

"It's going to take two of us. Find a branch to tie him up."

"Weakling. What do you think a man like Quintus Sertorius will do when he gets his hands on a pup like you?"

The hair on the back of my neck bristled. I pushed myself closer to the tree.

They searched around the creek bed, likely looking for a branch strong enough to support the buck's carcass.

They mumbled among themselves for a moment, and I couldn't understand them until one said, "They say he walked right into the Cimbri fortifications, challenged any man to single combat, and slew hundreds by himself."

"I met a cattle drover in the Forum the other day who said he fought with Sertorius at Arausio. Said he took a spear through the eye and then swam across the violent river with all his armor on."

Despite the fabrications, it was clear they were talking about me. There was no other Quintus Sertorius I was aware of, but certainly none who escaped the Battle of Arausio or swam the Rhone after losing an eye. In reality, it was a slinger's rock, not a spear.

They were looking for me. I couldn't know their intentions, but I could only assume the worst.

None of them looked particularly imposing. I may not have slain hundreds of Cimbri, but I could defeat the four of them.

But what would that solve? Someone sent them. I had my guess, but I needed to know for certain. Killing them would solve nothing but encourage my predator to send more men the next time. If I only had myself to look out for, I would have slain them and waited to ambush whoever else came next. But my first duty was to protect my family, and recklessness would only put them in more danger.

"Lies. Myths. Notice all of that started spreading around like a fire in the Subura when he was running for tribune? Just made up stories to get him elected, and even that failed."

More lies. It seems there was a great deal of conversation about me in Rome, but little of it was true.

A few of them laughed.

"Still, I wouldn't want to fight him alone," one said. "I heard he's a giant."

One hunter found a stick. They dragged the buck inland, its noble eyes staring up blankly at the canopy of trees. Then, they bound his hooves around the branch with strips of cloth.

"Bah! He's no giant. No taller than you or me," the archer said. "Saw him speaking in the Forum once."

"Strong though. He could split your head in two, Opimius."

"He's never going to have a chance now, is he? I'm going to put an arrow through his neck just like our friend here."

I expected more laughter to follow, but everything grew silent.

One of them stood taller than the rest, and it was he who approached the archer and put a finger in his chest.

"No. You won't," he said. "Sulla said alive. You want to shoot Sertorius in the knee? Go ahead. But if you kill him and I miss out on joining Sulla's conquest of Pontus because of it, I'll put an arrow through *your* neck."

There it was. I'd been right in my suspicions.

Lucius Cornelius Sulla, the Roman general who led his legions against his own city and conquered it, now wanted me dragged before him in chains.

I wasn't surprised. I led the resistance against his invasion, but even if he didn't know that, Sulla now had the power to eliminate the threat I posed to him. The only question was what method he intended to use. Execution? Assassination? Would he force me to support him, serve in his legions, advocate for his laws in the senate and on the rostra?

Regardless, he didn't want me captured to invite me to one of his symposiums. I would avoid capture at all costs.

"I hear you, Septus," the archer said. "It was just talk."

Once the large man was satisfied, he stepped away and they resumed their work binding the deer.

"Let's go," Septus said. "I'm starving and I want to get drunk. We'll resume our hunt tomorrow."

"For more deer or for Quintus Sertorius?" another asked.

"What do you think? Sulla will sail for Greece soon, and we can't join him unless we find that one-eyed wastrel."

"Sulla said his family's with him. What do we do with them?"

The large hunter answered, "We kill Barca and his gladiators. If his wife and child are with him . . ." He seemed to consider it.

"I heard she used to be a slave."

I ground my teeth to remain silent.

"What kind of man marries a slave?"

They laughed.

"Well, she should be used to chains. We can sell her."

"I heard she's beautiful. I might keep her myself," the large hunter said.

"Can we have a go first?" the archer said.

I clenched my bow with white-knuckled fists, the rough wood biting into my palms as I battled the impulse to move, to roar, to kill.

"Only nature to sell his sprout too."

"Some would pay a fortune to own a senator's daughter."

I waged a war in my mind and commanded myself to remain still. It required every bit of education in stoic self-restraint I'd ever received. I couldn't resist much longer.

Mercifully, they began to move away.

"Let's share a drink and discuss all the things we'll buy with our new fortunes."

They hurled the bound deer onto their shoulders and walked away, the sound of their banter fading into the rustle of the forest.

It would take me a day of hard running to get back to my family. Hopefully, Barca would return with something more from his excursion than news of imminent threat. Either way, we needed to keep moving.

SCROLL II

GAVIUS SERTORIUS—ONE day after the Kalends of Sextilis, 666 Ab Urbe Condita

The rock beneath me felt unstable, unreliable, like it might crumble any moment and send me tumbling to my death. I looked for something to hold onto but found nothing. Just Sulla, Lucullus, and me . . . and the accused man on his knees before us.

My ears buzzed, and it wasn't the murmur of the crowd. They were totally silent. My vision tunneled, but I wasn't in the sewers, I was on the Tarpeian Rock, overlooking the Roman Forum.

The city stretched out before us. I stared forward to steel my nerves, where the crowds blended into one solid mass of spectators. All of Rome was watching now, and they wouldn't tolerate any signs of weakness.

There must have been ten thousand citizens gathered, maybe more. Not many fled after we captured the city. Once we extinguished the fires, the bloodshed stopped. We didn't want to fight Romans. If they hadn't resisted, we would have spared them all.

That blood was on the hands of the man knelt before me. He started the bloodshed to begin with and then led the resistance, sending waves of citizens against us despite their inability to fight. Now, justice would be served.

Sulla wore his breastplate and helmet as if he were riding into another fight. No Roman general had ever worn his battle armor within the sacred city limits, as far as I'm aware, nor had it ever been necessary.

The consul stepped forward to the ledge, totally unconcerned about the rock's integrity and unafraid of falling. I summoned up some courage and nodded to Lucullus. We took a step forward and dragged Sulpicius between us.

A muted gasp spread throughout the city as the people caught sight of the tribune for the first time. I expected them to chant for his death the moment they laid eyes on him, but the crowd remained silent. We'd already exterminated his followers, so I knew no one would plead for his life.

Sulla began, "Citizens of Rome. It is a grim day." His voice rose like a war trumpet, his words carrying through the Forum and echoing in the Temple of Saturn and in the Curia Hostilia. "One hundred and twenty years have passed since Rome has used this rock. But there has never been a traitor more deserving of this fate than the man knelt beside me."

I pushed the tribune onto his stomach and placed my boot on his back. His toga was torn, disheveled, and covered in the blood of his battered lips and broken nose, and now the dirt of the traitor's rock. Sulla wanted Sulpicius to wear his Patrician's toga for his execution, even if he'd abandoned the nobility's cause when he fomented his insurrection.

Sulpicius mumbled something under his breath, as he had been since we dragged him from the carcer for his execution. Perhaps it was a prayer for some god to deliver him, but I assumed he was cursing me for my impudence, for laying hands on my superior. Arrogant men remain that way unto death. I applied more pressure with my boot until the breath was driven from his lungs.

"This man brought death and destruction upon Rome," Sulla said. "Many of you blame me. I understand. No general of the Republic has ever led legions against the city. But I swore an oath to defend Rome from her enemies. I don't care where those enemies were born, what family they come from, or what friends they have in the senate. If someone means to do harm to my city, they will die."

I stepped away from the tribune as Sulla grabbed a fistful of his long, curly hair and brought him to the edge.

Sulpicius grunted as he struggled against Sulla's might. But the opulent life of a rapacious tribune offered him nothing with which to resist Sulla's battle-won ferocity. The consul didn't even need Lucullus and me to contain him.

Sulla's voice was a lion's when he shouted, "Look at the city you betrayed!"

"I betrayed nothing. I betrayed nothing," Sulpicius said. But his cracking voice was little more than an airless whisper. Only we could hear it there atop the rock.

"Your greed and ambition brought Rome to bloodshed. Swords in the Forum!"

Mixed within the crowd, thousands of our legionaries stood and watched. The irony wasn't lost to me. It was Sulla—it was us —who led troops here. But Sulpicius left us no other choice. He remained the catalyst for all this chaos.

"Say something!" Sulla bellowed.

The people had been silent before, but now I could hear nothing but wind flapping through the banners atop the Capitolium and rustling through the cypress trees along the Via Sacra.

"I am giving you what no man in your position deserves: an opportunity to address the people you betrayed."

Sulpicius remained silent. He was known for his stirring, rabble-rousing oratory. Perhaps he'd simply run out of words.

He seemed to stare out over the Forum, his gaze settling on temples dedicated to gods who wouldn't come to his rescue.

The tribune cleared his throat. He raised his right hand as if he was about to give a speech on the Rostra rather than the Tarpeian Rock, and Sulla allowed it.

"I am a tribune of the Roman Republic!" Parched and rasping from his time in the carcer, his voice should have failed—yet it rose, steady and commanding, echoing through the Forum. "I am endowed with *sacrosanctitas*. No one may lay hands on me! The only man guilty of treason is the one who led his troops here, spreading fire and blood like ashes and wine at a funeral, the man who now accosts a Roman tribune."

I looked at Lucullus. Should we stop him? No one should be able to spread these lies about our consul before the Roman people. Why hadn't Sulla already tossed him from the ledge to the fate he deserved?

Lucullus shook his head. Sulla allowed this, and he must have had his reasons. He always did.

"I defended Rome with you. I beg you. They cannot defeat all of us if we stand *together*. *Defend* me now! *Resist* this tyrant, and help me *save* the Republic," Sulpicius pled.

He continued to use the rhetorical tricks he was famous for, emphasizing particular words of his smooth, crisp Latin. But the effects of his charm had worn off.

No one in the crowd moved.

Sulpicius knew his fate was sealed. That he would still try at this late hour just proved the depth of his arrogance. Sulla gave him a chance to repent of his crimes against the state and to die honorably, but he refused it.

Sulla brandished his dagger. He stepped in front of the accused, and for a moment, I couldn't see what he was doing. Moments later, Sulpicius was writhing on the rock as blood spouted and poured from his mouth, forever staining his toga. As a guttural cry escaped the tribune, Sulla turned to the people with Sulpicius's tongue in hand.

"This spread lies and corruption throughout the Republic. Those days are over, Romans. We are free of this demagogue forever."

He tossed the severed, bloody, wet tongue from the rock.

The crowd gasped and reeled back for a moment, until several young men and boys rushed from their families to take their turns stomping on the very thing that had brought Rome so much harm.

Sulpicius writhed and clutched at his face with his soft senator's hands. His eyes, wild and panicked as a boar caught in a snare, looked at Lucullus and me as if we could offer aid, as if we *would.*

I met his gaze and watched his panic with no remorse in my heart. Tribune or not, sacrosanctity or not, this is what he deserved. There should be no mercy for traitors. The pitiful man before me caused all this. It was his fault Roman blood stained my gladius.

Sulla knelt and dried his dagger on the tribune's toga before rising and saying, "I invoke the ancient accusation of *perduellio* on this man. High treason. Our ancestors threw traitors from the Tarpeian Rock. They burned the home of the accused. No one can mourn his death, including his wife and children."

As Sulla spoke those words, Lucullus gave me a nod. We wrapped up Sulpicius's flailing arms and dragged him to the ledge, his feet scraping against the stone as he resisted with the last of his strength.

The dizzying drop from the ledge might have turned my stomach—if the stench hadn't hit me first. The opulent tribune had soiled himself.

"Publius Sulpicius Rufus, you are condemned to death for *perduellio.* For betraying this Republic and the people who elected you." Sulla took him from us and held him over the edge. The tribune's feet dangled above death. "Your belongings are now property of the state. Mention of your name is now illegal. Drinking in your honor, celebrating the day of your birth, or acknowledging your accomplishments is now a crime. None shall don black to mourn you, none shall pray to the gods for your safe passage or place coins on your eyes. You will not be cremated or buried. You will be remembered only as a warning for those who might emulate you."

With that, Sulla released his grip. Sulpicius seemed to linger in the air, as if suspended. He would have screamed if he was able, but only muffled gargling escaped him before his body cracked into the stone of the Forum. The sound echoed throughout the Eternal City.

Despite my fear of heights and my distrust of the rock's strength, curiosity forced me to peek over the ledge.

I'd seen nothing quite like it. Each of his limbs appeared to be broken and twisted in different directions. The snapped, jagged edges of bone were stark white against the scarlet pool growing beneath him.

"Hear me now, Romans!" Sulla cut through the silence. "The extent of my mercy for men such as this is a swift death. A worse fate exists for the next man to threaten this great Republic."

The legionaries of Sulla's Fist shouted out in unison. Their swords sliced from scabbards in a sharp song of victory. They bashed them against their shields and glared at the mob until everyone joined them in celebration.

I stepped forward and raised my sword to the sky. "All hail Imperator Lucius Cornelius Sulla!"

"Hail!"

"Hail!"

At first, only the legionaries joined me, but soon every Roman man present cried out for the consul. The chanting continued long after I sheathed my sword and stepped back.

Eventually Sulla turned to us, and only then did his eyes reflect the joy of his victory.

"Give the people time to see the body up close. Each of them," Sulla said. "Let this image burn itself into the memory of every Roman for generations to come."

"Understood, consul," Lucullus said.

"Sever the head. Have the men place it on a pike by the steps of the senate house," he said. "Fix the mouth open. I want the people to see that the power of his voice is gone. Forever."

We nodded.

"Oh, and nail his tongue to the doors of the Curia. An effective reminder for any senator inspired by his example."

"As you command, consul," I said.

Fixing Roman heads on pikes, nailing a tongue to the doors of the senate house. I should be horrified. Revolted. The thought *should* revolt me, but I felt nothing. Nothing.

We saluted, and he returned the gesture.

As Sulla departed, Lucullus called after him.

"Should we leave the . . . the rest of his body where it is?"

Sulla considered it. "No. Throw it in the river," he said, "with the rest of them."

The gods forbid burying or burning the dead within city limits. Endless rows of ancestral tombs flanked every road to Rome, a solemn reminder of the city's enduring glory to all who came or went.

Sulpicius wouldn't receive burial or commemoration, but we still needed to take him outside the city limits. Lucullus knew an area near the Field of Mars where the Tiber slowed to an eddy, where water lilies usually found their rest and gave frogs a pad to croak from. Here foxes came and slept under the shade of poplars and took refreshment from the river.

Lucullus described the location with nostalgia in his eyes, as if he visited the spot as a boy and cherished his memory of the place. It seemed odd that he would sully the location with a headless corpse, but I didn't object.

The wagon rumbled and creaked as Lucullus ordered the legionary driver to stop.

"This is it?" I asked.

I looked out over the Tiber. Nothing Lucullus described was present. No water lilies, no frogs or tadpoles, no nestled foxes. The eddy was overflowing with corpses now. Hundreds, perhaps even thousands. The bodies of those who served Sulpicius, his "anti-senate" as he had called them. Our legionaries gathered them up and threw them in the river, but they had floated downstream and ended up here, bobbing alongside one another, each as bloodless and bloated as the next.

"This is it. Get him down," Lucullus directed the legionaries. "Toss him in."

I gazed down at the corpses and felt no grief, no horror—only shame. Not for taking Rome nor the part I played in their deaths but for the emptiness inside me. The dead deserved some feeling, some flicker of pity. But I had none to give. No sorrow. No sympathy. Just silence where my soul should have spoken.

War made my father a better man. After all he'd seen and done, he seemed to cherish life more deeply—man or beast, weak or strong, Roman or foreign. Some would call him weak. I didn't. I envied him.

Maybe war doesn't change us—it reveals us. Through it, I discovered in myself a profoundly cold heart. I could see this—and I disliked it—but I didn't know how to become someone else. I didn't know how to become like my father. Can a man truly change who he is?

The legionaries grabbed the headless corpse of the rapacious tribune. The hands which once made grand oratorical gestures to sway the mob, now swayed lifelessly beneath him.

"Seems like a waste of good water," I said.

"We don't drink from the Tiber," Lucullus said as he watched the legionaries move closer to the river. "It's too dirty to drink."

"Probably because we keep dumping the bodies of traitors here."

Lucullus chuckled. There hadn't been many reasons for us to laugh since the battle for Rome began. It was a welcome sound, but an unfamiliar one. Even Lucullus seemed surprised when the laughter escaped him.

He sobered. "It serves a purpose," he said. "Everyone should be reminded. Every few decades this sort of thing is required. It's like blood purging. It wards off the wolves at our door for a time, until we need to do it again."

The legionaries reached the bank.

I looked at Lucullus with confusion. "Perhaps my history is hazy, but I don't believe a legion has ever marched on Rome before. Certainly not in my lifetime."

He rested his hands on the hilt of his gladius and nodded. "Correct. We're the first. But this . . ." he gestured to the legionaries who now began to swing the corpse and count toward the release. "This has happened before, and it will happen again. It's the way of the world."

The legionaries released what remained of Sulpicius with a grunt. His body plunked into the water, sank down, rose back up, and floated to a halt beside his followers. It would remain there until the birds and fish picked it clean.

"I hope Sulla can change the way of the world, then," I said. "He can restore the Republic, or make it better than it ever was. Perhaps we can go more than a few decades without bloodshed. A century perhaps?"

No one trusted in Sulla's leadership more than Lucullus, but he didn't affirm my hopes. He was older and more experienced than I was. I'd fought in as many battles as him, but he'd experienced life in Rome far more than myself. Before joining the legion, he was an accomplished lawyer and a talented orator. His experience hardened him against hope.

"Good work, boys," Lucullus said. "Now, if we can only—"

Shouting downstream interrupted him, coarse insults that could only belong to some of our legionaries, followed by a high-pitched scream, and curses to make even a soldier gasp.

For the first time since we captured the city, my gut twisted with rage. I'd seen what legionaries did to the women of captured cities. I'd taken part. But we were in Rome. If one of our men laid a hand on a single Roman woman, I would cut off that hand and feed it to him. If Sulla let me, I'd crucify him.

I ran toward the noise.

"Gavius, it's no use," Lucullus shouted. "Not our concern, we need to return to the Forum."

"Go on ahead," I shouted back.

I knew he wouldn't, but no one pursued or tried to stop me either.

I crested a low hill and pushed through a tangle of overgrown oleander, their blossoms brushing against my arms. Just beyond, I saw the source of the commotion.

Two low-ranking legionaries were struggling to pull a woman away from the river.

She fought back against them like a wild boar, her thin limbs kicking and flailing against them.

"What's the meaning of this?" I said.

They didn't hear me. One of them wrapped her up from behind and told her to be still. She lashed out, pummeling him with both fists, then bit down hard on his thumb like a cornered wolf—ravenous, defiant, and unafraid to draw blood. The legionary cried out as the woman threw an elbow back into his nose.

"Come 'ere, little wench!" the other legionary shouted.

"Stop!" I used my battlefield voice, and both legionaries stood to attention, though one nursed his bloody thumb.

The woman didn't seem to hear me. She returned to the riverbank.

Closer now, I could see she was wearing the black cloth of mourning, a shabby old rag stretched over a small, thin frame. Wild, curly brown hair fell in tangled locks on her bare shoulders.

"What's the meaning of this?" I centered myself before them.

"Tribune, this . . . this *lupa* is mourning."

"And?"

They looked confused.

"It's illegal, sir. Consul's orders."

The other legionary pointed to the river. "That's 'er man there. She's in black on his account."

I took a deep breath and looked at the mourning woman. I could smell the wine on her breath even from a distance. She was mumbling to herself. When she looked over her shoulder in my direction, I could see that black streaks stained her face. Makeup of a Roman matron smeared by tears shed for someone she loved.

"I'll handle this," I said.

They exchanged a look. I'm sure their orders were to stop this exact behavior, perhaps from Sulla himself. But he was not here, and I was. I outranked them, and I wouldn't hesitate to pull rank if they didn't obey.

"Go. Move on. There are others to accost," I said. "You're released."

One of them stepped closer to me. "You'll . . . you'll tell the commander we did well?" he asked.

I asked them for name and rank and promised to put in a good word for them. That's what they were really concerned about in the end; it's what we all cared about. If Sulla was pleased with us, nothing else mattered.

When they departed, I stepped closer to the riverbank and took off my helmet. The woman still barely noticed me. She fixed her gaze on one corpse in the water, surrounded by several others. It was impossible to make out any of the dead man's features. I have no idea how the woman could have identified her husband in this condition. They all looked the same to me.

"What's your name, ma'am?" I asked.

She mumbled louder but did not address me.

"What's your name?" I said again, louder now.

She whipped her head in my direction, her eyes wide, blood-shot, and violent.

"What's it matter?"

I changed the subject. "Who was he to you?" I tucked my helmet under my armor, a sign of peace, I suppose. When she didn't answer, I continued, "A father? Brother? Lover?"

"He *was* my husband." Her words slurred together, but the bitterness contained within each of them was still tangible. "Now he's nothing. Now he's a corpse. Now he's food for the fish."

I hung my head. Still, no sympathy stirred in my breast for the dead man, but I felt for the drunk woman before me. Her husband's suffering was over, but her suffering was only beginning.

"I'm sorry for your loss, ma'am," I said.

She snarled. If she could have maintained her balance long enough to strike me, she would have. "What loss?" she said. "I'm not even allowed to mourn him. According to your commander, he was a traitor and a bastard. I should be thank"—she hiccupped—"thanking you for killing him. For taking our property and our home. For leaving me widowed and homeless, every shred of dignity gone."

Her anger dissipated into sadness. She wept into her dirty hands.

"No matter what he was, he was your husband. You have every right to your pain." I stepped closer to her. "Sulla may have rules about the color garment we're all allowed to wear, but no one can legislate what you feel in your heart."

"Well, those impudent"—another hiccup—"impudent bastards certainly feel different. They put their filthy pleb hands on me." She spoke to herself now as much as to me as her gaze shifted back to the body of her husband.

"It won't happen again," I said. "But I think you should leave. Others may not be as considerate," I said.

She stepped to the riverbank and let her toes dangle over the ledge. "Oh, I mean to leave," she said.

I exhaled. "Surely, you don't mean to jump," I said. "The water isn't but four feet deep. You'll do nothing but get yourself wet."

She said to herself, "I will embrace my husband and hold on to him until the water consumes me. His arms will hold me until my lungs are filled and . . ."

I could not hear the rest.

"What of your children?" I said.

She shook her head. "None. Only the two of us," she whispered. "And it shall stay that way forever."

"If you have no children, who will honor him once you are gone? Who will carry on his memory, remember his name?"

"Your consul made that illegal. I can't even celebrate his birthday."

I repeated what I said previously. "No one can legislate what's in your heart."

Every word I spoke felt foolish. Why did I care? I could walk away and let the traitor's wife join him in death. Rome would go on as if they never existed.

"He who has an army can legislate anything he wants," she said. "Including who lives and who dies."

I gritted my teeth. I sympathized with her and didn't want to see her take the next step, even if it was into shallow water. But I wouldn't tolerate anyone slandering Sulla.

"Sulla is not a tyrant," I said. "As Consul of Rome, he liberated the city from those who threatened our Republic. Now that the city is secure, we will establish order, and life in the city will return to normal."

She slipped a hand into the folds of her black stola and drew out a crumpled scroll, its seal broken and the parchment soft from wear.

"Are all you legionaries so half-witted?" Her words stung

despite the slur. "Or perhaps your commander simply doesn't trust you?"

I clenched my fists. Before speaking, I ensured my voice remained calm. "What do you have there?" I asked.

"One of the bastards who came after my husband left this behind. See—" She paused to compose herself. "Antonius got to him first. He didn't have time to read the list before the other assassins got him . . ."

"Give it to me," I said.

She continued, "They were in a rush to kill the next man," she said. "They must have all had lists of their own. But I found this one." She held it aloft but didn't offer it to me.

"Ma'am, give me the list."

"Surely, you have your own," she said. She unfurled the scroll, and her squinted eyes darted around it.

I heard of no lists. I was one of Sulla's most trusted officers, a high-ranking tribune and in his confidence. The drunk widow had to be lying. We were supposed to track down Sulpicius and Marius and no one else. The only others who needed to die were those who resisted us. Marius evaded capture, but his colleague was now headless upstream.

"There are no lists from Sulla." I shook my head. "Perhaps your husband made some enemies. Gambling debts? Money lenders? What about an old personal feud? Perhaps someone took advantage of the city's chaos."

She laughed. It was the piercing, bitter laugh of a heartbroken woman.

"Fortunate for your man, then," she said. "All the men on this list are Sulla's enemies."

She tossed the scroll at my feet.

As I hurried to pick it up, she said, "I won't jump. Not today. I'm too angry to die."

This was the rambling of a drunken widow. Most of our legionaries, including Lucullus, would have wanted her apprehended and punished for these false accusations, but they meant nothing.

I scanned the names on the list. If these were Sulla's enemies, he'd never mentioned them to me, apart from Gaius Marius and Sulpicius, whose names were atop the list.

The rest were men I'd never heard of, though each had approximate estate sizes beside them and a list of official capacities and accomplishments. These were important men.

"You never told me your name, widow," I said. "I'm Gavius."

She didn't answer. Instead, she turned and walked away, leaving the list of names in my hand.

I was about to throw the scroll in the river with the bodies, but the final name caught my attention. I'd missed it the first time, but now the words burned in my eyes.

Barca - freedman, former gladiator, and lanista. *Aided and abetted the traitors in resistance and in escape.*

I recalled the man from my father's home. Quintus Sertorius wasn't on the list, but his dear friend was. I told myself the list was fake, a widow's attempt at revenge or an ambitious man's misguided attempt to gain Sulla's favor. But I needed to know for sure. I needed to talk to my commander.

SCROLL III

Quintus Sertorius—One day after the Kalends of Sextilis, 666 Ab Urbe Condita

I traveled through the night. There was no time for sleep, no time for delay. Sulla's men could be on my heels, in the shadows trailing behind my every step.

The sun peeked over the hills in the east when I arrived on the second day, with stinging eyes and mud clinging to my tunic.

I didn't want to leave this quaint village. It was neither friendly nor inviting, but it was the perfect location for those in hiding like us. The village didn't even have a name, so far as I could tell. Only a few dozen others lived here, mostly old men. Not a single person had introduced themselves to us, no one had inquired why a young family and five gladiators had arrived here. Most of the locals kept their gaze averted and hoods drawn to cover their eyes. I wondered how many of them were refugees as well. Perhaps they were traitors, to Rome or to the rebels, in the civil war. Perhaps they were criminals or deserters from decades before. Regardless, their discretion was a boon.

I navigated through the rows of old homes, each constructed

long ago. Little stonework was used to build them, as the original settlers likely had no slave labor and had to do everything themselves. Strong, weathered lumber kept the homes erect through the summer storms and centuries of strife throughout Italy.

Even though each home looked nearly identical, I knew which one we rented. I'd stood watch by the shuttered window for two nights in a row before my hunt and became quite familiar with the immediate surroundings.

I entered to find my mother, wife, and daughter in the sparsely furnished room with only a single gladiator to protect them.

The young warrior was already in fighting kit, as if preparing to enter the arena any moment. As the morning sunlight poured into the shack, he jumped to his feet and readied himself to protect my family.

He exhaled with relief when he recognized my face.

"I was ready to lunge, my lord," he said, the accent of his homeland still prevalent despite several years in Roman captivity.

"I'm glad you didn't," I said. "That sword looks sharp."

A dozen gladiators came with Barca to Rome. Only four remained. The other three must have been hunting with Barca. The man left behind was a young gladiator from Thrace. From what Barca told me, he served in the Roman auxiliary before being enslaved. He and his father were both shackled and sold. Barca purchased them both and kept them together, though the young man's father did not survive the sands for long. Few of the spectators in Capua's arena knew of Thrace or found their culture particularly interesting, so the story became that this young man was a Spartan, an illegitimate heir to King Leonidas himself. Barca called him Spartacus.

"I worried you would not return," he said. "The *lanista* is still hunting."

"I hope he's delayed by the weight of a dozen bucks." I

patted his shoulder as a sign of gratitude for protecting my family. "I did not fare so well."

I looked beyond him to where Arrea sat on a simple cot with our daughter swaddled in her arms.

Shame overcame me. No infant should endure this; no wife should be required to flee for safety while her ankles remain swollen from childbearing. I had failed them. The least I could have done was return with something savory to eat, and even in this I fell short.

"How is she?" I sat down on the bed beside them.

My mother said, "She's finally asleep." Rhea sat in the corner on a simple, backless chair, stitching the toga I'd torn in our escape. "Each night she looked for you. She doesn't sleep so well without the strength of your arms."

My mother was a plain speaker. She did not intend to guilt me with her words, but I felt the weight of it, regardless.

"Hopefully she will not have to go without it for some time," I said.

Arrea leaned over, carefully so as not to disturb Toria from her sleep and allowed me to kiss her cheek.

I lingered there and smelled her hair, trying to draw strength from her presence for what I now had to tell them.

Waiting would only make it harder.

"I discovered other hunters on my path. I overheard them talking . . ."

"They were looking for you," mother said.

Despite living with my father in Nursia and having no experience in the cutthroat world of Roman politics, Rhea had a keen understanding of the situation we were in.

I nodded.

"Why?" Arrea did all she could to maintain her composure, to keep the fear from shimmering in her eyes or tugging at her lips.

"It seems they are following orders from Sulla." I looked away.

Lucius Cornelius Sulla had been a contentious name in our home for many years. He'd befriended Arrea and sent men to protect her and Gavius while I was fighting in Greece. She came to respect him and never understood my level of disdain and distrust for the man.

I had no intention of gloating; there was nothing to celebrate about what Sulla had done. I could tell the words hurt Arrea, but they also stirred in her heart the famous anger of a Gallic woman. Sulla deceived her. But there was nothing to be ashamed of, Sulla charmed many in Rome. Only now was the Republic waking up to his schemes and machinations.

"We cannot delay," I said. "I have no reason to believe those men followed me, but I expect there are others looking for us."

"Why does he want you alive?" mother asked.

A good question. The men specified taking me to Sulla alive. Since escaping the burning Eternal City, I'd received little in the way of news, but I expected there were many others Sulla ordered to be killed on sight.

"Sulla has always . . ." I considered how to phrase my words. "He has desired my service. My compliance. He's tried flattery and he's tried threats, and neither have worked."

Mother sighed and set down the half-stitched toga. "And now he can demand it at sword point." She rose and walked to our side.

Spartacus stepped closer to us. "Give me the order, *Dominus*. Send me to Rome and I'll bring you his head."

I smiled. I admired the young man's courage and recklessness. I wouldn't order the assassination of a Roman consul, even one such as Sulla. But even if I did, Spartacus wouldn't get within a hundred leagues of him. Sulla's legionaries filled the city. His officers—including my son—were always by his side.

"Let's prepare the wagons," mother said. She leaned over to kiss Toria and left a lingering hand of comfort on Arrea's shoulder before leading the way toward the exit.

Before my eyes adjusted to the light, I heard a sword ripping from its scabbard.

I brandished my own and looked to find the cause, but by then, my mother was already wrapped up and had a sword at her throat.

"Let her go," I said.

I'd witnessed the deaths of many friends in battle throughout my life. I'd seen conspiracies against the Republic, rebellions from our allies, and watched Roman legions march into the Eternal City. But nothing enraged me like seeing my mother in danger. I would kill this man without hesitation or mercy.

"It was remarkably easy to find you, Quintus Sertorius," the assassin said.

He was older, perhaps around my mother's age. His skin was weathered and darkened by years in the sun and wrinkled by hardship. But there was a youthful radiance in his eyes. Whoever he was, the years hadn't dulled him—he stood as battle-ready as any young man.

"Your quarrel is with me," I said. "Release her and we can address this as men."

The hair on the back of my neck stood up. I could feel others approaching behind me. I focused my mind. I heard three sets of feet shuffling through the village dirt.

While keeping the assassin in my gaze, I turned my head toward the doorway, where Spartacus remained with his sword drawn, ready to strike. I shook my head. One wrong move could get my mother killed.

The man looked perplexed. "I have no quarrel with you," he said. "I'm here to help you."

"You'll forgive me if I have trouble believing that. The tip of your sword is resting on my mother's throat."

He released her as if he hadn't realized what he was doing.

I reached out and pulled her to my side. Once I knew she was safe, once I assessed how many companions this man had with him, I would kill them all before they threatened my family further.

"Apologies," he said. "I'm a fan of the theater and haven't visited the Forum in many years. Is it decades now?" He shrugged. "I create my own theatrics."

"Go inside, Mother," I said.

She did not move. I stole a glance at Rhea. Her gaze was fixed on the man who'd accosted her, but with no sign of rage or fear. Her heart didn't even seem to stir, her breath was slow and deliberate.

I'd never known her to read philosophy the way my father and I had, but she was a greater stoic than anyone I'd ever met.

"You must be Rhea," the man said, with a deep, exaggerated bow. "You're as lovely as he always described you."

I wouldn't have been surprised for this assailant to know me. That he knew my mother's name was cause for concern. I instinctively stepped closer to her, careful to place myself between her and the assailant, while remaining prepared for an attack from the men behind us.

Spartacus's patience waned. The door burst open, and he charged out. His battle roar echoed throughout the quiet village as he lunged at the assailant, his Thracian falx sword poised overhead.

The older man's eye reflected no surprise or concern. He easily grabbed the young gladiator's wrist to halt the attack, kicked Spartacus's knee and spun him around.

"Oi! Calm down, lad. I mean you no harm. I'm a friend of her husband's."

He could have easily brought his sword to Spartacus's neck and taken his life, but he only pushed him forward to the dirt.

My mind raced like a cavalry stampede. What was this man talking about? None of this made sense.

"You're mistaken," I said. "My father is dead, and she's never remarried."

Before responding, the man leaned over and extended a hand, one the young gladiator didn't accept.

"Aye. It would be impossible to love another after Proculus Sertorius," he said.

My father's name coming from this man's lips burned in my ears.

"He is dead, yes," he said. "And I was sad to hear it. But he would have died on a ship in the Balearic Isles if it wasn't for me."

He lifted his chin, proud of the memory which seemed to flood over him.

I still maintained my focus, but for the first time, I eased the grip on my sword.

"You served with my father?"

He met my gaze. "Aye, lad," he said. "Good warrior, even better man. The only thing he spoke of more than Zeno and the other stoics was your family. He was the best friend I ever had." Either he was indeed an actor worthy of the Forum, or he was experiencing genuine nostalgia.

I was naturally skeptical, due to the man's arrival, but there was no way one of Sulla's henchmen could know so much about my father.

"Why did you threaten his wife then?" I asked.

Rhea's eyes remained on him, intensely curious but they revealed nothing else.

He bowed his head toward my mother. "I apologize, Domina," he said. "I hope I didn't frighten you." He turned his attention to me again, with sober eyes and a serious frown. "But I needed you to understand the position you're in. I needed you to listen to me."

I sheathed my sword. "I'm listening."

He stepped closer but maintained a respectful distance. "If I found you this easily, others will find you soon enough." He craned his head to look through one of the shuddered windows.

He was letting me know he was aware of Arrea and my child, and he didn't need to say it for me to understand.

"We were just planning our departure," my mother said. "What are you suggesting?"

He gestured to the men behind us, and they finally stepped out to reveal themselves.

They were all well armored, with swords, daggers, and bows bound strategically across their person for quick access. They weren't legionaries, but they were clearly professional warriors.

"Let me lead you somewhere safe. I have around two thousand fighting men in my employ, camped near Arretium. It's quite expensive to hire us, but I won't charge you a single denarius for shelter. None of Sulla's henchmen can threaten you or your family in my camp."

I considered the situation I was in, the situation Rome was in. A consul had marched troops against our city, crossing the sacred pomerium under arms. Rome had never seen such sacrilege. He set fire to our buildings and slaughtered any who resisted him. Now, he sent out assassins to kill or capture Roman citizens.

Part of me wanted to leave Italy. Take my family and sail far away, find somewhere safe and free of war. Perhaps there was another sleepy village like this one far enough away not to be drawn into every war, somewhere I could start anew and forget the man I was.

But I couldn't. I'd defeated many of Rome's enemies in my life, but none posed a threat as serious as Lucius Cornelius Sulla. My duty was to resist him. But first, I needed to ensure my family was safe.

"I don't even know your name," I said.

Two thousand armed men would be enough to protect my family. But first, I needed to determine whether I could trust this man.

"Where are my manners? My name is Fabius. Not part of the patrician family, mind you, but I still think it's a good name," he said. "I'm happy to answer all your questions, but time is of the essence."

"These men of yours . . . who are they?" Rhea asked.

He flashed a charming smile. "You'll meet them in time," he said. "If you mean to accept my offer, prepare your things. We should set out before midday."

I shook my head. "We are waiting on the return of a friend. I won't leave without him."

Fabius frowned. "I'm afraid you're placing your family in grave danger by remaining any longer."

"Sertorius!" the shout echoed throughout the small village. "Sertorius!" There was rage in the cry.

We prepared ourselves. Fabius and his followers gathered around us and brandished their weapons. I suddenly felt grateful for their presence, a swift change from their arrival.

The shouts came from the far end of the village.

I was relieved to find Barca and his gladiators rather than Sulla's assassins. Any relief I might have felt vanished when I noticed the blood dripping from his tunic and the bound captive limping behind him.

"It appears your friend has brought a guest," Fabius said. "If the locals didn't know your identity before, they do now."

I hurried toward them, anxious to address this and be done with it before we drew more unwanted attention to ourselves.

"What's happened?" I asked.

Barca was out of breath, a rare sight for a man so resilient.

"We discovered enemies in the woods. This man, this toad . . ." He reached back and grabbed a fistful of the captive's hair. Barca forced him to kneel at my feet. "He gave them information. They look for us, and he tells them we are here."

My heart beat like a war drum. "What became of them?"

Barca gestured to the blood covering him. "Dead. But more will come."

"It's time to leave this place," I said.

"And we must be quick about it, since everyone within miles now knows your name," Fabius said.

Barca grunted. "Who is this?"

"You may call me Fabius."

Barca looked at me and asked again. "Who?"

"He was a friend of my father."

"That does not explain why he is here."

Barca's eyes twitched between Fabius and the men behind him, who remained silent. There was something predatory that fell over him when he felt threatened or when those he cared about were threatened. It reminded me of the lions featured in the arena whenever magistrates could afford them.

"I heard about the bounty on Quintus Sertorius. I feared it was the son of a man I once loved dearly. Seeing that to be the case, I am here to help."

"And how did you hear this? Did this man tell you?" Barca jerked back the head of the wincing captive.

"That's actually quite simple. I was offered a great sum of money if I could track him down," said Fabius. "And, if I wasn't such a poor gambler, I'd wager you're the other man I was to look for. The freed gladiator of some repute and glory? Now a *lanista* and a man wanted for aiding the flight of Rome's enemies. Barca."

My friend's jaw twitched. "I am Barca."

His muscles rippled as he waited to see if that confirmation would cause Fabius and his men to lunge. Everyone remained still, save the captive who shivered and wept.

"And what did you tell them when this offer was made to you?" I asked. "Could you have led them here?"

Fabius smiled. "No one follows me, young master. I'm well-known for the quality of my work."

"You did not answer the first question," Barca said.

"Quite right. I did the only logical thing," he said. "I requested a downpayment for my services, and then set out to warn him," Fabius said.

Barca snarled. "Sertorius, this man is a bounty hunter and a liar. He cannot be trusted," he said. "He will lead us into a cage."

Fabius shook his head. "Bollocks! I could've sprung a trap if I had a mind to. I did not come alone, if you hadn't noticed," he said. "And I'm a mercenary captain by trade, not a bounty hunter."

I gave Barca a cautious nod. "It's true. If he meant to capture us, he had every opportunity."

Fabius bowed. "Now, if you'll allow me to lead you to safety, let's leave this place."

The tension in Barca's shoulders eased, but the scowl on his lips and the skepticism in his eyes remained apparent.

"What about him?" My mother pointed to the captive.

Barca replied. "I say we kill him before he puts us in more danger."

"I'm just a farmer," the captive said.

"Dead men can't speak," Fabius said. "I would suggest we learn what we can, and then we'll be on our way."

Fabius was right. We needed to know exactly what his orders were, and what Sulla's hunters already knew.

Barca attempted to intimidate the informant. His eyes flicked back and forth as he tried to think of more potent threats, but he was a gladiator. Barca's expertise was in shedding blood, not threatening it.

"Let me kill him, Sertorius," Barca said after repeated failures.

"Dead men cannot speak," Fabius said again.

"He will speak when he feels my dagger above his heart."

I took a different approach and knelt. "What's your name?" I asked the trembling captive.

He summoned up some courage and spit in my face. As I wiped the glob of saliva from my cheek, Barca pulled the man's head back by his hair and struck him.

"Enough, Barca," I said. "The man is clearly frightened. If

you tell us what you know, we will let you go without inflicting further injuries, to your body or to your honor."

The captive was short and thin, with a face that appeared youthful in some ways and weathered by decades in others. Despite his frame, he had the strong shoulders of a farmer and the tanned skin of someone who worked in the fields each day. This man wasn't part of some secretive network of spies for Sulla. How he became part of all this was precisely what I wanted to know.

"They know where I live. They know the names of my daughters. I'm not saying another word," the captive said.

"We are here, and they are not," Fabius said casually. "We must face our problems as they present themselves. Yes, your complicity here may put you at risk in the future, but if you don't answer our questions now, you won't live to see your beloved daughters again."

"I'm just a man." He squirmed beneath Barca's grip. "I know nothing. I'm just supposed to tell them if I saw a one-eyed Roman and a Numidian warrior coming through."

Fabius leaned closer to me. "They knew you were coming this way. I'm not surprised to hear they enlisted locals."

I had suspected this, but it was more important to know what Sulla's plans were and what information the man had already relayed to Sulla's hunters.

"You don't have a legion," the captive said.

"No," Barca consented, "but I have a sword."

He held his blade before the captive and allowed the sunlight to glimmer on his curved *khopesh*.

"The only thing standing between you and death is the nod of my friend," Barca said.

I was impressed with his use of Latin. Since he began studying with Arrea, his articulation improved each day. But regardless of his vocabulary, his words remained brutal. He meant what he said.

"I'll not tell you anything," the captive said, all but confirming he knew more than he originally suggested.

"I will carve out your eyes," Barca said. He tried to conjure up more potent threats. "I will nail . . . I will nail your tongue to a wagon wheel!"

"Go back to the deserts, your worthless whoreson!" Every time Barca pulled his hair, the captive became angrier.

Fabius looked at me. "Do you mind if I assist?"

I nodded my consent. Barca was getting nowhere with his threats, and my attempts at fairness weren't working either. Fabius could try, and then regardless of the outcome, we would depart.

Fabius flipped his dagger through the air and caught it gracefully by the hilt.

"Listen here, lads," he said. "Men are remarkable creatures. In my time, I've seen men eagerly accept death for honor, for love, for family . . ." Pine needles crunched under Fabius's boots as he stepped closer to Barca and the captive. "I've even known a few to endure unimaginable torture without uttering a groan. But there is one thing that causes all men to crumble. Something men care about more than honor, their homeland, their loved ones."

The captive watched Fabius with widening eyes. My father's old companion had yet to make a single threatening gesture, but the captive was more unnerved by his words than any of Barca's threats.

"What is this *thing* men care for?" Barca asked.

"His manhood."

The man ceased his squirming and became entirely still. Only his lips continued to tremble.

Fabius turned and addressed me, "You see, men will let the whole world burn gladly if it means keeping all their bits," he said, before returning his attention to the captive. "Listen here, lad. I'm going to geld you. My boys have been long at sea, and they've missed companionship. Tell my friends what they need to know, or I'll find you a husband."

I stepped forward, prepared to intervene. Even though this man sought to throw me and my people to the wolves, I couldn't stand by and watch this.

"Wait! Wait! The consul wants the cyclops alive," the captive cried out before I could say anything. "He wants the Numidian dead."

I stole a glance at my friend to gauge his reaction, but he revealed nothing. If he ever regretted all the sacrifices he'd made for me and my family, he'd never mentioned it.

"What does he plan to do with him?" Fabius pointed to me.

"*Gerrae*! You think they tell me that?" His eyes remained fixated on the dagger poised to make an irreversible cut. "The men who came just wanted to know when he arrived. They didn't want him harmed, at least not visibly they said. Wanted him shackled and taken to Rome. That's all I know."

"And what do *they* know? What have you already told them?" I asked.

"Are they aware he's here?" Fabius clarified.

"No," Barca said, maintaining his grip on the captive. "I slew the men he reported to."

Fabius eased the dagger forward.

"Stop!" the captive cried out. "There are others. Several. They know you're here, they know he's here. We were meeting to plan your capture. I wasn't privy to their plans, but they wanted to know your routine—when you eat, sleep, use the latrine."

I took a deep breath. "And those men you reported to didn't return," I said. "The rest will come soon."

The man nodded. "I'd expect."

No wonder the man had so bravely resisted us. He anticipated his liberation at any moment.

I almost ordered his release, but Fabius said, "There's something else. I can see it in your eyes. Speak."

He groaned but couldn't tolerate Fabius coming any closer.

"There are many searching for you two. At least one group is heading to your home . . . what is it?"

"Nursia?" I asked, my heartbeat quickening.

"That's it. If you want to avoid capture, I'd avoid returning."

"Release him," I ordered. "We must leave."

When Barca released him, the man massaged his tender scalp and scooted away from Fabius.

"When they arrive, you will tell them we've departed and have made our way for Brundisium. Do you understand?" Fabius said.

"No." I shook my head. "Don't be here when they return." I tossed a bag of coin into his lap. "Return to your daughters at once and take them to Capua. Stay there until all this is over."

He scooped up the coin and ran away.

"I'm not sure that was altogether wise, young Quintus," Fabius said.

I'd already forgotten about the captive or any threat he posed to us. My focus was entirely on Nursia.

"We will accept your offer of shelter, Fabius," I said. "But there's something we must do first. Everyone, gather your things. Let's leave this place."

SCROLL IV

Lucius Hirtuleius—Four Days Before the Nones of Sextilis, 666 Ab Urbe Condita

My foot sank into the mud up to my knee and I fell forward. The water engulfed me. I managed to wedge myself free and turned back to the others.

"This way," I said. "We need to keep moving."

I never expected to find myself wading through the salt marshes, but I didn't envision Sulla marching on Rome and naming Gaius Marius an outlaw either.

"This is ignoble! A disgrace," Marius the Younger cried out as he struggled to free himself from the muck. "Father, you are the savior of Rome. Surely your allies will rally to your cause."

There was no time for this, but Marius the Younger had continued to complain and plead with his father for the past two days. Our pursuers were close behind, and Marius was determined to sail away from Italy. In Numidia, the former consul said, he would raise an army of his retired veterans and those loyal to him for his service there. And he promised vengeance for what he now endured.

"Silence, boy," Marius grunted, the strength in his voice not at all diminished by the shame of his flight. "Unlike you, I wasn't raised in a villa. I came from the mud, boy. This is in my blood."

Despite the determination in his eyes and the command of his booming voice, Marius had never seemed so frail to me. He remained robust, his muscular shoulders and thick limbs not withered by age, but something changed in him when his former pupil marched on Rome. I'm not sure what the change was exactly, but I felt the constant need to stand by Marius and help him along, despite his protests.

I surveyed the area around us. The landscape was bleak and uninviting, even if we weren't fleeing for our lives. Gray skies loomed overhead, concealing the sun entirely, so that I couldn't even estimate the time of day. The air was thick with the smell of rotting vegetation and brackish water, some of which remained in my nostrils from the fall.

Frogs croaked nearby, waterfowl called in the distance, and insects buzzed all around us. So many mosquitoes rested on the bare flesh of my neck and arms that I'd all but given up on swatting them away. Everything else was silent, save the labored breath and whimpers of Marius the Younger, meaning our pursuers hadn't caught our trail.

But it wouldn't be long.

What would become of us if we were captured? Marius would be tried and executed. Marius the Younger would be exiled. What would Rome do with me? Not only was I abetting the escape of a man outlawed by the Republic, but I was also now a deserter.

My chest tightened as that word echoed in my mind. My grandfather would have disowned me.

But I refused to idle away in a legionary camp while Gaius Marius was chased down and persecuted. I left camp as soon as the news arrived, in search of the former consul. It only took me two days to find him, as his retinue of followers was anything but discreet. I convinced him to part ways with the others to speed up our escape and attract less attention, but we both knew hunters were close behind us.

"You're certain we're going the right way?" Marius asked.

I pushed through a tangled bunch of reeds and held them apart for Marius and his son to step through.

"No," I said. "But Aulus should return soon."

I wasn't ashamed of abandoning my post in service to Gaius Marius, but I regretted bringing Aulus along with me. He had no love of Marius, no feeling for him at all. But that's Aulus. He would endure shame and punishment to support his companions.

Before we left, I tried to talk him out of joining. The war with the Italians was all but over, I reminded him. Unlike me, he had a wife, and he could soon return to her with prestige and honor. But he refused. He would follow where I led, he said.

"Can he be trusted?" Marius the Younger asked. "Father, what if he's leading us right into a trap? We do not know this man."

Marius's son was in his mid-twenties but he spoke like a child. It confounded me that Marius the Younger inherited none of his father's toughness, strength, or intangible qualities.

Marius's reply was more to himself than his son. "I am not dying here," he said. "That is not my fate."

"What about Pompeius Strabo, father? He has a large army in Picenum, and he might yet come to your aid if you but ask him!" Marius the Younger continued. "How could any Roman refuse the man who saved the Republic from the Numidians, the Cimbri, and the Teutones?"

"Quiet," I ordered.

Marius the Younger grumbled to himself, likely displeased to take commands from a soldier like me, but his father complied so he did as well.

I focused my attention on the sounds of shaking reeds in the distance.

I gestured for father and son to crouch beside me, under the cover of reeds. Placing cupped hands around my lips, I made a bird call.

It was echoed back to me.

We continued this until the sound grew closer and closer.

I stood. "What did you find?"

Aulus drew closer, still catching his breath. Marsh mud covered him from helmet to legionary boots. Insect bites swelled his face and dotted his arms.

"Mud. Water. Reeds. A few dead fish."

Aulus was rarely seen without a smile on his face, nor heard without a witty joke at the ready, but these were absent today.

"There's no ship waiting on us, your highness," Aulus said.

His contempt for Marius was apparent, or perhaps it was for me, or simply the disastrous situation we found ourselves in. Aulus had few closely held political opinions, no allegiances to powerful families or politicians, but I suppose he disliked any man who put him in this situation.

Fortunately, Marius seemed oblivious to the edge on Aulus's words.

Marius grunted. "Flavonius will not fail me," he said. "The ship will arrive. And we will make it to Numidia."

"I'm relieved by your conviction, highness," Aulus said.

When he looked my way, I shook my head as a warning against this. Marius may be an aged, defeated, outlaw now, but he was still the Third Founder of Rome, and a six-time consul of the Republic.

"Where did he tell you we would find the ship again?" I asked.

"The salt marshes outside Minturnae," Marius the Younger answered for his father, clearly irritated at repeating himself.

The problem was that's exactly where we were and had seen no sign of a ship. No sign of anything but insects, frogs, and birds.

"A skiff will take us out to sea," Marius said. "If you're

looking for a trireme in this bog, you won't find it. That ship is waiting for us in open water."

Aulus exhaled. "I'm aware, sir. I was looking for the skiff, as you told me. But I've found nothing."

Splashing sounded in the distance. The shallow waters around us began to ripple.

"Get down," I said.

Whoever caused this disturbance wasn't close, but they moved in our direction. No one would leisurely peruse these swamps for pleasure. They were hunting for us.

I plucked a handful of reeds and distributed them.

"Beneath the water," I said. "Breathe through these."

Marius the Younger balked. "I'll not—"

His father grabbed him and forced him under.

We laid flat against the squelching mud to conceal ourselves.

I bit down on the end of a reed and tried to breathe through it. Little airflow passed through, and I was already out of breath from our journey. Panic crept in on me, but movement meant death. And not just for me, but for my friend, my hero, and his son. I prayed silently and asked the gods to give us divine resolve.

No one moved as far as I could tell, but it mattered not. They were upon us within moments. Following our tracks in the mud must have been easier to find than a boat that may or may not have existed.

"Get up!" I heard them say through the muffle of the water.

Marius stood first. His soggy toga was little more than a bundle of tattered cloth now, unflatteringly clinging to his form. Yet he stared down his pursuers defiantly despite this.

I rose next and brandished my sword. It didn't concern them. There were at least twenty men in their party, with two on horseback. A few starving legionaries, an old consul, and his impish son posed them no threat.

"That him?" one of the men on horseback asked the other.

"Doesn't look like him, does it? Too fat and old to be the man from the statues."

I could tell by their clothing and posture that the two riders were wealthy. Probably local officials who were important men in their own city.

"Is that you, Marius?" one of them said. "You the man who saved Rome from the Northern Menace?"

"Address him properly, dog!" Marius the Younger shouted.

The former consul said nothing but kept his gaze locked on the riders.

"That must be his bastard."

"I am no bastard!" Marius the Younger waded closer to them, wielding only a pointed finger as his weapon. "I am the son of Gaius Marius and Julia of the Julii Caesares. And I demand you show the proper respect."

The two riders looked at each other and exchanged a laugh. The rest of their men joined in. They were amused as much by the dastardly appearance of Marius as the arrogance of his son.

"That's them all right," one said.

The other squinted his eyes and focused his attention on Marius. "How does it feel, old man? To have been synonymous with kings and gods alike, only to die here in this bog a sad, tired, old vagabond?"

Marius didn't hesitate in his reply. "How does your first taste of real power feel? In this moment you might see a purpose to your whole meaningless existence, a chance to write yourself into history by the destruction of Rome's greatest son."

The rider snarled but didn't reply.

"Say the word, general," I said. "I will not let them take you."

Marius didn't respond, nor did he tear his gaze away from the officials, his eyes boring into them and judging their very souls.

I stole a glance at Aulus and gave him a nod to wait for my signal. He returned the gesture. This was not his fight, and I knew he would care nothing if the officials took Marius and left us there. But he would fight beside me. No matter what.

"So, who's going to do it, aye? Who's going to kill the great Gaius Marius? You?" He pointed to one official. "You? How about you, lad?" He gestured to one guard.

No one moved.

"My brother served you at Vercellae," one official said. "He spoke highly of you. Out of respect for him and the mother who bore us, I will not take your life. But he will." He gestured behind him to someone I couldn't see.

"Come, boy," the other official said.

A tall, young blond boy emerged from behind the riders, an executioner's axe in hand. He couldn't have been more than fifteen summers old, with not a hair on his chin or a wrinkle on his face. Despite his youth, he was large as a boulder and clearly strong as an ox. One swing of that axe could carve through stone.

"Do you recognize him?" one rider asked Marius. "Of course not. How could you remember one of so many thousands you enslaved after Vercellae? This one was a little runt, spared your sword only because he was too young to wield one. Isn't that right, lad?"

The boy said nothing but continued to churn his significant weight through the waters. There were tears in his eyes, and his plump lips trembled. I could not tell if he was frightened or filled with rage. Perhaps both, the two are dark horses that often ride together.

"*Tata!*" Marius the Younger ran to his father's side. "Don't let them do this." He begged with tears of his own, before turning to the officials. "Please. We are ludicrously wealthy."

The Cimbri slave boy waded closer.

Marius the Younger wept openly now, to the shame and frustration of his father. "We'll pay anything you like! You want a villa in Rome? Want to be a magistrate? When we reclaim the city, you can have whatever your heart desires!"

"General," I said calmly, "we await your orders."

I eyed the twenty men. We stood no chance against them, even with our combat experience. We would die here. But I swore an oath, not just to Rome but to Gaius Marius. He found me and brought me up from nothing. He gave me a chance when I was just an orphaned farmer's grandson. I didn't want to die, but I wouldn't hesitate to lay my life down for the tired, broken man beside me.

"Go on." Marius patted his son's back before pushing him away. The booming, commanding voice of our general was absent as he whispered, "I showed you how to live, boy. Now let me show you how to die."

Marius the Younger buried his face in muddy hands and turned away.

"General." I placed my fist over my heart.

"Tell them I died well," he said. "Don't waste your life on heroics. They aren't here for you."

He didn't bother to explain who "them" was, but he didn't have to. Gaius Marius had been living for his legacy since he was a young man, writing a line of his epitaph each day.

The former consul waded out and met the boy. The Cimbri slave towered over him. It was a remarkable sight. The conqueror of nations—a man with multiple lifetimes of victory in battle—staring up at the descendant of his vanquished enemies. And now the captive became the captor, the persecuted the persecutor.

"Go on, lad," Marius said.

Tears developed in my eyes, an uncommon sensation. I wanted to turn away like Marius the Younger, but refused to dishonor Marius in his final moments.

The Third Founder of Rome lifted his voice now, the boom of a war general echoing throughout the salt marshes. "Do it! If you deign to take the life of Rome's greatest hero, do it swiftly! Finish what your fathers could not and kill me!"

The boy trembled now, in contrast to Marius who remained calmer than the stagnant waters around us.

"I am Gaius Marius, the man who defeated your armies and enslaved your people! Gaius Marius the conqueror of Numidia, the vanquisher of the Cimbri and Teutones, the six-time consul of the greatest nation the world has ever seen. Do it!"

He offered up his neck for the killing blow. The boy raised his axe. I imagine he could barely see for the tears in his eyes.

"You look me in the eyes, boy! Let this face sear into your mind for the rest of your life, the vision of greatness before you in the moment you snuffed it out!"

The axe plunked into the water and the boy stepped away, finally allowing his tears to fall freely.

"Cannot," he said. "Cannot."

The officials lowered their heads.

"Who's it going to be then?" Marius's voice commanded, as it had on the battlefield and in the Forum.

The two officials whispered to each other.

Marius the Younger looked up, a touch of hope in his eyes despite the snot and salty tears streaming down the mud on his face.

"If someone you enslaved—someone who's people you destroyed—cannot kill you, neither can we," one official said.

His colleague added, "You indeed were a great man, Gaius Marius."

"No, I *am* a great man," Marius said. "I will stamp my foot, and legions will spring up all over the *Mare Nostrum*. I will take back my city. I will butcher the tyrant and his puppets. The people have always needed a Gaius Marius to save the city, and I'll do it again."

They offered no protest, despite how ludicrous the claims sounded from a man knee-deep in brackish water with weeds clinging to his excessive flesh and mud in his balding hair.

"We saw the boat you were looking for," one said. "About

three thousand paces that way." He pointed to the south; we had indeed been going in the wrong direction.

"I don't know where you're going, Gaius Marius, and I don't want to know," the other said. "But wherever it is, go there swiftly. Nowhere in Italy is safe for you now."

"If asked, we did not find you. Sulla's vengeance would be on us if he discovers we let you go."

Marius said nothing but kept his eyes on them until they turned away.

The officials clicked their horses to a trot, and the others trailed along after them, the Cimbri boy in the rear, still weeping.

Had I just witnessed the gods intervening? The officials didn't even mention Marius the Younger's promises. Why would they endanger themselves and give up on whatever bounty Sulla placed on his enemy's head? Because of the respect a Cimbri slave showed him?

Marius the Younger ran into his father's arms, and the former consul reluctantly embraced him. He patted his back to show the boy some comfort.

"How did you know they wouldn't kill you?" he babbled.

Marius freed himself and started south, expecting us to follow.

"I've seen my fate," he said. "And this is not where I die."

SCROLL V

QUINTUS SERTORIUS—THE Nones of Sextilis, 666 Ab Urbe Condita

Barca sent Spartacus and the other gladiators ahead on our only two horses. He instructed them to return to his *ludus* and prepare everyone for departure. Barca didn't ask Fabius's permission but made it clear his entire stable of gladiators would be joining.

The rest of us traveled by foot. The quickest path was the Via Salaria, but I knew Sulla would have men patrolling the popular roads. No, we would have to remain on paths less traveled, those only known to Sabines like my mother and me.

Our little party maintained the same formation each day. Fabius led from the front. As a captain, he claimed his sense of direction was exceptional, and by the end of the first day, I believed him. Barca remained in the back, his watchful eye always scanning the periphery and cautiously glancing behind us to ensure no one followed us in the shadows. My family and I marched in the center, along with a few of Fabius's guards.

We continued this process for six days before I recognized the landscape around us. Nursia wasn't far now. I might have taken comfort in that if not for the fear in my heart at what we might find. At least Barca's gladiators would be with us before we returned to my home, where bounty hunters might be waiting.

I shook the thought from my mind and turned to Arrea. "Would you like me to take her?" I gestured to Toria, who slept deeply in my wife's arms.

Toria would be six months old in a fortnight. She grew heavier every day, even as we grew thinner and hungrier. Arrea would've carried Toria always if she could, but I could see signs of exhaustion in her stride.

After considering my offer, she placed Toria in the cradle of my arms.

Despite our present circumstances, my daughter made me smile. The gentle plodding on this old dirt path lulled her to sleep, and she was accustomed to her father, mother, and grandmother passing her around.

I looked down at her and marveled like always. Her upper lip formed a perfect little bow, and it was always either grinning or pouting, only attuned to what went on in that little mind of hers. She'd recently developed a robust sense of humor, frequently falling into fits of uncontrollable laughter which caused us to do the same. Her eyes, now closed, were hazel like her mother's, but contained golden rings. When she looked at me, I felt a depth there I'd never expected from a babe.

"How are you faring?" I asked Arrea. "A few more hours and we'll be there. We can't tarry long, but you can rest in the shade for a watch."

Arrea stretched. Her back and hips gave her trouble on these long walks, though she rarely mentioned it.

"If she can do it, we all can." She gestured to my mother. "I'm fine, husband."

Looking at Rhea filled me with shame. Shame and anger. She was in her sixty-third year if she hadn't repeated a few along the way. She was a noble lady—not in birth but in character—and did not deserve all this. I would make things right, and I would give her the twilight years she deserved.

Fabius slowed his pace to match ours. "We should talk about what comes after gathering these gladiators."

We passed under the shade of some ancient oaks. Soon their leaves would turn and then fall, and winter would be upon us. And it would be a harsh one, I could tell from the mild nature of this Sextilis.

"There are many things we should discuss," I said.

I bobbed Toria in my arms and tucked the folds of her swaddle beneath her chin where she liked it.

"There is much I don't know about you, Fabius," I said. "Leaving that village with you was the only logical course at the time, but there is much I need to know before I trust your warriors with my family's safety."

He looked up at the trees in admiration and nodded. "I would have a lot of questions myself if an old bastard like me showed up and started making promises. Ask, and I shall answer."

Barca quickened his pace to join us. "I have one," he said. "What are you? You say you have an army, yet you are no general. You say your men were at sea, yet you are no merchant."

Fabius laughed. It was a genuine, hardy laugh, the kind that compelled others to join. "What am I? I am Fabius," he said.

"Perhaps he means your occupation," Rhea clarified.

There was no edge of accusation to her words, but my mother was a shrewd woman.

He nodded. "Understood, ma'am." He took his time before answering. He seemed more comfortable with silence than many others. "My father died before I returned from the Balearic campaign. On top of that, none of the coin I sent home arrived. The paymasters made a mistake, they said. They thought I died in battle, mixed me up with another unfortunate legionary. Before all that, I accrued considerable debts in my youth." He took a deep breath. "And the debtors came calling. I had nothing but my ancestral farmland and had no choice but to sell it. I ended up receiving my denarii but not until my debts were settled, and I had no home. So instead of behaving like a reasonable, intelligent man and buying a new farm, I purchased a ship."

Perhaps it was the gentle warmth of the midday sun or the breeze coming down from the Apennine slopes, but I found myself at peace listening to Fabius speak. He seemed intent on taking the long road to answering Barca's questions, but no one interjected. His voice was rich and melodious, carrying with it the hint of accents from all the places he'd traveled across the *Mare Nostrum*.

"I have been many things in my life, *lanista*, and few of them honorable. It's a shame I bear daily, that after knowing a man like Proculus Sertorius, I should go on to live intermittently as a pirate, a slaver, a criminal." He ran a hand through his hair. He kept it short on the sides, practical for a mercenary captain who presumably spent most of his nights sleeping under the stars but left enough on top to remind others he was once a striking figure, before life took its toll on him.

"And what are you now?" I asked.

"Most would say I'm a mercenary captain. I have roughly two thousand men under my command, and for the last ten years, we fought for hire."

I'd heard of mercenary armies in the past, but never one led by a Roman.

He seemed to know my thoughts and said, "When I returned from war, I had no home, no land, and no skills but sailing and fighting. Perhaps I should have learned a trade, but I was young and foolish. And I longed for the sea. I tasted battle on the open waters, and I wasn't ready to only experience that in memories."

"Then you should have continued serving your Republic," Barca said. "You should have returned to your own wars."

Fabius nodded. If he was insulted by Barca's comments or our questions, he didn't reveal it.

There was a touch of sadness in his eyes as he said, "After the campaign, Rome had no more use for me. They took what they could during the war and cast me aside when it was over." He turned to me to clarify. "I never blamed the Republic, you see. I blamed myself for not understanding the game we all play. I decided to play a different game, where the rules suit me better."

I didn't begrudge Fabius's choices. Many legionaries I'd served with returned from war to poverty and homelessness. I can't fault a man for forging his own path.

"And what about recently?" I asked. "I imagine feeding two thousand men is quite expensive. I assume you've been occupied as of late?"

Barca grunted. "Have you been in Italy, waiting to join the highest bidder?"

Fabius smiled. "Now, there you are wrong," he said. "We don't always join the highest bidder. We fight for the highest bidder who is *most likely to deliver* on their promises. We would have never joined the rebel cause, if that's what you mean. They were destined to fail. Besides, we've been occupied with work in the Anatolian Isles."

We exited from a tunnel of trees to see a small village in the distance. Perhaps *village* is too strong a word, as there were only three shacks there, and a few wooden barricades for sheep. Whatever it was, it lay in ruins. Dark smoke smoldered above the homes, despite the fires presumably dying out days before.

The lot of us grew silent as we passed by. Only then did I see the bodies, and the people crouched over them.

I turned their direction and almost offered my condolences, but quickly realized these individuals weren't mourning but scavenging. One cut the finger off a dead man and slipped the bronze ring into his pocket.

"I wouldn't look at them, young master," Fabius said, eyes forward.

"Surely these aren't agents of Sulla as well," Barca balked.

Fabius shook his head. "No, but they look starved, and we look tasty."

We continued as the scavengers watched us with wild eyes until they faded from view.

The sight lingered on in my mind, though, and my heart beat quicker every step we took. I wondered who was responsible, what provoked this attack, and if there were other victims along our path.

"You mentioned the Anatolian Isles," mother said, mercifully distracting us. "What fighting did you do there?"

"Protection, mostly," Fabius said. "The armies of Mithridates grow larger each day, and soon every stronghold in the east will wave his banner."

"You fought Mithridates?" I asked. I found myself eager to hear his response, for anything in the affirmative would have certainly been a lie. No mercenary army of two thousand could stand up against the King of Pontus.

He shook his head. "No. But his puppets are another matter. New warlords spawn every day it seems, content on taking cities and villages to offer him like wedding gifts. At first, we welcomed the constant stream of employment. But their power grew too strong, and we returned to Italy with fewer than we had when we arrived. I'll not go back there."

For a moment his face hardened. He remembered something that disturbed him.

"I've never seen power spread so quickly. His people think he's a god, you know? Perhaps he is." He rubbed at his face. Each crease, each line told a story marked by survival, of the harshness of living with no certainty—not even the next sunrise. "Either way, his armies will soon descend upon the Greek mainland. Corinth, Athens, and Sparta will all fall to him."

If correct, his prophecy would prove disastrous for the Republic, but my mind only fixated on one thing. Athens.

My dearest friend and mentor, Apollonius, was away on holiday there. He would have already returned to my side if it wasn't for the war in Italy, and now it seemed war would reach him there.

"What kind of conqueror is this Pontic king?" I asked.

Fabius shrugged. "It depends on the day," he said. "He enjoys the worship heaped upon him, and if he receives enough from the people of Greece, perhaps he'll show mercy. But he is capable of anything. Remind me sometime, when we're set up with a cup of wine, and I'll tell you more about how Mithrid—"

Each of us heard something in the distance. Instinctively, we all crouched. I passed Toria back to her mother and grabbed my sword.

A doe and two fawn sprang from the green overgrowth a few hundred paces ahead and disappeared on the other side of the road.

We all exhaled.

"We could've had a fine feast tonight if I'd been more prepared," Fabius lamented.

"As long as you're prepared for a fight," Barca said.

"I've never been caught unawares before," Fabius said. "I wouldn't be alive otherwise."

"My *ludus* is well stocked." Barca took the forefront now, trusting only his own eyes to scan the road before us. "If my men haven't cleaned out my granaries, we will dine well before our departure."

Despite having shoulders strong enough to bear the weight of an empire, there was a fluidity to Barca's movements, like a lion's graceful stalking as he watched for other predators on the path.

I maintained the grip on the hilt of my gladius for the remainder of our journey. We packed in closer together and prepared ourselves for the worst, but soon the high walls of Barca's gladiatorial school rose above us.

Odd . . . I usually heard Barca's *ludus* before seeing it. The clang of iron, the reverberation of clashing shields, and a constant chorus of shouts, grunts, taunts, and curses. But it was silent now. The gates were open, and no gladiators stood watch.

Barca sprinted ahead before I could suggest caution.

I unsheathed my sword and charged after him.

"Oi! Slow down," Fabius shouted after us.

"Stay with my family," I ordered.

I joined Barca on the training sands, half-expecting to find burnt bodies like we'd passed on our way.

But there was nothing. No sign of life, no sign of death.

"Spartacus!" Barca bellowed. "Crixus!"

Only echoes along the corridors of his empty *ludus* responded to him.

Barca searched everywhere for his men. He was so preoccupied trying to find someone he didn't notice the proclamation. Someone nailed the scroll to a training dummy at the center of the training arena.

"Barca," I said, and repeated myself until he heard me between his shouts.

He joined me and we read the letter together.

By order of the Senate and People of Rome,

This ludus *and adjoining villa are hereby property of the Roman Republic. The* lanista *known as Barca is an outlaw and enemy of the state, accused and convicted of aiding and abetting criminal resistance to the lawful Consul of Rome and in helping known enemies of the state escape justice.*

All gladiators in this ludus *have been sold to Lentulus Batiatus of the Capuan circuit. All household* servi *will be sold at auction on the Ides of Sextilis, in the Capuan forum. This* ludus *and adjoining villa will be sold at auction three days before the Nones of September.*

The Senate and People of Rome
One day before the Nones of Sextilis, 666 Ab Urbe Condita

For all his ferocity, and despite the sea's worth of blood he'd spilt, Barca's heart somehow remained unspoiled and pure, a child's heart buried beneath muscle and scar tissue.

He'd spent his life building this school, and now he'd lost it. But I knew the loss of his friends grieved him even more. Barca had no family of his own except those warriors.

"It was signed yesterday morning," I broke the silence.

Fabius and my family joined behind us.

"Whether it was one magistrate who arrived, or a legion of thousands, I would have butchered them all," Barca whispered.

I placed a hand on his rocky shoulder. "I'm truly sorry, *amice*. I grieve with you."

Guilt weighed down my chest and compressed my breath. This was my fault.

Barca must have rued the day I called him friend, the day he invited me to a simple dinner at his *ludus*. He was an ascending, ambitious, and ludicrously wealthy *lanista* then. Now he was an impoverished, homeless fugitive. An enemy of Rome.

"We must go," he said.

I expected him to say we should track down the gladiatorial caravan and liberate his men. How could I refuse him that after all he'd sacrificed for me?

Instead, he said, "If they've been here, they've been to your home."

That he could think of my family in a moment like this revealed the quality of his character even further, but he was right.

Guilty thoughts and self-admonishments for Barca's loss would keep me awake for weeks but now was not the time for it.

I burst from the empty *ludus* as quickly as we entered and trusted my feet to guide me home despite my occupied mind, and I trusted the others to follow.

My farm was little more than ashes and piles of burnt timber. Only the mosaic floors remained, covered in char and stained by the elements they were meant to be sheltered from.

My farm wouldn't have brought nearly as much coin as Barca's *ludus*, or perhaps they would have auctioned it as well. Or maybe Sulla wanted to make a point. Regardless, his agents left nothing of my home.

We made special memories there, like the first days of Toria's life. And I'd worked diligently on that farmstead to create the life I wanted for my family.

But surprisingly, I felt little pain sifting through the charred remains of my home. My wife and daughter were safe behind me, and as long as they remained safe, I would recover.

"Why would they even do this? What's their intention?" Arrea stared at the wreckage and blinked to keep her eyes dry.

"They wouldn't have done this without command," I said. "Sulla wants to make a point."

Fabius sighed. "I'm sorry this has happened, young master. If there's nothing you can salvage, though, we should be away. These embers are still warm, and we have no idea where they are or how many their party contains."

Mother came to my side and wrapped my hand up in hers. "This isn't right, my boy," she said.

I looked at my wife and daughter. "No. No it isn't," I said. "But Fabius is right. There's nothing left for us here. We have a long journey ahead of us. No sense in delaying to lament what's already gone."

Mother nodded. "I have six horses at the house. Should we mount up before departing?"

My family wouldn't have to make the entire journey by foot. I almost shouted out my gratitude, but I squeezed her hand and nodded instead.

We set off at once for my mother's domus, wasting no time. This was the home of my ancestors, where generations of Sertorii had lived, worked, and raised their families. This is where my father taught me philosophy by candlelight late into the night. Where my brother and I played with stick swords and dreamed of grandeur and glory. Where my mother rocked me back to sleep when I couldn't bear alone the weight of childhood nightmares.

I hadn't realized how much this place meant to me. I rarely thought of it, but somewhere deep inside, I'd always believed I would return—that when the legion no longer needed me, I would return here with my wife and children, raise horses, attempt to work the field again, and spoil my grandchildren on the land that raised me.

Whatever future I'd imagined here was gone, buried beneath ash and rubble. Claiming Barca's *ludus* and burning down my farm wasn't enough for Sulla's agents. They set the torch to my mother's home too.

Rhea fell to her knees and covered her mouth. I caught her and held her as she ran her hands through the soil our bare feet knew so well.

I knew she was thinking not of the building itself but of all those precious things contained within. Every memento, every physical reminder of my father here on earth was consumed by the flames.

We were all too exhausted and famished to weep, but Toria cried out for us. Her shrill cries carried over the burning property, as if she could feel the pain of our ancestors.

"I empathize with you, my lady," Fabius knelt beside us.

My mother couldn't form words.

I was about to respond for her, but a passing thought stole my attention. I recalled the initial purpose of our visit here.

The horses. The stables.

I released my mother and sprinted past the house, out toward the paddocks where we trained horses in my youth, praying to any god that would listen.

We had two stables. One for our stallions and another for the mares. The former was little more than a pile of rubble, but the lack of death's stench confirmed the horses were stolen rather than consumed. I made for the mares, who we kept away from the training ground so the stallions didn't misbehave when they were in heat.

I could have collapsed from relief when I saw the mares' stables still standing. Perhaps they'd simply run out of torches, but I prayed the horses were still within.

We needed them for our retreat, but more than that, my old warhorse Sura had been here when all this happened.

I'd always planned to return, to reclaim and ride her and her only for the rest of my days, but I hadn't had the chance. If something happened to her because of my negligence, I wouldn't be able to forgive myself, and my growing list of guilt could only grow so much longer.

I burst into the wood stables. The heavy stale scent of hay and horses still lingered, but even before my eye adjusted to the dark, I knew there were no horses within. I found my way to Sura's stall and hung my head by her empty post.

How could I find her? I contemplated numerous strategies, but I knew whoever had taken her and my mother's other horses would likely sell them at auction. She could be halfway across Italy now.

I heard something in the distance, and it wasn't my family. I craned my head and listened closer. It was a neigh. Then a snort. Horses!

The light engulfed me as I rushed back out, running blindly in the direction of the noise.

Over the crest of a small, overgrown hill, I found them.

Six steeds in all. Despite the matted conditions of her coat, I recognized Sura's silver-gray mane. I could never forget it.

"My girl," I said. "Sura."

She lifted her head weakly, her ears flicking toward me. Sura blinked slowly, but there was recognition in her eyes. She took a tentative step forward, her hooves dragging through the damp soil.

Tears pricked at my eye, tears I rarely shed for fallen comrades or for anything else, but for this animal who'd given me so much, who'd carried me through the Battle of Vercellae and Aquae Sextiae. For the steed who'd saved my life.

I reached out but allowed her to make the first approach. I expected her to be angry with my long absence. But to my infinite relief, she nuzzled my palm.

"I'm here now, girl," I comforted her.

She rested her head on my shoulder and nestled against me, unaware of her strength and nearly knocking me over.

I smiled until I ran my hands over her sides, where the sharp ridges of bones beneath her coat were growing prominent. She was hungry, her and the others.

Sulla's agents must have killed or scared off mother's stable boys.

I vowed to give her a king's feast as soon as I could.

"Horses!" Fabius led everyone to me.

"They're safe," I said. "Hungry, but unharmed, thank the gods."

"We will need them," Barca said stoically. "We must ride far from here."

"Yes," I said. "We can discuss the plan on the road, but we shouldn't tarry any longer." I noticed a small metal chest in Rhea's arms. It was charred, but otherwise undamaged. "What do you have there?"

For a moment, she smiled as if she wasn't standing in the rubble of her only home.

"Your father's," she said. "He wrote a lot during his time with the legion."

"Incessantly," Fabius chuckled. "While the rest of us rolled bones, he recorded history."

"I haven't been able to read them since your father's death, but I'm glad they survived. Perhaps it can help me remember his voice."

I'm glad Sulla's agents didn't destroy the metal chest. It

meant nothing to them, I'm sure, but it meant everything to us. It was all we had left of him now.

I embraced mother and took the chest from her. As I tied it down on the back of a mare, I said, "Mother, I had no idea you were stabling so many mares."

Her expression shifted in an instant—eyes widening, lips parting—as the weight of realization settled over her.

"We only had two," Rhea said.

I exchanged a look with Barca and Fabius. We all knew this meant the other horses belonged to our pursuers. They were still here.

"Mount up," I said. "We're leaving."

I helped Arrea climb onto Sura's back.

The sound of laughter filled the hills.

It was unfamiliar to everyone but me. I heard the same laughter in the woods a few days before.

Barca helped my mother onto another steed. Fabius, who'd held Toria to give us a break, now passed her up to my wife.

"Go. Now," I said. "Ride for Spoletium and don't look back. We will join you."

"But that's west, toward Rome," my mother said.

"Any other direction leads us into Picentes territory, and that's even worse." I sighed. "There is no other way."

"Quintus . . ." Arrea said. All she could do was shake her head.

"Go."

Fabius said, "If we take their horses, they can't catch us. Perhaps we should leave with your family?"

"But they can follow our tracks, and we must rest eventually," I said. "Mother, lead the way." I slapped the mare's hind end, and she shot off before anyone changed my mind. My wife and daughter galloped off in pursuit.

"We don't know how many there are," Fabius said.

"Five," I said, but didn't bother to explain myself.

"I suppose we can handle them then, a few cutthroats and horse thieves they are."

I led the way toward the laughter. My muscles coiled as they did before battle.

I yearned for vengeance. I yearned to punish these transgressors for what they'd taken from me, and more importantly, what they'd taken from people I love. The desire for vengeance is a weakness. An indulgence. I tried to remind myself—this was about our safety, not personal gratification.

We reached a vantage point, and I could see the five hunters walking up two hundred paces below. They'd reached a steep path, and they kept their gaze on the earth beneath them to keep their footing. They carried another deer.

Could they fight as well as they could hunt?

"Which one of you will do it?" I shouted.

They dropped the carcass. A thud reverberated through the hillside.

They looked up at us with confusion in their eyes and whispered among themselves.

"I hear you plan to capture Quintus Sertorius and kill his friend. Well, here we are. Come and claim us."

The big one led the way, eager for the promised reward, and the others followed.

They squared off from us about a hundred paces away, the perfect range for an archer.

I kept my gaze on the half-strung bow and said, "Who has the skill to fight me? Opimius? You, Caelius? Or what about Septus?"

Hearing their names caused a wave of panic to spread among them. The big fellow, the one they called Septus before, was the only one to keep his nerve.

"We're not here to kill you, Quintus Sertorius. We have great respect for you," he said. He spoke peacefully, but his eyes were violent.

"You're not? Your friend Opimius said he was going to put an arrow through my neck." My voice echoed through the hills.

They glared at one another, wondering how I could know this. I never intended to sow discord into their little band before slaying them, but I didn't mind it.

"It's only your friend who needs to die," Septus said. "The consul just wants to talk. He promised no harm will come to you."

"I've heard enough of his talk."

"Let's just go our own way," one of them said. "We haven't seen you, and you haven't seen us."

They expected to take us while we slept or used the latrines. They weren't prepared to fight us, man to man.

Septus turned and threatened the dissenter. "No!" he shouted. "You are coming with us. And so is the head of your friend." He brandished a long broadsword.

"Enough talk," Barca said. He charged for the man who wanted to claim his head.

The rest of them must have realized battle was inevitable. They readied their weapons and rushed in.

All my senses heightened. It seemed impossible, but I thought I could hear Opimius tighten his bow string.

"Fabius, the archer!" I dodged to the right to avoid the first arrow.

"Marked," Fabius replied calmly.

Two of the attackers approached, swords in hand.

I could see they were deliberating, trying to determine how to proceed. They didn't want to kill me, but they also didn't want to die.

They flourished their swords and waved them about like daggers, clearly more practiced with defending themselves in shadowy Roman alleyways than in sword fights.

One flashed his blade about, as if to distract me. But I never looked at the sword. Instead, I focused my attention on his eyes, knowing a flicker would come before a strike, and the strike before his death.

There it was. A subtle twitch, a man steeling himself against fear.

I stepped aside and swiped his sword away with my own. As he stumbled, I brought the blade down on the back of his neck.

He wasn't alive long enough to cry out.

The other attacker looked horrified. He'd never seen a legionary's precision, maybe he'd never watched a friend die.

As I prepared for the next assault, I turned to make sure another arrow wasn't aimed in my direction.

But Fabius's knife was already twirling through the air. It landed cleanly in the archer's throat. Opimius fell to his knees.

I felt the next man rushing me. I didn't see his eyes flicker, but I could feel the earth shift.

He came at me with an overhead swing, unpracticed and untrained. If the blow struck me, I would have died. He forgot himself and his mission to capture me, he could only think of survival now. I knew the feeling well and knew exactly how to avoid the frenzy.

I shifted away and let his sword dig into my family's soil.

He recovered quickly and lunged again without pause but also without reclaiming his balance. My blade ricocheted off his. His arm swung uncontrolled to the side.

I stabbed him through the gut.

He collapsed into my arms as if to embrace me, but I freed him from my blade and let him crumble to the earth.

Justice, not vengeance. Protection, not indulgence.

But they destroyed our home; now their blood watered our soil.

I found Barca standing over Septus. The fight was over, but Barca took his time.

The brute's hands were missing, his broadsword still clutched in their severed grips.

"Was it you who took my *ludus*? Did you steal my men?"

Fabius watched the interrogation nearby, the last of the attackers bleeding at his feet. His men stood behind him with bloody swords but without a drop of sweat on their heads.

Barca didn't wait for a response.

He slashed his sword through Septus's chest, first one way and then the other, leaving a scarlet X through his sternum.

Septus's eyes rolled back before Barca lopped off his head.

A gruesome display, but a warranted one.

Fabius was the first to speak after we sheathed our swords. "What shall we do with them?"

"Let them serve as a warning against any who seek to harm my friends and family," I said. "Leave them."

SCROLL VI

GAVIUS SERTORIUS—ONE day after the Nones of Sextilis, 666 Ab Urbe Condita

I'd never been inside the senate house before, and I wasn't permitted inside today. Only senators and foreign dignitaries could enter, but I was as close as any other man could be.

I stood at the precipice, just behind the velvet partition, with a stylus trembling in my hands.

Sulla had left two of his *servi* beside me, for the sole purpose of taking notes, but he wanted me to record my thoughts as well. This would be a monumental occasion, he said, and it should be recorded for posterity.

The Curia Hostilia looked modest from afar, blending in with the many temples and basilicas of the Forum. But the senate house looked massive standing beneath it. The stone facade glinted in the morning sun, polished the day prior to a dull shine. The servants had removed any blood from our previous conflict. The only reminder was Sulpicius's rotting tongue nailed to the center of the heavy bronze doors.

I looked past the gruesome reminder and marveled inside the

senate house. Elegant mosaics stretched throughout the vast corridor, depicting gods and men, order and chaos, and a subtle reminder about the fate of the hubristic. I was close enough to smell the polished cedar beams that stretched overhead, imagine the cool touch of Roman busts watching the proceedings in stern silence. I longed to run my hand over the floor, the shimmer of gold veins threading through the white marble slabs. I'd never longed to be a senator before, never even considered it, but a certain desire stirred in my breast as I waited for the day to begin.

This was power.

Three hundred senators, all in snow-white togas embroidered in the color of their rank and position, sat in rows of benches like actors awaiting their lines. The men, whose voices usually echoed through the Forum like thunder, now sat hushed, gripping the folds of their togas as if the soft fabrics could bring them security. Few of them dared to meet Sulla's gaze as my commander strode the floor and took his place beside Blind Lady Justice.

The statue held scales in her hand, and though her eyes were veiled, her expression was not without judgment. It was fitting for Sulla to stand beside her, as he would be carrying out her work today.

I turned to Sulla's *servi*. "Are you ready? We cannot miss a word," I said.

"Yes, *domine*," one said in an Eastern accent while the other bowed.

They'd better be right. Sulla gave us this task, and I would execute it with the same fervor I maintained on the battlefield.

I scribbled a few notes on my wax tablet: *Senators silent. Eyes downcast. Order restored.*

The silence failed to disturb Sulla. Instead, he allowed it to linger. Taking his time to analyze as many faces around the room as he was able.

Almost two weeks had passed since we liberated Rome, but

this was the first senate meeting since then, and therefore the Consul's first chance to address all his colleagues at once.

With a mixture of anticipation, fear, and excitement, they waited with bated breath. *What kind of conqueror would Sulla be,* they must have wondered. But I already knew the answer, I wouldn't have followed him if he wasn't Rome's savior.

Rather than paraphrase Sulla's speech, I'll include it in its entirety, as transcribed by Sulla's *servi* and edited appropriately for authenticity and effect by Sulla and me afterward:

Conscript Fathers, this is not a day of conquest, but of restoration. Rome, our beloved mother, has been reclaimed — not by a tyrant's hand but by the firm grasp of lawful authority. The streets beneath our feet, once troubled by riot and discord, now stand as witness to the truth: that the Republic can still be saved. We stand here not amid ruin, but on the threshold of renewal.

For too long, we have feared what might come to pass if legions ever turned their gaze upon Rome. Today, I put those fears to rest. I have marched not as a despot seeking power but as a consul bound by my oath — an oath to defend this city not only from swords beyond her walls but from corruption festering within them. The enemies of the Republic are not always foreign; too often they wear the robes of office and speak as friends.

But make no mistake — my presence here is not born of ambition. I come before you not as a tyrant nor as a usurper but as your elected consul. My sword was drawn to restore what others sought to destroy: the order, dignity, and traditions of Rome. The Republic is sacred, and it is my duty to ensure that it remains untainted by those who would twist it to suit their reckless designs.

In this spirit, I declare that all measures passed under the coercion of Sulpicius and Gaius Marius are hereby null and void. No law conceived in fear can stand beneath the light of justice. From this day forward, no Tribune shall thrust legislation upon the people without this Senate's approval. Let us reclaim our role as the rightful guardians of Rome's future, for it is here—within these walls—that the Republic finds her voice.

But we must do more than merely correct past wrongs. We must ensure that such chaos never takes root again. To strengthen the Republic, I will double the number of senators to six hundred, drawing from the finest equestrians and the most loyal patriots among us. In so doing, we shall extend the Senate's influence, solidify our honor, and ensure that the prestige of Rome stretches across every shore the eagle touches.

Furthermore, the tribal assemblies—breeding grounds for disorder—are abolished. Elections will now be held solely within the Centuriate Assembly, where the wisdom of seasoned men shall guide the will of the Republic. No longer will demagogues sway the ignorant masses with false promises. We must restore integrity to our institutions, and that integrity begins here, among you.

To foster prosperity and alleviate the burdens upon our citizens, I will remit ten percent of all debts, a gesture both prudent and just. Interest rates shall be curbed to prevent the rise of poverty, so that Rome may once again be a nation of wealth, not want. Let those who toil in service to the state find relief in the knowledge that their sacrifices are honored, not exploited.

Lastly, I pledge to establish twelve new colonies throughout the Republic. These colonies will be populated by our loyal veterans and urban plebeians, creating new opportunities for those who have bled for Rome. In these new lands, we shall plant the seeds of Roman order and discipline, spreading our way of life to the farthest corners of the known world.

Conscript Fathers, today marks not an end but a beginning. The Republic, shaken though she was, stands firm once more. I did not come here to seize power—I came to restore it to its rightful place. Let history remember this moment not as the day Sulla conquered Rome but as the day the Senate reclaimed her destiny. Together, we shall forge a future worthy of the name of Rome.

And let all who stand against this great endeavor, within or beyond these walls, know this: Rome endures, and the Republic shall never falter.

For today, the Republic rises once more—stronger, purer, and unyielding.

My written account includes notes about applause from the senators, where weeping could be heard, cries of thanksgiving, and hardy vows of sacrifice.

But I remember nothing of the sort.

Sulla neutered the tribunes by removing their ability to take a vote directly before the people. He increased the senate's power tremendously by doubling its size and making the Centuriate Assembly the voting body once more.

I expected cheering, weeping and vows of sacrifice, and so did Sulla, or at least he told me to expect it before he entered. But his promises were met with only silence.

The senate was known for its vigor and anger as well. One might have expected heckles and hisses in response to his promise of giving equestrians access to the senate rolls, but there was no visible or auditory response.

Perhaps they were only afraid. Certainly, they would rejoice later, when they realized Sulla was a man of his word. We believed it was only fair we added their joy in the margins of the speech's transcript.

I scribbled in my tablet: *Lingering silence. Someone coughing. Speech carried and delivered flawlessly. Tapping feet?*

None of these notes made it into the final transcript, of course.

But I only recall one senator speaking that day, and it wasn't until later when Sulla suggested they officially name Gaius Marius an enemy of the state.

Sulla hadn't expected opposition. Why should he? Marius was an unpopular man, hated by many, and the few friends he maintained were rotting in the Tiber or fleeing for their lives. None of them were in the senate house that day.

But an old Augur named Scaevola rocked to his feet when Sulla made this proposal. He was old, overweight, and frail. A younger colleague took his arm to stabilize him.

He aimed a bony, shaky hand at Sulla.

"I will never vote to outlaw a man who once saved Rome from destruction," his voice trembled like a reed in the wind, but he spoke each word with conviction.

There were murmurs of support throughout the senate house. No one else dared be as vocal, but Sulla appeared to be outnumbered.

He stepped to the center of the chambers and looked up at the old Augur.

"You should know, I have the right to enact this measure as a consul. I do not require your vote." The strength of his words forced the old man back to his seat.

I quickly wrote down: *Support for Marius? Old man, angry. Some support.*

But then the consul's demeanor changed. He smiled and extended his arms as if he meant to embrace the entire assembly.

"But I am not a tyrant. I meant only to put it to a vote. If you fine men disagree with me, I will uphold the law."

"Then why do you already have assassins out hunting for him?" Scaevola said from his bench.

I knew Sulla well enough to notice when rage flashed over him, even if everyone else missed it. But just like that, the moment had passed.

"Dear me," Sulla said. "My purpose is only to find Gaius Marius and bring him back to Rome. He is old, frail, and of feeble mind. It would damage Roman prestige to have so accomplished a man die in some sordid way in a desolate place."

Sulla did not bring up the matter again, nor did he request the measure be put to a vote. He could have had Scaevola thrown in chains and made it clear that any who dissented from his plan would receive similar treatment. But he did not. Sulla was just and fair, like the Blind statue now behind him.

The consul ended the day with several promises. He vowed to send his legionaries back to Nola on the next auspicious day. This was the first time the senators exhibited any visible relief.

I added to the tablet: *Senators relieved we're leaving. Afraid of legions? Proof of Sulla's intentions. Some men whispered to each other after announcement.*

He then clarified that in the coming months he would permit the consular elections to proceed as normal. He would not be running for consul again, instead he would honor Roman tradition. He might support a candidate, but he wanted a free election, the same as always.

Again, he clarified, he was no tyrant.

Despite the lack of vocal support for his promises, Sulla's speech that day was a masterstroke.

He gained favor with an angry crowd of plebeians by promising to build colonies for them. He won over the equestrians by promising to open the senate to them, which negated any anger they might have felt about the remission of debts owed to them. His promise to increase senatorial power twofold would guarantee the support of patrician families for the rest of his life, whether they felt confident enough to voice it that day or not.

The only group who could continue to hate him after that day were the ten tribunes, and those who sought to use that position for their own power. But he accepted this gladly. If he was a tyrant, he once told me, he would eagerly abolish the position altogether.

I turned to Sulla's *servi*. "Did you get all that?" I said.

They nodded. "Every word."

I expected for Sulla to linger for some time, addressing any senators who wished for a private word with him.

But most of those old men poured out and pushed past me. I listened intently to see if any of their whispers were malicious, but each of them stopped talking the moment they saw my armor.

Sulla exited soon thereafter with only a few of his closest supporters.

He wore his famous smile, his back as straight and chin as high as those statues he passed by. But I could sense an edge to him. Something beneath the surface, like boiling water.

"Well done, consul." I saluted.

"Was everything recorded properly?" Sulla said. His words were spoken with a cheerful tone, but something beneath was sharp as a knife. "I need a cup of wine, then we shall reflect on our message."

He descended the steps from the Curia, in the direction of his home on the Palatine rather than the *comitium* where senators usually convened after a concluded meeting.

"Consul, if I may have a moment," I said.

He stopped and turned.

Sulla always made time for me, or I wouldn't have asked. But there was something in his eyes that said I needed to make it quick this time. His patience had been tested.

"Something to report?" He maintained his smile the best he could.

"I met a woman by the river," I said. "She was mourning the death of her husband . . ."

I pulled out the list and walked closer to him so no one could overhear.

He shook his head and took the list from my hand.

"Those who mourn say many things, Gavius," he said.

He seemed to already know what I was about to say.

"Yes, I just . . ."

"Not here," he said.

"It was only the last name that concerned me." I lowered my head. I knew Sulla well enough to realize I needed to stop pressing, but my concern gnawed at me. He trusted me, he cared for me. Right? He would understand.

Sulla looked at the list again, crumpled it, and slid it into the folds of his consular toga. He placed a hand on my shoulder, his grip stronger than usual when he met my eyes.

"He helped Sulpicius and Gaius Marius escape justice," Sulla said.

My eyes must have reflected my concern. Was he talking about my father or Barca?

He shook his head. "The gladiator must be dealt with. Your father's name isn't on the list, is it?" He patted my face. "No harm shall come to your family as long as I'm around." Then he turned. As he departed, I was barely able to hear him say, "Do not ask me this again."

I hadn't asked a question yet. My mind swirled. Had he confirmed the authenticity of the list?

Perhaps it wasn't my place to know. My father was safe, Sulla promised, and that was all that mattered.

I closed my tablet, hung my stylus, and hurried after the consul.

SCROLL VII

Lucius Hirtuleius—One day after the Nones of Sextilis, 666 Ab Urbe Condita

A salty mist settled on my lips, but all I could taste was bile. The air was wet, but my mouth was dry as old bones. I hated ships, and I hated sailing. By the time the coastline appeared on the horizon, I decided I hated all bodies of water, too, save Nursia's stream where I bathed as a child. I longed for that simple time when civil wars, exile, and desertion were not concepts I'd ever considered.

I collected what little saliva I could and spit it over the rail of the bireme. Most of it dripped down my chin. Perhaps looking down at the ship would be the best way to steel myself. We didn't have much further, and I desperately wanted to arrive before emptying my already barren stomach into Neptune's sea once more.

The waves slapped hard against the ship beneath me. Salt had eaten away at the timbers, leaving streaks of gray where the rest of the vessel was a rich brown. The wood groaned with each rise and fall; the incessant noise I feared would be seared into my mind forever.

This was a vessel of necessity, not luxury. It wasn't proper for a man of Marius's stature and achievement, but we didn't exactly have a fleet of options available to us.

Speaking of the former consul, he came to my side and clapped me on the shoulder. He was totally oblivious to my predicament and had displayed no sign of distress on the voyage himself. I couldn't imagine the former consul had spent too many nights at sea, but he seemed impervious to damn near everything. Hunger, sleeplessness, sea storms, exile, civil war . . . he still wore a rueful smile.

"Almost there, general," I said, my own words almost gagging me.

"You've seen a Roman triumph, but wait until you see how the Numidians celebrate conquering heroes," he said. "Have no doubts, there will be feasts, festivals, and games in my honor. A brief reprieve before we return to finish this." The smile slowly faded as he considered what lay ahead. Regardless of how lavishly we were treated upon arrival, Marius remained singularly focused on destroying Sulla and saving the Republic.

Frayed, stiff ropes creaked above us, their knots barely holding the sails as they flapped against the wind. And this was the best weather we'd experienced. The seas weren't favorable for the journey, but we had no choice but to depart when we did. Stay and die or escape and fight back against the sea. As landfall came slowly into view, I could admit to myself we'd made the right decision, but there were a few moments along the journey where I'd regretted not accepting an honorable death in the marshes rather than enduring Triton's wrath.

"At the moment, general, I have little concern for festivals and games, but feasts . . . that sounds nice."

We'd eaten nothing but bread for days, and most of it was soggy and molding after the storeroom flooded on the night of the second storm.

I finally dared to look toward the coast. It was an explosion of color after so many days of nothing but ship, sea, and sky. In truth, it was little more than sand and the tops of weathered trees, but it was as pleasing as seeing the most beautiful woman in Rome. The sun beat down relentlessly, as if centered directly above the shoreline, casting everything in a sharp, golden light. I was forced to squint but would continue to admire it even if it blinded me.

"Land ahead," Aulus said from the helm.

For someone who'd spent no more time at sea than I had, Aulus had been remarkably durable through the storms. But though his stomach remained strong, his eyes reflected a heaviness uncommon to him.

Marius the Younger joined him at the front. He raised his voice so we could hear him over the winds. "I should like a hot bath before anything else, father," he said. "Do the barbarians have hot baths?"

"Yes, yes," Marius said. "Baths, wine, women, meat." Then, he lowered his voice. He meant to speak to himself, but I overheard as he said, "And they have an army."

"I shall enjoy myself, then," Marius the Younger said, his first words absent complaining since our flight began.

"Tonight, we are kings. Soon enough, we will return to Italy as conquerors."

Land drew closer.

"I thought we were landing near Carthage?" I said.

Marius's smile returned, now more rueful than before. "You're looking at Carthage." He nodded to the shore.

I'd heard the stories—every Roman had. Our greatest enemy brought low by our ancestors. Marius's mentor, Scipio Aemilianus, was the one who carried out this final destruction.

Regardless of knowing the fate of Carthage, seeing it was another thing entirely. Now, only a shadow remained. The shadow of something strong enough to challenge the might of Rome.

Broken columns jutted from the earth like splintered bones, all dyes and paints faded away from years of exposure. There were no great walls, no vast mercantile port, no golden citadels like Roman children hear stories about. It was an eerie sight, as ghosts still lingered above the ruins, waiting for us.

Before I could make sense of why the sight affected me, I spotted the grand procession lining the shore.

"Your hosts await us, father!" Marius the Younger shouted, as giddy as a young boy.

The captain and his sailors began shouting orders to prepare for landing.

The Numidians stood in formation, tall and lean, their skin a deep bronze beneath gleaming armor. I was surprised to find that there was no uniformity to this Numidian army. Unlike the legion, each warrior had his own style. Some wore metal breast-plates, others leather or chainmail. Some held aloft tall spears, their tips shining like a sea of stars, while others bore large rectangular shields or longbows.

The bireme slowed to an excruciating pace. I wanted to be off that vessel as badly as I wanted to breathe, and we were so close.

But what I saw next stole my attention from even the incessant churning of my stomach. It wasn't the Numidian army that gave me pause but the beasts standing behind them. Three elephants, their massive bodies towering over the assembled men. I'd heard stories of course—but I never knew if they were real or just myths like gorgons and cyclops. But they were real, and before me in the flesh. Enormous is an understatement, with scars and deep wrinkles marking their rough gray skin, their tusks long and curved like massive scimitars.

I couldn't imagine how a group of them charging into battle wouldn't rout even the bravest of armies or how it wouldn't cause the earth to cave in.

I wasn't alone in my awe. Marius clasped his hands behind his back and stiffened his posture. He expected a grand reception, to be honored as a hero, and seeing these elephants must have felt like a fitting tribute, perhaps a promise to use them in his service should he only ask.

This entire army, and the three beasts, were all centered around a single man on camelback. This must have been the Numidian king. Rich reds, blues, and golds were woven in intricate patterns through his robes, and the carpet draped across his steed's humped back was nearly as ornate. A crown of polished gold rested on his head, something I never thought I'd see as a Roman legionary.

The Numidians were known for their dynastic pride, and it was clearly on display with how they protected their king but also allowed him a place of reverence and seclusion within their midst. This pride was why Marius felt so confident of our welcome, their dynasty would be forgotten and buried like the ruins of Carthage if it wasn't for him.

Marius the Younger hurried back to us. "Father, I thought you said the king was old?"

Looking again, I could see the Numidian ruler was young, little more than a boy, if I could tell from the distance.

"He is, he is. This must be the young prince," Marius said.

His son crossed his arms. "They insult you already. The king should be here, kneeling before the man who saved them."

Marius's face hardened. "I said he's old, boy," Marius said, taking a firmer tone with his son than he usually did. "He probably can't rally from his bed, let alone travel to Carthage to greet his guests. They will honor us properly; have no doubt."

The sailors hurled ropes over the wooden railing, and the bireme came to a groaning halt.

Aulus and Marius the Younger stood by the lowering exit ramp, waiting on the general to depart first. But it was my responsibility to protect him. Despite his connections here, Numidia was a foreign land, and I didn't yet trust their intentions. If they meant us harm, there was nothing I could do to stop them, of course, but duty demanded I die first in such an event, so I led the way instead.

Stepping off the ship, I tasted the enormity of Carthage for the first time. Yes, it was little more than rubble and ash as I'd seen from a distance, but its sheer size was boggling to the mind. The port area alone, now nothing but broken columns and dead earth, was larger than most cities I'd seen.

I prepared myself to announce Marius's arrival, but I felt a hand on my shoulder.

The old general whispered, "Give me your cloak."

I leaned in closer to make sure I understood him correctly.

"I look like a peasant. They need to see I'm still a warrior."

"Quick about it, legionary," Marius the Younger said.

I unfastened the pin and swept the cloak over Marius's shoulders while the Numidians watched us in silence.

"Make way for the great Gaius Marius. Six-time consul of the Roman Republic, the Third Founder of Rome, and the liberator of Numidia!"

My voice carried over the ruins, the wind now calm compared to at sea. I wondered if the last time a Roman shouted Latin here it was cries of "burn, burn, burn" as they leveled the great city.

The prince and his army remained entirely still, as if posing for someone to sculpt the scene into a triumphal column.

"Perhaps they don't understand you," Aulus whispered.

Marius stepped forward now.

"What a magnificent army! Oh, the glory we can win together!" Despite his age and condition, Marius's voice remained as powerful as it was when he led legions at the Battle of Vercellae.

The prince nudged his camel forward. A bizarre, guttural bellow escaped the beast—something between the rumbling groan of a sick ox and the enraged bray of a donkey—as it carried the prince forward.

At least twenty men on foot joined the prince, surrounding him and his beast.

My chest tightened. A friendly welcome wouldn't have

required such protection, would it? Perhaps it was just their way. Marius didn't seem to think anything of it.

Their party came to a halt a cautious distance away from us so that voices still needed to be raised to hear one another over the distant winds of the sea and the crashing of the waves.

"Are you the one they call Gaius Marius?" the prince said. His Latin was so crisp and clear it might have been uttered from a patrician's son.

Marius grunted, quietly enough that only we near him could hear. "I know I don't look like the Third Founder of Rome, but aye, I am Gaius Marius."

The moment Marius uttered those words, archers around the kings army tightened their bowstring, aiming the jagged tips for the former consul.

I pulled my gladius halfway from its scabbard and stepped in front of Marius.

"What is the meaning of this?" Marius asked. Incredulous and irritated, but most of all the Numidians perplexed him. "I said I *am* Gaius Marius."

"Return to your ships," the prince said. His words were firm, but something else lingered there as well. Was it remorse? Shame? Empathy?

The better question was whether it mattered.

"I demand to speak to the king!"

I kept my eyes on the archers before us, but knew the veins on Marius's neck were close to bursting. Like the power of his voice, his famous rage was undiminished.

"You are speaking to him," the young man said.

Marius did not reply for a long time. I imagine he was considering all the possibilities, considering everything this meant.

"Your father is dead?" he finally said, his tone changing dramatically.

The newly anointed king lowered his head. "He is."

Marius pushed me aside and stepped forward, exposing himself to grave danger but apparently unconcerned by it.

"I grieve with you, King Juba," he said. "I know you will honor his legacy."

Juba nodded. His acting was either as refined as his Latin, or he was genuinely grateful.

"He lived well and died well. A Numidian can ask for nothing else."

"As a friend and ally of your father, I'm obliged to tell you that King Gauda would have welcomed us with open arms. He would want you to do the same."

The young king lowered his gaze; he couldn't look at us now.

"I know," he said.

I saw the tension in Marius's shoulders release. I stole a quick glance back at Marius the Younger and Aulus. There was no such relief on their faces.

"Come," Marius said. "We will ride to Cirta together, share a cup in honor of his memory. I have many stories to tell you of our time together on the battlefield."

The king only shook his head.

"My orders are to kill you," he said, "and to ship your head back to Italy, packed in salt."

I revealed my sword now. I'd always vowed to bring as many of my enemies with me when I died, but I knew all four of us would drown in a sea of arrows before taking the first step. Whatever was left of us would be squashed like insects by the camels and elephants.

"Orders? Orders!" Marius raged. "You are the King of Numidia! You take no orders except from the Roman Republic, and I AM ROME!"

The king's guard readied themselves as if we posed them a threat.

Juba himself remained unafraid, but his heart was visibly wounded.

"I wish it were so," Juba said.

He finally summoned some courage and looked up. "You must return to your ships immediately."

Marius lunged forward. I managed to stop him from charging to a brutal death.

"I saved your dynasty, boy!" Spittle flew from his lips as he raged against me. "If it weren't for Gaius Marius, you'd be nothing! Dead, forgotten, rubble, lower than the ruins beneath us!"

Juba interrupted, "Yes, and because of this I spare your life," he said. "This may cost me my own, but I will allow you to live for the sake of my father."

Marius continued his onslaught. "The entire Numidian Kingdom, erased, buried by the sands of time if it wasn't for me! ME!" The veins in his neck threatened to burst. "Me! Gaius Marius! A curse on your entire kingdom for betraying your savior!"

He aimed his sinister left hand at the king as he uttered the curse. I wondered if they even knew what this meant, but we did.

"Be reasonable!" Juba finally challenged Marius's volume. "Sulla owns Rome now. He sent messengers to every nation on your *Mare Nostrum*." He brandished a scroll from his ornate robes and tossed it to the dirt between us. "He made it clear how much Gaius Marius's captor can gain and how much his abettor will suffer."

Marius was finally out of breath.

I said, "If you fear Sulla, then help us defeat him! Help us reclaim Rome, and we will be in your debt as your people are to Marius."

Juba shook his head. Each of our rebuttals increased his resolve.

"Too many of my people have died for the struggles of other nations. No more."

"Your people? All your people would be dead and rotting if it wasn't for me!" Marius began again.

"Return to your ships," Juba said. "Return to your ships.

Return to your ships." He repeated himself again and again, raising his voice over Marius's insults and objections.

Aulus came forward and shouted, "How long? How long do we have to depart?"

Marius prepared himself for a new tirade against Aulus for interrupting, but King Juba spoke first. "Your ships must be gone by first light, or we will have no choice but to obey the lawful order of the Roman consul and have you all executed."

Aulus, bravely or foolishly, wrapped his arms around Marius and started pushing him back the way we'd come.

"The winds aren't favorable," I said. "We'll die in those waters if we attempt the voyage so soon."

In reality, the winds didn't concern me as much as where they might take us.

Juba frowned. "The winds are unfavorable to Gaius Marius everywhere," he said. "I will sacrifice that your gods change their mind and alter his fate."

Marius, surprisingly, allowed Aulus to lead him away. He'd given up on berating the king, and now only mumbled to himself as he stumbled away from the port.

"We have nowhere to go. You're killing us!" Marius the Younger cried out. "Same as if you'd butcher us here. Please!"

Juba's camel groaned as if it attempted to clear a blocked throat. Within that foreign noise there was a coarse humanlike grunt, as though the creature itself half-mocked our plight in its strange, throaty yowling.

"We must go." I tugged at Marius the Younger's wrist.

The king had already turned his beast around and trotted back to his army. They turned their backs to us.

What now? Where could we go? Marius spoke of nothing but Numidia since the moment our flight began. He had no other options as far as I was aware, no alternative, no secret army waiting for his command to help us liberate Rome.

For the first time since I met him, Marius lost his strength. He fell from Aulus's grip and onto a broken Carthaginian column.

He propped himself up and stared out at the sea, knowing somewhere on the other side of that water, the man responsible for all this was alive and well in the city he helped save, rejoicing in the thought of his death.

The once-great Roman slouched on the broken ruins of the once-great city and mumbled to himself.

"Orders, general?" I asked.

"What do we do now?" Aulus said more poignantly.

I thought Marius was responding quietly, so I leaned in closer.

I strained to hear the same three words uttered in repetition like an ancient prayer or a new curse.

"Kill them all. Kill them all. Kill them all."

SCROLL VIII

QUINTUS SERTORIUS—TWO days after the Nones of Sextilis, 666 Ab Urbe Condita

The journey to Spoletium was a short one by horse, but it took us the better part of three days by foot. The sun was about to rise again by the time the colony came into view.

I said a prayer of thanks, first for the sight of my family waiting by the gates and second for the hope of a moment's rest.

I didn't feel well. My limbs began to tremble the moment we departed Nursia, and my fingers and toes went numb. The sensation was like the experience of blood loss, but even after Barca and Fabius checked me for a second and third time, they discovered no injuries.

In truth, I knew what caused the disturbance. I was a father now. So much depended on my survival, and I refused to imagine what would happen to my wife and child if I fell. I'd fought in battle after battle since I was old enough to shave, but I never had this much to lose before.

I took a deep breath and summoned up all the strength I could. There was more to do before I could rest my weary bones.

Arrea hurried toward me when she spotted us in the distance. Toria started flailing her limbs wildly when she saw me, along with a chorus of coos and babbles that almost made me forget our predicament for a moment. Almost.

"Quintus," Arrea said when she could find no other words.

"My wife." I pulled her into my embrace, Toria between us, and gave them both a kiss on the head.

Only when I stepped away did I notice the dried blood I left on her arm and forehead.

"I'm sorry," I said.

Arrea placed a hand on my cheek. "Never apologize for protecting us," she said.

She passed Toria into my arms as our daughter grinned, revealing the tip of one tiny tooth.

I held her close as she patted at my face and tugged at the uncharacteristic stubble of my beard. I smelled her hair and rubbed a dirty thumb over her shoulders. She was safe. My wife was safe. Nothing else mattered.

I led our band closer to the gates, where my mother remained with Sura and the other mares.

"They need water and food," she said, always thinking of our horses before herself.

I peered inside the city walls, which were little more than a barricade to mark the limits of the colony. The citizens began to stir, lighting lanterns to illuminate the dawning streets. Goats bleated and shopkeepers hung up crudely made signs, prepared for the day to begin.

The locals didn't seem to know about Rome's plight or the war across Italy. Fires hadn't blackened any of their buildings, and I saw no bodies in the street. Spoletium was too small a prize for Rome or her former allies to consider during the war, and Sulla ignored it now.

"They'll have it," I said.

Fabius joined us. "It pleases me to find you well, my lady," he said, before turning to me. "My men are camped two days' march from here; we can make it in one if we all mount up."

"We should keep moving," Barca said. "I do not trust this place."

"Not everyone is blessed with your endurance, brother." I looked at my mother. "We need the rest and something to sustain us for the journey. I am the only one likely to be recognized." I imagined how warm and pleasant a tavern bed would feel. "I'll remain outside the city walls with the horses, and make sure they're cared for. All of you, go and find somewhere to rest. We'll depart at nightfall."

Barca's eyes hardened. He didn't like the plan, but eventually he nodded. "I will keep them safe," he said.

I reached for my belt and plucked off my coin purse. It was light but contained enough to provide what we needed. That tiny pouch was all the denarii I owned, save my domus in Rome. Had Sulla burnt that one down too?

I passed the coin purse to Barca and closed his hand around it.

Fabius clapped me on the shoulder. "I'll go with you," he said. He turned to his men. "Look after them, understood?"

They nodded in response.

I savored one last moment with Toria before handing her to my mother. She fussed and reached out for me, but a few tickles beneath her chin was enough to pacify her for the moment.

"We stayed off the road as best we could on the way," Rhea said. "There's a stream and green pastures just west, over the crest there." She pointed.

"I'll take them there." Before they left, I said to Barca, "Find us a guide, someone who can lead us to Arretium on paths only the locals would know."

I watched them turn and enter the city, before they vanished into the growing throng of citizens.

"I suppose let's feed some horses, then," Fabius said, cheerfully ignorant of our predicament, or resilient enough to endure it with a smile.

The morning air bit my cheeks as I led Sura and a few other horses down an uneven path. Sura's silver coat gleamed in the soft light, glistening like she was covered in morning dew, her hooves crunching against fallen leaves.

Fabius trudged along awkwardly behind me, doing his best to keep up. The pair of mares he led seemed less inclined to cooperate. He might have been a master of arms and sea, but he remained painfully unskilled with horses.

"It's times like these I miss your father," Fabius said.

"I miss him most of the time."

"He had a maxim, your father," Fabius said. "What was it? *Fight bravely, serve faithfully, sacrifice everything, and* . . . bollocks. What was the rest?"

I could almost see my father's kind eyes peering down at me.

"He maintained several sayings like this," I said. "He knew just when I needed to hear each one."

"Well, whatever it was, when things were the hardest, that's when you wanted Proculus Sertorius by your side. No panic in him, no fear. Just focused on the task ahead," he said, nostalgia in his voice. "And the sound of his laughter would cheer us all up about now."

"I can't recall the sound of his laughter," I said.

A disturbance interrupted his response.

"Oi! This horse tried to bite me," Fabius shouted. "Are they all spiteful little harpies like this one?"

I suppressed a smile. "I suppose you didn't ride much during your years at sea?"

"Beasts make unwelcome ship companions," he said. "Can you imagine the smell?"

"They're wary of you, Fabius. I can hardly blame them; you hold those reins like you're dragging cargo onto a ship."

"Aye, that's all I know," he said. "I'll take a deck under my feet and sails over my head. Horses are beautiful, but they're dangerous. Like massive dogs that can kick with the power of a battering ram."

"Horses are animals of prey. Fearful and cautious by nature. If they display violence, it's because they're afraid or uncomfortable. Earn their trust, and you'll have a companion for life. Just don't stand behind them."

I thought about my dog, Pollux, and was glad Apollonius took him to Athens, where they were both safe from all this.

"And how might I earn their trust?" he asked, before clearing his throat and changing the tone of his voice. "My lady, I am a friend. You are much larger and stronger than I am, and you have no reason to fear me."

"Did it work?" I asked.

The mare snorted.

"I suppose this one has issues with trust," he grumbled.

"Dogs give their loyalty because it's in their nature. They trust easily. Out of love for us, horses follow us into battles they cannot possibly comprehend, but it doesn't come easily. We must earn it."

"They sound a bit like mercenaries to me," he said.

I laughed, the first genuine laughter I could remember for weeks. "Horses won't betray you for a better offer."

He stopped walking until I turned around and looked at him. For a moment, I thought I'd offended him, but he said, "Turns out you remember the sound of your father's laughter after all," he said. "You just heard it."

We reached the stream. Clear, cold water babbled over smooth stones. I released the reins and allowed the horses to approach the bank, tails swishing happily. Fabius did the same and all the steeds lowered their heads to drink and pluck at small flowers growing along the creek bed.

Fabius broke the peaceful silence. "I think this is the most you've spoken since the day we met," he said. "Either you really like horses, or you've been lost in contemplation."

"Both." I kept my gaze on Sura to make sure she found what she needed.

He stepped to my side. "Some say I'm an even better listener than I am a mercenary captain. If only listening paid well."

"My thoughts are what you'd expect of a fugitive," I said. "I wonder if Sulla has officially named me an enemy of the state. I don't know whether I'll ever be able to set foot in the city I've given my life for. I wonder if he burned down my domus in Rome like he burned down my farm . . ."

Fabius looked at me, blinking, and waited for me to continue. He knew there was more.

"Part of me thinks I should take my family and leave this place. Forever."

Fabius shrugged. "Not a bad idea. You don't owe Rome anything else. Look at you," he said. "Covered head-to-toe in scars. You gave an eye for Rome, and we only get two of those, you know?" He sobered. "It's hard to outrun Rome, lad. I know. I've tried. But maybe there's somewhere out there."

I shook my head. "No. I can't leave. If I abandon Rome now, all the sacrifices I made—and all the sacrifices of those I served with—will be for nothing," I said. "I cannot leave Rome in the hands of a tyrant."

"What will you do about it, then?" he asked. "What *can* you do?"

"We travel to your camp. I won't consider anything else until I know my family is safe," I said. "Then I wait. I cannot stand up to Sulla alone, not rationally. Not ethically. I hold no power. But someone will resist him eventually, and when they do, I'll be ready to join them."

Fabius exhaled. "Permission to speak freely, young master?"

I nodded.

"I'm afraid you don't understand the gravity of this situation," he said. "Rome is broken. It's not just Sulla. He may have set the precedent, but even his death can't change that. The moment he marched his legions into Rome with swords and torches, the Republic you love died. Someone else will come along and follow his example. Rome can't be repaired. It can only be destroyed and built anew, stone by stone."

I finally turned my attention away from the horses. "What are you suggesting?"

He frowned. "Nothing," he said. "Nothing specifically. But I've seen what tyrants do to people. In the east, I witnessed bodies piled higher than any temple in Rome. I saw entire tribes erased from memory. And in all my years, I've never seen someone defeat a tyrant by waiting."

"What would you have me do?" I asked. "If I raise an army and march them on Rome, I'd be no better than Sulla."

"Rebels are only victorious when they become as ruthless as their oppressors."

"I am not a rebel, Fabius. Sulla is."

He lowered his gaze. "You're a good man, Quintus Sertorius. A good man like your father. But good men don't win wars. Ruthless men do."

"My goal is not to win a war, Fabius," I said. "There is no war. My only purpose is to save Rome."

His voice was little more than a whisper now. "Do you not hear yourself?" he said. "I'm afraid we're already at war and you don't know it yet."

My chest tightened in anger. I wasn't upset with Fabius, but because I knew he spoke true. And I knew eventually my heart must accept what my mind already perceived.

"I will not allow my city to be raped and plundered again. I refuse to have more Roman blood on my hands."

The horses noticed the tone shift in our conversation and investigated for a moment before returning to their sustenance.

"And I would never try to change your mind," he said. "But you must think strategically. Considering only your next move is how you end up dead, and how I lost a fortune gambling." He placed a hand on my shoulder. "You need to raise an army. At the very least, an army allows you to negotiate from a position of strength."

"How? I am no magistrate. I have no authority. And how would I compensate an army? Sulla burnt down my farm and likely sold my home and everything in it. Even if he didn't, I don't have enough to fund a legion."

"I assume you've men all over Italy who fought beside you for years. Many would rally to your banner."

Sura trotted up from the stream, satisfied. She nudged my arm for affection.

"And how would I compensate them except with promises I can't keep?"

"You're not the only Roman patriot, Sertorius. Some men will join you because they believe it is right."

I took a deep breath. That I even considered Fabius's advice revealed much about the situation I found myself in.

Fabius smiled. "My mercenaries are not so patriotic. They fight for coin," he said. "However, I'd wager there are countless benefactors throughout Italy who'd happily invest in someone who might repulse Sulla. And this is a bet I believe I'd win."

The horses finished eating and drinking and returned to us one by one. The sound of the bubbling stream was almost mocking in its serenity. But my mind was a rushing torrent, a consuming flood.

I could take my family and run away. I could hide in some foreign village outside Rome's reach and live out my years in peace. But how could my wife and daughter respect such a coward? How could I respect myself?

Someone needed to save the Republic. Who would stand up if I didn't?

SCROLL IX

GAVIUS SERTORIUS—THREE days before the Ides of Sextilis, 666 Ab Urbe Condita

Dawn's first light stretched across the Field of Mars, casting long shadows over the legionaries of Sulla's Fist. Our men, disciplined as ever, stood in formation for the first time since we stormed the Eternal City. The spread wings of our silver eagles reflected the morning light, which I found ironic. Our enemy, Gaius Marius, standardized the use of legion eagles.

Most men would have trembled in awe and terror standing before this army, but to me, they were not shadowy, bloodied warriors, but brothers. *Amici*. We would fight together again soon, but Sulla wasn't done in Rome.

The air was cool and crisp, a gentle breeze carrying with it the first sting of winter and the faint scent of legionary armor.

In the distance behind them, the city of Rome rose like a sleeping giant, its temples and columns jutting out into the azure sky like blades of grass.

I was the only tribune at Sulla's side that morning, an honor I cherished. Sulla allowed no other junior officer to stand before the legions.

On the commander's other side, his friend and co-consul, Rufus, shifted apprehensively. I liked Rufus, but I found it difficult to see him as Sulla's equal.

Lucullus and Crassus, both senior officers now, also stood close by with plumed helmets tucked under their arms. They exchanged an uneasy glance; they'd been arguing about Sulla's decision all morning.

Crassus ignored whatever warning Lucullus whispered to him and stepped forward.

"It is my responsibility as an advisor to state my concerns about this decision," he said.

The sun peeked through the morning clouds long enough to reveal Sulla's amusement.

"Speak freely," he said.

"Keeping the army in Rome until we're ready to depart for Greece would be prudent," he said.

Lucullus looked down, and I averted my gaze back to the legions, who continued to wait silently.

Crassus voiced the concerns of many senior officers in Sulla's legion, though no one else spoke to him so directly. Perhaps it was his high-born status, but Crassus never held his tongue on an opinion he felt strongly about, and Sulla never chastised him for it. That Crassus brought Sulla a private army of skilled cavalry didn't hurt.

Crassus continued. "Your laws have passed, but they remain in incubation. And they have many detractors, as you well know. They hide behind smiles for fear of your legionaries but will strike like vipers when you're unprotected."

To challenge Sulla, and to do so publicly, was unthinkable for me. I would have stumbled over my words, or my knees might have buckled. Crassus, however, had not a drop of sweat on his thick brow.

"The legions need not enforce your law, or exact punishments," Crassus said. "Their mere presence is enough."

Sulla tapped his chin as if he was considering it, though I knew Sulla wouldn't change his mind once he set it. Even Crassus must have known that, despite his inability to silence himself.

"Hmm," he said thoughtfully. "Lucullus, what say you?"

Lucullus wasn't frightened of Sulla—or anything else as far as I could tell—but he always showed Sulla the utmost reverence.

He directed his reply to Crassus. "The legions have served their purpose. We liberated Rome from traitors and criminals. Our next objective is to liberate the East from more traitors and criminals."

Sulla nodded along. "Interesting. Tribune, thoughts?" He turned to me.

I'd listened to other officers debate the decision but never formed my own opinion. I expected Sulla to ask his co-consul for his opinion before that of a simple tribune and didn't know what to say.

Sulla often tested us with questions. These tests weren't malicious. He meant them for our edification, our training. Still, I wanted to give the *correct* answer—whatever would impress Sulla most.

"We will be vulnerable without the legions . . ." I formulated my words carefully. "But we will be away for a long time. Years maybe. If we want the peace we established to hold until our return, we'll need the support of the people. I believe sending the legions away will earn not only their support but the people's love, Consul."

"The people's love? Very good," Sulla said, either satisfied or amused. "Very good, all of you." He clasped his hands behind his back and surveyed the legions. "Lucius Cornelius Sulla is not a tyrant. The people must know this. I refuse to keep soldiers in the streets like some common despot."

Even Crassus knew better than to challenge him again.

Sulla continued, "It's interesting, freedom. Step back for a moment and consider it sometime. Watch the people as they exercise their *freedom*." Sulla's eyes narrowed. He stared out over his army, but he saw something else. "They're so quick to sacrifice order for chaos, not appreciating the consequences. And for what? So they can vote? So they can choose? Choice is only an illusion. They're so easily swayed by a polished tongue, and more often by a heavy coin purse. Their will has been obsolete so long they've forgotten how to use it."

I listened intently, as did everyone else. Sulla seemed to forget us.

"Freedom. *Freedom*. It's an idea. Another illusion. The people gain so little of its rewards and so many of its burdens." Only now did he turn to us, careful to meet each of our gazes before he said, "I will give the plebs and the proles what they desire. They can have their freedom. And Sulla's Fist will not return to Rome until they beckon us home and beg us to remain."

I didn't understand what he meant and didn't have time to make sense of it. The light finally broke and the clouds retreated. The dawning sun illuminated a sea of glimmering armor and helmets before us.

I noticed a strange look in Sulla's eyes. I'd seen it, oddly enough, in the gaze of the vagabond prophets who visited our camp, promising to tell legionaries their future in exchange for a few bronze coins. It was the look of someone who knew exactly how events would unfold, or at least believed they did.

"Before we begin the day's proceedings, I have one final motion to pass as Consul." He reached within the folds of his toga and revealed a neatly wound, thin scroll, sealed with red wax. He passed it to his co-consul. "The tribune is correct that we shall be away for some time. While we're gone, my allies won't be safe. This order grants you the rank of proconsul after our term of office ends. You will be taking over command of Strabo's army in the north. You'll be safe there until I return."

Rufus grinned like a child on his birthday.

"My friend and colleague, I thank you," he said. "I shall lead well."

"A prudent move, Consul." Crassus nodded approvingly.

Sulla nodded. "The war with the tribes has come to an end. Others will fight to have the army disbanded and your rank stripped from you. If that happens, they'll drag you through the courts so the plebs can spit on you. I'll ensure that doesn't happen."

He stepped forward and his posture shifted slightly. He prepared to address the men.

"Soldiers of Rome!" His voice carried throughout the Field of Mars. "Men of Sulla's Fist!" These words were even more powerful, and the men announced their pride with a stomp of their right foot. "There is little glory to be earned in defeating the treasonous and traitorous. No man has ever celebrated a triumph for defeating a renegade comrade. Regardless, you served with honor and distinction. Forgetting parades, praise, and plunder, you liberated Rome, as surely as those who crushed Hannibal at Zama!"

The men stomped again.

My chest swelled with pride. Being a warrior of Sulla's Fist was the highest honor of my life. I wouldn't allow politics to distract me from that.

"But you know what does come with parades, praise, and plunder? Defeating foreign kings and showing our enemies that Rome alone rules the *Mare Nostrum*!" I could barely hear those words as the legionaries erupted.

I always attempted to maintain a stoic composure when standing before the legion, but I couldn't resist the smile stretching across my wind-bitten face.

"And that's where we're going, men. Mithridates has spread his corruption far and wide, amassing hordes of treasure like no Roman has ever seen before. And now it's *ours* for the taking!"

The volume impossibly increased.

"We will reestablish Roman authority throughout the east, as we've reestablished it here." The cadence of his words slowed, and the men fell silent as well, waiting patiently for him to continue. "But first, we must leave our fair city, free and protected—as it should have been when we arrived—to prepare ourselves. The people are afraid. And why shouldn't they be? What they endured under the demagogues is unfathomable!"

A chorus of shouts rang out from the legions: "Traitors! Cowards! Usurpers!"

Sulla continued, "So now, we must assuage their fears. We will depart. They are watching you, if you look . . ." He pointed to the Roman cityscape around the Field of Mars. "In their huts, hovels, and insulae, they are watching to see what the men of Sulla's Fist will do. Let us show them that we are Rome! And when they next witness us, it will be in a triumphal parade, with chariots overflowing with gold behind us, and Mithridates's head on a litter!" Sulla unsheathed his sword and thrust it in the air. Every warrior present did the same.

As the bellows of their excitement continued, he turned to Lucullus.

"Send the signal," he said.

Trumpets blared, a mournful note slicing through the noise and the morning air.

As the *signiferi* hoisted their banners, the legionaries of Sulla's Fist turned in perfect order and marched away from Rome.

I followed Sulla's example and kept my sword raised until the last man disappeared from the field.

"Now that is how you send off an army," said Lucullus.

Crassus was obviously disappointed. Sulla's charisma failed to change his opinion.

Rather than addressing it again, he and Lucullus donned their helmets, buckled them, and saluted the Consul. They departed once Sulla returned the gesture, though Lucullus delayed a moment to nod a goodbye in my direction.

Sulla watched in silence until everyone departed.

"Now we can begin," he said.

I'd almost forgotten Sulla's true purpose of the day was not just to send away the army but to host the election for his successors. It seemed such a minor concern with everything else involved. How could someone replace Sulla? After all he'd done for Rome over the past year, I believed he should be reelected, without delay.

But Roman custom dictates no man should serve as consul more than once in a ten-year period. Gaius Marius broke this tradition, of course, holding the consul's chair for four years in a row previously. My commander valued tradition too much for this. I admired his desire to restore the balance of power, but I wished he'd reconsider anyway.

Sulla gave me directions for the day, which primarily consisted of standing, watching, and waiting to be called on. He and Rufus made their way across the Field of Mars to the freshly constructed platform and took the center.

Citizens began to appear once they were certain no more legionaries remained. They moved to the voting area cautiously, like deer approaching a clearing where they'd recently seen wolves.

By the time the sun reached its zenith, the Field of Mars was filled to capacity once again, with Roman citizens this time rather than legionaries. The people were noticeably quieter than the latter, which I considered unusual.

Soon enough, the candidates arrived. Some in luxurious litters and followed by retinues stretching back to the Tiber, and others walking upright with only a handful of *servi* and attendants in their wake.

Regardless, all of them appeared insignificant, inconsequential men to me. No man of Sulla's stature stood among them. Perhaps that's what the commander wanted. Even though these men would replace him in office, none could overshadow his greatness or accomplishments.

Once every candidate found their place, Sulla addressed the

people from the speaker's platform.

"I stand before you today not as a conqueror but as a servant of the Republic. You've just witnessed something remarkable today, whether you realize it or not."

His voice carried as effortlessly as when he spoke to the legions, but the pitch was different, and his cadence altered. I marveled at his ability to craft a resonating message, and deliver it flawlessly, no matter who he addressed.

"It was never the barbarian at our gates that Rome feared most—it was the Roman within, the one who might crave ultimate power too deeply to surrender it once claimed. Well, Lucius Cornelius Sulla did claim that power. More than any man before me, I could have eliminated my enemies. I could have named myself king. I *could* have ultimate power, and yet I give it back to *you*." He made a throwing gesture out to the crowd. "Just moments ago, I sent the Republic's strongest army away to prove that power—*true* power—belongs to you and you only. To the people of Rome!"

He spoke different in private, of course, where he proudly claimed all real power belongs to the senate and magistrates, not bread bakers and shopkeepers. But he delivered the line with complete conviction, and the people responded. Now I heard the boisterous cheering I'd heard stories about.

"This is your Rome. This is your Republic. It is my duty to defend it, from enemies within and without, and nothing more. Your duty is to select your representatives, and you will do so today. Let me reassure you: Whatever the outcome, Lucius Cornelius Sulla will honor and uphold it!"

Whatever fears the crowd arrived with had vanished with the morning chill, all at a few words from my commander.

The centuries lined up, the columns stretching from the ballot box to the Tiber, and voting began.

The candidates shifted nervously, calculating each gesture they made as if it might somehow affect the outcome of the election now. Sulla simply watched. He seemed to be playing a different game than his colleagues, a game only he understood. A game he'd already won.

The air was thick with tension as we walked through the Forum. The rising sun settled on top of Saturn's temple and cast a golden hue over the city.

Sulla led the way, his stride purposeful and his toga immaculate despite the chaos of the past several days. I trailed behind him, along with Rufus and the rest of Sulla's retinue.

Sulla's following was noticeably smaller than it had been previously.

The consul's lictors flanked our party, each with a tight grip on their fasces as they eyed the gathering crowd and dared them to make a sudden move.

We passed vendors as they set up their stalls before the Basilica Aemilia. They whispered to one another and watched us pass, their murmured conversations muted by the sound of our footsteps on the Via Sacra.

I'd followed Sulla to several meetings of the senate now. I'd followed him many places. And even when we were in the middle of a bloody war, he'd always stopped to greet passersby. He usually maintained an easy, controlled gait, lolling back at times to share a joke with us. But not today.

He hadn't laughed since the election. The people didn't vote for Vatia, the candidate Sulla openly supported. Not only that, but they elected his political enemy. Some man named Cinna, whom I'd never heard of before. A political nonentity, someone of relative unimportance. But the results infuriated Sulla regardless because Cinna was a known associate of Gaius Marius.

"The people didn't elect Cinna on merit," Sulla had said.

"They voted for him to spurn *me*." I recall the snarl on his face. "After all I've done for them."

The other consul-elect was a man named Gnaeus Octavius. Sulla called Octavius a dullard, an unaccomplished man elected because of his name and the accomplishments of his ancestors. His only noteworthy characteristic was his zealous devotion to the gods, a growing rarity among the noble houses.

My commander returned freedom and power to the people, only for them to spit on him. If they truly appreciated his sacrifice, they would have elected Vatia, and Cinna would remain a nobody.

So Sulla told no jokes today.

The Curia Hostilia loomed ahead, its stern facade casting a long shadow over the Forum.

Today was Sulla's last day in office. His consulship was a historical success. Not only had he crushed the rebels, but he had also liberated Rome from Marius, Sulpicius, and their supporters. All this in the span of a single year.

Then, Sulla kept his word and upheld the Republic's laws, even when offered unprecedented power. This walk to the senate house should have felt like a triumph, but instead it felt like we marched under the yoke.

As we began to ascend the steps to the Curia, I could feel the weight of Sulla's mood. I'd seen him jubilant, and I'd seen him enraged, but his silence unnerved me most.

He entered the senate chambers without turning to address us. Even I had no idea what he intended to do that day.

I stopped at the threshold of the ancient chambers along with the other nonsenators and the *servi*.

I prayed Sulla would handle the exchange of power and be done with it. I stayed with my commander to fight Rome's enemies, not be embroiled in her poisonous politics. I yearned for battle.

A hush fell over the chambers as Sulla strode the floor to his curule chair. Even without his legions, Sulla inspired fear in his enemies and, on this occasion, perhaps even his friends.

A priest barred the door with a rope partition, and Sulla began the day's meeting.

I scribbled notes onto a wax tablet, as I had previously, but this time without any clear instructions on why. Sulla would not be giving a speech. He would merely preside over the exchange of power, or perhaps he would disrupt it. Recording either wouldn't benefit him.

Light stretched across the Forum, but the chill in the air deepened as the meeting continued. Senior senators and former consuls were each given a turn to address the congregation. I tried to remain focused but daydreamed about being on campaign. I yearned for the weight of my lorica and to rid myself of this infernal toga. I remembered the feeling of sun on my skin, the wind pouring over me like a current as I charged with Bucephalus into battle.

I remained preoccupied with these thoughts when I was nearly knocked from my feet. I stumbled, my tablet and stylus crashing and sliding across the stone.

A robust middle-aged man had shoved passed me and was entering the senate house. By the stains on his tunic and the matted knots in his hair, I deduced he was one of many starving beggars on Rome's streets. I tried to reach out and restrain him, but I refused to cross the sacred boundary myself, knowing the penalty was steep. He charged ahead to the center of the chambers.

The senators rose to their feet immediately, clamoring and squawking like an angry flock of birds.

"Sacrilege!" men shouted.

One voice rose above the rest, "Who dares interrupt this august meeting?"

The beggar tried to speak, but no one could hear him over the tumult.

Only Sulla seemed disinterested in the intrusion. He simply studied the man.

"Arrest this pleb!"

Only now did the man make himself heard, "I am no pleb! I am Gaius Sentius!"

I'd never heard the name, but apparently the senate was familiar with him. They murmured to one another in confusion.

"Good Sentius, why have you abandoned your province?" one senator asked.

"Why have you returned in this . . . sordid way?" Another turned his nose up to Sentius's appearance.

Sentius tried to summon a little pride. "My province is overrun."

Everyone fell silent with those few words.

"Mithridates's forces have taken the Hellespont. He has captured Greece. All of it."

"That's impossible," one of two consul-elects, Cinna, said. "He can't field an army large enough to conquer the entire peninsula so quickly."

Sentius met his gaze, and even from outside the senate house, I caught the faint curl of a smile on his dusty lips. "Aye, but he has several armies. Not that he needed them, mind you. Most of the Greek cities abandoned us and joined Mithridates's cause without raising a sword."

The news terrified the senators. Infuriated them. But it thrilled me. Sulla would act quickly now, and we'd be fighting again in a matter of weeks.

"What about Athens?" asked an old senator with a wrinkled face.

Sentius frowned. "It belongs to Mithridates now."

Sulla strode over to the disheveled man. "We applaud you for bringing us this news, but this is neither the time nor place for it. Today is for celebrating the election of our upcoming consuls."

Sentius separated from Sulla and shook his head at the senators. "I didn't come to tell you about the defeats; I came to tell you what Mithridates did when he was victorious."

Everyone waited patiently, but Sentius was having trouble composing himself.

"First, he ordered the death of every Roman citizen in Asia Minor. Then, he ordered his new Greek allies to follow his example, as a symbol of their loyalty to his cause and their eternal enmity to us."

Every inch of my flesh tingled with rage. Had I the chance, I would've stormed into the Curia itself, grabbed Sulla, and begged him to lead us to Greece instantly. I'd never desired vengeance so profoundly, so deeply. I understood the tales of Achilles now.

For once, Sulla was as stunned as the rest of us. If he really could see the future, he'd overlooked this event.

"How many?" one senator managed to ask.

"Reports estimate eighty thousand."

"Eight thousand?" someone cried out.

"No, eighty thousand," Sentius corrected. "And that's just the men. Every woman and child with Roman blood met the same fate. They even killed our slaves and freedmen."

By now, the message carried back through the throng of gatherers in the Forum. The Roman people cried out and tore at their togas. Perhaps some of them had friends and relatives in those foreign countries, but the rest mourned the loss of Roman prestige, the loss of Roman power, and the elimination of so many citizens.

I'm not sure how long this continued, how long the senators argued among themselves. The next thing I recall was Sulla leading the two consul-elects, Cinna and Octavius from the senate house. They passed right by me and carried on to the rostra, the people parted before them like they carried the plague.

Sulla addressed the people first. I should have recorded his words, but everything spun around me, the marble and the brick and the columns and statues. I could think only of this foreign king and what he did to Rome.

Sulla didn't address the massacre. Instead, he formally introduced Cinna and Octavius as their new consuls.

I remember the smug look on Cinna's face, with a piqued brow and a satisfied grin. I would have hated him in that moment if I had any hate to spare, but I no longer cared for the senators and their game of politics. I would save my rage for Mithridates and his followers.

Sulla then announced he would leave for the East immediately, to a chorus of praise from the people and a rush of excitement from me.

But first, he stopped and addressed the two men who would replace him.

"I ask only one thing before I depart to avenge our fallen and restore our Republic. Swear, here and now, before the gods and the people of Rome, that you will not destroy the harmony I've sacrificed so much to build. Swear that you will uphold the laws I passed and not use your power to sow chaos in my absence."

The tears and praise fell away from the people as they grew silent and waited. Cinna and Octavius both lingered for a moment. What would Sulla do if they declined? No law required them to take such an oath.

But, eventually, both men raised their right hand and made Sulla's vow before the gods and the people of Rome.

Sulla remained unsatisfied. He snapped his fingers and shouted something to a nearby servant, who ran to the rostra and handed him two stones. He passed these to the new consuls and said, "Cast these stones from the rostra, as a symbol of your oath. And let all know this—if you break it, you'll be cast from Rome as you cast away these rocks."

Cinna's eye twitched, but both men complied.

If Octavius was truly as devoted to the gods as his reputation indicated, we could trust he would keep this oath. Cinna, however, couldn't be trusted.

Sulla knew this but said nothing else. He stepped down from the platform, his movements brisk.

"We leave immediately. We'll sail from Nola with the first favorable winds," he said when we reconvened with his retinue.

I fell in step behind him, and we departed the Forum. The senate, the elections, the oaths—all simply a prelude. The true battle—the only one that mattered—remained in the shadow of Athens and the ambitions of a foreign king.

SCROLL X

ARREA—THREE DAYS after the Ides of Sextilis, 666 Ab Urbe Condita

I didn't know where I was when she woke me. I guess it didn't matter. Our tent was too dark to see anything, but I could feel my husband's warmth beside me, and I could hear Toria's cry elevating as she wiggled against the restraints of her swaddling cloth.

For once, I woke up before Quintus. I often reminded him she woke because she was hungry, and he lacked the equipment to feed her. He would laugh but always remained awake with us anyway. Fortunately, this time his eye remained shut. He needed the rest.

"Shh . . . there now, little one." I took Toria in my arms and peeled back the blanket layers.

That brought a smile to her tiny lips, one I could see even in the darkness. She cupped her pudgy hands around my face and patted enough to wake me sufficiently.

Beside our bedrolls, we had nothing in the tent save a stool in the corner. That's where I took my seat and tried to feed Toria.

Unlike most nights, she refused to latch. Sometimes it took a few tries, especially in the dark. But on this night—over two weeks into our journey from Spoletium to Fabius's camp outside Arretium—she seemed totally disinterested.

Instead, she babbled and pointed to the tent flap and the night air beyond it. She'd just discovered the use of her index finger recently and made constant use of it to direct my attention.

As her frustration and excitement grew, so did her volume, and soon I hurried to do as the little tyrant commanded.

The light of a still-smoldering campfire poured into the tent when I pushed back the flap. I stopped there and looked at my husband.

He was sound asleep. I couldn't recall the last time I'd seen it. For days, he'd stayed awake for guard shifts that weren't his, allowing Barca, Fabius, or one of the mercenaries to sleep, despite their protests. His vigilance was remarkable. He always kept his eye on our guide and on the road before us.

But I could see the strain wearing on him. Even then, as he slept deeply for the first time in weeks, his teeth remained clenched and his brow furrowed. Quintus spoke of his dreams rarely, but I don't recall any of them being pleasant. I doubted whatever ran through his mind in that moment was peaceful.

Quintus found me (or I found him) after a battle. My master and his compatriots had wounded Quintus gravely. Despite the fear I felt in that moment, when an armored, sword-wielding man barged into my master's hut, something compelled me to help him.

I cleaned and dressed his wound and assisted in his recovery for weeks. At the time, it seemed ludicrous. I should have run; most slaves in my position would have. But it was the best decision I ever made. And except for the baby girl now swaddled in my arms, I was prouder of saving Quintus Sertorius than anything else I'd done in my life.

I wished so badly that I could heal him now. If there were a balm, a bandage I could apply, to fix the broken state of my husband's beloved Republic or mend that which bleeds inside him, I would.

Even when he smiled, even when he giggled with Toria, tickling her with the stubble of his beard, or nibbled on her toes, I could see the sadness, the burden in his eye. I wondered if it would ever go away.

But still, my heart leapt when I looked back at him, sleeping on our cot. It was no easy life, being the wife of Quintus Sertorius. But in the end, I would be able to say what most Roman matrons cannot: My husband was a good man, and he truly loved me.

And it didn't hurt that he was handsome. Strikingly so. His sun-tanned skin was darker than any of my people's. His hair was the color of roasted chestnuts, though a few specks of gray developed above his ears when he allowed it to grow long enough. He'd found little time to shave during our flight, and his dark beard had grown out. Most of his fellow senators considered beards to be barbaric, reminding them too much of my people, but I liked Quintus's. That it tickled our daughter and made her laugh only made me like it more.

He'd be forty in two years, which would make him old by Gallic standards but in his prime to the Romans. Quintus remained vigorous, but life's strain was aging him. I knew the cause of every crease: this one from the death of his father, the next from Arausio, that one from all the times he'd spread the ashes of his companions. More than a few wrinkles developed directly from the political turmoil we found ourselves in. Fresh ones seemed to form each day as he worried for our safety.

Each line revealed his heart, how much he cared. I loved him more for each, though I wished they weren't necessary.

Toria kicked and squirmed until I stepped out and allowed the flap to close behind me.

The air was thick with late-summer humidity, though a faint coolness indicated the arrival of an early autumn. Smoke and fog

fought for supremacy above our little camp, both making it difficult to see, but Toria delighted in this.

The chirp of crickets and the hum of cicadas in the tall grass
excited her the most, as she pointed each time she heard
something.

We always maintained one guard to watch the camp, but I
saw no one at first. Perhaps it was Quintus's turn, but he simply
couldn't keep his eyelid open any longer.

No, he wouldn't do that. He'd fight through sleep like a line
of enemy infantry to make sure we remained safe.

Toria and I stepped through the cloud of fog and roiling
campfire smoke until we spotted Barca on the far end of camp,
facing out into the night.

"Do you mind if we join you?"

To my surprise, we startled him. Barca wasn't accustomed to
surprise, and it didn't please him.

"You crept up on cat's paws," he said.

"I don't think I've ever seen you caught unaware before," I
said with a furtive grin. "Lucky for you I was not an assassin."

"Hmph." Rather than saying anything else, he reached over
and picked up a towel to dry the sweat from his forehead. An
unsheathed dagger lay beneath.

He never directly answered my question, but I found my seat
on a stool beside him, and he didn't object.

When he saw Toria, he smiled.

"Has the little warrior come for inspection? I assure you
both, I am wide awake, and my gear is in proper order." He
attempted a Roman salute that would have made Quintus
laugh.

Toria reached out for him. She rarely objected when others
held her, but she asked for no one outside the family save Barca.

"Would you like to hold her?"

He considered it, then shook his head. "Must remain
watchful."

We settled into silence as the fire warmed our backs. A cool, moist wind wafted toward us from a pond or stream somewhere in the distance. And the insects continued to sing.

Above, the moon freed itself from the cover of gray clouds and illuminated Barca's face. Something was different. He usually wore anger like a cloak, his eyes radiating half-restrained intensity. Every movement seemed on the verge of a pounce. But tonight, I sensed more sadness in him than anger.

"What are you thinking, gladiator?" I said.

I thought my calling him that might provoke a chuckle or a retort, but it didn't.

He remained quiet so long I assumed he had no interest in talking or hadn't heard me.

"I've always had purpose," he said. "I've had direction my entire life. Now I do not."

I thought about responding, but I could see his mind at work. He was processing something and only my silence would permit him to do so properly.

"My first memory was of my mother . . . well, perhaps she was a wet nurse. The slave-women raised all of us collectively. I never knew which one birthed me. Was it the same for you?"

"I wasn't born a *servi*," I said.

He winced. "Taken when older, then? Probably harder. We accepted fate from the first day because it's all we knew." He crossed his arms and fixed his gaze on something—nothing—in the distance. "This woman, whoever she was, said I would grow to be big and strong. It was not a compliment. She said I couldn't be a house slave. I would frighten the matrons." His gaze shifted to the stars above. For a moment, he seemed to forget that Toria and I sat beside him. "Only two possible outcomes, she said. I would die in the salt mines, or I could die in the arena. In the arena, I would last longer, and at least I would die with a full belly."

He remembered us when he heard Toria coo.

"I dedicated my life to fighting. I started brawls and found myself in trouble with my masters. I took beatings, but it was for a purpose. I needed them to see. And they did. My efforts proved successful when they sold me to a *lanista*."

"Much better than the salt mines." I'd heard the stories and shuddered at the thought.

"They said it was my eleventh birthday when they sold me, but I doubt anyone kept count. When I arrived, I found a new purpose. To perfect my craft. To deceive more effectively, strike with more strength, move with more finesse. I needed this to survive the training pits, and I did. By the time stubble grew on my chin, I entered the arena."

I realized how still Toria had become. Surprisingly, she remained awake, listening intently as if she could understand him.

"Next, I devoted myself to earning the attention, respect, and admiration of my *lanista*. No small task, despite my fighting skill. I knew it would be the only way to earn freedom."

He reached down and scooped up a handful of dirt and let it sift through his fingers. Did it remind him of the arena? Of blood on the sand?

"I soon realized that the more I won, the more coin my *lanista* made. By success, I made myself indispensable to him. He would never grant me freedom that way."

He paused, and I feared he wouldn't continue. But I wanted to know the rest. Barca rarely spoke of himself, even less often about his past. I couldn't expect this opportunity again.

"How then? How did you earn it?" I asked.

"Through the love of the crowd." He almost whispered the words, as if he could hear them chant his name. "I became an entertainer. I ensured they would cheer so long and loud, eventually my master would have no choice. And it worked."

"Go on."

"By Roman standards, I was still a young man when I received my wooden sword. But I had no skills. I knew nothing but how to fight. I didn't know where to go. What to do. So . . . I continued fighting for my master. Only now he paid me." He looked me in the eyes. "My purpose became to earn a fortune. To one day be richer than the man who paid me.

"In time, I had enough to start my own *ludus*. I focused solely on making the greatest school possible." Something agitated him as he spoke and he shifted on his stool. "Others judge me for becoming the thing I loathed, but my life was the sands. How else was I to help other boys who were too tall and strong, who scare Roman matrons? How else could I mold them into warriors rather than skeletons in the salt mines?"

I grabbed his hand and squeezed it. Toria reached for him, too, as if she always wanted to comfort him.

"You needn't explain to me, Barca," I said. "Quintus and I have *servi* at our villa in Rome . . . or at least we did. All we can do is treat them with the kindness neither you nor I were afforded."

The touch confused him, but I think he appreciated it as well. He nodded.

"That was my purpose when we met. My men. I worked as hard for my gladiators as they worked for me. I thought that would be the rest of my life. I thought I would die with the same vision fixed in my gaze." His rigid jawline twitched. "But that changed when I met your husband," he said.

One might expect his words to carry anger or regret, but I heard none.

"He called me 'friend.' No one ever called me that before, especially not a Roman."

"Quintus is a good man," I said. "And he cares for you. More than a friend, like a brother."

"And then you taught me how to read, how to speak too. And that . . ." he stopped.

Barca looked away. "But I care nothing for this Republic. It would suit me to watch the Roman wolves devour each other. I only ever wished to protect your family. And it pleased—no, honored me—that *I* could protect." He jabbed a finger in his chest with pride.

Unable to remain still, he jumped to his feet and paced before us.

"But now my school is gone. All I've built has crumbled. I have nothing." His words slowed and his volume decreased as he continued to talk. "I have no plan. For the first time in my life, I am without purpose."

I felt tears welling up in my eyes and did my best to blink them away.

"Barca, I am so sorry for everything you've endured. You've lost so much only because you helped us."

He frowned. "I am not a slave. Not any longer. I make my own fate. No one is accountable but those who stole from me."

I nodded. "I admire your spirit, Barca. Always have. But you sacrificed everything for us—"

"Not everything," he said. "I'm still breathing."

For some reason, that made me laugh, which finally forced a single tear to roll down my cheek. "And good, let's keep it that way, yes? Don't go sacrificing your life."

He held up his chin. "I'm not dying anytime soon. Death cannot have me until He earns me, and He hasn't yet."

Boasting seemed to please him, and the tension in his shoulders eased. "I shall hold the little warrior now," he said.

Toria didn't need convincing. The moment I stood up, she stretched her arms out to him.

Barca took her into his large, scarred arms. He held onto her like precious, fragile treasure. He fidgeted, unsure exactly how to keep her comfortable, and looked to me for guidance.

But I learned many lessons about instructing when Barca taught me the basics of fighting. I leaned back and crossed my arms in playful mockery, leaving him to figure it out on his own.

Toria wrapped her pudgy arms around his neck and eventually settled in. He didn't seem to mind when her drool dripped down his shoulder.

"You still have a purpose, Barca," I said. "I'm convinced much of this life is a bleak affair, but it's better with you in it. The gods still have a purpose for you, even if you don't know what it is."

His eyes narrowed, not in anger but focus. "Yes," he said. "First, I will escort this little warrior to the safety of camp. Then we will discover what the gods have in store for me."

He craned his neck to look at her. Toria was already fast asleep in his arms.

SCROLL XI

LUCIUS HIRTULEIUS—SIX days before the Kalends of September, 666 Ab Urbe Condita

I woke to the sound of scraping steel. Slow. Steady. Unrelenting.

Blinking against the dim light, I sat up on my cot, the smell of damp wood and salt thick in the air. A single flame flickered above a tallow candle beside me, dimly illuminating the cabin's cramped walls. Seated on a weathered barrel, Gaius Marius hunched over his work, the light glimmering on the blade as he dragged it across a whetstone.

"You don't sleep well," he said without looking up. His voice was low and flat, disturbing neither his son or Aulus who continued to slumber across the cabin. "Do bad dreams trouble you?"

No dreams troubled me, but I slept poorly regardless. How was I supposed to rest on this old vessel? It swayed beneath us endlessly, the boards groaning like an old man rising from bed. The rowers and sailors on the deck above snored louder than any legionary camp I'd slept in, and that was no small feat. No, I didn't sleep well at sea.

But in the glow of that dim light, it wasn't the sea or the sailors or the creaking wood that troubled me. It was him, the man seated by my cot, the Consul of Rome turned fugitive, the man sharpening his blade in the middle of the night.

I rubbed the sleep from my eyes but couldn't clear the grumble from my throat. "If I was dreaming, I can't recall them."

Marius smiled faintly, though it never reached his eyes. "Even through all this, I sleep soundly." The whetstone hissed as he ran it across his blade again. "I used to toss about like you. Not so long ago, my dreams made me . . . restless."

The groaning cabin seemed to shrink, and the stale air within grew heavier.

"When I was a young man," Marius said, "I served in Hispania, against the Numantines. Ever heard of Numantia?"

I'd heard of it, but only from Marius himself, as he'd told me endless stories about the war over the years. Could he not recall our conversations? Was the question rhetorical?

I simply nodded.

"Brave warriors, they were. Brave, and by the end of the war, they were desperate warriors as well." His voice continued to lower so that I had to lean forward to hear him. "Do you know what desperation does to men, Lucius?"

Of course I did. We'd fought in countless battles together, and I'd seen desperation in the eyes of the defeated more times than I could recollect. He knew that, so I didn't reply.

He answered his own question. "Desperation makes men unpredictable. Dangerous. To defeat a desperate foe, one must become just as dangerous." Mercifully, he set the whetstone aside and examined the edge of his *pugio*, rotating it so the flame shimmered along the polished steel. "Scipio Aemilianus himself gave me command of a single maniple to deal with some of these desperate, dangerous men. It was my first position of authority."

"Is this when he told the officers you were his successor?" I asked. Marius had recollected the event to me more times than I could count, his eyes always gleaming, reflecting the campfire they sat around when Scipio Aemilianus made the claim.

He continued as if he hadn't heard me. "The enemy tribe took shelter in an abandoned camp twenty miles from Numantia. Our scouts reported there were over eight hundred of them. Eight hundred desperate, dangerous men. I had one hundred and twenty at my command. I spent days trying to develop a strategy that would allow us to defeat them. But I couldn't. It didn't seem possible."

Realizing Marius had no intention of allowing me to fall back asleep, I swung my legs over the side of my cot and leaned closer. I'd heard many of Marius's stories about Hispania but couldn't recall this one.

"But Scipio trusted me to see this through. I knew he gave me enough men to carry out the order; I only needed to discover how. Eventually, the solution came to me. I promised the desperate men clemency. If these eight hundred men laid down their arms, we would allow their women and children within the besieged city to evacuate. We would even see them safely to Lusitania, where they could live without fear of Roman retribution."

He paused, as if waiting for a comment. Before I could speak, he abruptly continued.

"All eight hundred of them laid down their arms and came out, half-starved, with only torn rags to protect them from the elements. Fear in their eyes, they met us in a mountainous ravine. Do you know what I did then, Lucius?"

He balanced the dagger's tip on his forefinger, a prick of blood welling up around it.

I swallowed. "You executed them."

He looked at me then, his eyes sharp as the blade. "They were too many to be killed by hand. Even disarmed, these pitiful creatures might have overwhelmed us," he said. "So, I burned them alive."

The words lingered between us like smoke. I couldn't break his gaze, the weight of it pressing down on me like stone.

"I'd heard nothing like their screams. And they lingered on much longer than you'd expect. Fire doesn't kill as quickly as the sword. But it was war. It was necessary. I couldn't return to Scipio except in triumph. This was about survival; it was about my future. But that didn't stop the decision from haunting my dreams. For years I stirred through the night, like you do now." For the first time, he turned his dagger and aimed its crimson tip at me. "So, what is it that keeps you awake, soldier? What decision haunts you?"

He leaned forward, his shadow stretching across the floorboards.

I was suddenly aware of how close we were. I felt the urge to leave for the top deck, where the air wouldn't be so stifling. I glanced over to Aulus, hoping he would stir, but—unlike myself —he slept soundly.

"Nothing comes to mind," I said, but the words felt fragile.

"Nothing?" Marius's lips twisted. "A man who's done nothing shameful in war? You'd be the first I've met."

I frantically searched my mind for a story to reciprocate his but came up with nothing. I had little in life to be proud of, but my conduct as a legionary was one of them. I did only what duty and honor compelled.

I'd certainly never burned eight hundred unarmed men alive.

"Perhaps sleep still grips me," I said. "Ask me again tomorrow, and I'm sure I can think of something."

"Allow me to assist," he said. "Have you ever broken your word? A sacred oath? Have you ever betrayed someone who put their trust in you?"

He wasn't making simple conversation, swapping war stories like we used to. No, he had a purpose. His dark gaze penetrated me, searching for answers, but I didn't understand what he wanted to find.

"I've always kept my word," I said. "The gods have never given me reason to break it."

Something tugged at Marius's lip. "So, you would forsake a vow if hardship bade you? If opportunity presented itself? Perhaps a memory isn't what disturbs your sleep, but a plan."

I understood him then. "I would never betray you, general," I said.

"Betray me?" He tilted his head. "I never said that."

"You didn't have to," I said, the sleep in my voice now replaced by frustration. "You've circled around it since you woke me."

"And so? Can you blame me?" He picked up the whetstone and began his work again, quicker and more aggressively than before. "I have a price on my head. The tides of fortune have swayed. I could hardly blame you for betraying me and taking that reward."

It felt like a shield bashed into my chest. I'd sacrificed everything for Marius. I even became a deserter to protect him, something I'd never have entertained in a hundred lifetimes otherwise. I waded through swamps, spent countless nights on this *Dis* cursed ship, and narrowly escaped execution in the ruins of Carthage.

"I could have betrayed you in Italy but didn't," I said. "I have no need for Sulla's bounty. I made an oath to you, and I will keep it."

The words hung in the air, and for a moment, I didn't know how he'd respond. He set the blade and whetstone down. He stood and pinched the candlewick between his fingers, snuffing out the flame with a faint hiss.

In utter darkness, he said, "We are both desperate men, Lucius. And desperation makes men dangerous. I needed to be certain."

I released a breath I didn't realize I'd been holding and leaned back on my cot. My back and shoulders relaxed, but they seared from tension. Marius appeared to be assuaged, and I couldn't accost him for the insult. I had nothing else to say.

His barrel scraped against soggy wood as he stood.

"Get some sleep," he said. "You'll need it today."

Going back to sleep wasn't an option. The swift thud of my heart wouldn't allow it.

"There isn't much to do on this ship," I said. "I'm sure I'll have time to rest throughout the day."

I couldn't see him but felt him pause by the door. "We're leaving the ship, Lucius. The captain made me aware. He means to abandon us on an island today."

I shot back up. "What? I thought your client secured us safe passage?"

"He did, but only to Numidia. I haven't a single denarius left, and the captain will hear no more promises." His voice remained low, steady, almost peaceful. I sensed no urgency or concern, nothing to indicate he understood the precarious position we'd soon be in.

Pale blue light stretched across the cabin as Marius departed.

My mind reeled as I stared up from my cot into the darkness above me.

Was this how the story of Gaius Marius would end? Stranded, starving on some hollow rock while Rome continued without him?

The whetstone's hiss lingered in my ears, soft as a death knell carried on the wind. Sleep never returned.

SCROLL XII

Quintus Sertorius—Five days before the Kalends of September, 666 Ab Urbe Condita

Our journey to Arretium would've only taken a few days had we traveled back to Rome and taken the Via Cassia north, but that would have meant death for Barca and imprisonment for me.

Instead, we traveled through forests, hillside mountain paths, and bogs, following the blind guide Barca hired in Spoletium.

I recall little of the journey. Exhaustion clouded my mind. I could scarcely sleep, even when Barca or Fabius volunteered to take watch. I never let the blind guide out of my sight and watched for signs of betrayal. I always kept my sword at the ready, in case I spotted something in the distance.

But nothing warranted my fears, thankfully. No one accosted us on the road, and the blind guide accepted his payment and set off barefoot back through the same paths he led us.

But the effects of exhaustion lingered with us all as we arrived on a hilltop fourteen days after departing Spoletium. Fabius's mercenary camp rested in the valley. Perhaps it was our weary limbs that forced us to pause there on the crest of the hill, or perhaps it was amazement at what we saw.

I shielded my eye against the late afternoon sun and considered the camp. It was unlike a legionary encampment. I saw no orderly rows of tents laid out to a prefect's mathematical precision. Instead, Fabius's camp sprawled across the valley floor like a festival ground, scattered with colorful tents, cooking fires, and makeshift pavilions. Yet, despite its looseness, it wasn't chaotic.

Fabius's mercenaries maintained a different kind of order here—one built from necessity rather than regulation. Even from the distance, I could see men move purposefully between the fires, sharpening their weapons and carrying supplies. Banners fluttered in the breeze, a mix of old faded legionary standards, colorful flags of nations across the *Mare Nostrum,* and hastily sewn insignias that likely meant nothing but to Fabius and his men.

And they were singing.

Not marching songs or battle chants. I could barely make out the words, but these were bawdy, carefree tunes, accompanied by the disorganized clatter of makeshift drums. Laughter echoed throughout the camp—loud, unrestrained, and unafraid. This looked more like a gathering of Thespians than a war band.

"Here it is," Fabius said. "My traveling Babylon."

I shifted Toria to my other hip and glanced at my wife. Arrea placed her hand in mine. Her dark hair had fallen loose from its braid during our journey and flew wildly over her shoulders, bits of twigs and leaves mixed in. Our trek exhausted her, but her eyes remained sharp as she studied the camp below.

"They seem . . . cheerful," she said.

I nodded. "Mercenaries have every right to be happy, I suppose."

She looked confused. "Why?"

"When you only fight the battles of others, you have no battles of your own," I said.

Toria squirmed and babbled in frustration. I ran my fingers

gently through her soft, dark hair. She'd grown immensely since we left Rome. She now desired to explore and experience the new world around her. My daughter wanted to move. Toria no longer wanted us to carry her about all the time. The freedom of camp would please her more than anyone.

Fabius waved us forward and led us down toward the camp.

Arrea studied me. "Do you resent them for that?"

I considered my answer. "So long as men live, we'll fight one another. Mercenaries exist to serve that function, a purely trans-actional enterprise, simple as buying a loaf of bread at the market," I said. "I don't blame the individuals but wish we lived in a world where their craft wasn't valued."

As we followed Fabius at a brisk pace, I looked down and brushed Toria's cheek. She blinked up at me. Something humored her—perhaps my disheveled hair—and she giggled. After she gained her first tooth, three more rapidly appeared. They caused her to drool like a mastiff until it ran down her cheeks and pooled on my arms, but—at least for the moment—they caused her no pain.

Arrea wasn't finished with our conversation and got to the heart of it. "Do you trust them?"

We had no choice but to accept Fabius's offer when he first arrived. We were short on supplies and on the run with enemies on our heels. I didn't fear Fabius turning us in to Sulla. If he intended to collect Sulla's reward, he'd had opportunities. But did I trust him for more than safe passage? Could I trust his men?

I wasn't certain if I trusted Fabius or not, but I *wanted* to trust him. I felt closer to my father in his presence.

"Of course I do, my love," I lied.

I would remain cautious, but I wouldn't force Arrea to share in my burdens.

Barca, who'd watched our flank for most of the journey, moved up alongside us.

"This is no army," he said. "This is a circus."

"This circus can offer protection for now," I said.

Barca didn't reply, but his jaw tightened. He grew more reserved with each passing day. I missed his banter, his direct manner of speech.

Fabius's pace quickened as we grew closer, showing no signs of exhaustion from our journey. His stride was that of a man coming home.

As we reached the edge of his camp, the first mercenary spotted him.

"Fabius!" one shouted.

Others joined in and soon every mercenary in the camp rushed toward the gate.

"Did you miss me?" Fabius shouted.

They swarmed around him, laughing and clapping his back. They embraced him as first among equals rather than as a commander like I'd expected.

I marveled at the ease with which he navigated through the crowd. He called out each man by name, adding in a joke or insult when he could. Fabius was like a king without a crown.

The mercenaries were so rapturous at their leader's return, they scarcely noticed us. At the very least, I was grateful they cast no unkind looks in our direction.

We followed Fabius to the center of camp, where a raised platform of crates and barrels served as a makeshift rostra, or theater stage, depending on the occasion.

Fabius leapt gratefully on top, and waved us forward, offering a hand to my mother.

"Brothers!" he called out. "My comrades. How good it is to see you! The freest men on this scarred rock we call earth."

As we joined Fabius on stage and faced his army, I scanned the crowd. These men were formidable warriors with a lifetime of experience in battle. Unlike the uniformity of the legion, where each man looked identical aside from slight variations in the kit to designate rank, each man here presented himself unique. Some had old, boiled leather breastplates while also wearing ornate silver helmets with high plumes. They'd not been issued their arms and armor but had taken them from fallen foes.

If I was such a man, how much would I charge for my services? How much compensation would I expect to risk death and dismemberment for a cause not my own? My throat tightened when I considered what the expense would be for two thousand such men.

"Yes, we are free, lads," Fabius continued. "We are who we decide to be. We no longer must bear those names given to us when we were the unwelcome sons of unworthy fathers, when we were merely citizens. We are free to fight, to eat, drink, and make love!"

I now noticed many women scattered throughout the crowd, almost as numerous as the mercenaries. Whether they were campaign wives, family members, or prostitutes, I did not know, but they drank of the same wine and cheered as fervently as the men.

"And we choose who to fight for. My friends, we have guests."

They cheered, although they still didn't know us.

"We're unfit for their company, but we shall do our best to pretend we are. The man before you is Quintus Sertorius, veteran of the Cimbri wars like many of you."

I carefully handed Toria to my wife and stepped forward to greet the mercenaries.

Roman crowds felt duty bound to erupt with applause at the mention of the Cimbri wars, but the victory didn't compel enthusiasm from the mercenaries.

They reacted more when Fabius said, "And I'd wager any amount of coin he could beat any of you in a duel."

I forced a smile and raised my fists, which his men seemed to enjoy.

"His good friend, Barca, who some of you likely made a fortune betting on when he was king of the arena, joins him. As does his family." He made his hand like a knife and aimed it out at his warriors. "If any of you so much as disrespects the earth they walk on, I shall castrate you myself and nail what's left of you here." He stomped on the makeshift stage.

Despite the threat, his men remained in good humor. Something told me they knew to listen to Fabius instinctively, threats or not.

"Now, for those of you who've been too drunk to notice, Rome has had some strife in these recent days."

This elicited a great deal of laughter and catcalls from the mercenaries. Unsurprisingly, Rome's discord didn't concern them.

"Unlike us, Quintus Sertorius is an honorable man who wants to use his time here on this rock to improve the world. We are going to help him do so, whatever that means."

The men cheered now. They likely assumed I planned to hire them, and the mercenaries were ready for their next contract.

"Now, I will allow our illustrious guest to address you himself." He gestured to me and stepped aside.

I had nothing prepared to say. I still couldn't think clearly. My stomach gurgled, and all I wanted to do was taste the olives and wine everyone else enjoyed.

Instead, I took a deep breath, composed myself, and stared out over the scarred, sunburnt, and smiling men of Fabius's army.

Despite their wine-induced good spirits, they sobered enough to listen to me, curious as to what I might say or adequately practiced in making their patrons feel important.

"Your welcome honors me," I began. "I am grateful to each of you. Nothing is more important to me than my family, and with warriors like you around us, I know they are safe from those who might harm us."

I looked to Fabius to see if that was enough, but he gestured for me to continue.

"You are welcoming an exile," I said. "A man named Sulla

led Roman troops against his own city. I led the resistance against him, and for that, he sent followers to capture me and kill those I care about."

Fabius nodded for me to go on.

"The Republic is in flux. No one knows what will happen next. But . . ." I looked back at my family and felt a pang in my chest. "But I fear fighting lies ahead."

I considered my conversation with Fabius, as I had many times over the past two weeks. I knew he was right.

I would exhaust every alternative possible to bloodshed, but if that failed, Rome would need these mercenaries if we hoped for any chance of defeating Sulla and his loyalists.

"If it comes to that, I will need good men beside me. Rome will need good men. And Fabius says you're up for the task."

They pounded their chests and grunted rhythmically.

I took a deep breath and continued. "When I joined the legion, I had other opportunities in Rome. I could have avoided the bloodshed and the sacrifice, but I believe my calling was to serve the Republic."

I refrained from using oratorical gestures as I would speaking in the Forum. These men weren't interested in theatrics, they wanted honesty.

"I was young and naive. Part of me was also prideful. I never said it aloud, but somewhere in my heart I felt superior to the men who joined out of necessity. Many of my comrades joined not out of love for the Republic but because they were hungry. Others, because they were tired of sleeping in the rain. Or because they had no inheritance and no land. The legion offered them an escape, an opportunity."

They listened closely. I could almost speak at normal volume, as if having a personal conversation, now that the camp was quiet and still.

"But the legion humbled me, and I quickly discovered my error. Many of these men who joined for nothing but self-interest, became finer soldiers than I'd ever dreamt of becoming myself. They fought harder, endured more, questioned less, complained not at all. Some sacrificed more, some of them sacrificed everything. I realized that it matters not *why* you serve but *how* you serve. I am here to say: I don't care why you fight but only that you fight with courage."

For the first time, many of Fabius's men nodded along.

"Whether coin, glory, or something else inspires you—none of that matters to me. If civil war lies before us, I'll need men who fight hard, who stand their ground when bodies collect at their feet and the chaos of battle swallows everything around them. I need men who won't blink when the odds are stacked against them. Does that describe you?"

They erupted, making up for their previous silence. The women let out war cries of their own, as if they planned to join us on the battlefield.

I stole a glance behind me. Arrea looked awestruck. I couldn't tell whether the topic of another war terrified her, or if the mercenaries' support inspired her.

Toria pointed at me and watched with wide eyes, saying '*tata, tata*' over and over again. Barca stared out into the distance with a fixed gaze and a hard face. Fabius gave me a nod of encouragement. My mother dabbed at her eyes.

I considered what I could promise them. Even patriotic legionaries desired compensation. What could I possibly offer?

Fabius's men had no desire for citizenship or for land. I yearned for peace, a quiet life away from swords and battlefields. These mercenaries would've taken a different path if they shared that desire. They fought not because they had to or because duty compelled them but because they wanted to. I could see in their eyes the desire to live this way until their last breath and to be compensated well for the time they had left.

When we spoke by the stream, Fabius suggested that benefactors would support us. I prayed he was right. Otherwise, this was all for naught.

But they didn't ask about payment now, and I didn't mention it. That was a problem for another day.

"Hard times might lie ahead," I said. "Before this is over, we may shed blood beside one another. But for now, let us drink."

The mercenaries cheered and sang an impromptu song.

I stepped down from the makeshift stage.

I wasn't a consul. I wasn't even a praetor. My term as legatus expired months ago. I held no authority. Only a burning desire to save the Republic before it was too late. Nothing gave me the power to raise an army. I needed to remain cautious. I still didn't know if Sulla named me an enemy of the state or if he conspired against me in shadows. Regardless, some would call this speech illegal.

Criminal.

Treasonous.

My family gathered to address me, as did Fabius. I nodded along as they spoke, but my mind was fixed on prayer.

I prayed for guidance, wisdom, and strength. I asked the gods to spare Rome a civil war. I begged them to present another solution.

The gods didn't respond, but I knew their answer.

Civil war began the moment Sulla marched his legion through Rome's gates.

I left my family in our assigned quarters with Barca, who insisted on keeping watch over them himself. Toria was fast asleep in her mother's arms before I washed off my face and departed. Even Rhea rested on a cot in the corner, perhaps dreaming of our home before others reduced it to ash. I wanted to join them for a brief reprieve, but I knew it was important to meet the mercenaries. Speeches can only do so much. Fabius's men fought for coin, but if it came to that, they would fight harder for a commander they believed in.

I followed Fabius through the camp. The scent of roasted meats filled the evening air, mingling with the tang of smoke from a hundred campfires. As the sun lowered in the west, shadows stretched across the uneven ground. Fabius's "traveling Babylon" was alive and boisterous—laughter, clattering dice, the rhythmic strumming of lyres. Men shared skins of wine freely and raised their voices in bawdy songs that echoed throughout the surrounding hills.

Fabius introduced me at each campfire. I ignored the growling of my stomach as I watched a boar rotate on a spit, juices dripping into the fire below. Hunger gnawed at me like frostbite, but I ignored their offers to sit and join. There were two thousand men, and I wanted to shake the hand of each one if I could manage it before collapsing.

We moved on to another fire surrounded by six or seven men and just as many women. They looked up as we approached, and Fabius greeted them each by name.

"Borsus, Rufio, Panates," he said, "This is Quintus Sertorius, our leader."

I extended my hand to each and offered a curt nod to the women, not knowing or seeking to find out their station.

These were rough men, scarred from a lifetime of fighting for survival, but their eyes conveyed an intelligence that belied their coarseness.

"I heard about you," one said. "Is it true you fought off a hundred Cimbri at Arausio?"

"And then swam across a flooded river in full kit with a spear in your eye?"

I smiled. "A hundred might be an exaggeration, but each Cimbri warrior fought like a hundred. And it was a slinger's rock in my eye, not a spear."

They nodded, some impressed, others skeptical.

"Is it true fifty thousand Romans perished that day?" another mercenary asked.

My smile faded. "More."

The casualties were so high they lost all meaning. Whenever someone asked of Arausio, I thought of my brother, of my friends. I remembered Titus, Pilate, Flamen, and all the others. And I remembered their faces.

"I can't fathom what that would even look like."

They returned to their meals, not much empathy in their eyes, but that suited me just fine. Tales of service to Rome would win me no friends here.

As Fabius led me on to the next fire he said, "You'll win them all over, if you keep speaking to them like that."

The next gathering we approached was smaller, and the group around it was older and more reserved. They eyed me with a mix of curiosity, suspicion, and indifference.

One of them, a man with a crooked nose and a sharp gaze, spoke up. "Tell me, Lord Sertorius, do you think this rebellion of yours could actually work?"

I knew immediately he'd served in the legion long ago, I could see it in his posture and by the look in his eyes. I assumed he'd been a mercenary for many years as well, and probably survived this long by being cautious with who he worked for.

I met his gaze. "This isn't my rebellion. It isn't a rebellion at all. Sulla broke the law when he took Rome by force," I said. "He's continued to abuse his power by the destruction of property and the ordered assassination of Roman citizens. His legions grant him too much power now, but soon enough Rome will join in opposition to him and pass down judgment for his crimes."

Another shrugged, unconvinced. "Call it what you like, but it's no small task we have before us."

"The greatest task before Rome is to ensure justice is served without shedding further blood," I said. "But if it comes to a fight, we can win. I've never led my warriors into a defeat before, and I don't intend to do so now."

I wasn't certain if this or anything else could convince them, but they seemed satisfied for now.

One skewered a piece of roasted meat and passed it to me. I tried to remember my manners as I tore into the charred flesh before Fabius led me on.

It wasn't long before we reached a larger fire, surrounded by a mix of men playing dice and others sharpening their various weapons. At the center sat a man shaped like a draft horse, a mountain of rippling muscle with a barrel chest and a booming voice that seemed to vibrate the earth beneath us.

"Ah, here we are," Fabius said. "Sertorius, this is Gallus. One of my finest captains."

The large man looked up, a grin splitting his braided beard. "I'm looking forward to fighting with you," he said. "Though, part of me regrets leaving Greece. We could be making a fortune with all that chaos."

Fabius laughed and changed the topic but then stopped. "What do you mean? What chaos?"

Gallus and the others gave us a confused look "You haven't heard?" he said. "Everyone's talking about it. Mithridates took the whole damn peninsula. Every banner in Greece belongs to him now, either willingly or by conquest. They put every Roman to the sword. You really haven't heard? News spreading like a fever on a trireme."

My vision tunneled around Gallus. I couldn't see or hear anything else. But I wasn't seeing the massive mercenary, I saw Apollonius. If Gallus spoke true, I could only imagine what my dearest friend experienced in Athens. I encouraged him to take this holiday in Greece to get away from war and bloodshed for a time, but instead I sent him into the lion's den.

"What of Athens?" I managed to say.

Gallus shrugged. "First city to join Mithridates is my under-standing." He kicked back on a log and crossed his legs. "The Pontic king put some puppet leader over the 'birthplace of democracy' to give the Greeks the illusion of autonomy. But it's Mithridates in control, everyone knows it."

"At least he's the one who organized the massacre," another mercenary put in.

"Did they execute freedmen?" I asked.

Fabius tilted his head at me. Of course, he didn't know about Apollonius or why I would ask this question, but I'm sure everyone around the fire could see the fear in my eye.

Gallus pulled and stroked his coarse beard. "The news-readers don't hold freedmen in much regard, commander," he said. "Don't recall them mentioning it specifically. But if those former slaves declared themselves as Romans, I'd say they're hanging from a tree just the same as the trueborn."

Fabius placed a hand on my shoulder. "I grieve with you," he said. "I may no longer count myself as a citizen, but I was born and raised in Rome, and I have no desire to see her people killed in such a sordid way."

"Rome will have vengeance," I said.

My mind drifted to Apollonius again. The loss of my farm and even my ancestral home paled in comparison to the grief I'd experience if I lost my friend. I'd relied on him for years, but perhaps I needed him now more than ever. He was the closest thing I'd had to a father since my own died. Had I lost Apollonius now too?

Gallus clicked his tongue. "Rome always does get her vengeance, aye? But it may be some time waiting. That Sulla will set sail with his legions any day now, and he doesn't have a fraction of the manpower he'll need to defeat the Greek and Pontic forces. We would know. They're vicious little bastards."

Another mercenary, a young man not yet twenty years old, stood and gestured to me. "You should rejoice, commander. Your enemy will fail in the East. In the meantime, Rome is ripe for the plucking. Without the tyrant and his legions, we'll make short work of the city defenses. You could take Rome for yourself, if you so desired."

I'd never been one to doubt Sulla. He'd overcome great odds before. But he would be eager to punish these transgressions, and this attack on Roman prestige during the last days of his consulship was not only an insult to the Republic but to his honor specifically.

If he sailed prematurely and died in a futile war, Roman freedom would be better for it, but I wouldn't rejoice. Countless legionaries would die in the process, and my son among them.

"Excuse me," I said. "I should retire and get some rest. It's been a pleasure, and I thank you for the report."

I almost saluted, but remembered the gesture meant nothing to them. Instead, I nodded and turned to leave. When I did, I saw Barca standing directly behind me. I wondered how long he'd been there.

"Sertorius," he said. "May we speak?"

I thought about asking for a moment alone. I didn't know where I'd go or what I'd do—only that I needed to quiet the storm in my mind. I'd trained myself to appear calm, no matter what I felt. But I was unraveling.

Still, after all he'd done for me, I couldn't say no—not with the grim look in his eyes.

"Of course, *amice*," I said. "Walk with me."

We marched side by side through camp, slow enough that I could wave and nod to as many mercenaries as I could, but fast enough that I wouldn't be forced to stop and talk.

"You know someone in Athens," he said. "This man is your leader, yes?"

"Not a leader in a traditional sense. He has been a mentor to me. A teacher. Almost like a father."

He nodded. "I understand this. And I heard what that man said. Your mentor-teacher is in danger."

I clasped my hands behind my back to keep them from trembling. "It appears that way," I said. "I can only pray he's still alive."

Even speaking this way made my chest burn. I wanted to tell

all these mercenaries we would abandon our plans to retake Rome and instead sail for Greece with the sole objective of saving my friend. I would have, if I could. At any personal cost or sacrifice, Apollonius deserved nothing less. But I couldn't abandon the Republic, and my friend wouldn't want me to.

"I had a teacher-mentor once," Barca said. "He fought my worst impulses. Made me a better man. But he was cut in the arena. The infection killed him, and I was worse for it." He stopped walking and waited until I halted and met his gaze. "I won't allow that to happen to you."

I furrowed my brow. "What are you saying?"

"This is not my fight, Sertorius. I was planning to depart soon enough but refused to do so until I knew you and your family were safe. I do not like these mercenaries, but you are protected from Sulla's wrath here." His face was severe as a scarred statue. "But you will not truly be safe until your teacher-mentor has returned to you."

I shook my head. "*Mi amice* . . ." I placed a hand on his shoulder. "That is out of our hands now," I said, wishing the words didn't need to be said. "He would curse me for risking anyone's life in a hopeless attempt to rescue him so far away."

He placed his hand on my shoulder in return but squeezed it much harder. "There is no such thing as hopeless," he said. "You taught me this. You advised me the way Apollonius advised you. I will bring him back."

"Barca, we're talking about Athens. Have you ever been to Athens? Or Greece for that matter? There are armies everywhere and killing with impunity." I wanted to plead with him. His offer was brave, but it was reckless, dangerous, and I needed him alive too.

Uncharacteristically, he smiled. "Sometimes it's better to not be Roman," he said. "I'll be safer in Greece than Italy."

Perhaps he was right about that, but his plan remained foolish.

He reached behind him and pulled a leather pouch from

beneath his cloak. "I have a bit of coin left. More than enough to buy passage to Greece."

"There is a war on land and sea, Barca. Few ships will brave the waters these days."

"You should know better," he said. "Those men said Sulla will depart soon. Merchants and peddlers swindling wares will sail like a full fleet behind him. One of them will allow me on."

He was right about this, too, but still my heart resisted.

"We don't even know if he's still alive."

"And we won't know until I go."

"Barca, listen to me." I met his gaze. "I may have lost one friend already. I cannot afford to lose another. Not now."

I failed in my attempts to sway him. He did not blink.

"I know my purpose again. And this is it. I can go with your blessing, or I will go without it."

SCROLL XIII

ARREA—THE Kalends of September, 666 Ab Urbe Condita

It was early, and the sun was just beginning to rise when we woke and wrapped ourselves up. The hardiness I developed in the cold winds of Gaul had long since left me, worn away by Italy's gentler winters. The chill nipped at my face and clung to my bones, so I wrapped Toria up in another layer, and followed the others to the gate.

Today was a sad day. Barca was one of my only real friends. I made few during my time in servitude, and life as a Roman matron presented me with fewer companions than one might think. Who else among the senators' wives was once a slave? Who else was freed by the man she married? None that I knew of. Most of them were born in Rome and knew nothing of what life looked like outside it. They didn't need to address it. In their eyes, I was intrinsically and irredeemably beneath them.

And now Barca was leaving. For a noble cause, of course, the only sort of calling that could lead him away from us. I wanted Apollonius—one of my only other dear friends—returned to us, but I prayed there was some other way. None presented itself in the few days before Barca planned his departure, and this morning would be his last with us.

He was the first one at the gate. He'd already saddled his horse and was brushing her off when we arrived.

"I prefer to avoid goodbyes," he said. "I planned to leave in the quiet of night, but I couldn't leave without bidding my little warrior farewell."

He smiled when I pulled back the fold around Toria's head and let him see her.

She was still asleep, unwilling to wake until she was good and ready. But there was a dreamy smile on her lips as Barca brushed back the soft wisps of hair above her brow.

"I would have fought for you, little warrior," he said. "I would have slayed thousands at your command."

Toria babbled and shifted softly in my arms. She was just becoming old enough to recognize people and know the ones she liked. Born with her father's kind nature, she tolerated almost everyone, but Toria had a special fondness for Barca. She would miss his presence.

Quintus shifted beside me. Roman men are taught to restrict emotions, but this didn't burden my husband. Still, he tried to contain his sadness that morning. This goodbye was harder for him than most. He relied on Barca, as a warrior and as a friend.

Barca shook Rhea's hand and bowed to her. He always treated her with almost divine reverence.

"Look after them for me. Will you?"

Rhea smiled. "I will, if you also vow to look after yourself." She knelt and kissed his scarred cheek. "Be safe."

A morning wind picked up and blew through my uncombed hair as Barca turned to me.

"Remember your training, lady," he said. "I laugh at any fool who gets in your way."

"And you remember your reading. Study your alphabet when you can or you'll forget it."

He laughed a hearty laugh; the kind I hadn't heard from him

in months. A dangerous task lay before him, but this was the most unburdened I'd seen him.

"I don't know how often they use Latin where I am going." He tapped his forehead. "But I will never forget."

At last, he turned to my husband. They embraced but said nothing else until Barca swept gracefully atop his horse and took up the reins.

"Will you return?" Quintus asked.

Barca sniffled, he never did like the cold. "Who knows where the gods will lead us," he said.

And that was the best answer we could hope for, given the circumstances.

"Perhaps we can finally have that dinner we planned so long ago," Quintus said.

The smile faded from his lips as soon as he uttered those words.

Perhaps he remembered that both of our homes were gone. Even if Barca returned and they restored the Republic, nothing would ever be the same again.

Barca nodded and led his horse to a trot.

He didn't make it very far before Sertorius shouted, "I can never thank you for all you've done."

Barca spun his horse around and faced us.

"No. You cannot," he said. "But you don't need to." He placed a fist on his breast. "*Mi amice.*"

My husband made the same gesture. "*Mi amice.*"

Barca faded from view.

We stood there, time standing still, hoping he'd change his mind and return. And to our surprise, a rider did appear. But it wasn't Barca.

Instead, I recognized the rider as one of Fabius's top lieutenants, a giant named Gallus. If I wasn't in such poor spirits, I might have laughed at how he dwarfed the horse beneath him.

"Morning to you, commander," Gallus said cheerfully with a nod to my husband.

"*Ave*, Gallus. Enjoying a morning ride?" I could sense skepticism in Quintus's voice. Perhaps he was wondering what Gallus was doing outside the fort so early.

He was trusting by nature, my husband, but life taught him to be suspicious for our safety.

Gallus pulled his horse to a stop. "I've been riding, and it's the morning, but can't say I've been enjoying it, sir," he said. "Just returned from a brothel in Arretium, and I'm currently regretting every decision I've ever made."

One couldn't tell it from his smile, but the bags under his eyes suggested he hadn't benefitted from much sleep.

"I hope your time was enjoyable. A lot of hard work lies ahead," my husband said.

"I had my fun, but I had my purpose too," he said. "There's nowhere in the world better to receive your news than the brothel. Did you know that? How do you think I came to know about the affairs in Greece? And I've brought more succulent morsels for you today, commander."

"Oh? And what would that be?" Quintus asked.

"Rome just held elections recently. Thought you'd be interested in the victors."

Quintus looked at us over his shoulder. "I wasn't aware the election had taken place so early. Who are our newest consuls, then?"

Gallus smiled. "The names mean nothing to me. But given what I've heard, they might just mean something to you," he said. "One man is named Octavius, someone irrelevant and simple-minded from what the whores tell me. The other, though, is a man named Cinna. You know him? Even the door guards know he's no friend of Sulla's. I assumed the news might be welcome to you."

For a moment I registered nothing in my husband's eye, but then he smiled.

"What is it?" I asked. "Do you know him?"

Gallus nodded and led his horse on through the gates while my husband collected himself.

"I know him," he said. "I never figured him for a consul, but yes. I know him well. Perhaps the gods have good things in store for us after all."

I didn't understand, but I delighted in my husband's smile. It'd been so long since we'd received hopeful tidings. Perhaps this was the turn we'd been waiting on. I only wished Barca was here to hear it.

SCROLL XIV

GAVIUS SERTORIUS—THE Ides of November, 666 Ab Urbe Condita

Legionaries are many things.

We are engineers—the way we construct forts like cities, monuments to the god of war, in a few short hours.

We are carpenters—legionaries construct and raise not only our own tents but the hundreds of other structures required within a military fortress.

We are cooks—legionaries prepare meals each night, unlike citizens who have *servi* to do so for them.

We are comics—sometimes legionaries must entertain a crowd of their brothers and know how to elicit laughter.

We are merchants—legionaries establish the prices and relative cost of everything in camp. Even after a few months under the standard, most legionaries can haggle or barter with the best in the Forum.

And we are trained killers. We're particularly good at that.

But legionaries are not sailors.

Of course there are individual units that specialize in naval warfare, but men of the battlefield have no tolerance for the open sea. I heard more complaining during those three days sailing than I had in over a year and a half at war.

I hated it just as much as the rest, but as a tribune, I knew I couldn't reveal this. Still, I emptied my stomach like all the others, leaning over the trireme railings and holding on tight when we hit a wave.

Mercifully, we arrived on the third day. The ships groaned to a halt as they dashed through the rocky beach. Then we began the tedious work of securing the vessels with anchors and ropes.

I wanted to kiss that grainy beach the moment I touched ground. Everything continued to sway around me, and I prayed the sensation would dissipate soon. I'd never been on a ship before, of any kind, let alone a massive legionary trireme. And I'd also never left Italy, never seen a foreign land.

Yet here I was, staring out over a world I knew nothing about save the stories I savored as a child.

Lucullus called after me, "What do you think?" He scrambled down the rope ladder and joined me on the beach. "Not what you expected?"

I scanned everything around us. There was little to take in save an endless landscape of dust. It was as if we'd arrived in a god-sized bowl, filled with nothing and surrounded by the jagged mountaintops.

"This is Greece?" I asked.

Lucullus wiped sweat from his brow. "Epirus, to be exact. Greece proper is south, but don't worry, you'll see it soon enough." My friend had visited Greece before, several times in fact. As a young man, he'd studied rhetoric and law here and was happy to remind everyone of his experience.

"Even in Epirus I expected more . . . life."

Lucullus nodded. "Hard to imagine the king here once posed a greater threat to Rome than any other. But where is Pyrrhus now?" Lucullus clapped me on the shoulder. "This is what we do to our enemies, Gavius. Don't forget that."

He stepped away and left me in the vast emptiness with my thoughts.

I'd expected to arrive in a bustling port overflowing with merchants and drovers, or a throng of citizens cheering our arrival. At worst, I expected a force of Mithridates's loyalist to welcome us with battle. Instead, we found nothing but dust and mountains.

I didn't consider myself naive, but I realized my expectations were often wrong in these circumstances.

There was too much to do to consider it any longer.

I passed out orders for camp to be set up immediately. Sulla and all of us who followed him were eager to shed blood, but that would have to wait. We were damp, hungry, and still reeling from sea sickness.

But, as I said, legionaries are experienced engineers and carpenters, and within a matter of hours, they constructed the bulk of the fort and hoisted their tents to decorate the barren landscape.

Sulla ordered an officers' meeting in his freshly constructed praetorium, and I was excited for it.

I'm unashamed to admit my highest priority for the day was to earn back some of Sulla's favor I felt I'd lost. He hadn't greeted me warmly in weeks. Perhaps it was only our circumstances, but a briefing of officers was the perfect opportunity for me to say something witty and clever to impress my commander. It'd worked for me before.

Upon entering, I marveled at the state of Sulla's headquarters. That morning, only dirt and broken shells rested here. Now, braziers illuminated the massive tent, revealing tapestries depicting the general's many victories. The light glistened on the marble busts of Sulla ancestors. A large wooden table—with a sandbox etched into the middle and already filled with sticks and small figurines—dominated the center of the room. I spotted no chairs around it, as Sulla claimed the mind is clearer when standing or walking.

Sulla said, "Come, come." He warmed himself by a brazier, already reading over some scroll, probably something about provisioning. Battles are won with full bellies and lost with empty ones, he always said. "We have figs over there, and some cheese if you'd like."

Each of us, no matter how reserved or bashful, lined up to take a turn at Sulla's offering. We'd had nothing on the ship but bread, and most of it was soggy and salty by the end of the first day, despite our efforts to protect it.

I joined Crassus and Lucullus in line, along with several other officers I didn't recognize. Although the legionaries of Sulla's Fist unanimously supported our decision to march on Rome, many of our officers deserted. This led to many internal promotions, such as my own, but it also forced Sulla to bring in new officers from other armies.

I wouldn't allow newcomers to surpass me.

"Our guest should soon arrive." Sulla rolled up the document. "There's someone I want all of us to hear from."

"Who is this guest?" one of the new officers said.

Sulla stared the officer into silence. "I was about to tell you," he answered.

Sulla seemed different lately. Perhaps it began when we marched on Rome, but his demeanor shifted again when we received the news about Mithridates and his treachery in Greece. I knew he was under a tremendous amount of pressure. The fate of the Republic once again rested on his shoulders, an unfathomable burden to bear. I did not blame him for it, but I noticed the change. Besides shorter, less affable responses, he drank more. Not only was his wine dark and unwatered, but the quantities continued to increase.

The only vice I'd ever seen in my father was an affinity for strong wine, and now I understood why. Stupefaction offers a delightful reprieve to the overwhelmed.

"Our guest is Publius Rutilius Rufus. Do you recall the name? Some of you may be too young to remember," Sulla said.

"Former consul," Crassus said, dry as the figs on his plate. "Rome exiled him for extorting the provinces."

"Correct." Sulla nodded. "And since then, he's lived in Mytilene."

When we failed to understand what this meant for us, he clarified.

"Mytilene is within Mithridates's territory. He likely knows more about our enemy than any Roman still alive."

"Despite his legal circumstances, this is a former consul. A man of great probity and respect," Lucullus addressed the officers. "Nearly eighty years old with a lifetime of service to Rome. Remember to show your respect."

As if on command, the tent flaps opened. A haze of dust came first and filtered the late-day sunlight, and the former consul stepped in next.

I assumed Lucullus spoke incorrectly. I couldn't believe this man was eighty years old. I spotted no wrinkle on his face, from laughter or frowning. His frame was thin and his arms sinewy. His hair was silver and kept short like a legionary's, and he wore no jewelry or other trappings of his former station. Still, he stood with the dignitas of a former consul rather than a current exile.

This was not a man but a statue of stoic virtue brought to life.

"I greet you," he said with only the faintest of nods.

"Dear Rutilius." Sulla stretched out his arms to the former consul and gestured for him to join us. "Would you care for some wine?"

"No," Rutilius answered brusquely.

We were shocked by the rude answer, but Sulla was unperturbed.

"I thank you for joining us. These last few weeks must have been very difficult for you."

"Yes," Rutilius said.

Outside the tent, I could hear the dull thud of legionaries hammering stakes and clanging iron tools.

"Well, please join us by the table. Come," Sulla said. "I have many questions for you."

"I will provide answers," Rutilius said.

I studied the man's face and wondered if he didn't like our commander. The shortness of his responses would generally indicate this, but there was no animosity in his eyes that I could see. Perhaps it was simply his way.

"My inquiries are around Rome's enemy. Mithridates."

Rutilius blinked and waited for the first question.

Even Sulla seemed a bit surprised by Rutilius's lack of interaction.

"We've heard reports he orchestrated the murder of eighty thousand Romans across Asia Minor and Greece and somehow managed to accomplish this in a single day." Sulla placed his hands on the table and balanced himself on his fingers. "Is this true?"

My stomach lurched at those words. It's all anyone could think of or talk about since the news arrived, but I became weak every time someone uttered those words. Unfathomable. Unbelievable. Unacceptable.

Rutilius said, "Yes." And for a moment I thought this was all he would say, but then he added, "Though my belief is the number was much higher. No one can calculate such losses with any certainty."

Sulla shook his head. "Remarkable. How do you think he accomplished such a feat?"

Rutilius stepped closer to the table. "He didn't find it difficult. Most cities in Greece and Asia Minor were eager to conspire with him. In those few that weren't, he promised freedom to the slaves who killed their Roman masters. He vowed to eliminate all debt to those who slayed Roman debtors."

I set aside my plate. I remained hungry but lost my appetite. Many of the murdered Romans had lived in the east for generations. They were neighbors, perhaps even friends with those around them. And yet at the first opportunity, those they trusted rounded up and slaughtered them.

I would have my vengeance. I would win back Sulla's favor and accept the inevitable offer to exact Roman justice. Nothing else mattered to me.

"Brilliant," Sulla said. To my surprise, he was smiling. "We're dealing with someone extraordinary, aren't we?"

"Yes," Rutilius said.

"Did you see these atrocities yourself?" a new legatus asked.

Sulla said nothing, but this breach of conduct angered me. We all knew no one should interrupt Sulla during a discussion like this.

Rutilius turned to the legatus. "Yes. I was sacrificing at the Temple of Artemis in Ephesus when the killings began," he said. "I prayed when Romans flocked into the temple. Like us, the Greeks and Anatolians believe no blood should be spilt before the gods. They thought they would find sanctuary in the temples. They did not. The men, women, and children, clung to the statue of Artemis as the locals stormed within and slew them. They dispatched the children first, then the women. They saved the men for last, so they might witness the evisceration of their families."

For the first time, I saw a hint of emotion in Rutilius's old, weary eyes. He looked through the officer, seeing again whatever he witnessed on that day.

"And how could you survive such catastrophe in this place?" Lucullus asked. He, too, broke procedure but simply couldn't resist asking what we all wondered.

Rutilius turned sharply to my friend. "I buried my sword in the sands of Mytilene's beach and vowed to never use it again," he said. "But I poured oil on myself and offered myself for the slaughter. The people there are grateful for my work to spare them abusive taxation during my time as governor. They took a vote and decided I am no longer Roman because of my exile. I was prepared to die with the other Romans, yet they refused to kill me. There were no other exceptions in Ephesus."

I felt the snarl forming on my lips, so I lowered my gaze. I heard the chainmail shift around the room as officers shuffled uncomfortably.

"Weren't you accused of extorting the Asiatics? And then convicted?" an officer I didn't recognize asked.

"It's well established that the trial was a sham. I was guilty only of resisting our tax collectors who exploited these provinces, and so they convicted me of the very thing I ended."

"Dear Lucullus," Sulla said. "It's not Rutilius's responsibility to throw away his life needlessly. This wasn't the battlefield. Better to live, nay?"

I couldn't understand why Sulla pardoned this. We were taught it was our duty to fight or die in such events, but if Sulla accepted Rutilius's answer, we all would as well.

"The Ephesians took me to Mithridates personally after they spared me," Rutilius added, unashamed. "I expected him to do what they could not. Instead, he invited me to dine with him."

A hushed gasp fell over the praetorium, but the look on Sulla's face was one of delight. Did I notice a touch of envy in his eyes as well?

"You shared a cup with this barbarian?" Crassus asked with no effort to hide his distaste.

"No," Rutilius said. "I did not drink. I only listened."

"Did he explain why he massacred our people?" I blurted out. "Did he explain why he would murder so many innocents when we have military targets available for his wrath?"

The answer that came to mind was the king's cowardice. I wasn't prepared to accept any other answer. That's what slaughtering civilians was—cowardice—and nothing more. When they fought someone who could fight back, they would pay for it.

Rutilius shifted his stern, gray eyes to me. "He didn't need to. He wanted us to know how much the world hates us, that our crippling taxation would be our downfall. He wanted to make it clear that nowhere in the world is safe for Romans but in Rome itself. His hope is for us to withdraw from his lands so he can continue with his aspirations of empire."

Cataline laughed. Rutilius shot his gaze to the young tribune, unamused.

"I'm more interested in hearing about the man himself," Sulla said. "Tell me, what was he like?" Sulla took a sip of wine and settled in as if listening to political gossip at a symposium.

Rutilius seemed surprised by the question. "Extraordinary size. Physically imposing. He's considered wrestling in the games at Olympia, and I expect he could win."

My commander savored every word. "What of his appearance? Is he handsome?"

I thought I heard Rutilius chuckle, which surprised me. "Ever seen a statue of Alexander the Great? Imagine the marble chipping away, and Mithridates is the man who would emerge. He's aware of his similarities and keen on maintaining that image."

Sulla leaned back and clapped his hands, unable to contain himself.

I didn't understand how any of this was helpful intelligence in our war against him, but Sulla must have a purpose, right?

"And his personality? What was it like dining with this king?"

Rutilius's eyes narrowed. Perhaps he was just as surprised by these questions as I was. "He is kind. He laughed often. Attempted to empathize with me for the Roman plight, and offered his apologies for 'what must be done'."

"Kind? He slaughtered thousands of innocent children . . . and men and women. The world has never seen anything like this," I whispered.

But Rutilius heard me. "I said he was kind. I did not say he was good."

Sulla ignored the interruption. "And how did the king become this way? What of his past? I know so little and I'm intrigued," Sulla said, although that much was clear. "Did he speak of that?"

"He spoke of little else," Rutilius said. "His father was murdered when Mithridates was a child. His mother became regent while he and his brother came of age. His mother favored the younger son and tried to kill Mithridates. He escaped and survived off the land for years. In the wilderness, he claimed to have experimented with poisons to the point he is immune to them all."

"Impossible." Crassus shook his head. "He would have died in the wilderness and his little legend would have ended there if he'd so much as tasted poison."

Rutilius continued, "Once he became of age, he returned to Sinope and executed his mother and brother. He took the throne. He's ruled uncontested since."

"What else?" Sulla asked.

Rutilius shook his head. "There is much to say. He is more myth than truth, I suppose, and I am growing weary."

"Tell me everything." Sulla's tone became stern for the first time.

Rutilius took a deep breath. "He is descended from Darius and Cyrus through his father, and Alexander the Great through his mother. The Macedonian king dreamed of a Greek-Persian hybrid empire, and Mithridates is the culmination of this. He wears Alexander's cloak and rarely takes it off."

Rutilius paused and thought about what else might be pertinent in this strange line of inquiry. Sulla waited. "They say a comet blazed through the sky at his birth and another the day of the Roman massacre. He claims lightning struck his cradle as a babe, and he survived with only a diadem-shaped scar on his forehead. The Greeks believe he is a god. They call him Dionysius. The Asiatics call him liberator and Eupator."

"What does that mean?" a new officer asked.

"Good father," Rutilius said plainly. "Both Greeks and Easterners believe he is the promised king of prophecy that will overthrow Rome and establish the hybrid empire Alexander envisioned."

"And what do you think?" Lucullus questioned, his hand on the hilt of his gladius.

Rutilius looked at my friend but did not answer.

Crassus cocked a brow. "You speak as if you admire the man."

Rutilius nodded. "Indeed. If he were born a Roman, he would make a fine consul."

I crossed my arms. "But he wasn't born Roman. So, he isn't fit to lick our sandals."

I stole a quick glance at Sulla to see if I'd impressed him with the comment, but he didn't appear to have heard.

Lucullus abruptly slammed his hands down the table. "So, this man is immune to poison, and lightning, too, apparently. He is tall, strong, and possesses great stamina. Descended from the purest royal families of the Greeks and Asians alike and is worshipped as a god by all the people in his kingdom. Does this king have no weakness we can exploit?"

It was the first question worth asking, in my opinion, but Rutilius didn't have a good answer.

"He is also paranoid and does not trust easily. You cannot defeat him by ploy or plot. Therefore, I do not believe you can win. You will lose this war, Cornelius Sulla."

We all took a collective step closer to him. If Sulla gave even a nod, I would have killed him myself for this treason. Exiled or not, he was Roman. To speak this way in our own camp infuriated me. Whether it was fair or not, in that moment I saw in Rutilius the object of our betrayal, as if he was responsible for the massacre himself.

"How dare you come and—" Lucullus began.

Rutilius interrupted. "You do not have enough men. They outnumber you ten to one. If you include their forces in Asia Minor, perhaps a hundred to one. You cannot win."

The former consul spoke these words without emotion. What

he lacked, we possessed in abundance. Only Sulla remained as calm as our guest.

"Thank you, dear Rutilius," he said. "I welcome your insight and appreciate your concern. However, I will be victorious. I always am." He looked around the praetorium and addressed his officers for the first time. "Mithridates is my first worthy adversary. Crushing him will be my greatest accomplishment."

Generally, Sulla's unwavering confidence gave me strength and comfort. But after everything Rutilius shared, Sulla's proclamation sounded foolish. It sounded like hubris.

"Where will you go now?" Sulla asked Rutilius.

"I will travel to Smyrna, where I'll live out my last days and finish composing my history of Rome. I am almost done." He smiled for the first time. At least Rutilius took delight in his writing.

Sulla balked. "Surely not," he said. "It's not safe for a Roman in Smyrna, or anywhere else for that matter. If you're willing to renege on your vow, I would gladly welcome you on my staff. I could benefit from your wisdom, and of course your legal status and prestige will be restored to you upon our victory."

I wouldn't fight beside someone who expected our ultimate failure, but I wouldn't have to.

"No," Rutilius said. "I made a vow, and I will keep it."

Sulla's eyes flashed. "Fine. Thank you for your time. You may go."

No one nodded or saluted to Rutilius as he departed. No one shook his hand. But his presence and his prophecies still lingered with us as he departed.

"Imperator, may I enter?" a voice sounded from the tent just moments after Rutilius's departure.

Sulla took a deep breath. "Yes."

Sulla snapped and a slave brought him dark wine, not in a simple cup but in a massive chalice.

A messenger entered. He bowed, knelt, and extended a scroll. This clearly wasn't his first time delivering messages to important men, but he wore no armor or the crest of a legionary emissary. He was a civilian, but from where?

Sulla nodded at me. I snatched the letter from the messenger's hands and passed it to the commander.

The messenger stood, but didn't depart, confidently ignoring the presence of everyone but Sulla. Perhaps he expected additional compensation for his troubles.

Sulla broke the seal. For a moment, I saw the tug of a smile on his eyes.

"Our timeline accelerates," he said. "Bring me parchment. Emissary, I will send you with a reply. And coin."

I wondered if he wanted us to leave. Perhaps he was too distracted to dismiss us. But, without looking up, he pointed at Lucullus and me.

"You will take the fourth legion and advance south. Mithridates northern-most army is two days' march away. If you hit them fast and hard, you can steal our first victory."

I nodded, relieved and excited to have my vengeance.

"Understood, commander," Lucullus said. "We'll depart first thing in the morning."

"No," Sulla said. "You'll leave now."

I peeked through the tent flaps. Most of the sunlight had faded and darkness would be upon us shortly, but neither of us would refuse Sulla's orders.

"Do not fail me."

We knew not where we were headed or what enemy forces we would find, but we set off regardless.

The war with the promised king of Greece and Asia had begun.

SCROLL XV

Lucius Hirtuleius—Four days after the Ides of November, 666 Ab Urbe Condita

The wine was cheap and sour, but after two months of drinking stale water and regret, it tasted like Falernian grape.

I leaned back against the rickety wooden bench and swirled what little remained in my cup, trying to summon up the courage to drink the rest. Across from me, Aulus hung his head and watched the vibration of his wine, as if searching for answers within. Marius and Marius the Younger sat on either side of us, drinking their third and fourth cups respectively.

The tavern reeked of sweat, fish, and stale ale—an establishment that had never been respectable, not even in its prime, which must have been before my great-grandfather's time. The building was constructed from driftwood and sun-bleached planks, each one filled with visible knots and cracks. From the markings on the wall and floorboards, I assumed the tavern had flooded in the past.

It took us several days to realize where we were. Eventually, we pieced together that we were either in Sardinia or some other island close to it. Either way, this tiny coastal settlement was unwelcoming.

We eventually found work, which was a miracle considering that the settlement seemed to contain three slaves for each citizen.

Marius, the six-time Roman consul, the man named the Third Founder of Rome, found menial dock work. He hauled sacks of grain onto ships that would sail to Rome without him.

Aulus and I repaired fishing nets for a short, angry Cilician man who paid us in bread and insults.

Whether or not Marius the Younger did anything to contribute to our cause, I can't recall. But he shared the meager fruits of our labor—sour wine and stale bread—all the same.

"This is no way for a consul to live," Marius the Younger said to himself, his words slurred.

Aulus smiled without mirth. "None of us is a Roman consul."

When my friend spoke, which was increasingly rare, it was generally a half-concealed insult to Marius. The former consul was not as sharp as I remembered him, but he was more unpredictable. One of those comments would cause a rift between us if Aulus wasn't careful.

I tapped the table beside Aulus and when he looked up at me, I shook my head.

"Rome is a fickle whore," Marius the Younger spat. "One day you're her greatest hero, and the next you're shoveling shit on some godsforsaken island."

"Please keep your voice down," I said.

So far, we hadn't attracted any unwanted attention. Even Marius himself maintained an inconspicuous profile, which I feared he wasn't capable of doing. The last thing we needed was for these angry, drunken locals to become aware of his identity, and more importantly the hefty bounty on his head.

I knew our time would run out eventually. Despite our

efforts, we didn't fit in. Every local man in the tavern had a beard longer than a horses' mane and coarser than hogs' hair. A lifetime spent on the water had made their skin scaly, and the burgeoning sun left them dark as night.

"Rome is fickle," Marius said. "But if you call our homeland a whore again, I'll break one of your fingers." The old consul drained what was left in his cup. He snapped his fingers for another while counting his coin to see how many more we could afford.

Not much. Soon our stale bread would be devoured and all the wine we could afford consumed. Then, we would return to the bungalow where we'd found cheap shelter, and rest until it was time to report for our meager duties once more.

What was our plan? What was Marius hoping for? Perhaps he wanted me to find an opportunity, to find his way off the island. If so, he placed his trust poorly. I was a bodyguard, meant to protect him from the agents of Sulla who sought his death. I was no guide, no visionary. Perhaps Aulus would have been better suited for the role, but he cared less and less about our predicament each day.

"Rome's fluid nature can be a curse, or it can be a blessing. Today, I am declared a Public Enemy of the Republic, and tomorrow I may be consul again, adored and cheered by the entire mob," Marius said. "You'll understand when you are older."

Marius the Younger was a coward and a fool. I didn't care for him and couldn't understand the love Marius showed him. Perhaps I would show the same kind of unconditional affection for my own heir, but I'd like to think I would still possess the clarity to see apparent flaws, and work to correct them. That was the kind of love the man who raised me, my grandfather, showed.

The thought saddened me. I'd nearly died a hundred times or more in battle, and more recently in the swamps outside

Minturnae, on the ruins of Carthage, and on our voyage to—and isolation on—this desolate island. Death had never concerned me before. I possessed the unwavering belief that I would die when the gods ordained. Believing I could do nothing to shorten or extend my destined time alive, I found no reason to worry about dying as many other men do.

That might have been the first moment I truly considered everything I would never experience if my life were snuffed out now. Thirty-five years I'd been on Terra Mater, and all I had to show for my time was years laboring on my grandfather's farm and nearly twenty years of killing on the battlefield. I knew nothing of women, and even less of children, but I'd always expected to have a wife and child at some point. If I die this day, in the Sardinian tavern, my only regret in the afterlife would be never experiencing that.

I loved a woman once. A strong beauty, named Andromache, I met on my campaign to Greece. At least I thought it was love, though I had nothing to compare it to. I think she loved me too. She invited me to stay with her in Greece, and I invited her to return with me to Rome. We both chose duty to our people over any potential future together. I believed we made the right call, but if I died as a deserter in this forlorn place, it would seem my sacrifices were all for naught.

But I thrust the idea from my mind and took a drink. If I married and had children now, I would likely leave them the way my father left us. Orphaned and widowed. I wouldn't allow that.

With family in my thoughts, I said, "Aulus, what do you think your wife is doing right now?" I cautiously glanced at the door behind us, determined to stay vigilant even when no one else would.

He chuckled, but it was unpleasant. There was no smile in his eyes or on his lips. "Gods only know." He drained the rest of his cup.

I glanced around the room. Establishments like this keep the lights dim to conceal the identities and activities of those within. Locals filled the tables in the center of the dingy tavern, but twice as many *servi* lined the walls. They sat with bowed heads, not even whispering to one another, staring at their bare feet and waiting on a command. I wondered where they hailed from, what brought them here. Their masters had squeezed out whatever life previously dwelled in them.

The tavern grew quiet. The rancorous laughter evaporated, and the clatter of rolling dice halted. I looked for the reason why.

Three men entered, locals by the looks of their beards. The others must have known them and showed respect or fear by quieting themselves at the arrival.

The three men seemed not to notice. They took their time stripping off their cloaks and leather-working gloves and hung them from a nail near the door.

One of the three turned and looked directly at our table. His chest was bare and exposed with his tunic pulled down and tucked into the belt at his waist. His belly protruded like a boulder, thick and tight as if it was all his body could do to keep the seams together. But there was no mistaking the man's strength. Each finger on his hand was thick and the knuckles knotted like tree branches. His broad shoulders looked capable of holding the world as well as Atlas.

I hadn't seen anyone like this man since we fought the Cimbri, where their entire army possessed such traits.

The wooden floor creaked and groaned for mercy with his every step. He drew near.

Only one stool remained open at our table, and this giant took it. He plopped down with tremendous force; it was a wonder the dilapidated wood could bear his weight.

The stench of fish, grease, and salt consumed the table, though I did my best to ignore it. Marius the Younger, on the other hand, leaned away as if gasping for air.

He sized each of us up. The look in his eyes was slightly curious but mostly bored.

"Greetings," I said.

Instead of replying, he reached down and unbuckled the woodcutter's axe from his hip. He hoisted it in the air and let it fall to the table. The thud reverberated throughout the silent tavern, and Aulus's wine nearly spilled.

Marius and I exchanged a glance, before placing our own weapons on the table.

"You are not from around here," the man said.

A sheen of sweat developed on my brow, cold as the Tiber in late winter.

"No," Marius admitted.

"We don't receive visitors often."

The tavern proprietor hurried to the table and poured wine for our guest. The cup's size matched the man's, probably three times the volume of our own. The host began to depart but the giant slapped the table with his meaty hands and waited for our drinks to be refilled as well.

"That's a shame," Aulus said. "Every traveler should experience such a quaint, welcoming village."

The giant grunted, and I could swear it shook the table.

"Strangely enough, another foreigner showed up on our docks recently." The man gulped from his cup and ignored the purple wine dripping through his beard like dew in a spider-web. "Looked a little bit like you four," he said.

I could only assume he meant someone without a long beard and the idiosyncratic skin of these sea people.

"We are the only members of our party," I said. "Perhaps the other traveler was simply passing through, as we are."

He burped into his arm. "No," he said. "No, that's not it. He didn't stay long, just came to deliver a message. Said a man named Gaius Marius was somewhere on the water and we should keep an eye out. Probably has a few companions or guards with him." The giant looked directly at me. "Said one of them might be missing a hand."

The salty air grew thicker. This giant knew who we were, and we knew it.

"Gaius Marius was a six-time consul of Rome." Aulus swirled the wine in his cup. "Surely he wouldn't be caught, dead or alive, in a place like this."

The giant fixed his gaze on Marius. "Messenger said Marius is desperate. A war hero or something, in his time, but a tired old man with muddy sandals now." He leaned forward and placed his hammer-like elbows on the creaking table. "Still, the price on his head is a war hero's bounty."

Marius didn't avert his gaze. Even in his old age, he was usually the strongest, toughest man in any room he entered. This giant dwarfed him, but he didn't seem to notice.

"I'm honored then," Marius said. "Though I don't think any amount is sufficient for the man who kills the Third Founder of Rome."

I deflated like an old wineskin and prepared myself for the violence to come.

The giant smiled. "Good. I feared you would deny it like a coward." Seeing that Marius finished his cup, he stretched across the table and refilled it with his own.

I kept my eyes on his hands, which were close enough to grab his weapon any moment he chose to. Although I refused to turn around, I could feel the giant's two companions stepping closer to the table as well.

"At least you can die with your dignity," he said.

Marius grunted. "Oh, I'll die with dignity as I have lived with dignity, but I'm not going to die today."

It took a few moments for his words to sink in, but eventually the giant chuckled. His followers were quick to do so, and soon the entire room joined in.

"I'm not sure that's up to you, is it?" the giant said. "It's not even up to the Fates, or the gods, or whatever you people believe in. It's up to me. The fish have been elusive this year, and I need gold. With what your friends in Rome are going to pay me, I'll never have to cast a net again."

Marius stood abruptly. For a moment I thought this would be the catalyst for our fight, but the giant seemed amused and curious, so he let Marius talk.

"I am Gaius Marius. The Third Founder of Rome, conqueror of the Numidians, Cimbri, Teutones, and so many other tribes and nations I don't care about enough to recall."

Marius was as famous for the power of his voice as he was for his conquests, yet it was even stronger now. It was as if every syllable rolled out for some reverberating war drum deep in his chest.

"I forgot myself for a moment and believed I could blend in here and find a brief respite on my voyage. But even in this forgotten, godless, dilapidated, shit-stinking village I am known. I am Gaius Marius, greater than any you've laid eyes on before and ever will again. Consider yourself blessed by Fortuna." He spoke with such confidence, even I believed him, despite knowing the desperation of our position. The former consul scanned the room but fixed his gaze on the many *servi* lined up along the walls. "Slaves, I am the man who conquered many of your tribes and nations. If it wasn't for me, your people might have been victorious. Even now, Rome might have destroyed. Without me, you might have roasted flesh over the fires of the burning Forum and enjoyed all the abundance fate has denied you."

The slaves shifted uncomfortably and looked away as if his gaze burned their skin. They were unused to being addressed directly, especially by a man like Gaius Marius.

But Marius did not relent.

"I am Gaius Marius. I have the power to create and the power to destroy and today I offer you a blessing greater than your gods have ever given you, one you've done nothing to deserve but have every opportunity to claim."

The giant's smile fell, and his curiosity seemed to fade. He glowered at the *servi* along the walls. The other masters snapped their hands and slapped their tables, shouting for their property to avert their gaze and not listen.

"I offer you not only your freedom, but a seat of authority and power within the Republic that conquered you. Take up arms alongside me. I will lead you to Rome and give you spoils you couldn't fathom, control of your own destiny, and prestige among a people who currently scorn you. I offer you the chance to become your own masters and the master of others. All I ask is that you bring me the head of this man." He pointed at the giant. "This frog-spawned wretch so craven as to threaten the life of Gaius Marius, so arrogant as to fashion himself the arbiter of fate."

The giant stood, reminding us all that he still stood over Marius despite the power of his voice. He drained his wine and threw the chalice across the room. His booming laughter followed the clatter.

"I allowed you to speak so that everyone here might see the depths of your desperation. What a potent reminder how fragile men become in old age, how far we can all fall if glory doesn't swallow us up beforehand."

He took hold of his woodcutter's axe. Marius didn't move, but Aulus and I stood and took hold of our blades. Marius the Younger remained seated, frozen in fear as the color drained from his face.

"My offer doesn't just extend to you slaves. You poor, you indebted, you destitute wretches tired of living on the discarded bones of rotten fish. Come with me and become kings."

The giant laughed again, but only his two companions joined him. The other village citizens remained silent. My mind raced trying to piece together the promise that Marius made and all its implications, yet there was no time for that. Instead, I focused my attention on the other masters and wondered if their silence was an indication of growing concern or if any of them considered Marius's offer.

"I'll be generous too." The giant tightened his massive hands around the axe hilt. "I'll make a promise I can keep. Help me cut this old man into tiny bits to feed our fish, and I'll share some of the bounty with each—"

Before he could finish his offer, a young slave pounced on his massive shoulders. With a howl of a wolf loosed from his cage, the young man plunged a table fork into the giant's neck, again and again.

The giant threw back his elbow, casting the slave across the room and crashing down on a table. But several others replaced him. The *servi* pounced on the giant like a pack of starving dogs tearing at a bear.

Screams echoed throughout the musty tavern as chaos developed all around us.

One of the giant's companions lunged at me with the rusty point of his sword aimed at my stomach.

I was rusty from inaction and exhausted from hunger and hard labor, but I'd trained all my life for moments like this. Nature took over.

I sidestepped the attack at the last moment, and the blade whiffed past me. Aulus sprung into action along with everyone else who sought to aid us.

I sent an elbow into the attacker's nose. Blood spewed immediately, but he didn't seem to notice. He stabilized himself and prepared for another attack.

He displayed his aggression fully as he slashed wildly at my chest. My continued evasion frustrated him; he wasn't used to fighting anyone who fought him back.

He rushed in and threw a shoulder into mine. I recoiled, but he lost his balance as well. I jabbed him with the nub of my left arm, and I generated enough force to push him onto our table. Cups clattered on the wooden floorboards and sour wine mixed with the giant's blood.

When my foe regained his footing, he stabbed at me again, this time with half the force of his original attack. I batted away his sword with my own, and it flew from his limp wrist across the tavern.

Defenseless, he tried to scramble away, but slipped on the uneven floor. He only held up his arms as I thrust my gladius through his stomach until it hit the wood beneath him.

I watched him until the fight died in his eyes. When I cast up my gaze, the tumult was all but over. The few living masters who hadn't joined us moaned and pled for mercy. The *servi* dispatched them without precision or discipline, but with plenty of fury. Eventually, they all fell silent.

Everyone stood, breathless and shaking, holding onto their bloody cutlery and waiting for what was next. These poor wretches had been deceived, manipulated their entire lives, but still I saw hope in their eyes as they looked to Marius to see if he would keep his vow. The few citizens who joined us trembled more than the rest, perhaps expecting the wrath to be turned on them next.

Marius spread his arms to them all, like a father greeting his triumphant sons.

"We have work to do," he said. "Go throughout the village. Liberate the rest and make it known that my offer extends to any who accept it. The sword awaits those who don't."

Elated at Marius's steadfastness, the men, women, and even children among them roared their approval and stormed out of the tavern.

Now only we four remained, save the tavern proprietor who crouched by his counter. He covered himself with outstretched hands and wept. From the dampness of his tunic, I assume he soiled himself.

Marius turned to him with an absent look. "Are you joining us?"

Eventually the proprietor managed to nod.

"Good. Go on then. Liberate."

He stood, stumbled, stood again, and then sprinted from his establishment with the vigor of a man half his age.

Marius's suicidal plan somehow worked. After our near escape in the marshes, and now this . . . I wondered if the gods truly favored him as he always claimed, even in our desperation.

Aulus threw down his sword and turned to the former consul. "What, by all the gods, do we do next?"

Marius, without pause or deliberation, said, "We build ships. Then we return to Rome."

SCROLL XVI

QUINTUS SERTORIUS—SEVEN days before the Kalends of December, 666 Ab Urbe Condita

The valley ahead was shrouded in dust. It rose in swirling clouds above the crude wooden palisade of the Marsi fortress, thick with the stench of sweat, fire, and unburied dead. On Sura's back and atop the hill, I surveyed the battlefield and watched the last of the Marsi rebels pour out of their stronghold.

Even from a thousand paces away I could tell they were weak. Malnourished, desperate men, clad in mismatched armor and wielding whatever weapons they'd salvaged over the past two years.

Our war against the rebels was all but over. They had no hope of victory, and Rome's offer of clemency expired months prior. This would be their final stand, and I assumed they knew it. Otherwise, why would they march out to face us so ill-prepared?

I turned to Fabius, who rode beside me, no more comfortable on his steed now than he'd been previously.

"Poor bastards," Fabius said. "They'll break the moment we press them."

I squinted. "I wouldn't be so sure. They have nowhere else to run."

I tightened my grip on Sura's reins. She stamped the ground impatiently. Perhaps she remembered battle and was eager for it to begin, but probably not. I reached down and stroked her mane and hummed a low note quietly enough only she could hear. We hadn't galloped into the fray together for many years. Would I fight harder to protect her, or would my concern for her safety be a liability? I wasn't certain, but her presence steadied me regardless.

As the Marsi continued to form up, I broke away and rode around our formation to address the men from the front.

Our ranks had grown by nearly a thousand men since we began this expedition. Most were veterans who fought beside me in Gaul, Greece, and against the Italian rebels. Their support and loyalty to me meant a great deal, but I sometimes wondered if I needed more who joined me for political ideology than personal sentiment. I needed warriors more loyal to the Republic than to me.

I steadied myself before the thousand new recruits, who formed the center of our formation. I remembered many of them from over the years and wished I'd been able to address each more properly since they joined.

The past month kept Fabius and me quite busy. I spent much of my time running the mercenaries through battle drills. They were hardened warriors to be certain, but they'd never fought against legionaries. I needed to teach them the weaknesses of Roman formations, which I knew intimately, and also the few vulnerabilities in legionary armor. Despite my distaste for the subject, and concern for how they might wield this knowledge, I knew they needed to know this before we took Rome. More than anything, I taught them proper discipline. I refused to release a pack of wild savages on the Eternal City. I would not burn our buildings and monuments as Sulla had.

We spent the remainder of our time congregating with local elders, tribal leaders, and other wealthy locals who might support our cause. Some enthusiastically rejected us for fear of Sulla and his supporters. Some apprehensively supported us, but only after we vowed to keep their participation secret. One of these wealthy benefactors rode on the other side of Fabius today, as he wished to see our competency in battle before throwing his support behind us.

That's one of the few reasons we were here, on the battlefield staring out at a few thousand starving Marsi holdouts. This was not a battle fought for honor or the protection of the Roman people as all the others, but one of practicality. Until we received more support, I needed to compensate Fabius's men, in bloodshed and in coin. I wouldn't allow them to sack Roman settlements, but the Marsi fortress on the other side of the valley was theirs for the taking after we conquered. In addition, fighting Rome's enemies further legitimized my stance of being a true Roman. The Republic must know I wanted to restore the Republic, not repress it, when I returned to the Eternal City. My fight was with Sulla. I had never and would never turn my back on Rome.

If this battle earned us the support or faith of additional benefactors, all the better.

I addressed the men, "Today we end a war," I called out. "There are more battles to come, but with this victory we take out the thorn in Rome's side so we might focus our efforts on those who harm the Republic most."

They knew whom I spoke of and let out a roar to show their support.

"The Marsi have nothing left but hatred, and hatred will not stop your swords. Hold your lines, trust your shields, and heed your centurions. Victory belongs to the disciplined!"

I turned toward the enemy. They'd abandoned their fortress

now and lined up more like a starving pack of wolves than a military formation.

It was time. I raised my sword and aimed it toward Fabius. He donned his helmet and led our wealthy benefactor, who remained at a healthy distance from the line, toward one of the flanks he would lead.

I circled behind our formation and gave the order to advance. It wasn't necessary to move far. The Marsi charged, wild and desperate without formation or cohesion. The discipline of the rebel armies I'd fought previously was gone. All that remained was rage and desperation.

They smashed into the interlocked shields of my front line, and even over the tumult I could hear the curses they leveled at us. They cursed us to Hades, called us tyrants, murderers, oppressors. And their blades cut as sharply as their words, but my men held firm.

Sura reared back and shook her head, the sounds of battle returning to her for the first time in nearly a decade. I steadied myself and attempted to calm her while I shouted out my orders. I called for a line rotation swiftly, and then another. My veterans were hardy, but they were out of shape and couldn't be counted on to hold for long. I needed the front ranks fresh until the Marsi attack slowed.

"Centurion, centurion!" I shouted, and at last the officer turned toward me. "Send reserves to the left flank."

He hesitated. Most of my officers had been Mules during their previous service, and they were unused to offering commands. Only two of them had crests for their helmets to designate their rank.

Eventually he remembered his station and nodded.

The mercenaries on the right flank held strong, but they faced the least resistance. It was difficult to judge them from my vantage point in the center, but from what I could see, their discipline pleased me.

Fabius, leading the left flank, pushed forward to a bitter

contest near a line of rocks where the enemy claimed high ground. But soon our reserve lines reinforced them.

The Marsi were losing on all three fronts. Only a few hundred of their men had fallen, by my estimation, but the battle's fate was already decided.

Most armies fled at this point. Perhaps a tactical retreat to regroup and find better positioning, sometimes a full-on flight. But the Marsi continued to fight, refusing to break. They would die here, and they knew it.

"Rotation, rotation," I shouted. It pleased me when the front transitioned seamlessly and swiftly at my command. They were improving before my eye, rediscovering all the tactics that kept them alive through all the countless battles we'd waged in the past.

Fabius's men won decisively on the right, and their line surged forward. Only moments seemed to pass before they crashed into the flank of the Marsi center.

We rolled up their line like a scroll.

Instead of throwing down their weapons and pleading for mercy, the last of the Marsi rebels fighting on Fabius's left flank fought harder. Some of them bit at our throats, others grabbed hold of blades even as they pierced them, forcing the steel deeper into their own guts just to cut their killers in return.

Hatred kept them alive this long, but it could not sustain them. The last Marsi rebel fell screaming beneath a dozen swords, axes, and spears.

The battle was over.

The smell of decay filled the air as we strode through the ruins of the Marsi camp. The embers of their fires still simmered. Pots of stew rested on spits where they'd been cooking when the rebels heard the trumpets announcing our arrival. I authorized the men to take whatever they desired, and I didn't need to tell them twice.

I jumped off Sura's back and ran my hand along her soft flank. I hadn't needed to ride her into the fray this day, but I knew the time would come soon. She seemed to know this, too, as I interpreted her snorts as anxious.

Fabius found me. He wiped sweat from his brow and nodded to the benefactor trailing along behind him.

I don't recall this patrician's name, but I do remember the soft fabric of his clean toga and flush of his rotund face.

"What a spectacle," the man exclaimed. "My wife will never believe I've been in a proper Roman battle!"

I gave him a measured look. "I hope you approve of our efforts."

His sagging jowls bounced as he nodded.

"I approve, and I enjoyed it, my dear Sertorius. Positively splendid."

I extended my hand. At first, he didn't seem to understand what the gesture meant. Eventually, he extended his soft, limp hand.

"Can we count on your support?" I asked.

"I believe in your cause, my good man. I do. And I believe in your capabilities as a warrior." He looked up and pursed his lips in feigned contemplation. I hung on his words, and that pleased him. "And I trust you're just the one to give Sulla's boys a lesson in respect. Yes. I will personally fund this fine force. Twenty thousand denarii, in exchange for your heroic service to Rome. I expect this generosity to be rewarded with a position of importance in our restored Republic."

Given the size of his latifundium and the great wealth he so readily boasted of, we'd hoped for more. Twenty thousand denarii would pay the mercenaries for little more than two weeks.

"I thank you. Rome thanks you. I will not forget your generosity."

The patrician beamed, fortunately oblivious to my disappointment.

Fabius forced a smile as well, knowing fully we needed more coin, and soon. But he led the patrician away to show him the Marsi camp, as if there was more to see then the musty bedding and weathered equipment of a now-dead army.

I returned to Sura. As an officer, I had much to do after any battle, but if it was my choice I would ride my horse somewhere quiet and sit alone with her for a while, thinking and not thinking, feeling and not feeling.

I laid my forehead against hers and tried to enjoy a brief moment of that, but as soon as I closed my eye I heard my name.

"Quintus Sertorius?"

I turned to find a man I couldn't recall. There was nothing remarkable about him save the sharpness of his eyes.

"I am Sertorius," I said.

He wasn't threatening, but he clearly wasn't a man of my legion so I placed a hand on my gladius hilt.

"The women in your camp said I'd find you here." He reached into a leather satchel slung over his shoulder and materialized a letter. "I have something for you."

I watched his movements carefully. "You came from camp? You should have waited there. We would have given you food, rest, and shelter. Where did you hail from?" I accepted the letter and looked at the seal.

"You'll have to read the letter to find out," he said.

I ran my thumb over the cool, stamped wax. The paper was of fine quality, and although I didn't recognize the seal, I knew it came from someone important.

"This must be urgent news indeed."

He smirked. "I'm the greatest courier alive, sire. You need something delivered, something important or . . . secretive. I'm your man. Swamps, plagues, flooded rivers, bands of rebel warriors . . . makes no difference to me. I always get the job done. And I'm compensated well for it."

"A valuable skill. Perhaps I'll employ your services sometime."

"Do you know a man named . . ." He brandished a wax tablet and analyzed the writing. "Fabius? Have a letter for him too. Different patron."

"Two arrows in one shot. A lucrative job."

He grinned.

I pointed toward the mercenary captain. "Right that way, the handsome man who somehow looks twenty and sixty at the same time."

He offered a casual nod and left me with the letter.

The courier's demeanor offered no insight into whether this news was a fortune or a curse, but perhaps he didn't know the contents.

I wasted no time breaking the seal and unfurling the letter.

Before reading the contents, I scanned the bottom and spotted a name. Cinna. An old friend and, more importantly, one of Rome's two consuls. Interesting.

Dear Quintus,

What times we live in. We've sacrificed everything for Rome, and now our own colleagues expel us from our own homes. Compelled into exile, forced to take shelter from despots and usurpers. But I know neither of us will allow this to continue. We've fought too hard and too long to allow the whims of others to control our destiny.

I've heard tell you're raising an army. Small but impressive from what the little birds chirp. Oh, I sacrifice a hundred bulls for it to be so.

We are of one mind. I intend to do the same. By the time you reach me, I'll have a force of my own. I'm establishing camp a half-day's ride north of Beneventum. Join me.

I relish knowing we will fight together again. Let us reclaim our Republic.

Lucius Cornelius Cinna, The RIGHTFUL Consul of the Roman Republic

Dictated on the Nones of November, Six Hundred and Sixty-Six Years from the Founding of the City.

I let my head back and laughed. A belly laugh, a deep genuine one that eased the battle-tension in my shoulders.

I didn't know why at first but couldn't stop myself. The notion of Fortuna favoring me was infinitely humorous.

I heard the dirt crunch behind me. "Good news?" I turned to find Fabius with an excited smile of his own.

"I think our luck has changed," I said. "A friend of mine is raising an army of his own. He beckons us to join him."

Fabius let out a low whistle. He couldn't resist throwing his arms around my shoulders. "Remarkable," he said. "Unbelievable."

"Together we can—"

He continued. "It's remarkable that such good news could arrive and yet still not be the best we receive today."

I craned my head.

Fabius grabbed me firmly and kissed me on the forehead. "Coin, Sertorius. Coin! A donor has vowed an . . . *enormous* sum of money."

"How much?" I asked, hardly believing what I was hearing.

He ran through the numbers in his head. "Three months. Three months for the entire force."

Fabius must have studied mathematics in his youth. I couldn't begin to calculate the sum.

"From whom? Who did this? And why?"

He shook his head. "An anonymous donor. Says he fears retribution . . . understandable I suppose." He looked over the letter again. "But he assures us we have his full support. The coin should arrive by wagon, at night, within the next three days."

I knew better than to trust this. The gods heaped obstacle after obstacle on us for so long. I'd been betrayed before; allies deceived me. I told myself to remain skeptical, but what would I do differently if I refused to trust a hope? Turn away such a vast sum of money and such overwhelming support? I could only remain vigilant and hope that fortune's tides finally turned in our favor.

Despite my reservations, I exhaled, slow and deep.

"Let's return to camp then. When the shipment arrives, we set out for Beneventum."

With our combined forces and enough coin to sustain us through the end of winter, we might be able to force the senate to negotiate. We could hold Sulla and his loyalists responsible for the crimes and restore order to the Republic.

For the first time since I watched our temples burn under Sulla's torchlight, I believed it was possible.

SCROLL XVII

Gavius Sertorius—Two days before the Kalends of December, 666 Ab Urbe Condita

Bodies piled high on the Greek plain. The late-Autumn rainfall had been relentless, but we further nourished the fields with blood. The once-green grass became a trampled, muddy grave. The fight began less than an hour before, but already the Pontic forces were breaking.

I gripped my gladius and steadied myself on Bucephalus's back. My breath was ragged, and sweat slicked my brow as I surveyed the battlefield. Our left flank, the one I commanded, initiated the Pontic collapse. Now, the rest of their army began to crumble like a rotting foundation. Their lines buckled under my order of advance. Their spearmen broke their lines as Sulla's Fist pressed forward in tight, near perfect formation.

I could see their banners across the battlefield, each depicting a blazing comet. They wavered.

"Loose ranks, loose ranks!" I shouted, and the centurions relayed my order.

Dust spread across the plains as the Pontic cavalry retreated first, whipping their mounts furiously as they departed. Their infantry followed, and not in a disciplined withdrawal. No, it was an outright rout.

"*Roma Victrix*!" I raised a fist to the heavens.

My first victory in a position of command as an officer of Rome. By all the gods, nothing had ever tasted so sweet.

"Mark time," I ordered as my men continued taunting our fleeing foes. "Hold fast."

I spun Bucephalus round, which seemed to disappoint him. He seemed to miss the fray as much as I did. I scanned the rear of our forces for Lucullus's silver eagle and somehow spotted it through the haze of dust and smoke.

Kicking Bucephalus to a gallop, I cut across the battlefield, avoiding the wounded, dying, and the dead as best I could.

I found Lucullus on our right flank near a ruined stretch of ground where the fighting had been thickest. Dirt and sweat streaked his face, but his expression was sharp as ever. He shouted orders at his officer in a manner reminiscent of Sulla, just as careful to not allow excitement to diminish our discipline as the general himself.

Only when he spotted my arrival did he allow himself to smile. "If that's the best Mithridates can throw at us, we'll be celebrating a triumph in Rome by the Kalends!"

His men roared.

We both knew this was only the beginning, and the foreign king would present far greater challenges to us before we could defeat him. But there was no use in mentioning it now. I allowed myself to join them in the elated revelry of victory, if only for a moment.

He led his horse to a trot until he reached my side. He reached over and clapped my shoulder while our horses investigated each other.

"I saw your flank. Masterful work, Gavius. Sulla was right to trust us with this command."

The hope of Sulla's approval and praise was even sweeter than the taste of victory.

"We have them on the run, and they aren't stopping." I pointed out the obvious.

Lucullus's gaze swept over the field, his eyes narrowing as he refocused. "Even after their casualties, they outnumber us two to one," he said. "Any smart general would regroup, claim strategic ground, form a rear guard . . . but they aren't. They're truly fleeing, aren't they?"

"In the direction of Athens, if the battle didn't turn me around."

He turned to one of his centurions who remained at attention nearby.

"Send scouts to track their every movement," Lucullus ordered. "I want certain confirmation they're headed to the city."

He turned to me, unbuckled his helmet and removed it. Running a hand through his sweaty hair, he said, "That force was commanded by Archelaus. Mithridates's second-in-command. Every report I've received indicates he's a talented veteran commander. He wouldn't flee from a smaller force unless he knows he can't defeat us."

"Unless he's leading us into a trap," I said.

He glanced at me. I could see his mind grinding, considering the glory of conquering the foe, and juxtaposing that with the fear of annihilation and dishonor.

"You think so?"

I didn't hesitate. "Yes," I said. "I feel certain of it."

I wasn't one to rely on intuition often but rather the orders of wiser men. Whether this confidence came from the hubris of victory or the battle-won wisdom I'd gained myself I didn't know. But the shift felt nice.

Lucullus grunted in acknowledgment. His eyes flickered toward the fleeing army and the horizon. Athens lay ahead, not yet visible but looming like a giant in our minds.

I could see him debating what to do.

"What would you do?" Lucullus asked.

As my superior, he was in primary command here, and he'd earned that right. He'd fought beside Sulla and commanded flanks before I swore my oath. His decision was final. That he would ask my opinion meant something. Perhaps I'd grown wiser after all.

I straightened. "We should wait for Sulla," I said. "Reform, regroup, prepare . . . then follow Archelaus to Athens and crush them."

The boundless glory of annihilating this Pontic force enticed us both, but my assessment was correct, and he knew it.

"Agreed." He nodded.

I would have followed his orders regardless, but that he trusted my judgment filled me with immense pride.

He disseminated the order to halt and secure the perimeter. The centurions ensured our men obeyed swiftly and efficiently. I rode back to my left flank and passed along the same orders.

Sulla was only a few days behind us. When he arrived, we would march on Athens.

He would reclaim the birthplace of democracy, and I would secure the victory.

SCROLL XVIII

LUCIUS HIRTULEIUS—TWO days after the Nones of December, 666 Ab Urbe Condita

The sea was golden in the morning light, the rippling waves catching the first rays of sun like scattered coins. The coast stretched behind me, rugged and wild, the kind of beauty men can never tame. Jagged cliffs jutted out over the water's edge. Morning mist shrouded the rolling green hills beyond it. A few gulls drifted lazily above, oblivious to the chaos unfolding on this shore over the past two weeks.

I ran my hand over the worn wooden rail of the dock, staring out over clusters of our ships in the harbor.

On Marius's orders, we attempted to build ships of our own. The effort didn't last long. It swiftly became apparent that constructing seaworthy vessels required more than nailing wood together. By the end of the first week, Marius redirected our orders to banditry.

Any merchant foolish enough to land here, any fisherman caught in the wrong tide, any traveler cursed by Fortuna to see

Sardinia on the horizon—we took their ships, their supplies, and usually their lives.

I hung my head and stared down at the water and the tiny fish swirling around in a cascade of bubbles beneath me.

Lucius Hirtuleius had never been a thief.

I was a legionary. An officer of Rome. A man raised by his grandfather and taught by his companions to live with honor.

Yet I'd devoted my life to serving a man who declared himself a savior and outlaw in the same breath. I stood on the docks of a village we butchered and drained dry and watched as a ragged band of fugitives and freed *servi* prepared our sails for war.

"There is no dignity in this," I pled with Marius. "This is not our way."

"Then tell me a better way," was Marius's only reply. "I will alter our course if you can give me one viable alternative. How else can we return to Italy? How else can we save Rome?"

I came up with nothing.

Sertorius was the strategist. He was brilliant enough to find a solution, one that preserved our *dignitas* and spared innocent lives. But despite all my effort to do the same, I came up with nothing.

So, I did what I'd always done. I followed orders. Like a good soldier.

The docks became alive with movement. Marius's five hundred "warriors" scrambled onto the decks of our stolen ships, loading barrels of water and wine and sacks of grain, each of which belonged to someone who joined Marius willingly or died defending them.

Voices in a dozen different languages rose from the ships, mingling with bursts of laughter that carried easily on the salt-tinged wind. They were eager to begin our voyage, for their lives to mean something. To taste what they'd never tasted, to drink what they'd never drank. Their plan was simple enough I suppose. The women and children would remain in this village with only a handful of protectors and no masters, as the rulers of the village, enjoying whatever supplies we didn't require for our journey. The men would sail under Marius's command and help restore him to power and glory, which he would use to bestow gifts and rewards upon them. His promises remained vague, but if he fulfilled even half his vows, these unfortunate sons of foreign nations would be greater than Roman consuls.

Footsteps shook the deck. I turned to find Aulus beside me.

"You look troubled," he said.

I sighed. "How could I not be troubled?" I leaned over the railing, spit, and watched as the tiny fish scurried.

Aulus smirked, as he usually did despite the circumstances. "It won't surprise you to discover I share your concerns, though I have the good sense enough not to dwell on them. Instead, I voice them in little quips the old man is too absent to interpret."

We stood in silence for a moment, watching as a group of former slaves struggled to load a heavy crate on a nearby merchant vessel. They weren't soldiers, not honorable legionaries of the Republic.

"This gang cannot retake Rome," I whispered.

"No," Aulus agreed. "But they'll usher Marius to his next destination, where he'll narrowly escape death again and somehow be stronger for it."

The weight of our course pressed heavier on my shoulders. Italy. Rome. We would return not as recalled exiles but as conquerors—at least in Marius's mind. I should've been excited to take Rome back from a tyrant, but I only felt dread.

Aulus shifted beside me. "You should board. You'll be leaving soon."

"I suppose we should," I said. "Let's pick our vessel."

"I'm not coming with you," he said.

I turned to him sharply. "What?"

He gestured to a fisherman's vessel moored at the far end of the harbor. "Marius doesn't want to take that one. I'm going to take it."

I shook my head. "Aulus, you can't—"

"I can, and I will." His face became sullen. "I never cared for Marius, or any politician, to be honest. I thought I might come to worship him as you do on this voyage, but I've only come to resent him. Sulla, Marius . . . I don't care who sits on the curule chair. Let the fools fight it out."

I tried to respond, but he cut me off again.

"Lucius, I have nothing waiting for me in Italy." I noticed a hint of sorrow in his voice, something often beneath the surface of his smile but rarely allowed to manifest.

"Of course you do," I objected. "You have a family. What of your wife? She's been waiting on you for years while we fought the rebels. Even if you abandon Marius's cause, as is your right, you should sail with us and return to her."

He sighed and looked up at the gulls. "I received a letter not two weeks into our campaign against the rebels. Her father found a better match, someone with grander prospects, probably wealthier, someone not wasting his best years fighting a war with little chance of advancement or opportunity."

My chest ached for him. He'd often complained about his ill-suited marriage, but I could see the pain in his eyes. "Aulus, I didn't know . . . I am—"

"They didn't ask for the dowry back, which pleased my father." He chuckled. "I suppose I should be grateful."

"Aulus . . ."

"It doesn't matter." He shook his head. "I wasn't a good husband anyway. Family was never my calling."

I wondered for a moment what he felt the gods had designed for him. He abjured the local politics of his father, he cared little for war and conquest, dreaded the shackles of marriage. The aching in his heart seemed to manifest from the yearning for more but the inability to find what it was.

"Nothing waits for me in Italy," he reiterated. "But I have unfinished business elsewhere."

I already knew the answer, but I asked anyway. "Where?"

"Hispania."

After his twin brother, Spurius, betrayed us in the war against the rebels, Sertorius nearly killed him. Instead, he allowed him to escape with his life to Hispania.

The Insteius twins had been inseparable from birth. Aulus never had the opportunity to address the betrayal with his brother or make amends, if it was even possible. He'd hardly mentioned Spurius since Sertorius sent him away. I never discerned whether Aulus hated his brother for the betrayal or Sertorius for sending Spurius away, but it didn't matter. I knew my friend. I always expected this to happen eventually.

"I'll never know peace until I find him, Lucius," Aulus said.

"Hispania is a vast land, untamed and wild. How do you expect to find him?"

Aulus grinned. "Do you know any barbarians who bathe as often as Spurius? I'll follow the smell of olive oil and women's perfume."

I laughed. The memory of their endless banter brought me joy despite it feeling like a lifetime ago.

"And what will you do when you find him?"

Aulus sobered and shrugged his shoulder. "Don't know. I suppose I'll decide when I lay eyes on him for the first time."

I tried to find the words to stop him. Aulus would stay if I asked—if I said I needed him, he wouldn't leave. But that would be a lie born of self-interest. I feared I would never see him again, but I wouldn't betray a lifelong companion just to spare myself the ache of his absence.

"You should come with me." Aulus placed a hand on my shoulder.

As if on command, Marius's voice carried over the dock. "Come on then! Move it. Time to set sail now. Lucius!"

I turned to my companion as Marius's orders continued. "I wish only that I could," I said.

He nodded. "I knew you wouldn't. I see the growing resentment in your eyes, but you're still devoted to him, aren't you?"

I breathed deeply as I considered it, then nodded.

"Go then," he said. "Keep sacrificing the required number of pigeons, and the gods will guide you as they always have."

I punched his shoulder before clasping his arm and pulling him close.

"Safe travels, *mi amice.*"

He clapped my back. "In this life or the next, *mi amice.*"

Aulus and I turned in opposite directions. I faced away and followed Marius's voice. By the time I reach my vessel, Aulus had unfastened the ropes and pushed off. The wind caught his sail, and he drifted out into the golden horizon, west toward Hispania and whatever the Fates had in store for him there.

I hoisted myself onto Marius's ship just before his men raised the gangplank. We set sail for Italy. I knew our destination, but not where it would lead. It was in the hands of the gods now.

SCROLL XIX

Quintus Sertorius—Six days before the Kalends of January, 666 Ab Urbe Condita

The wind crept down from the hills, threading its cool fingers through the folds of my cloak. I could feel the first sting of winter taking hold in the countryside. The leaves that remained on the few scattered trees clung stubbornly, brittle and brown, while most had already perished and now littered the stone road beneath Sura's hooves. The smell of damp earth and woodsmoke from some unseen farmer's hearth nearby mixed with the scent of horses and leather.

We waited at the crest of a low ridge overlooking a wide valley, silent but for the occasional snort of our mounts or the rustle of dried grass. My mother rode on my left, Arrea on my right with Toria bundled in her arms. It was a common sight by now, but it still impressed me that Arrea had become such a skilled rider that she could manage her steed with one hand while comforting Toria with the other. Fabius rode one of our most docile mares, though she seemed to become more frustrated the longer my poor riding friend remained on her back.

The rest of our army waited behind us, probably wondering if we'd be making a new camp with new allies, or if we'd be returning in disappointment.

Each of us fixed our gaze on the far end of the valley.

We were here to unite with allies, which should exceptionally improve our odds of victory. Cinna's letter should have instilled nothing but confidence in all of us, but there was still an air of tension that lingered among us.

Fabius broke the silence. "He said he'd be coming this way, yes?" He shifted in his saddle and rubbed the exposed flesh of his arms for warmth. "Do you think he's changed his mind?"

I ran my fingers through Sura's mane. "I served with Cinna in the North for years. His son was like a brother to me. He won't change his mind."

I spoke honestly, but the longer we waited, the more anxious I became. Winter was coming soon, and if we didn't act, the slow grind of the season would defeat us rather than Sulla's loyalists in Rome.

Then, from beyond a copse of bare elms, a small cluster of riders emerged.

"There," I said.

No one said anything else, but I think we were all equally disappointed by what we saw. A few dozen horsemen perhaps, nothing more. I could see Cinna among them. His plain, hunched posture was distinct against the battle-hardened warriors around him. His appearance was modest even in consular armor and riding a magnificent warhorse.

I was relieved to see my old friend, but . . . was this all he had?

But then, from the tree line, the rest began to appear.

Hundreds, then thousands, of legionaries appeared, countless columns of legionaries each moving with discipline and purpose. Their standards fluttered in the cool afternoon breeze. A sea of shields glinted in the sunlight, and the red cloak of the Roman legion hung from every shoulder.

A light breath escaped me. "He's done it," I said. "He raised an army."

Fabius's laugh cut through the wind. "I can only imagine the look on Sulla's face if he could see this."

I nudged Sura to a trot.

"Who do you want with you?" Fabius said.

"I'm going alone," I replied.

"But you don't know if—"

"I do." I nodded to Fabius and my family before quickening the pace down the slope.

The valley between us was open and quiet, remarkably quiet given the size of our forces on either side. I smiled as I saw Cinna follow my lead and leave his vanguard behind and trotting off to meet me alone.

We met in the open, with only the hills and pale sky above as witness. The lazy croak of a raven perched on one of the skeletal trees lining the edge of the valley signaled the beginning of our discussion like a trumpet.

Cinna directed his horse closer and regarded me. Despite his shining armor and expensive cloak, he was as unremarkable as he'd ever been. A touch shorter than most, lacking strong muscles or any excess fat. His high-plumed helmet concealed his balding, ruddy hair.

His eyes looked grim. Perhaps Cinna had endured as much difficulty as we had since the chaos spread through Rome.

"Sertorius," he said flatly.

I dipped my head and placed a fist over my heart. "Consul."

"I should have you reprimanded," he said.

The words felt like they came from someone else. Of course, it would have been right for a consul to accost me for raising an army without the auspices of the senate, but this didn't match the tone of his letter at all.

"I'm sorry?" I said.

"I've always thought of us as friends." He dropped the reins and crossed his arms. "And yet you do me a great insult."

I tilted my head. "Please, inform me of my grievance and I'll set it right."

I still couldn't tell whether Cinna was playing at a joke or if he was serious. Either way, he seemed different.

"Word spreads quickly. I'm told you have a daughter now."

"Yes . . . yes I do. Toria is her name."

"Neigh a year old now?"

I was becoming more confused with each word. "Only a few months shy. Hard to believe."

"And yet her uncle Cinna has not been invited to meet her!" He let out a laugh and pushed his horse close enough so we could shake hands. I laughed, relieved that his game was over.

"A grievous insult, I'll admit." I gripped his forearm. "Between all that's happened recently, we've found little time for friendly visitors."

He waved off the comment. "Together, we'll set all that right. We'll rid Rome of the tyrant's influence and then enjoy those pleasantries we've been so long denied."

"Consul, what happened?" I asked. "Only a few short months ago I received word of your election, and the next thing I heard, you'd been exiled."

He laughed. "I betrayed Sulla, that's what happened. He had us swear an oath of loyalty to him. Can you imagine the vanity? I had no choice but to accept, but I thought it rather obvious a vow made under compulsion should be nullified." He shook his head. "I expected my consular 'colleague' to help me restore order, but he holds that oath sacred. Imagine this, he hates Sulla as much as we do yet serves as the tyrant's faithful puppet."

"You 'betrayed' Sulla?"

He shrugged. "I sought to repeal his legislation and name him a criminal for his war crimes against the state. But Octavius and the senate are determined to keep Sulla's chair warm and waiting for him until his return." He pointed at me. "But we'll address that. Yes, we will."

"I'm ready," I said. "With our combined forces, perhaps the senate will negotiate."

He cocked his head. "You know them as well as I do," he said. "They aren't going to relent until we've left them no other option."

I sighed. He was right. Common sense wouldn't be enough to compel them. Pride, spite, and fear of Sulla would require them to resist as long as they could.

"I've seen them, Sertorius," he said. "We have no choice but to besiege the city."

I couldn't find the words, so I nodded then.

"Once the city grows hungry and the plebs start howling for their blood, Octavius and the senate will capitulate. Or so we can hope. But if it comes to fighting, we'll make short work of them," he said. "There's not but two thousand fighting men left in the city, and most of them are children or old men."

"Reinforcements will interfere," I said.

He nodded. "Undeniably. Though, with Sulla's legions toiling in Greece, we can crush any force remaining in Italy."

I sobered at the thought of "crushing" Roman troops, but I would do what was necessary to save the Republic.

"How many men do you have?" he asked.

"Just shy of four thousand," I said. "Two thousand mercenaries and nearly as many veterans from Umbria, Latium, and thereabouts."

"Four thousand? Impressive," he said. "I have nearly three thousand Roman legionaries, and over two thousand auxiliaries from the Picentes tribes. Bastards are so eager to make up for the atrocities of their rebellion, they'd have sent their women and children to fight for us if I'd asked."

"Together, we have an imposing force," I said, and meant it. With an army of ten thousand at our command, the senate wouldn't be able to hold us off for long. "We'll fight as one."

He gave me a firm nod. "As we should."

"And you and I will serve together as equals?" I asked. "I

won't lead an army against Rome unless I determine how they're used."

Cinna was an elected consul. Despite the senate exiling him and replacing him in office, he had all the legitimate right of command, and I had none. But I had far more battlefield experience than Cinna. I hoped he recognized this.

I wanted to save the Republic without destroying it in the process. I wouldn't sign my name to another slaughter of the Roman people, so everything depended on his response.

Cinna wasn't an ambitious or dangerous man, but power corrupts. As a subordinate, I wouldn't be able to set things right.

He nodded fervently but looked away as he said, "Of course, of course. You've raised a fine army. Far be it from me to strip them from you. Yes, you and I. Equals. Brothers-in-arms as we were so long ago."

Only then did he look my way again, with his familiar, gentle smile stretched across his face.

"I'm honored to stand beside you, consul," I said. "Our camp is three days' march behind us. I see no reason to return if you're ready to unite."

Cinna shrugged. "Our camp *was* on the other side of this valley," he said. "We deconstructed this morning. Let's march on Rome."

I didn't know whether to smile or curse or pray or weep. But he was right.

I looked around. Soon this valley would be choked with mud and sleet. Soon Rome would receive supplies for the winter, allowing them to hold out against us for longer. The time for preparation had passed. Now came the hour of action.

"Agreed," I said. "To Rome then."

PART II: PERDUELLIS

He cursed the gods for giving him the victory . . . with the same sword wherewith he had slain his brother, he stabbed himself in the heart, and falling upon his brother, was burnt in the same flames.

— VALERIUS MAXIMUS, V 5.4

This incident struck everyone as a great condemnation of the civil war and changed their attitudes. Nobody was able to refrain from tears."

— GRANIUS LICINIANUS, 35.20

So much livelier among our ancestors was repentance for guilt as well as glory in virtuous action.

— TACITUS, HISTORIES 51.1

SCROLL XX

GAVIUS SERTORIUS—TWO days after the Nones of January, 667 Ab Urbe Condita

The city rose before us like a myth brought to life. The limestone walls shone like a white laurel, washed clean by the ceaseless rainfall. Athens was older than Rome, older than memory, older perhaps even than some of our gods. Somewhere within that sprawling maze of stone, brave men first dared to speak of democracy. Somewhere in those open marketplaces and on shaded porticos, wise men first considered the nature of life and what it means to be good.

And now we'd come to conquer her.

I stood atop a ridge overlooking the plain and the city below. Even if I climbed to a peak twice as high as this one, I still wouldn't have been able to see the breadth of the ancient city.

Around me, legionaries threw off their packs and wrung rainwater from their clothing. I'd released them to eat, but for the moment, excitement distracted them.

We marched more than four hundred miles to reach Athens. Most of the legionaries—myself included—were simple men from the Sabine hills, the marshland of Latium, or the farmlands of Capua. They'd never ventured this far from home, never even considered the possibility of seeing Athens, the setting of many childhood lessons and bedtime stories.

To conquer it meant infinite glory. Immortality.

Lucullus joined me on the ridge and crossed his arms. He looked tired. We all were, but he was just as excited as the rest of us.

I spotted Sulla farther down the slope, near the temporary camp where our engineers began siege preparations.

Sulla had remained focused since we departed Epirus, though his good cheer returned from time to time. I found it impossible to know whether I would find him sullen and irritable or carefree and affable when I approached him.

None of us would dare speak of this to one another out of respect for our commander, but I could sense tension from the other officers when they approached Sulla as well. Only Lucullus seemed unperturbed, constantly reiterating that all things would settle down once we began the siege.

I looked forward to that. I missed our friendly interactions, the way he looked after me like a son. If the siege didn't set things right, I was determined to do something, anything, to win back his trust.

I could hear only the muffle of Sulla's words as he pointed at various points of Athens' high walls.

Soon, we would cut off the roads, find a way to blockade the port with few ships at our disposal, and starve them out. Athens would be ours, and then we could continue our fight into Asia Minor. We would retrieve everything Mithridates had stolen from us.

But then the messenger arrived.

He galloped up behind us on a dirty colt. The poor beast wheezed from exhaustion. Foam dripped from its chin.

The rider—a scrawny man in Roman kit—appeared as

exhausted as his steed. He lost his footing upon dismount and collapsed.

Some of the legionaries laughed. I hurried to his side.

"From where do you hail?" I said. I considered chastising him for the poor care he'd given his horse, but I could see from the gaunt features and leathery skin of the rider that he'd ridden out of desperation.

He sucked wind and rocked himself to his feet.

"I scarcely remember," he said. "First Asculum. Epirus. Thessaly. Boeotia! I've been following you for weeks."

"Bring him some wine. Figs and cheese too," I ordered. "Quick."

As I helped the messenger to his feet, I considered his words. First Asculum? The man had followed us all the way from Italy? Whatever news he bore was important.

I turned to Lucullus. "Send for the commander," I said.

By the time the messenger finished his second cup of wine and a handful of figs, Sulla and several other officers arrived.

The commander was in good spirits, despite the interruption.

"What is it? What is so important as to disrupt my preparation?"

I gestured to the hapless messenger who scrambled to pull a sealed scroll from his satchel.

He fell to one knee, lowered his gaze, and held the scroll aloft.

Sulla sighed. "Bring wine. I'm parched. Three amphorae. No, four. Cups for every officer, today is a day of celebration."

The messenger remained on one knee. The moment was drawn out. It became awkward. "Would you like me to hand you the scroll, general?"

Sulla reached into a bowl of fresh grapes from the Greek countryside. "Hermes," he said to the messenger. "Can you read?"

The messenger looked up. "W-what's that, sir?"

"He asked if you could read," Crassus said, joining Sulla at his side.

"Yes, or . . . or, as well as the next man, I suppose."

"Read it for us then," Sulla spoke through a mouthful of Greek delicacies.

I accepted a cup of wine. I thought the messenger could use another before trying to recite a letter, but he stood and composed himself.

"Should I b-break the seal, sir?" he said.

"Go on," Sulla commanded.

I nodded to a nearby legionary. "Take his horse to feed. Go."

The legionary was disappointed to miss the letter but obeyed.

The messenger broke the seal, delicately as if he was performing some sacred sacrifice, and unfurled the scroll.

He cleared his throat.

To Lucius Cornelius Sulla, Proconsul and Defender of Rome,

It is with solemn gravity that I inform you that my friend and your former co-consul, Quintus Pompeius Rufus, did in fact arrive at my camp to take my command in accordance with your orders. Naturally, I received him with all the dignity and respect due a man of his station. Preparations were underway for the ceremonial transfer of command.

My eyes flickered to Sulla as the messenger read aloud. His expression was unreadable, but he stopped chewing. He was listening intently now.

Tragically, as Rufus stood before the assembled men to speak, a bolt of Jupiter's lightning struck him dead where he stood. The gods, in their infinite and inscrutable wisdom, it seems, had other plans than you and I.

Sulla remained still, but I could see the chalice in his hand was beginning to shake. Fresh Greek wine spilled out over the rim and onto his ringed fingers.

I have consulted with the augurs, and each agrees this is a divine sign that the gods themselves favor my continued command. I have elected to remain in leadership out of respect for the gods themselves.

Please accept my condolences; I know Rufus was dear to you.

In friendship and discord,

Gnaeus Pompeius Strabo, Commander of the Picentes Legions

A long silence followed. No one dared be the first to break it. Only the messenger moved, falling to his knee once more.

I knew little of politics, but even I knew "struck by lightning" meant assassinated.

Sulla didn't speak. He didn't scream. Instead, he paced to a nearby *servus* and snatched an unopened amphora of wine from his grasp.

He smashed it against a wooden table and didn't seem to notice the broken shards piercing his palm or the blood dripping with the wine down his forearm.

Somehow his face remained eerily calm, fixed in stillness like a wax death mask. But his eyes—his eyes were wild.

Crassus was the only man brave enough to speak up. "I grieve with you," he said without emotion. "Shall we return to the siege efforts, general?"

Sulla turned back toward Athens.

With his attention diverted, I gestured for the messenger to depart—quickly—and he didn't protest.

When Sulla whipped back around to us, his eyes were wide and unblinking.

His voice was even as he said, "There will be no siege," he said.

Lucullus stepped forward, cautiously but as confused as the rest of us. "General?"

"We take the city now."

No one objected. No one responded at all.

He pointed at Lucullus and me. "You will lead two legions to Piraeus. Cut the city off from the sea. Secure the harbor. Destroy everything that might aid their survival. No food, no ships, no mercy."

I opened my mouth to protest, but instead I only said, "Moving, Imperator."

Only a short time before, I would have been thrilled to learn the battle was upon us. It wasn't the order that chilled me but the matter with which it was given.

Sulla had always been unpredictable; it was the very trait that terrified his enemies. Yet he'd never been impulsive, until now.

Was this the man who outwitted the Numidians and the Cimbri and the rebels, or someone else? Had Strabo's veiled insults unnerved him? He'd lost a friend, to assassination no doubt, and was too far away to seek vengeance. But why should that have any bearing on our strategy in Greece?

Lucullus gave a serious nod. "We'll see it done."

"With the rest of our force, I will take those walls." He pointed back at the limestone walls. "Today. No siege towers, no sappers. Just steel, might, and balls."

Lucullus and I saluted the general even though he wasn't looking and returned to our men, who enjoyed their afternoon meal in blissful ignorance.

"This isn't what we planned," I whispered, almost to myself.

"No," Lucullus consented, which surprised me.

"Is he unraveling?" I found the courage to ask.

"Maybe," Lucullus said, "Or maybe he's still three steps ahead of us all."

I didn't reply.

We both felt the same way. The line between calculation and madness had grown thin.

And now we marched straight through it.

For the first time in weeks, I saw no rainclouds above us. Perhaps that was a good sign. Still, the sea wind stung with cold salt as Lucullus and I advanced toward Piraeus, Athens's lifeline to the sea.

Bucephalus, my brave warhorse and most loyal companion,

breathed in heavy snorts; his hooves thudding with purpose as we pushed forward.

Lucullus and I rode in the center of the formation, Roman steel moving in front and behind us like a tide.

We led our columns to the west first and then would take the path south directly to Piraeus's outer gates. Still, we could not go far enough to escape the gaze of Athens's high walls. I could still see the limestone glimmering as the drums sounded alarm within the city. Horns blared in uneven intervals, desperate and shrill.

My heart thudded beneath my breastplate, and I clenched my fists. I wasn't nervous for the battle to come but recognized the enormity of the moment. I peered around at the simple land around Athens and recalled stories of the men who fought and died here long ago.

Pericles, Alcibiades, Theseus, and so many others. Some said even the gods visited Athens in the flesh long ago, and that Athena herself dwelled there still.

I remembered a story Apollonius told me as a boy that . . .

His name interrupted my thoughts. I wondered what Apollonius would think if he could see me now, leading an army outside the walls of his beloved Athens.

I eased the tension in my shoulders and stretched my arms.

Apollonius would support me, no doubt. He was as much Roman now as he was Greek or Jew and had been since my father liberated him from bondage. What Mithridates and his loyalists did to the Roman people was unforgivable, surely even a Greek-born man like Apollonius would agree. The Pontic army were barbarians, and we would slaughter them like barbarians.

"They are scared," Lucullus said. We rode side by side, but because of the speed of our march and the force of the sea wind, we had to raise our voices to be heard.

"Good." I spit in the direction of Athens. "Let them experience what every Roman in the east felt when Mithridates organized their slaughter."

Soon, we could see the gates of Piraeus grow into view. The walls lacked the elegancy of its sister city, but they were still high and strong. With two large stone towers on either side of the gate, it would be no small feat to take the gate without proper equipment.

What was it again? Steel, might, and balls. That's what we had to take the city.

Lucullus and I continued to improvise a battle plan as we narrowed our columns to enter the ravine leading straight to Piraeus's gate.

"First cohort lost six men to flux last week," I said, cupping a hand over my mouth so he might hear me better. "Let the second take the initial assault."

Lucullus nodded. "I watched your fourth cohort's second century training yesterday. They're greener than the rest, took most of the new recruits after last reinforcements. I would prepare extra reserves there."

"Agreed," I said. "How much resistance should we expect? I would wager the bulk of enemy forces will be protecting the city."

Lucullus frowned. "I'm not so certain. If they lose Piraeus, the city will be ours eventually too. Without reinforcements from the sea, they'll anticipate doom. The fighting here will be fierce."

I was pleased to hear it. I wanted Mithridates to throw his finest at us so we could extend our first display of Roman power.

"If we storm the gate, we might be able to force the breech before they can prepare proper defenses. They can't fit more than . . . say, fifteen archers in each of those towers. As long as they can prepare no oil or boulders to send down on us, our *testudo* can hold long enough to crush the gate."

For a moment, I considered the valley we traversed. Shouldn't it be a pond of rainwater after the past month?

"Hard and fast," Lucullus interrupted my thoughts. "Any hesitation, and they'll dig in their heels. With open access to the sea, it could be some time before we can take them."

Were that to happen, a length siege would generally be an acceptable alternative. But Sulla made it clear he wanted to take Piraeus and Athens today, and his word was law for Lucullus and me, despite our reservations.

The path grew even narrower as we neared Piraeus. I ordered for our columns to condense. The road leading to Piraeus's gate only allowed ten men to stand abreast. That might work in our favor, pitting Rome's best against theirs, and I liked those odds. Still, I cautiously glanced back at how far our line extended.

Lucullus and I exchanged a glance. Neither of us liked how exposed our flanks were.

We crested a final hill before the outer defenses, just outside of an archer's range. Enemy guards heaved the massive gates closed, but now I spotted the forces arrayed against us.

I raised a closed fist, and our centurions carried the order to halt backward and forward through the column.

My gaze fixed on the Pontic warriors to the west of the closed gates. A copse of scattered trees stood between us, restricting my ability to access their number.

I did notice these warriors were better equipped and more impressive than those we'd fought a few weeks prior. Each man I could see was well armored in plate mail like I'd never seen before. Each bore a curved blade and a broad shield. They partially concealed their faces with bronze, white crested helmets.

If they hadn't carried out the execution of every Roman in Greece and Asia, I might have sought to learn from them. As things were, I was eager to shed their blood.

"Could these be Mithridates's own warriors?" I asked, able to speak more softly now. "They're . . . different than the last."

Lucullus shrugged. "It's possible. We won't know until we search the bodies of the fallen. Are you ready?"

I expected Mithridates to be protected within Athens' high walls, probably hiding in the Acropolis. Most kings enjoy pampered conditions while their subjects fight, until no one remains to die for them.

I hoped Mithridates was braver than most kings. I wanted nothing more than to be the man who killed the Pontic king. I could only imagine Sulla's delight if I brought him the head of his enemy.

"I'm ready," I said. "On your signal."

He raised his hand, two fingers extended. Just before he dropped it to initiate the advance, he paused.

"Wait," he said. "Do you see that? East of the gate."

He directed my attention until I spotted them.

A myth came to life before my eyes, a vision I'd conjured in my mind countless times as a child. Greek hoplites, arrayed in splendor with pikes twice—no, three times—the size of any man.

They didn't look like soldiers of this world, but like figures lifted from some mosaic. Ghosts of Macedon, men forged in the fires of Alexander's wars, brought to life.

Lucullus's face hardened. "I don't know how he's done it. Mithridates united ancient enemies against us."

I straightened and forced myself to stop admiring the men I'd soon kill.

"The despot can resurrect whatever long-dead armies he'd like; they aren't ready for our charge."

Lucullus gave me a nod, grateful for the reassurance, and raised his hand once more.

"Advance!" the centurions shouted, the call snaking back and forth through the formation as the line began to move the same way.

Lucullus and I pulled away from the center and rode with our guard to our position of command on either side of the column.

When the third cohort of my legion clashed first with the hoplites, I wasn't certain what to expect. How could one penetrate a defensive line when the enemy spears were longer than battering rams? I reminded myself that legionaries defeated the Greek hoplites long ago, and we would again.

Back then, Rome's superior cavalry won the day. We didn't have the same advantage, with only three hundred riders at the rear of our column and little space in this valley for them to operate.

But we had Gavius Sertorius and his warhorse Bucephalus. That would suffice.

I leaned forward and whispered to him, "It's time again, my boy. Let's fight together."

As the front lines formed the fray, I prepared to send reserves to the far left of our flank, where we were weakest. But from my vantage point, some five hundred feet away, I could see they didn't need it.

Our line braced against the initial assault well.

The legionaries impressed me. This was Sulla's Fist. Of course we could destroy hoplites and Pontic cutthroats.

"Stand fast by center," I shouted. Others relayed the orders, but the legionaries only needed to continue as they were. Centurions called for line rotation at proper intervals, and the transition was handled with precision and excellence.

I called for a runner. "Go to second century, tell them they'll be leading *testudo* once we clear the path to the gates."

"Moving, tribune!"

Our front lines continued to push forward, a steady and measured advance, but an effective one the enemy seemed ill-equipped to handle.

Already the hoplite force panicked. Despite their impressive prebattle display, we found them unprepared.

Perhaps Sulla was right. I could barely contain myself. The man was some sort of prodigy, a genius, a demigod! Even with his most impulsive, seemingly irresponsible orders, he somehow divined exactly what would lead us to victory. Our swift action was the very thing that would make Athens ours.

Greek and Pontic warriors rushed back to the gates,

hammering their fists and weapons against it. They cried out for the guards to show mercy and allow them entry.

I smiled and exhaled. Sulla would be proud.

But then they broke the dams.

I heard the roar first, low and distant but distinct even over the tumult of battle. Then a torrent of water flooded the ridge behind us.

A cry of panic rose from our reserves as a wave of dirty rainwater and debris swallowed them. The current tore through our line like a knife through parchment. Soon the entire ravine would be a churning, chaotic swamp.

Our two hundred cavalrymen received the worst. I can still hear the shrill pitch of their horses.

My thoughts scrambled. I knew I should be shouting something, giving some command to restore order if nothing else. But I was utterly stunned.

Mithridates must have captured the winter's rainfall to build a floodplain and waited until we arrived to release it. This must have been an arduous task that required nothing short of brilliance from Mithridates and his generals, but in the moment, it looked more like magic. Like divine vengeance, like Neptune riding his four-horsed chariots to swallow us whole.

To make matters worse, Greek peltasts appeared from the trees. They weren't abundant, but each had three sharp javelins in hand. With our reserves crumbling—some simply trying not to drown where the water was deepest—it didn't require many of these ambushers to sow utter chaos.

The front line held firm—for now, still dry and unshaken. But the momentum shifted. Every Greek and Pontic warrior returned to the fight. Those who recently fled like frightened cattle charged back into the fray with fury, raw and terrible fury.

They looked more like the Spartans of Thermopylae than the cowards we'd seen only moments before.

It was all a ploy. The Easterners had been one step ahead of us from the very start.

Bucephalus stamped anxiously at the dirt beneath us. Water flooded over his hooves, moving fast.

He bucked in increasing heights.

"What do we do, boy?" I think I said, but everything around me blurred, as clouded and indiscernible as the muddy flood of rain water.

I led Bucephalus up the side of the ridge a few feet to calm him, while I tried to collect my own composure. I looked across the narrow battlefield to find Lucullus, hoping only to imitate his own actions as I found myself lacking any of my own.

Before I could spot him, I heard the sound for retreat. He didn't wait for my feedback this time, and to seek it would have probably delayed things too long. And what could I have said? Even as the water leveled out along the ridge, it would be knee-high by the time it reached the gates. We could maintain the front line with utter heroism, hold off arrows and javelins with our *testudo*, but it would be impossible to muster enough strength to take the gates down now.

So the retreat began. No, not a retreat. The rout.

I watched as our ranks scrambled onto either side of the ridge line, doing all they could to protect themselves in the scattered flight as the peltasts circled them like venomous snakes.

"Retreat!" I finally managed to shout. "Retreat!"

Bucephalus stamped beneath me, waiting impatiently to gallop away from the flood. But I couldn't move. I couldn't tear my gaze away from the gates we'd so recently marched against. I'd never fought in a losing battle. Sulla's Fist had never lost a battle. I couldn't believe it, I refused to accept it. I almost charged past our fleeing troops to fight by myself.

A javelin cut through the air just beside me, close enough to whistle in my ear.

We marched right into their trap. We were never close to victory.

Bucephalus stopped waiting on my command and carried me away with the rest of our men.

We reconvened in our half-built camp. I ordered centurions to conduct roll calls, but men could scarcely find their own standards, let alone fall into orderly formation.

The *medici* rushed to assist. Instead of bandaging wounds or removing hopeless limbs, they pumped water from the lungs of those unfortunate souls who sank into the mud for too long.

We saved some. Others died with blue faces and swollen eyes.

Considering the brilliance of the enemy surprise, we escaped with minor casualties. It might take days before we could tally up the true number, but I estimated something close to three hundred missing from our ranks, several more gasping for air as we reconvened.

More concerning was the loss of our cavalry. I spotted no more than twenty warhorses returning to camp. I refused to believe than one hundred and eighty of our best steeds had died in the current, but where they were now, I did not know.

Even so great a loss as this could have been acceptable if we'd taken Piraeus. But we hadn't. We lost.

I failed.

"Runner! Messenger! Envoy!" I shouted, searching for somewhere to tether Bucephalus.

Finally, a legionary arrived at my side. He was little more than a boy, so young he couldn't properly conceal his dismay as good legionaries are trained to do. From the look of his kit, he'd been in camp rather than the front.

"Go to the stables. Take whatever tired old thing you can find and ride out to Sulla. Find out if he wants us to reinforce him when we're able, and where," I said.

The small boy could only nod his head, but I could see in his eyes he wasn't hearing anything I said.

"Go!" I barked.

He sprinted off, forgetting his salute, which felt infinitely unimportant at this moment.

"Boy! Find another runner to go with you." I shouted. "Someone must return with Sulla's reply if you perish."

While the camp swirled with chaos and the men struggled to regain order, I found Lucullus at once—he alone stood tall among the slumped and weary. His greatest gift was never in command or strategy but in the art of concealment. Behind his pale eyes, he buried fear, doubt, and despair. He wore a mask of unshakeable resolve.

Despite my confusion, dismay, and piercing disappointment, I commanded myself to do the same. The men looked to us for strength.

I said nothing when I arrived at Lucullus's side. He continued giving orders, his voice even but somehow still distinct over the chaos of camp.

When the centuries began going through the rolls, he turned to me.

Despite his calm tone, I heard pain in his words. "They laughed," he said. "As we retreated. They laughed at us."

"I know," I said, though I recalled no sound but the cry of our horses.

Lucullus swallowed. Rubbed his chin. He twisted his family signet ring around his swollen finger.

"They played music, Gavius," he said. "I heard instruments, people singing."

"I know," I said. "I know."

I found nothing else to say. I would not place the blame on Lucullus, but I also couldn't speak accusations against Sulla.

"If Sulla is victorious . . ." I stopped to correct myself. "*When*

Sulla is victorious, he will consider this loss as a small sacrifice compared to the greater achievement. Even though we failed to take the port, our efforts forced Mithridates to separate his forces between Athens and Piraeus. Perhaps the thinning of enemy ranks gave Sulla what he needs to take the city."

I looked for any sign of the runner I sent, but it was not the young boy who arrived when the gates parted open.

It was Sulla, and behind him marched the survivors of Sulla's Fist.

If not for the mud and blood and limping veterans, I'd still have known of Sulla's defeat from the look on his face. He grew more pale as he aged, but in this moment he was whiter than our cloaks.

I expected to find calculated madness and steadfast obsession for justice in Sulla's eyes if ever I saw him defeated. More recently, I might have expected fury.

Neither were present now. He simply entered through the gates, his head held high but his gaze fixed on nothing. His gait was even, steady as he walked directly past us.

No battle speeches. No angry declarations or vows of Roman vengeance.

He pushed back the leather flap to his praetorium at the center of camp and disappeared within. Alone.

SCROLL XXI

QUINTUS SERTORIUS—FIVE days after the Ides of January, 667 Ab Urbe Condita

In the early days, everyone upheld the sanctity of war season with the same respect and reverence they afforded oaths and sacred holidays. Everyone knew fighting ended on the Ides of October, regardless of the strategic merits of continuing or who benefitted or suffered from the reprieve. Neither friend nor foe broke that sacred, unspoken understanding.

Wars were different then, or so I've read. Wars were fought for honor, for survival even. They weren't personal and contained none of the hatred and rage of our own. One tribe against the next, one nation battling another for the right to continue existing. Rome gained some of her oldest and most faithful allies this way too. Back then, it was still possible to shake your enemy's hand and look him in the eye after a victor was declared.

Not so now. And after a lifetime of fighting, I doubted things were ever so simple.

Regardless, we couldn't afford to maintain the same practices of our forebears in those stories. Cinna and I conferred with our officers on the matter, but we quickly established that the siege of Rome would have to begin immediately, despite the onset of winter. Even with the support of our anonymous benefactors, I couldn't afford to compensate the mercenaries for an entire season of sitting and waiting. And if I didn't pay them, they would find other employment.

We established the siege on the Nones of January, and I knew it would remain until we saved Rome or we were all dead.

The Eternal City and the surrounding area was too large for us to establish a traditional siege wall around it. The quaestors estimated the amount of wood such a feat would require, and they claimed we'd have to cut down every forest and sacred grove in Central Italy.

"We don't need to conduct a full siege," I told Cinna. "Taking the city by force is our last resort. We have only to blockade the roads, and the people will force Octavius to open the gates and negotiate."

Cinna and I divided responsibilities among our two armies, and I passed orders down to Fabius and my centurions. We had no choice but to spread our ranks thin. Even foregoing a traditional wall, we had a great deal of land to cover.

And despite not facing resistance from those in Rome thus far, we still needed to make each step with caution. A large Roman army remained just northeast of the city, and my reports indicated the commander was none other than Sulla's friend and former co-consul, Quintus Pompeius Rufus.

Strangely enough for one so close to Sulla, Rufus hadn't threatened us thus far. Regardless, I ordered my scouts to watch his camp both night and day. If he intervened, he would find me ready.

We blockaded all roads to the south and east of the city. We had much more to accomplish, but now the senate understood our intentions.

But eleven days after we arrived at Rome's gates, our trumpets sounded alarm. Fabius and I were planning our next objective when the first blare echoed throughout the camp. Two more followed.

We burst from my praetorium into the windy chill of the winter morning. I buckled my helmet and listened closely.

It was clear an army was arriving, and not from Rome itself nor from the north where Rufus's legions camped.

"Our scouts will need to be questioned about this," Fabius said as we hurried toward the gathering legionaries. "We haven't received a single report of an additional force in the south."

I took note of his concerns, but I said nothing. Instead, I focused on finding Cinna, who was also gathered there before the legionaries and staring out in the same direction as everyone else.

Once I reached his side, I shouted out orders for my legionaries and mercenaries to form orderly lines. We didn't know what was happening yet, but we'd be prepared for whatever it was.

"Have you any idea who might be arriving?" I asked.

He shook his head, though I noticed a poor attempt to conceal a wily grin.

"Are you certain?" I said again.

He shrugged. "I have a vague notion. I suppose we'll find out soon enough."

I turned toward the south. My long-distance vision wasn't keen, but I could already see men pouring through the wooded hills in the distance like a swift-moving fog.

"Centurions, roll call. I want every standard accounted for," I shouted.

As those arriving grew into focus, I was left with more questions than answers. This clearly was no Roman army. It didn't look like an army of any kind. Instead, it reminded me more of the angry mobs of the Forum that grew more common every year. I could see they were armed but not with the gladii of legionaries. Even squinting, I couldn't tell exactly what most of them wielded, but they appeared to be crude weapons of foreign origin. As far as I could tell, they bore no protective armor or chain mail. Most seemed to be dressed in nothing but woolen tunics, with the occasional man bearing a cloak.

"Perhaps this is an armed gang of foreign patriots come to join us?" Fabius said sardonically.

I ignored him and kept my gaze on the growing force. Whoever this was, it unsettled me greatly.

From their midst, I spotted a lone rider on horseback. He was adorned no richer than the rest of the foot soldiers around him, but the rider held his head aloft, his back straight, with the prideful presence of someone who'd accomplished great things.

I still needed to squint to make out the features, but I already knew who this was. Gaius Marius was arriving, and he'd brought a strange group of warriors along with him.

I gestured for Cinna to follow me away from the others. Once we were out of range from eavesdropping legionaries, I said, "Is that Gaius Marius?"

He couldn't contain his smile any longer. "It certainly is," he said.

I looked down and rubbed my eye. "Why is he here?"

Cinna tilted his head. "He's come to join us, *amice!*" He was almost rapturous and totally oblivious to my concerns.

My relationship with Marius was a difficult one, one I've detailed in previous scrolls. In my youth, I loved him like a father and faithfully served him. Yet, the strain of the years since left a blemish on these happier memories. Perhaps I'd misjudged him from the start, or perhaps the life and age had changed him. Regardless, I considered him dangerous and unpredictable now. His ambition matched Sulla's flame for flame, and the insatiable hunger driving him was no less consuming.

"This is unwise, consul," I said. "I must advise against this."

Cinna placed a hand on his chest and his chin dropped. "I'm desolated," he said. "To be honest, I thought you'd be thrilled. I was always under the impression you and Marius were still friends and allies."

I sighed. "I have no animosity toward the former consul," I said. "But I no longer trust his intentions. The past ten years made one thing clear: Marius is willing to unleash chaos and depravity to get what he wants."

Cinna nodded, but it was clear he didn't take my concerns to heart. "Of course, he's made some mistakes. Political mistakes, of course. Who hasn't? Perhaps his advanced years have made him ill-tempered, but he's as sound a battlefield strategist as ever. We could use that sort of man now."

I delayed my response so I could consider his position. But in the end, I only shook my head.

Marius gave me my first commission in the legion. I served him for years. He would never accept me as anything but a subordinate.

I wouldn't be able to restrict his reckless impulses. If we took back Rome, what turmoil would follow with Marius unchecked?

"Consul, look around you," I said. "We can succeed without Gaius Marius."

He crossed his arms, tiring of my resistance. "You may be right. The two of us can win without him." He flicked his wrist toward the nearing army. "His band of ruffians provide no value, I'll concede that. But this isn't simply about *taking* Rome," he said. "This is about taking and *holding* Rome. It's a delicate thing, Sertorius. I am the legitimate consul, but I'm known by few and loved by fewer. You are a respected war hero but hold no real power. Gaius Marius is like you in this, but he has a great name. The people are quicker to forget his recent transgressions than we are, and many still worship him as they did when he saved Rome from the Cimbri invasion. We need him for a sustainable victory. Each of us must play our part."

I sighed. Cinna would understand if he could see the visions in my mind of blood in Roman streets. But, failing that, I couldn't convince him.

"Besides," Cinna said, shifting his gaze toward Marius's force. "He has come on my invitation. We can hardly refuse him now."

My chest tightened. I forced a smile. "I hadn't known. Of course we cannot reject him if he came by your request."

We were supposed to share command as equals—but if that were true, he wouldn't have made this decision without me.

I couldn't change it now, though. Gaius Marius had joined us, but I remained determined to save Rome from unnecessary bloodshed, regardless of the enemies I made in the process.

Marius, on his lone horse, arrived before us with his small army close behind.

He looked down on us and took a deep breath. His deep, resonating voice carried over our combined forces. "Let's save the Republic."

The wind knifed through our half-finished palisades, carrying with it the chill of winter. The bare oaks and cypress trees stood like brittle skeletons against the gray sky, their twisted limbs creaking under the weight of a thin frost. Behind us, smoke curled from the scattered fires of our siegeworks, and the dull ring of hammers and the clatter of shovels filled the still air. Legionaries worked tirelessly all around us in the frozen mud, their breath fogging with every labored exhale.

Before we began proceedings, I spotted an old friend among Marius's rough band of warriors.

"By all the gods . . . Lucius?" I said.

My dearest companion was as pleased to see me, though less surprised. He wrapped me in a firm embrace. "It's good to see you, *amice*."

Lucius meant as much to me as anyone, and his arrival excited me as much as Marius's concerned me.

"I thought you and Aius were still serving in the—"

"Much has happened since we last spoke," he said. "I'll regale you with many hair-raising stories of heroism and triumph over some wine tonight." He nodded behind me where Cinna and Marius were gathering. "But for now . . ."

I clapped him on the shoulder and turned to my co-commanders. Cinna had our men construct a crude wooden table near the siege lines. In the center was a shallow box filled with the loose dirt dug up from our trenches.

Before deliberations began, Cinna prepared a rudimentary drawing in the box. In the center was the city—Rome—and the crude outlines of its roads, hills, and the encircling Tiber, each drawn with a soldier's practicality rather than a mapmaker's precision.

As Cinna finished his drawing, he pulled his cloak around his arms to brace against the cold. Marius—still dressed more like an escaped *servus* than a former consul, seemed indifferent to the chill. This, at least, hadn't changed as he aged. Some inner fuel concealed him against the elements.

"Looks more like a cracked eggshell than the Eternal City," Marius said with a grunt.

Cinna began, "Supplies are still entering the city from the Capitoline and the Palatine. We've sealed all roads to the southeast, here." He marked off each path we'd previously taken. "Once we capture the northern roads, the city will be properly strangled."

Marius took the drawing stick from Cinna's hand. "You're forgetting one thing." He tapped the open area to the west of the city. "Ostia."

Rome's port city of Ostia was indeed unguarded. Marius was correct that supplies could enter the city there, but would it be enough to warrant our attention?

"As the days get colder, fewer and fewer vessels enter Ostia's docks," I said. "If any supplies should come from Ostia, they would be negligible."

For the first time since his arrival, Marius looked at me.

I wasn't sure what to expect. He'd wavered between nostalgic affability and bitter coldness in our recent interactions, but here I felt neither. I saw only disregard in his eyes. It left me wondering if he simply considered me of little importance now or if he truly did not remember me. I'm not sure which I preferred.

"Anything which reinforces the city is important," Marius said. "If the nobles were wise, they'd be here on their knees capitulating as we speak. But they aren't wise. They'll have to be reduced to eating the polished leather of their sandals and their house pets before they'll be willing to kiss our feet." He stabbed the stick into the dirt where Ostia would be.

"You may be right," I conceded. "But I remind all of us that most in Rome are not our enemy." I pointed at the poor drawing of Rome in the box of dirt. "Mothers, children, old men, veterans who served with all of us . . . those who have no love of Sulla and his tyranny. These will be the first to starve." I met Marius's gaze. "They will die before the nobles do."

Marius grunted. "We understand the implications of siege warfare," he said. "My question is: what are you doing here if you don't accept the costs, Quintus Sertorius?" There was an edge to his words as he spoke my name. He remembered me after all, though it appeared he recalled none of our fond memories in this moment.

I nodded, perhaps he was right. Was I willing to accept the repercussions of this siege? I had no other choice. "I understand this as well, general Marius," I said. "I learned much of this serving under your eagle. My intention is only to remind everyone here that our plan is to retake Rome with as little loss of life as possible. If we make it clear to everyone in Rome that their only hope of surviving through the winter is for the nobles to accept terms of surrender, the people will force their hand."

Cinna appeared more like his old self for a moment, fading into silence as he looked back and forth between Marius and me.

When I mentioned my time under Marius's banner, the old general's aggression faded for a moment. Still, I knew he wouldn't change his mind.

"We will spare as many of the people as possible, but I'll show no mercy to those who support Sulla and benefit from his treason. Neither should you. These traitors stole Rome. They deserve every punishment and violation imaginable."

"Sulla bears sole responsibility for the indignities Rome endured," I said. "I'm sure many in office are just as repulsed by Sulla's actions as us but too afraid to fight back. We may call them cowards, but not traitors. We shouldn't label anyone a Sullan loyalist unless they declare themselves so. From the moment we formed this alliance, our directive was to—"

"Excuse me," Marius cut me off like he had when I was a simple legionary under his command. "This alliance just began. Whatever the two of you agreed upon before my arrival is of no consequence now."

Cinna interjected before I could, "We will press them, but with great care. Time is on our side, I believe. Sulla is quite distracted in Greece—"

"With *my* war," Marius added.

"Yes, the war Sulla stole from Marius occupies him in Greece and will for some time, perhaps even years."

I thought of Apollonius, trapped in Athens. I thought of Barca and his mission to save him, if it wasn't already too late. And I thought of Gavius, serving under Sulla's banner. I could have drifted away from the conversation and contemplated all this, but I wouldn't allow it. The present moment demanded my attention.

Cinna continued, "Sulla's allies in the city know they cannot last. Perhaps they could survive through the winter, but they can't hold out until Sulla returns. They will bend the knee. I'll reclaim my consul's chair, and then I will repeal Sulla's laws."

"Agreed," I said. "Though we must remain cautious, lest we

become like Sulla in the process. We are liberators, not conquerors."

Marius crossed his burly arms and grunted. "I am nothing like Sulla."

Men digging trenches nearby swore as they wrestled with the frozen ground, their shovels striking rock-hard earth.

"My scouts continue to watch on the Roman army to the north." I drew a circle with my finger in the dirt box. "They report six legions there."

"And this army . . . it's commanded by Sulla's friend Rufus, is it not?" Marius said.

A wry look spread over Cinna's face. "Actually, I have something exciting to report," he said. "Rufus died no more than a day after his arrival in camp. The reports indicate lightning struck him, but we all know what that means. Gnaeus Pompeius Strabo remains in command of this army."

Marius and Cinna both chuckled at Rufus's demise.

"Excellent news," Marius said.

They both appeared delighted that Strabo remained in command.

I wasn't so sure. I witnessed Strabo's avarice and duplicity firsthand while serving in his legions. He wasn't in an open alliance with Sulla, or anyone else as far as I knew, but that didn't make him any less dangerous. He brought his legions closer to Rome for a reason, one we didn't understand yet.

"I've heard of this Pompeius Strabo," Marius said. "Bastard will join whoever offers him the most coin."

"Then we should be the first to make an offer, and a generous one," Cinna said.

"I'm not so certain," I said. "I served under Strabo in the early days of the rebellion. You are right that greed endlessly motivated him, yet he's pragmatic. Coin alone might not be enough to sway him. He is waiting to see which way Fortuna's wind blows. He'll join the side he feels most likely to win."

"Then that returns me to my previous point," Marius said.

He grabbed the stick and stabbed it one, two, and then three times where Ostia would be. "I will take Ostia. You will take the northern roads. Cinna will maintain siege efforts here. Within a week, we'll control every access point to the city, and Strabo will have no choice but to join us."

"Ostia has grown these last few years," I said. "It's not well guarded, perhaps, but it will take a strong advance to take the port city. Perhaps I should lead my men there."

My primary concern was for the Roman citizens who called Ostia home. Simple folk, fishermen, merchants. They didn't deserve Marius's ire.

Marius shook his head. "No. I served as grain monitor in Ostia once. I know every crack and crevice of that port, grown or not. I'll take it with a few dozen men if I must."

Cinna nodded. "Marius, your knowledge of the port city will be invaluable. Sertorius, you should have no trouble taking the northern roads with the strength of your forces. Are we all in agreement?"

"I agree on this plan of action," I said. "Though I would ask one thing. General Marius . . . will you vow to deal fairly with the people of Ostia? They are not our enemy."

Marius rolled his eyes, then raised his right hand. "I vow to treat the people of Ostia as they treat me upon my arrival. I will meet smile with smile or sword with sword. Their fate lies in their hands."

I found his oath wholly unsatisfying, but there was nothing else I could say.

The three of us stood there around the dirt drawing of Rome for a few moments longer.

I wanted to save Rome. I feared Marius wanted to punish it. And Cinna stood there awkwardly between us, trying meagerly to strike the balance.

Then we departed with only a few nods shared between us. I was the last to leave, stealing a moment's glance at the city walls in the distance. The spires and arches stood proud against the gray sky. Rome's beauty remained through everything she'd endured the past year, and yet . . . when I silenced my mind, I could almost hear the gurgling of bellies and the whispered prayers of the common people sheltering beneath these monuments, of everyone trapped behind those high walls.

It would be a long winter, and unless I could control my allies, it would be a bloody one.

The campfire burned low, its orange glow flickering against the cold, damp air of the Roman winter. The smell of the burning wood was almost enough to overcome the scent of the wet, scattered earth around us.

Our siege efforts were finished for the day, though the distant groan of wagons and the muffled voices of legionaries still carried faintly through the night.

We sat close to the fire, bundled up but smiling. Rhea was wrapped tightly in her shawl, nursing a cup of watered wine. Arrea rested on a sawn log beside me, her head on my shoulder.

Across from us was the man of the hour, my childhood friend, Lucius Hirtuleius. Our reunion delighted him just as much as it had me, but he paid me no mind now. His attention was entirely fixed on the bundle of cloth in his arms.

Arrea had wrapped Toria up so tightly, only the pink tip of her nose and her dark, curious eyes were visible in the campfire's light.

"By all the gods," Lucius said with a grin, "It feels like she arrived just yesterday. Yet she's already become a little queen."

Lucius had preciously little experience with children, but he made up for it with enthusiasm and delicate care.

Arrea chuckled. "Yes, a little queen. She can also be a little tyrant when the mood catches her."

Lucius leaned toward Toria and made a silly face, earning a

giggle. Despite our circumstances, she was a happy child. I could already see Toria developing a unique sense of humor, which delighted all of us.

I took a sip of wine. In this moment, I was happy. Thoughts of Gavius, Apollonius, Barca, Marius, Cinna, and the fate of Rome still lingered in my mind, but I was determined to enjoy the present.

Lucius said, "Thank Venus she has Arrea's smile and eyes. Shame she has your eyebrows, Sertorius. The poor babe."

We laughed.

"I like them. They make her expressive," Arrea said. "Her brows speak the words she cannot."

"It's good to see you all. I"—Lucius hesitated—"I wasn't sure when fate would bring us back together."

"Difficult times," I said. "I'm still waiting on these grand tales of heroism and daring."

He looked up and squinted, overcome by wanderlust. "How can a simple soldier such as I recall the tale? Do I have the right words to explain how we waded through bogs to escape capture, how we swam to a vessel with arrows and stones splashing the water all around us? How can I explain the precarious nature of our arrival in Numidia, to a great welcome party by a foreign king, only to be turned away again? And then, I have no words to describe how we survived by the work of our hands in a small Sardinian village only to earn ourselves the following of thousands and fresh vessels to carry us home."

We laughed at Lucius's poor attempt at theater, but Toria listened with delight in her eyes. She'd not seen Lucius since she was an infant, but he brought her comfort and happiness, as if her heart recalled what her mind could not.

"Numidia you say?" Mother smiled. "Tell us you did not go looking for elephants."

Lucius smiled, but I knew him better than myself. I saw the sorrow lingering beneath. Lucius never lied, even in jest. What he told us was true, even if embellished. Now I wondered what he chose not to share, what aspects of his journey with Marius wouldn't have fit within his grand retelling?

"I didn't have to look," Lucius said. "I saw them the moment we arrived. Sadly, we found little but misfortune after that. The Numidian king turned us away. Our journey became more arduous from there, Aulus barely . . ." Lucius's voice faded. His eyes focused on the fire between us.

"Aulus was with you?" Arrea asked.

He nodded. "For a time. But he chose not to return. He sailed elsewhere." Lucius remembered himself and changed his tone. "He departed for adventures of his own in distant lands."

I smiled. It was a genuine smile but one that contained all the sadness of Lucius's. I didn't need to ask where Aulus went. In my heart, I always knew he would one day sail for Hispania to find his brother.

"I hope at the end of his journey, they find peace," I said.

Lucius nodded. "So do I."

For a while, we said nothing more. Whatever remained of Lucius's tale was better left for a different time. Instead, we enjoyed the crackle of the fire and the faint songs of my legionaries around nearby fires of their own. The scent of pine needles burned in the flames, mingling with the aroma of wine and leather.

Lucius was the first to break the silence, as if he couldn't bare his own contemplation any longer. "I worry about my brother," he said. "I didn't bring Aius with me when I departed. He . . . he wouldn't have understood. Probably didn't understand why I left either."

"Aius was still with the legions in the Umbrian hills, right? No fighting in those parts since you left, as far as I'm aware," I said. "I'm sure he is just fine. Probably lecturing some fellow officer on the nature of Nicomachean ethics if I had to guess."

Lucius sighed. "True. After I left, they shuffled the legion about, though. Some reinforced Strabo, others joined Sulla's forces . . . gods, can you imagine Aius serving under Sulla?"

"The Senate discharged most of them, I believe. Maybe he's back in Nursia as we speak?" I said.

Mother refilled her wine, took a sip, and then stood by the fire to warm her hands. "No matter where he is, we'll find him," she said.

Rhea never claimed to be a seer. She didn't know the future better than any of us, but her words never failed to soothe.

"I hope so," Lucius said. "I'm the only reason he joined the legion. Brought him on as a junior officer. I thought it might change him. Harden him, prepare him for the way the world is . . . I was wrong." He raised his eyes and looked at me. "He's not like us."

Toria sensed his sadness and began to fuss.

Arrea rose. "That's my signal," she said. "If we fail to heed the warning, Lucius, our queen will become a tyrant presently."

Lucius whispered something in her ear and handed her to Arrea. Neither of them wanted to part.

"And what is it you're telling my daughter?" I said with mock disapproval.

He held up his arms in surrender. "Just passing along some insight on her father."

Rhea said, "Arrea, I'll join you."

Arrea whispered her thanks. "Toria has become quite difficult to put down at night. Before long it will take a small army just to change her cloth and tuck her in."

"Rhea, you're welcome to rejoin us once you've wrangled the queen effectively," Lucius said.

After losing both his parents, Lucius found a quiet anchor in Rhea—someone who gave him the warmth of a mother, the counsel of a sister, and the strength of a father. He relied on her as much as I did.

She smiled. "Thank you, my boy. I'll let you men enjoy a bit of time together." She turned to me. "Do you recall that chest we found in Nursia? I'm going to read some of your father's letters tonight," she said. "It's been too long. I'd like to hear his voice tonight. Until tomorrow, my heroes."

After they departed, I told Lucius about escaping Rome, meeting Fabius, recruiting the mercenaries, and the alliance with Cinna.

He sat beside me with our last amphora of wine in hand and refilled our cups.

"And that brings us to today, when you arrived with general Marius. I'm not sure how much this changes our plans, but time will tell."

By now, even the more rambunctious of my mercenaries had ceased their singing and fallen asleep. The quiet of the winter night settled fully around us.

"You don't trust him," Lucius said. "Marius I mean. You don't trust Marius any longer?"

I took a sip of wine to consider my answer. Marius found us both when we were young and needed leadership. We'd both worshipped him and served him faithfully. But Lucius hadn't witnessed Marius's political actions as I had. I envied that Lucius could still admire Marius as I once had. It's comforting to trust in a hero so completely.

I hoped Lucius would change the subject, but he waited patiently for my reply, his eyes glistening in the firelight.

"I fear his recklessness. I fear his desire for vengeance."

He predictably stiffened. Lucius was careful with his wine except on rare occasions, but he drained the rest of his cup and quickly refilled it.

"Gaius Marius saved Rome once. He can again. The people will rally to him, to us."

I nodded. "His name will give weight to our cause, I agree."

"And yet you still don't want him here?" He stood and moved to the fire. He warmed his hand over the flames, but I knew it wasn't the desire for warmth that compelled him. He could never sit still during moments of conflict.

"Lucius, I loved him once too. Perhaps I still do, in some

ways. He shaped us into the men who sit here by this fire." I sighed. "But I can't allow fond memories to cloud my judgment. He isn't who he was, Lucius."

He spun to me. "The things he did for us, Quintus . . . that compels a loyalty time can't erode. We owe him."

Despite disagreeing with Lucius, I admired his simple, unwavering devotion. It was one of his best qualities, but one that could bring him more harm than good if not tempered with caution.

My voice remained calm as I said, "He's dangerous, Lucius. He's erratic. I want to believe he shares my devotion to the Republic—but there's a fire in him I've seen before, and it burns with more than just patriotism."

Lucius took another gulp of wine. "And shouldn't he desire vengeance? He's the Third Founder of Rome, and yet his enemies cast him out like a common criminal. Sent headhunters out with the promise of a few coins to butcher him in his sleep! You didn't see it, Quintus, what they did to him. I witnessed a six-time Consul of the Republic wade through marshes and breathe through broken reeds to avoid—" He noticed his pitch increasing, and slowed himself.

"You're right, Lucius. I wasn't there. I cannot blame him for desiring vengeance," I said. "But will Marius distinguish between who deserves his wrath and who doesn't? He's long displayed a willingness to crush anyone in his way."

"That's what makes him a great general," Lucius said.

"And it makes him a dangerous politician."

When he didn't reply, I continued. "Sulla used an army for vengeance against his political enemies. And yet the Roman people suffered most, and that's why we are here. We must not make the same mistakes."

I feared I'd gone too far. His fists clenched.

"You cannot possibly be comparing Marius to Sulla? The tyrant was outmaneuvered and couldn't handle his loss. Marius seeks justice for Rome."

"Intentions don't matter," I said. "Justifications don't matter. Only consequences."

My words utterly perplexed him. "Are you really suggesting that Marius is capable of slaughtering his own people? You believe the man who saved the Republic on numerous occasions —the leader who raised us into 'the men who sit here by this fire' could be a tyrant?"

"I believe we're all capable of it, Lucius," I said. "If any man can become great, he can also become evil."

He shook his head but said no more. Some of his anger faded like the cooling flames.

I drank the remainder of my wine and set the cup down on the log beside me. "I didn't mean to spoil our reunion. Your safe return means more to me than anything else," I said.

Lucius sat beside me again and tossed a twig into the fire.

"He is different now . . . different than he was. I know better than anyone."

I could have asked for clarification, but he would have shared if he wanted to. Instead, we poured more wine and stared into the fire.

Eventually, I said, "We're about to retake Rome. How we do so will determine the future of the Republic. Every one of us must be better than Sulla. We must reject base instincts: greed, ambition, and the desire for vengeance."

Lucius shifted and rubbed his weary eyes with the nub of his arm. "I made a vow, Quintus. I promised to serve him. I abandoned my post to protect him. Lucius Hirtuleius is a deserter. I cannot be an oath-breaker twice over."

I placed a hand on his slumped shoulder. "You did what you thought honorable. No one can fault you for that," I said. "We swore our oaths to the Republic. Not to Marius. Unquestioning loyalty to one man—that's what drove Sulla's legionaries as they torched our city, convinced all the while of their own virtue and heroism."

Lucius said nothing. He didn't need to.

I looked up at the moon. I hadn't stayed up this late—at least by choice—in a long time.

"I should retire," I said with a sigh. "We march north in the morning."

He sighed. "I suppose I should get some rest as well. I'm coming with you."

"What?" I said, hopeful I understood him correctly.

He turned and grinned. "You are leaving, and I won't let you go without me again."

I squeezed the back of his neck, then refilled both our cups of wine. "Then we can remain a little longer. One last drink before we liberate the Republic."

Beneath a sky of frozen stars, we shared the last of our wine. No words left, no jokes worth telling—not with the dawn so close and war marching behind it.

SCROLL XXII

GAVIUS SERTORIUS—FOUR days before Kalends of February, 667
Ab Urbe Condita

After our defeats at the gates of Piraeus and Athens, Sulla's Fist
returned to our original plan. We began the methodical execution of siege warfare.

Our men carved trenches, created embankments, and erected
palisades. Anywhere the Roman legion went, we altered the
earth forever, but rarely to the degree we impacted Athens.

Sulla made his intentions clear: Athens would surrender, or
he would starve them into submission.

We felled every strand of timber within one hundred *iugera*—
forests and fields untouched by human hands for centuries—to
fuel our siege. Old oaks said to have once whispered secrets to
priests during the Peloponnesian War now served as battering
rams. Sulla said nothing should be spared if the wood was
strong. We reduced the sacred groves of Artemis and Dionysus
to stumps.

Legionaries are superstitious by nature. Some wondered if
the Greek gods might punish us for our indiscretions. But Sulla

gave the orders without ceremony, as routine as instructing the men to polish their chain mail.

He addressed the matter only in private.

"The gods won't reject us this gift," he said. "Any true god on Olympus should be crying out for our victory, to punish their reprobate, wasteful denizens."

Sulla often referenced the will of the gods as a powerful factor in his own command. His cavalier approach to the sacred earth around us surprised me, but he made it clear this was not another impulsive decision.

He never mentioned our defeat—we didn't expect him to. Shame and anger still smoldered behind his eyes, but when he summoned the officers at the end of January, we found him composed, sharp, and cold as ever. His purpose that day wasn't to discuss drawing swords but to partake in something rarer: a battle fought with words.

Sulla instructed us to leave our weapons, shields, and helmets behind.

"I want them to look on Roman faces. Let them see we do not fear them," he explained.

Sulla led us out through frostbitten fields, up toward the northernmost gate of Athens. We passed by the broken remnants of his recent battle there. We kept our gaze lifted, ignoring the splintered Roman shields beneath our feet.

We stopped just a few hundred feet from Athens's gate, which towered above us, looming larger than I'd ever imagined from a distance.

Guards heaved open the massive gates, and three Greeks stepped out.

Lucullus leaned toward Sulla. "Imperator, I see archers on the wall. We're in range."

Sulla kept his steady gaze on the Greeks. "I'm aware, dear Lucullus," he said. "That's precisely my intention."

The Greeks, and their Pontic allies, had already proven to be treacherous. What honor could they possess if they were willing to slaughter thousands of innocent men, women, and children for no other reason than to provoke our anger?

I regretted not bringing my shield. I had no way to protect Sulla if they decided to let loose their arrows.

Sulla didn't waver.

The three Greeks wore their traditional himation, which reminded me of the Roman toga. Fine designs threaded the fabric, and I noticed the jewelry that glimmered around their necks and on their fingers.

Perhaps the senate would've taken them seriously, but wealth and ostentation failed to impress the legion.

Show me a scarred veteran with resolve in his eyes. I'd listen to him. I doubted these three weaklings had anything to say worth hearing.

"Greetings," they each said.

"I expect you understand Greek?" one said.

Most of us did, and Sulla was an expert, but his reply was in Latin. "You'll address us in our tongue here," he said.

They sighed but nodded in acceptance.

The oldest, grayest of the three stepped forward. Before speaking, he tilted his chin slightly, raised his right hand and set his feet a certain pace apart. His eyes flickered as if he was summoning memories of all his oratorical education.

I heard Crassus snicker, but the rest of us waited.

The old emissary began a long-winded invocation of Athen's storied past—of Themistocles and Miltiades, Socrates and Aristotle, of Marathon and Salamis. He spent much of his lecture reminding us that it was the Greeks, Athenians particularly, who saved the west from the Persian invasion.

"If not for our illustrious forebears, you'd be wearing trousers and worshipping Mithra," he said.

Until then, Sulla had listened patiently, but he couldn't ignore the irony of this last statement. "And yet you—their progenies—accept Mithra and trousers willingly."

One of them replied, "We aren't wearing trousers."

Sulla shrugged. "Only a matter of time when you bow to Eastern kings."

The leader tried to ignore the interruption and continued his rehearsed speech.

Nothing but drivel. He discussed the greatest of their ancestors, but I heard only desperation in his voice. Maybe these pampered fools hadn't experienced crippling hunger or unbearable thirst yet, but their people had. Otherwise, they would've remained in the safety and opulence of their palaces.

Athens hadn't prepared for the siege. They didn't have enough to last the winter. Or, if they'd stocked their granaries enough to care for their own, they hadn't planned on feeding an entire army of Pontic warriors as well.

It'd only been a few weeks since the siege began in earnest, and with Piraeus's port still open, they still received some resupply. But men's stomachs begin to grumble after even a few days without food.

"The home of Mother Athena holds an indissoluble place in the divine story of civilization."

"And?"

Sulla's words cut through the lecture like a knife.

The emissaries, baffled, shared a panicked look.

The youngest stepped forward. "We've heard you are a cultured man. Someone who has passion for our culture. We ask only that you show mercy and fairness to the creators of so much you respect."

"I may enjoy your wine, your poetry, and the cleverness of your language," he said. "But *you* created none of this. You are the lesser sons of greater men."

I watched Sulla as he replied. That look in his eye was more apparent than ever. A wolf smelling blood.

"I did not come to Greece for a history lesson," Sulla said flatly, "but to reduce rebels to obedience."

No fury. No bluster. Only ice punctuated his words.

The three emissaries recoiled as if they'd been struck by an arrow. The eldest flushed—in anger, astonishment, or in shame —that his message failed to deliver.

"Go back to your starving city," Sulla said. "I know you cannot outlast the winter. If you capitulate now, I will deal fairly with you. Roman mercy. If you do not, and I must storm your crumbling walls by force, I will *eviscerate* you. Roman vengeance."

They remained there, wide-mouthed and flabbergasted for a moment. Nothing needed to be said, but we wouldn't turn our backs on them. They would leave first.

While we waited for their pitiful departure, the youngest emissary summoned a little courage.

He aimed a bony finger in Sulla's direction and said, "A ship arrived yesterday," he said. "Through our *open* port at Piraeus."

The jab stung. Lucullus and I both cast down our gaze.

"The visitor brought news from Italy. Rome is under siege." He smiled smugly and waited for our reaction. Only Sulla remained entirely still. "Your city bleeds now, as ours does, and it's your own hands holding the blade."

A rustle of panic passed through our line of officers. My stomach clenched up. Did the emissary speak true? I prayed this was a wicked lie and nothing more.

"And what great army have these traitors gathered?" Sulla asked, disinterested.

The third emissary, perhaps emboldened by our first reaction, said, "It's said to be impressive. How many was it, Antipater? Ten thousand men?"

The eldest smirked. "I believe so. How many legionaries do you have, Imperator Sulla? How many will remain after our conflict?" he said. "And each day, more of your countrymen gather to their banner. Even if you departed today, they're likely to outnumber you. The longer you wait, the greater the odds against you."

Sulla didn't respond or react.

Lucullus broke the silence. "Who leads them?"

He spoke out of turn, but we all wanted to know the answer.

If the Greeks intended to unravel us, they'd succeeded. I wanted to know who sought to destroy everything we sacrificed to build. I wanted to carve their names in my mind and prepare their destruction.

"Powerful men, I'm told," the youngest emissary said, hands gingerly placed on his hips now. "The first is a consul. Cinna, I believe. The other . . ." He paused for effect, letting the name strike like a dagger. "Gaius Marius. I believe you're well acquainted."

I braced for Sulla's reaction. I expected him to erupt, for those veins in his head and neck to appear and his skin to blanch. I thought he might bash the emissaries to death with his own two hands.

But Sulla only laughed.

"An exile and a fat old man?" he said. "Marius will keel over before he reaches the gates of Rome, if his poor horse doesn't give out first."

Sulla's lack of reaction disappointed the delegates, but they weren't ready to let the matter go.

The eldest continued. "They are not alone," he added. "There is another. A Roman commander called Quintus Sertorius. It's said he's a hero of your legions, worshipped and loved by your people."

All our officers turned to me. My jaw tightened and the blood drained from my face. My vision tunneled. I looked down at my feet and tried to remain steady, but my father's name echoed in my mind, and the breath caught in my lungs.

"I believe it was this man who already won a great victory outside Rome itself," the third emissary said.

My father.

My father.

Attacking Rome.

Joining those outlaws, criminals, those oath breakers! Betraying, destroying all that we'd sacrificed for. I could not believe it. I would not believe it, I thought. But I already did.

Maybe he should've been on Sulla's list after all. My own name disgusted me.

The Greeks took delight in our dismay.

The eldest emissary said, "I don't believe we need to outlast the winter, Lucius Cornelius Sulla. I think we only need to outlast you. When your city falls, what will happen to your wife and children, after what you've done? What will become of your friends? I've heard your enemies are as vicious and maligned as you are. What would you do?"

Sulla took his time responding. He let his gaze linger on each of their faces. "I'll remember each of you," he said. "When we burn down your city, I will find you. And when I do, I will take each of you right over there." He pointed to the slope just before the city. "And I will have each of you crucified. I might hammer in the nails myself. They'll pierce you here, and here." He gestured to his wrists and feet. "Crosses will line this road for miles."

The Greeks left before saying another word.

I continued to look at the ground, unable to lift my head or shift my gaze.

Once the emissaries disappeared into the city, I expected Sulla to make the fullness of his rage known. Rome besieged in his absence? Surely this would provoke an ancient hatred deeper even than the one created by the assassination of his colleague.

And what did this news mean for me? Would Sulla cast me out? Would he consider me a traitor for my blood and my nomen?

Instead, he placed a hand on my shoulder. "I grieve with you," he said. "My father was a drunken fool. That's almost as bad as a traitor."

I couldn't bring myself to look at him but nodded in understanding.

He didn't press me, and—mercifully—neither did the other officers.

Caught in a haze and a maelstrom of revolting thoughts, I followed them back to camp.

Before we entered, Sulla said, "The time to strike will be soon. We need supplies. Arms. Materials. Gold. Sack the temples. All of them."

Lucullus blinked. "Even Apollo's shrine at Delphi?"

"Tell the priests we're borrowing it to save their homeland from Eastern invaders. Once Athens is restored and Mithridates rots on a cross, I shall return the gold."

No one resisted Sulla's orders.

Only Crassus spoke. "What about the siege of Rome?" he said flatly. "What is to be done?"

"Nothing to fear, good Crassus," Sulla replied. "The gods have tested us, but their favor shines on us now. All is going according to plan."

SCROLL XXIII

Quintus Sertorius—The Kalends of February, 667 Ab Urbe Condita

The night air was cold, sharp, and still. Each foggy breath hung in the air like a ghost. I rode alone to the sound of Sura's hooves muffled by the dew-wet grass, my eye scanning the gentle hills ahead for movement.

This was a foolish thing to do—perhaps the most dangerous ride I'd taken in years. But I was compelled by a letter I received, written by a hand I knew well. The message came from Pompey, son of commander Strabo.

Their legions remained abject and neutral, even as I'd taken the northern roads over the past two weeks. They'd given no indication of what they might do until the letter arrived, and therefore I couldn't ignore it.

Pompey's words were the simple ones of a soldier. A request to meet at night, under the stars, just the two of us. No escorts. No guards. No warhorses or ranks of legionaries standing in shadowed reserves. Pompey concluded the letter with an oath that he would uphold this request.

I might have been a fool to believe him, but I did. Whether or not Pompey was worthy of this dangerous trust, I didn't know, but I refused to be the one to break a vow.

Under different circumstances, perhaps I would have waited or suggested a less-dangerous alternative. But another scroll arrived shortly before Pompey's with news of Ostia. As I'd feared, Marius had taken Rome's port city with great violence. Although he was adamant that the resistance was fierce and he had no recourse but to fight, he didn't bother explaining why he gave his band of ruffians total liberty to sack a Roman settlement.

It was clearer now than ever before. I needed to end this war swiftly. Not simply because of the payment expected by my mercenaries, and not due to the actions of those who resisted us. On the contrary, I needed to end the war before my own allies made a mockery of our cause and brought more suffering on the Roman people.

If Marius and Cinna forgot themselves and their oaths, they would become my enemies, too, and I was swiftly running out of friends.

Pompey and I served together against the Italian rebels a few short years ago, though it felt like a lifetime since then. He was young at the time, but fearless. Strong, loyal, sharp-eyed, and above all, just. I remembered the quiet nights we sat beside each other and looked up at the stars when neither of us could sleep. These memories alone compelled me to reject any fears for my own safety and ride out to meet him.

At the top of a rounded knoll, right where he said I'd find him, Pompey sat atop his horse. Alone, save a vast blanket of stars in the sky. His cloak flapped gently in the wind as he stared at the heavens above.

I approached carefully, reins loose in my fingers. No movement in the dark. No glint of steel. No hidden shapes among the brush. I wouldn't lower my guard, but it appeared my faith was well placed.

"You came," he said as I neared, without turning his head.

"I did." I eased Sura to a halt a few paces beside him and dismounted. My legionary boots crunched softly in the cold grass.

He clambered off his steed as well, to meet me face-to-face. Instead of shaking my hand, he pointed to a bright cluster of stars above us.

"We spoke of that once. Do you recall?"

I followed his gaze. "The Pleiades," I said, proud of my recollection.

He smiled without turning. "I hoped you would remember."

"The six sisters, I believe you said."

"Almost. The seven sisters."

"I never could spot the seventh," I said.

We stood in silence for a moment, surrounded by the hush of the Italian countryside, the occasional flutter of night birds' wings, and the rustle of wind blowing through olive trees below.

Finally, Pompey turned to me. I recognized my friend plainly in the moonlight, but he'd changed since I'd last seen him. He was only twenty years old with the face of a youth. Time hadn't aged him, but war had. The heaviness I once glimpsed behind his laughter now appeared on the surface in the shape of his silence.

With tired eyes, he said, "I'll be direct, Sertorius. My father is undecided on how to proceed."

He paused for me to respond, but I allowed him to continue.

"He doesn't trust Sulla," Pompey said. "Not since he marched on Rome. But he has no love for Marius or Cinna. And his feelings for you . . ." He trailed off for a moment and looked down before adding, "were never warm."

"Unfortunately, your father and I never saw eye to eye," I said.

We both knew that was an understatement.

"Despite your disagreements, my father did come to respect you while you served with us. He knows you're a man of your word, and he trusts you uphold your oaths. I needed no proof, but you coming here alone as I requested is further evidence of your honesty."

I knew none of those words ever escaped Strabo's mouth, but I hoped at least the sentiment was true.

"He's willing to join you, Sertorius," Pompey said. "On one condition."

"What are his terms?" I stiffened.

"My father will join you with all six of his legions if you agree to make him consul after our victory. And we would be victorious. He would bring with him six legions. The senate would be forced to surrender. Rome could be ours without bloodshed." He turned away and clasped his hands behind his back. "But you must guarantee his election. My father's enemies would crush him with frivolous lawsuits without the consul's immunity."

Although this was a pragmatic request by someone who understood the gravity of our circumstances, I knew this was a lie. Strabo sought only to improve his own position and power and was using the Republic's chaos to achieve it.

I cleared my throat. "You know as well as anyone that we cannot guarantee who wins elections," I said. "We are taking Rome to restore freedom to the people, not diminish it further. When we retake the city, elections will be fair and honest again. Though I will not and cannot guarantee anyone's success, I can vow the full weight of our support. I'll ensure Marius and Cinna agree to this before arrangements are made."

Marius or Cinna would have agreed to Strabo's original terms. I doubted they had any moral scruples with rigging one more election if it guaranteed our victory. Yet, I refused to do the same, no matter how much Strabo's support might bolster our position. I would not trade Sulla's tyranny for a new one.

Pompey's broad jaw clenched. "I was instructed not to leave without a guarantee."

I studied him closely. The lines at the corners of his eyes, the weight pressing down on his shoulders. I could see his shame. He knew I was right, and I believe he resented what Strabo ordered him to do. But such is the power fathers can have over their sons.

"That is something I cannot offer," I said. "Yet, there could be alternative solutions. My allies have already agreed to compensate Strabo handsomely for his support. Marius's silver mines in Hispania should provide more than enough to secure Strabo the finest advocates in Rome should a lawsuit appear, and as many estates and villas as he desires besides."

I wasn't thrilled at the prospects of bribery either, but if Strabo had no more loyalty to Rome than the mercenaries who served me, than I was willing to pay for his assistance in the same manner.

But bargaining with Rome's freedom was not an option.

Pompey exhaled, his breath rolling out like a stormy cloud. "You know he won't accept."

"I assumed."

If Strabo wanted to be consul again, a rigged election would be the only way to achieve it. The people elected him once, when he was only a ludicrously wealthy, no-named outsider. But all of Rome knew him now, and he was universally scorned. After years of avarice, greed, and incompetence as a general, no amount of support would be enough.

A long silence followed. I wouldn't change my mind, and Pompey wasn't authorized to accept alternatives.

At last I said, "Do you agree with what he's doing, Pompey? Do you believe his support should only be thrown in with those who would offer him the greatest reward? This is the future of our Republic at stake."

He refused to look at me, staring up instead as the stars reflected in his eyes. "My opinions are of no consequence. I'm a soldier. Soldiers follow orders."

I sighed; the cold pressed in tighter now. "No doubt Sulla's men said the same thing."

He turned his back to me. "You do understand what happens next, don't you?" he said. "If he cannot join you, my father will throw in his lot with Octavius and the senate. With his support, they might yet resist you. No doubt they would be grateful enough for his support they would not hesitate to support his bid for consul."

I knew he was correct. But I offered to support his bid as well, just not guarantee it. The senate might be willing to do so. I was disappointed by my young friend's admission, but he knew his father well, and spoke true.

"I understand," I said.

Twigs snapped beneath his feet as he made his way back to his horse. He took hold of the saddle but hesitated before pulling himself up.

"I wish this had gone differently," he said.

"So do I," I said.

Surprisingly, he turned back around. I thought for a moment he was extending a dagger, but it was only an open palm.

He still refused to look at me, but we clasped wrists—firmly but without joy.

Then he mounted up and rode off into the darkness. I watched the trail of frozen dirt fly up behind him and looked up again one last time at the stars.

I knew I wouldn't see Pompey again until we met on the battlefield.

SCROLL XXIV

Gavius Sertorius—One day after the Kalends of February, 667 Ab Urbe Condita

The night winds brought no rain for once. Campfires burned low, their glow flickering across the orderly rows of legionary tents and the weathered faces of night watchmen. The stale air smelt of burnt pitch, steel, and sweaty men—just like every night during the siege.

I'd just finished reviewing the troop rotations along the eastern ramparts and delivering the day's requisition scrolls to the quaestors. As I did every night, I marched through camp to Sulla's praetorium.

I expected the usual routine: a stiff nod from Sulla, possibly a few additional orders, or a dismissal to rest or take the evening rounds.

As I entered the dimly lit command quarters, I could see that tonight was different.

Sulla stood alone at the center of the tent. The maps and ledgers remained untouched, his writing stylus abandoned on the center of his large oak table. A half-full amphora sat nearby.

The commander's face, usually taut with grim duty, seemed almost . . . slack. Not weary exactly but contemplative.

"Good evening, Gavius," he said.

I looked around at the corners of the praetorium to see if any other officers were lurking nearby. Surprisingly, only Sulla's *servi* remained there.

"Leave us," Sulla instructed them.

They passed by with bowed heads and left the two of us alone in the praetorium.

I'd never seen him dismiss his attendants before. My hands began to sweat. I wondered if Sulla finally wished to speak more directly about my father. I feared what he might say.

"Will you sit with me?" he said.

"Of course," I answered.

He pulled over a second chair and gestured to it. In one swift motion, he swept the maps and ledgers from his table with a careless hand. Grain tallies fluttered like wounded birds to the ground as he sat across from me.

"Wine?"

"Of course, thank you," I said. I was naturally skeptical of drinking with Sulla, as lately it had made him far more volatile. But refusing the offer wasn't an option.

He said nothing at first, only raised his cup. I raised mine. We drank.

We sat in silence for a moment, warmed only by the candle-light and the steady rhythm of distant snoring legionaries.

After we were half through our cups, he said, "How are you, Gavius?"

I hesitated. I'd come to expect such inquiries into my well-being long ago, but Sulla had scarcely looked my direction since we arrived in Greece, since we marched on Rome actually.

"I'm well, Imperator." I forced a smile. "Nothing to complain of."

He turned his head slightly. "You're a worse liar than your father."

The words were a lash, but his voice lacked venom. I didn't reply.

He smiled sadly. "I apologize. I spoke in jest, but some wounds are best left bandaged for a time," he said. "I meant only to check on your well-being. If anyone understands difficulties with fathers, it's me."

His eyes stared through me. He took a sip.

"I appreciate your concern, commander," I said. "I've focused my attention on the siege."

"My father was a drunk. A profligate gambler. A miscreant. The sort of nobleman who still clung to his heritage, wearing his vomit-stained patrician's toga even as his debtors dragged him through the courts."

Sulla swirled his wine and looked into the flame as he spoke.

"We lived in the Subura," he continued. "Have you ever been there? Makes the Aventine look like Elysium. Our street reeked of the sewers beneath us, though the other tenants smelled worse. Fights, muggings, stabbings took place outside our windows. My mother tried to shutter them before she died, but they broke in some scuffle or another, so I learned to watch. My father could afford no tutors, so I let those chaotic slums teach me about life."

He grew quiet. I wasn't sure if he wanted me to reply.

"My father brought home whores and cutthroats and called them friends. I detested their company even more than the proles outside our doors, so that's where I spent most of my time. The locals probably thought me a simpleton. I'd stand there and wave at any passersby while those in my home were drinking themselves into a stupor. I hoped to find a companion, but none in the Subura could afford friendliness."

When I finished my cup, he quickly refilled it, something his *servi* usually did for us. That was a great honor, but I was touched most by his confiding in me. I expected him to lecture me about my father, but instead he spoke of his own.

"A hard way to grow up," I said. "That makes your climb to power all the more impressive."

He smiled. "That's where I met him. Did I ever tell you about him?"

I shook my head, unsure who he meant.

"A little cat. Thin as old cloth stretched over bone. Gray with tiny white paws. I don't know where he came from, but once we met each other, he came every night. He seemed to understand the debauchery taking place in the home of the Cornelii Sullae, and kept the young scion company during it."

The silence grew heavier. He finished his own cup and refilled it. Sulla was drinking to capture his words rather than to escape the thoughts as he'd done recently. I allowed the silence to continue and listened intently.

"He watched after me, I believed. He was always there. Kind. Asked nothing of me, though I would give him what little scraps I could just to see his tail swish." He chuckled to himself at the thought. "But one evening he did not come. I waited and waited, but my feline friend did not arrive. I strayed farther from our home than my father allowed, but I knew he wouldn't come looking." He buried his face behind his cup for a moment. He inhaled deeply before continuing. "I found him tucked into a crevice near the sewer. Some of the other youths in the Subura had decided to chase him. Found a chicken bone in the gutter and killed him with it for sport."

He turned to me then. As the candlelight sparkled in his eyes, I saw something in them I hadn't seen since I first joined his legions outside Capua. It was more than sadness, than anger. More ancient.

"I became a man that day, not when I eventually dawned my toga virilis or grew my first beard. I realized I was alone. I realized no one was there to protect me. No one would come to save me. I would have to create my own fate, and I would have to be as ruthless as the rest of the world to claim it."

I said nothing, too enraptured by the weight in his words.

Sulla leaned back in his chair, balancing the cup of wine in his palm.

His voice was colder now. "I've tried playing by the rules, Gavius," he said. "I've tried to follow the law. Protocol. I've done things as we're told to do. And where has it led me? It allowed corrupt men to take over our city and steal away our command, forcing us to take it back with blood on our hands. Then, I trusted men like Strabo to give his command over to Rufus as the law commands. And for my trust, for my fool's hope, he died. Just like my furry friend."

He glanced into the flickering light. "No more. I see now that I was wrong." He turned to me again. "There is no justice except the justice we create, Gavius. No mercy, only strength. And if we don't use it, others will. You understand this, don't you?"

His voice was soft, filled with fatherly concern, like it had when he took me on as his own in Italy.

My heart had slowed to a steady thud. I hadn't felt this calm since before we marched on Rome. I could have remained there for hours listening to Sulla.

"I understand," I said. "I'll follow you no matter what, commander."

He nodded, genuinely grateful. No one as powerful as Sulla needed the approval of his subordinates, but it filled me with strength to know he sought mine anyway.

Whatever reservations I'd felt these last few, hard months was gone now. I refused to speak and disrupt the peace of our discussion, but I would have sworn my oath anew, to Sulla and the Republic, right then if I could have.

"I'll not mention your father again," Sulla said, "unless you ask it of me. I wish only for you to know that I understand. The decisions of our fathers often reflect on us, but we create our own fate. If I was constrained to my father's, I'd probably be in a gutter myself by now. You make your own fate, too, Gavius."

His words settled on me as heavily as the wine. I nodded.

"Your wisdom inspires me, Imperator. I will make my own

fate. No, I've already made it. My fate is to follow you, to glory and conquest, as long as I'm able."

He smiled.

We spoke of simpler things then, though I don't recall the contents of our conversation. We sipped wine together for quite some time, and I remember thoughtless laughter shared between us. It was as if the Sulla I'd seen the past few months had absconded, replaced by the man who mentored me when I first joined the legion.

We carried on this way until the flaps of Sulla's tent opened.

I frowned, half expecting the other officers to interrupt, but it was only a guard, rigid as a spear.

"Apologies, general," he said with a crisp salute. "Two Greek men request an audience with you."

Sulla rolled his wine-darkened eyes. "I'm enjoying good wine and conversation with our tribune here. Tell them to speak with Lucullus or Crassus. Anyone but me."

The guard hesitated. "I tried that, Imperator. They refuse to speak with anyone but you. They insist it's urgent."

The commander sighed theatrically and looked at me. "When is it not urgent? You see, Gavius? Not a moment's peace." He slouched in his chair and waved a languid hand. "Bring them in."

Two men were pushed inside, into the light of the candelabrum.

I stood and turned my chair around so I could face them. It was an awful sight.

They were walking corpses—skintight across bone, like Sulla described the poor cat from his youth. Their faces were hollowed by hunger and desperation. Their Greek chiton hung in soiled tatters over their scrawny limbs.

"I hope you know Greek," one rasped, his voice little more than a whisper. "We know Latin naught."

Sulla nodded and replied in their tongue, "I do. Speak."

The exchange continued in Greek—beautiful, complex, difficult Greek. I could barely speak it, but thanks to the lessons Apollonius gave me as a boy, I could understand what they said.

I listened intently and tried to keep the wine from distracting me. The two Greek men spoke directly and without affectation, unlike the emissaries we'd met with a few weeks prior. They came not to beg for their lives but to discuss the future of their people.

"We are not your enemy," one of them said with a weak voice. "The people of Athens have no love of Mithridates. We took no part in the deal with Pontus. It's only a few corrupt noblemen who brought us to this sad pass."

Sulla frowned. "Sadly, this is often the case. A few bad men in power can bring strife and calamity upon an entire people."

"They do not speak for us, sire. If you can find a way to silence them, you'll find Athens—and all of Greece—ready to honor our time-tested allegiance to Rome."

"Alas, you reach the heart of the matter," Sulla said. "If I could only silence Athens's reprobate leaders, all this trouble could be avoided. But how am I to do so? Are you offering to wield the liberator's knife yourselves?"

"We aren't assassins. We're simple folk. But . . ." the first man said.

The second stepped forward and quickly reached the purpose of their visit.

He spoke with urgency as he described a place along Athens's high walls where the defenses were weakest.

"Indistinguishable to a casual observer, but it was damaged when the Macedonians came here over two hundred years ago. The ramparts were repaired but remain cracked and unsteady. Athens's walls have been vulnerable here all this time, yet none but carpenters and architects, like us, know of it."

Sulla's fingers drummed the rim of his cup, slowly, methodically.

"If you attack there, the wall will collapse," the other Greek said.

"You're certain?" Sulla asked.

"We would not risk coming here otherwise," the first Greek man answered.

Sulla stood abruptly and joined us on the other side of the table. Both Greek men jumped with a start, but Sulla only smiled toward them.

"You'll both be rewarded. Handsomely."

The Greek men blinked in disbelief. Despite this promise, their eyes reflected no hope. Perhaps Athens's condition rendered hope impossible.

"To begin with, I'll see you provided a warm bath and a full meal. Enough to make your bellies forget they were ever empty. Then gold. Once your city is freed, you'll live like kings."

Both men fell to their knees and kissed Sulla's feet, covering them with snot and tears.

"Oh thank you, thank you, sire," they cried.

"Rise," Sulla said. "If you speak true, all this and more will be yours. Sulla rewards his friends as completely as he punishes his enemies."

"We must return," one of them said, nudging the other. "We will gratefully accept all you have promised, but first we must return to our families."

Sulla raised a hand. "Give your name and theirs to my guard. When the city is taken—and it will be taken—they will be spared. But if you go back now, you're liable to die with the rest."

The Greeks' weary eyes widened.

"Besides," Sulla continued, "if you're lying to me, a common death wouldn't do for the two of you. I'll need to prepare something special for your punishment."

The two men exchanged a glance, unsure if they'd been honored or sentenced.

"Oh, do cheer up, men," Sulla said. "We'll waste no time following your advice. You'll see your loved ones soon." He turned to me, "Gavius."

I stood at once, careful not to sway from the lingering effects of Sulla's strong wine.

"Wake the sappers, bring them here immediately. Have the engineering detachment prepare our heaviest rams and all our diggers. I want every torch and flammable thing trained on that weak spot. Have the distances measured tonight. Tell Crassus I want his siege ladders, whether they're finished or not. We'll begin preparations at dawn."

"Yes, Imperator," I said.

As I turned toward the wall, Sulla called after me.

"And Gavius?"

I looked back.

"There will be no quarter given this time. No mercy. Only strength, only the justice we create, remember? Make sure your men understand."

He didn't wait for a reply, and I didn't give one.

"Now, let's talk more about Athens as I have a feast prepared for my new allies," Sulla said to the Greeks as I departed.

I stepped into the frozen night, stars glittering like shattered glass above the city we now prepared to burn.

No quarter given. No mercy. Only strength. Only the justice we create.

Sulla's words echoed in my head. Even with wine still heavy in my belly, I was ready.

The morning air was cold enough to freeze the breath in my lungs, but that didn't stop my flesh from burning. With excitement, with fear, with anticipation. Enraptured, we stood before the mighty walls of Athens, near its weakest point.

There would be no space for cavalry in the breach, so I would fight on foot along with ten thousand men of Sulla's Fist behind me. And Sulla himself, as brave as any commander Rome had ever seen, would lead us into the fray himself.

For two weeks, our sappers dug like moles, forging a network of winding, timber-braced tunnels, lining the walls with firewood and oil along the way.

Every piece of gold we'd confiscated from Greek temples was spent on this siege. Every piece of hewn timber put to use. We'd done all we could do, and there was nowhere left to dig. It was time.

Sulla and I stood alone before our forces as the leading officer of our sapper detachment came to us, his face streaked with mud and his eyes hollowed out from days underground.

"She's ready, Imperator," he said, his voice hoarse.

Sulla's pure white cloak fluttered in the morning breeze. I knew it would be crimson with the blood of our enemies by nightfall. His armor and plumed helmet gleamed in the light of dawn, a statue of Mars come to life.

He gave no speech. Sulla knew we were either ready or we were not. While the sappers dug, we'd rehearsed the battle cadence relentlessly. Every man in the legion was now determined to prove Sulla was right to put his faith in us again.

If the Greek turncoats spoke true and the walls crumbled, victory would be ours that day.

"Light it," Sulla said without ceremony.

The officer nodded, panic and excitement on his face as he saluted and returned to the tunnel entrance.

He grabbed a single torch nearby and carried it as cautiously as a newborn toward the kindling.

He paused for a moment. Perhaps he needed to catch his breath, perhaps he wanted to check the bundling of wood first or the saturation of oil. It was difficult to tell from the distance, but I think his lips moved rhythmically in prayer.

Then he let the torch fall. The first spark was ignited as the officer paced slowly away from the tunnel.

The ground beneath us groaned. Was that it?

The silence lingered, stealing my breath and suffocating me. Had our sappers failed? Had the Greeks lied to us?

I stole a glance at Sulla. His iron gaze remained fixed on the glimmering limestone walls before us.

Then thunder cracked, a rolling boom that echoed in my chest—thunder not from the sky but the earth.

The tunnels collapsed. It began nearest us first, and I watched as the wet earth caved in on itself all the way to the walls.

The damaged section shuddered, splintered, and with the moan of a dying Titan, gave way. Entire slabs of masonry crumbled, breaking free and crushing the ground beneath, a cascade of dust and debris rushing forth from each burst.

Time and meaning evaporated as I watched. I don't know how long the walls continued to fall. It might have been only moments, perhaps days. I'd never seen anything like it. Horrifically beautiful, violently divine. A gap opened in the once-impregnable walls.

Just as Sulla ordained, the space was wide enough for one full cohort to march through, side by side.

Finally, Gaia stopped her mewling and the earth cried no more. The booming crashes were replaced with the roar of legionaries behind me.

I didn't wait for the order—I gave it.

"Forward! Into the breach!" I raised my gladius to the sky.

The first wave surged past. Sulla and I fell in line with their ranks, swords drawn and shields raised. I could feel the men rally, strength growing like a building tidal wave, because Sulla was with us.

As we neared the wall, a cloud of dust and debris enveloped us. It shrouded my vision like the darkest of nights and choked my lungs, but we pressed on.

This would be a battle of gritted teeth and blood on the stones. No mercy.

The cloud dissipated as we climbed over crumbled ruins and into the city. Greek hoplites awaited us, prepared.

Thousands of them flooded the city space, each with a bronze breastplate and a pointed Corinthian helmet. Their choice of armor was fitting, for Rome once annihilated Corinth, and the same fate awaited them today.

The hoplites marched, shoulder to shoulder, spears lowered, to meet us at the cusp of the breach. They shouted curses in their tongue as our front line crashed into them.

Behind and around them I heard the rally cry of Pontic troops, the ululating cry that would have sown terror in the hearts of any foe but Sulla's Fist.

But the first enemy presence I feared that day were the archers in the high towers above us, where the wall hadn't fallen.

I watched as shielded men on our front line shot back, like the force of a battering ram struck their chests, with only an arrow in their sternums. The man directly in front of me received an arrow to the eye. He collapsed, screaming. I stumbled over him but knew the rest of our line would trample him before he could reach safety. These are the sacrifices legionaries make in war.

"Shields up! Testudo!" Sulla shouted.

I echoed the call, and so did our centurions.

Arrows rained down over us, the thud like an angry hailstorm from Jupiter himself. Intermittently, an arrow would shred right through the wood of one of our shields and pin it to the arm of the unfortunate legionary wielding it.

But still we pressed on.

Another two men before me fell to the edge of Greek spears. I found myself now at the front. It was irresponsible for an officer to place himself in such danger, especially so early in the battle. But with Sulla nearby, I could not resist. He would be able to witness my bravery firsthand today.

"Remember what they took from us, men! Avenge our fallen and send these barbarians to Dis!"

I locked my shield with those beside me and maintained close spacing to avoid the mistakes of those who fell before me.

I wedged myself between two Greek spears and pushed forward enough that they couldn't be drawn back to strike me. I severed them both, rendering them useless.

The hoplites wielding them threw down their broken spears and brandished daggers. The hoplite phalanx thrives on discipline and order. My purpose was to take that from them.

The two hoplites abandoned their own shield wall and rushed ours. I found myself a few steps ahead of the line, no shield brothers beside me for protection now. But I knew they were watching me, and so was Sulla.

The two hoplites advanced against me with little room to maneuver but fire in their hearts. They chanted something at me in Greek, I said nothing to them in return. I waited for the first hoplite to lunge. As if he was still wielding that massive spear, he extended his reach beyond control. They didn't know how to fight knuckle to knuckle like Romans do.

He found poor footing on the broken stone beneath us and left himself vulnerable. I stabbed my blade through the thick of his arm. I drew it back across his throat. He spun from the force, blood spraying out in a whirl behind him.

I ducked beneath my shield just in time to avoid a stab from the other hoplite. The steel ricocheted off the top of my *scutum* with a metallic clang. His next attack came swiftly and connected beneath my arm.

The force drove breath from my lungs, but the dagger wasn't enough to pierce Roman armor.

His third attack was a desperate slash that sliced through exposed flesh at my elbow.

I couldn't assess how deep or grievous the injury was, but at least for now I maintained a firm grip on my shield.

I thrust its buttress into the hoplite's face. He staggered back. That Corinthian helm concealed much of his face, but I could see blood trickling down from his chin.

He drew back his dagger for another flurry of stabs, but my gladius reached his thigh first.

It was a superficial wound but enough that he buckled to his knees.

I drove my blade down through his collarbone. His grimy fingers clutched at my arms until they lost strength and he collapsed.

The legionaries roared behind me. I couldn't afford to turn and look, but I thought I heard Sulla's famous laughter among them.

I fell back into the protection of our line, but I'm not sure it was necessary. The Greek front already faltered.

Pontic troops rushed in around them to take their place, but now we had our first opportunity to advance.

"Now, Gavius! Now!" I heard Sulla's order.

"On me, on me!" I shouted.

The right half of our formation splintered away from the left. Sulla remained, I marched away with the right, as we'd practiced so many times.

We'd expect for me and my legion to face the strongest resistance, but that didn't appear to be the case. The Pontic warriors clashed with Sulla's line and the hoplites retreated deeper into the city to regroup. We faced little more than stragglers on our way to the gatehouse.

I ordered for our ranks to thin out as we passed through a maze of Greek homes. Soon we reached a clearing, and I saw the famous gates of Athens before us.

I couldn't imagine how we'd have toppled those walls, no matter how many trees we felled or battering rams we built. Fortunately, we didn't have to.

"Second cohort, up!" I shouted.

Again our ranks divided. We formed a tight cluster formation close to the gates themselves while five hundred of our finest stormed up the dark stairwells to the gatehouse.

I collected my breath and scanned the cityscape for any sign of oncoming Greek defenders. Above us, wailing sounded from the archers and tower guardsmen. I didn't need to call for report or turn around to know the second cohort had been victorious.

The gates groaned as they slowly split and rolled open. On the other side of those gates, Lucullus and Crassus waited on top of their fine steeds, our remaining cavalry behind them.

We split to allow them entry. I saw the smiles on their faces as my companions led the stampede forward. And behind them, the other twenty thousand legionaries of Sulla's Fist poured in.

"Into the city!" Lucullus shouted.

The men cheered like we'd already won the battle.

In a way, we had.

The fighting carried on for several hours, maybe more. The Athenian defenders did all they could, but they could not stand up to the full might of Sulla's Fist once we entered the city walls. The few who remained retreated to the towering Acropolis, where Athens would make her final stand.

We let them go. They could have the Acropolis for now—we had everything else.

The Pontic forces seemed to thin out and disappear. They must have fled to their ships in Piraeus, with hopes of sailing away and replenishing their army. No doubt Mithridates was among them.

His escape meant the war would continue, but the battle was won.

It was over. And now the real bloodshed began.

Athens burned.

Nothing was spared. Smoke curled into the sky in great black ribbons, swallowing temple columns, the sloped clay roofs of Athenian houses, and the silent faces of statues whose names I didn't know.

At Sulla's command, the leash was off. The legionaries hunted like wolves, loosed upon the city with permission to plunder, to scorch, to satisfy every hunger. And they did so with fervor.

I wouldn't have known my way around Athens even before the siege, but now I was positively lost. I accepted this, though, for I had nowhere in particular to be. I ambled through the burning streets, holding a torn strip of cloth to my bleeding arm, and watched everything unfold around me.

A shopkeeper screamed as two legionaries burst through his door. A woman clutching a babe was dragged through the Agora by a fistful of her hair. Fires leapt from stall to shrine to villa to temple, climbing over ancient stones and licking the edges of mosaics once designed to honor philosophers and poets.

Long before we set these streets on fire, Socrates strode them. Pericles. Euripides. The same marble where democracy was born now ran red with the blood of its hapless descendants.

And I—I just watched.

It wasn't sorrow I felt. Not entirely. The Athenians made their decision when they sided with Mithridates, when they swore an oath to fight beside a king who slaughtered eighty thousand innocents in a single day. And I lost men in this siege. Few enough that history would remember this as a staggering victory for Rome, but camp would still be emptier and quieter than the night before.

We tried to warn them. Sulla made it clear what would happen without complete surrender. They'd chosen resistance. They chose war, and now they saw what that meant.

Still, a knot settled in my gut that ached more than my arm as I passed the corner of what I believed was a schoolhouse. Its walls were charred and broken. Children's toys—clay animal figurines, marbles made of acorns, a small wooden chariot—lay splintered on the stone, stamped flat by Roman boots.

I reminded myself that this was justice. I just wished justice didn't always have to scream so loud.

A voice called out to me, "Tribune! Joining the festivities, are you?"

I turned to find one of my legionaries standing in the open doorway of a home. He clutched trinkets to his chest, struggling to keep them all from falling.

"They made us do this. Left us no choice," was my only response.

I continued walking.

It wasn't my intention to find Sulla, but I meandered right up to the temple steps where he'd established a temporary command post. Officers and scribes worked around him, as well as *servi* who busied themselves pouring wine and providing supplication after our hard day's work.

Sulla's cloak was stained with dust and blood, but his smile was radiant. His icy eyes reflected the distant fires and all the joy total victory can bring.

Two familiar figures waited at the foot of the temple steps— the Greek men who revealed the wall's secret to us.

They looked different now. Washed, clean shaven, and richly clothed, but their eyes radiated disbelief and horror.

Sulla noticed them and stood with outstretched arms.

"You are men of your word," he said in Greek. "The walls collapsed, just as you promised. A gift from the gods and from you. You'll be rewarded handsomely, rest assured. Your families are being secured as we speak, and no harm will come to them, on my honor."

As I climbed the steps to Sulla's side, one of them said, "This . . . this is not what we expected." His voice trembled like a reed in the wind.

Sulla tilted his head. "No?"

"We believed you came to restore order. To free Athens from the yoke of the East."

The other said, "We came to you not only for ourselves and our families. We came on behalf of Athens's people. The ordinary citizens who didn't choose this war, who did not want it, and did not support your enemies."

The first Greek said, "We thought aiding you would afford us mercy."

Sulla's smile waned, but it didn't vanish. He spoke patiently, as though correcting a child. "I understand your concern. Truly, I do. But you are not magistrates or strategoi . . . you aren't authorized to speak on behalf of the people. This . . . this is war." He gestured to the chaos all around us. He descended the steps until they were on equal footing. "You men are patriots, but so am I. I'm also a general. When a city is taken by assault rather than surrender, it becomes property of the men who took it. This is Roman custom, but we did not create it. This was the Greek way long before it was ours, and some other, long forgotten tribe before that. This is the way of the world."

One of the Greek men stammered, "Yes . . but, but in times of—"

Sulla interrupted, "Is that not so, Tribune?" He turned to me.

I released the bloody cloth from my arm and stood at attention before I responded.

"It is," I said. "The two of you provided useful information. Yet it was our legionaries who climbed over the rubble, who bled and died to take these streets. The men you see looting are still mourning the loss of brothers. Now they seek comfort and the reward for their sacrifice, their victory. It is their right."

My response pleased Sulla.

The Greek men said nothing. Their faces tightened, but they didn't weep.

Sulla smiled again, warmer now. "Come now. You will receive great honor, more than you could have dreamed of. When the city quiets, I shall host a feast to rival the Bacchanalian revelries of Alexander. You and your families shall join us as guests—no, as allies and comrades. Eat. Drink. Seek rest. The future of Greece forever changed today, and you can be part of what comes next."

He motioned for his guard to lead them away. They didn't resist or say anything further. Their shoulders sagged as they departed.

Sulla turned to me. He placed both of his hands on my shoulders, looked at me, and then drew me close. What other general would have shown so much affection? What other tribune would have been worthy of it?

"We've done it, Gavius. We've broken the Athenian resistance, and the rest of Greece will soon follow. We've defeated their armies and carved our name into the marble beside theirs. This day will be remembered."

I nodded. "Yes, Imperator. You've won a great victory today."

He cocked his head to the side. "You don't seemed pleased."

Smoke stung my eyes. I blinked.

"Just tired from battle, sir."

He noticed my wound. Taking my hand, he raised my arm and inspected it.

Sulla shrugged. "Tired and wounded are both ailments for which wine is the cure. And we have much to drink. Let's celebrate like we did after our victory at Nola. Remember?"

I smiled at the memory, though something in me still felt cold.

The thought of drinking, feasting, and games of dice brought me no joy in the moment, strangely enough. I just wanted to sleep.

But I'd sought my commander's approval and attention since we arrived in Greece, and finally I had it. I would pantomime victory joy if I had to.

"Come," Sulla said, striding toward the smoky streets. "Athens is ours, now let's enjoy it."

I followed him and did all I could to ignore the broken children's toys beneath our feet, the cries in the alleyway, and the echo of philosophers who once believed virtue—not victory—was the mark of true greatness.

SCROLL XXV

Lucius Hirtuleius—Two Days after the Ides of February, 667 Ab Urbe Condita

"Do you have everything you need?" Sertorius asked.

He always made the effort to speak with his men before battle, and I'm sure it brought the rest as much courage as it brought me.

"I do. I'm ready," I said.

He comforted his horse, Sura, named after my mother whom he never met. I watched carefully and tried to perform the same soft touch behind my steed's ear, but he just shook his head and snorted. Sertorius was a far better equestrian than me, that's for certain.

We scanned the legionaries forming up before us. I looked up and estimated the time by the height of the sun. Strabo's forces could arrive any moment now.

"You know, *amice*, if I had known about your clandestine meeting with Pompey, I would have stopped you."

He smiled. "Any reasonable man would have."

"It was reckless. Foolish. Even though you served with the

man and trusted him. . . . I would have stopped you," I said. "I'm glad I didn't know. I'm glad I couldn't get in the way. Now we know we did everything we could to avoid what's going to happen today."

He sobered. "We did."

There was nothing else to say. We'd prepared our stratagem in advance; now we had only to follow through with it. We saluted each other before he galloped back to the center. Sertorius would command there while the mercenary leader, Fabius, controlled the right flank. I would lead the left.

Fierce winds howled from the east, shrieking through the gaps in our ranks and spinning our standards. I'd need to keep an eye on that today, winds can change the tide of battle.

I looked down. The hard earth was slick with half-thawed mud and a thin layer of trampled snow, now ground down to a paste by a thousand marching feet. I knew positioning would be important. If my front ranks started slipping in the sludge, my whole flank could collapse.

Behind us loomed the Colline Gate, shadowed by the wide arm of the Servian Wall, which had protected Rome for centuries. Today, its ancient stones would spectate the civil strife that now clouded her glory. Of course, no Romans actually stood on the walls to watch us, but I knew the entire Republic was cautiously waiting the outcome of the day's battle.

We hoped our victory would force Octavius and the senate to see the futility of their position, and encourage them to surrender. Our defeat, on the other hand, would bolster their resolve and encourage them to hold out longer, regardless of how many within the city suffered.

Sertorius and I knew we had to win this day.

I heard the horns before I could see the legions. At first, I wondered why our musicians were so far away from our line before reminding myself we were fighting Romans today. They looked like us, talked like us, announced their arrival like us.

The legions of Pompeius Strabo moved methodically into

view across the field. They were trained. More experienced than our own soldiers. If we won today, it would not be for the size of our army, the brutality of our warriors, or the skill of the mercenaries, but the leadership of Quintus Sertorius and his officers.

I stole a glance at the center and watched for Sertorius to give the signal.

I echoed it to my flank. "Advance!"

We began our march down a soft embankment, almost as silent, disciplined, and dreadful as our enemy.

The pilum volley initiated the battle. Their jagged tips crunched against shields and screaming men, as we let our own pila fly.

Then came the rush. Both armies increased pace until the two front walls crashed into each other. I said a silent prayer of thanks that we met on slightly higher ground than the enemy.

Steel met studded shield, flesh met earth, the frozen sludge drank Roman blood. Order could dissolve into a desperate, grinding melee at any moment if we weren't careful.

I surveyed the field. I could see the engagement completely from my vantage point behind our lines. A useful advantage, no doubt, but I would have preferred to be on the front.

"Send in the third cohort to reinforce the first!" I ordered.

The balance of the fray ebbed and flowed like a current that couldn't decide whether it wanted to wash away the beach or escape it entirely.

The battle was still young, but no advantage could be seen clearly thus far. Mars and Bellona declined to make their intentions known.

I remained on the ridge above our flank, shouting orders, sending runners, watching for opportunities that rarely came.

Sertorius trusted me to command his left wing, and I refused to fail him. I glanced over at the center whenever I could and found relief when I saw his standards, unmoving, above the battlefield. I knew my friend was there, gracefully planted on Sura's back, bending the shape of this battle to his will.

"Shields to the left, shields to the left!" I ordered when I returned my attention to my own men.

Surely, one side would show some sign of weakness soon.

But the hours ground on, and neither side faltered. The bodies piled up and formed a mound beneath the fray, and yet both armies fought on.

I looked up at the sun again, only to find it retreating behind thick winter clouds as it began its descent, casting a grim, amber light over the battlefield.

Gods, how long had we been fighting?

"You!" I shouted at a runner.

He hurried to my side and stared up at me with wide eyes.

"Go to Sertorius, ask for direction. Night will fall soon. We must press or withdraw. I await his command."

The runner nodded vigorously and sprinted off, sure-footed on the muddy earth.

I tried waiting for the runner to return, I truly did. But I watched as the exterior of my wing began to fold back. The first rank fell, and like a tidal wave, it pushed back on the rest. In moments, Strabo's front line had reached my third.

I tried to find the runner, tried to spot Sertorius in the chaos, but I found neither.

Instincts took over.

I leapt from my horse. He was a good steed but my expertise was fighting on foot. I gave him a pat and turned to my guard.

I'd barely come to know them since Sertorius made me an officer, but they waited patiently for my orders, and I knew they would follow.

"On me," I said.

And they didn't hesitate.

We drew our swords, and charged into the storm.

I had no shield. Hadn't used one since I lost my arm in Greece, leaving a clean stump that still ached with the memory of a hand. But I'd learned long ago how to fight without it. What others perceived as a weakness, I would use against them.

"What's wrong, legionaries? Are you afraid to fight for your Republic?" I shouted as I reached the front lines.

I had been able to see the battlefield stretch out clearly from my previous vantage point, but I hadn't seen the devastation in its totality until I reached the line.

"Hirtuleius is with us!" someone shouted.

Most of them barely knew me, but they seemed to rally at the call.

"Come then, let's end this," I roared. "For the Republic!"

My men rallied the call, but then Strabo's did as well. Both sides seemed infuriated by the other's claim, and the melee intensified.

I pushed my way to the front line. Wedged in between two shields in our shield wall, I stabbed my blade over it with precision gained from many years of experience. Short, brutal strikes, strong enough to split the rings in the enemy chain mail, swift enough they couldn't take my other arm.

The reserves from both armies must have pushed in. We collapsed into the enemy such that we almost became one line. It seemed nearly impossible just to find enough space to strike with swords. In lieu of that, I used my shoulder, my elbow, my head, the nub of my arm to disorient Strabo's legionaries around me.

"The future of Rome is decided today!" I shouted. "The Republic's fate rests on your shoulders."

Perhaps it was my words, or perhaps it was seeing an officer fighting beside them as a brother-in-arms, but our front lines rallied. The centurions called for rotation, and the second line rushed to the front, eager to answer my call to heroism.

I found enough space to free my sword arm, just in time to parry a strike meant for my ribs. A piercing ring echoed as my foe's gladius flew off. I let out a battle cry as I stabbed my own blade beneath his exposed armpit.

"Show them what true Roman might looks like," I said.

I could scarcely get the words out before another enemy legionary sought to strike me down. Before he could deliver the final blow, I threw my pommel into his nose. Disoriented and likely blinded, he staggered until the men around me finished him.

I felt our line begin to surge forward. We might be able to win the flank after all.

A gray shroud began to envelop the battlefield. Night was almost upon us, though the last of day's light allowed me to spot the shimmering crest of an officer near the front.

This was no ordinary centurion. This man was a tribune.

He stood firm even as his men faltered. He shouted orders, though they were meek and unheeded. I could see his gear was polished and unblemished from the day's fighting. He was likely a reserve officer sent to reinforce the enemy flank.

I'd seen many true warriors across the battlefield in my life, and this was not one of them.

Also during my many years of service, I'd seen many armies falter. Nothing made warriors route quicker than their standard falling or witnessing an officer's death.

I knew what I had to do.

One more fallen Roman and Strabo's forces would retreat. We would win the flank, and then we could reinforce Sertorius and Fabius. We would win the day, and Rome would be ours.

It felt like the entire war came down to me in that moment. I'd never felt more certain of my singular purpose.

I broke from the line and charged the officer.

He turned at the last moment, barely able to lift his shield to deflect my blade. I stabbed again and again. He made little effort in the way of attack, instead he continued to stagger back and recoil from my assault.

I left myself vulnerable to the other enemies around us, but there is something ancient about two men meeting in single combat. No one on either side decided to intervene.

The young tribune stumbled. For the first time, he tried to thrust at me, but his assault was clumsy and slow. I batted his shield away and drove my blade into his thigh.

A sharp cry escaped him. I kicked him in the chest and he collapsed to the mud.

I stood over him and drew back my gladius, and then I buried it in his chest, pinning him to the earth.

My men erupted. They surged forward. Enemy swords and shields sunk into the mud as they turned and ran.

I almost stood and joined the pursuit, but I turned again to the officer. He fought poorly, but honorably, and didn't deserve unnecessary suffering. He earned the mercy of a swift death.

A helmet partially concealed his face, blood and grime painted the rest. Something about the dying officer's eyes reminded me of my own. Something in the shape of his jaw that seemed familiar.

But even before my mind could perceive his identity, my body knew. The recognition—the acceptance—didn't come gently. It tore through me like the very sword I'd used to slay the enemy officer before me. The noise of war dissolved into black silence too vast to comprehend. The world tilted, the weight of existence pressed in on my chest, and the battlefield vanished.

I squinted against the growing darkness and searched his face for eternity.

"Aius," my brother's name escaped me.

His limbs thrashed against his will. I brought him into my arms and wiped away the blood bubbling in the corners of his lips.

"No, no," I whispered. "No."

I originally meant to dispatch the officer quickly, but that was before realizing he was my brother. Now I frantically tried to recollect everything I'd learned from *medici*, for some remedy or divine method of salvation.

His eyes widened when he stared up at me. Utterly perplexed. I saw no anger or resentment. I deserved his hatred, yet I found none.

But I hated myself. Deeply, violently, more than I'd ever hated anyone or anything in my life.

But in my brother's eyes, I saw nothing but confusion. Then resignation.

"Aius, no . . . weren't supposed to be here." I buried my forehead into his and rocked him. His eyes bore into mine until whatever makes us alive was gone. "How . . . no, no."

I cradled him against my chest, the way I'd carried him around when we were children.

I didn't care about the battle anymore, or the war, or Rome, or freedom, or life.

It left me—my voice—rising above the clash of steel like a wounded god's lament, too terrible to be mine.

SCROLL XXVI

ARREA—TWO DAYS after the Ides of February, 667 Ab Urbe Condita

The sky was a bruised gray above the valley, the kind of color that weighs heavy on the heart even without grief to anchor it. The growing cold seeped into the bone, sharp and unrelenting, but the men on the battlefield didn't seem to feel it.

They stood like statues around the funeral pyres they'd prepared. Dozens of them, maybe more, each built with care and reverence.

My husband insisted they would burn not just their dead, but the enemy's too. They would give Strabo's men a proper burial, as each Roman is due. A special pyre was prepared for Aius, the only tribune believed to have fallen on either side that day.

Quintus approached Aius's pyre. Soot streaked his face, his jaw clenched tight. He used his torch to ignite this first pyre.

I stole a glance at Lucius. His cloak hung loose about his shoulders, unfastened, stained, and torn. His face was bloodless, his empty gaze fixed on the wooden frame where his brother's body lay, wrapped in a scarlet soldier's cloak.

Sometimes I forgot what these men left on the battlefield, but I saw it on full display now. I understood why Quintus returned differently each time he fought.

And my heart wept for them. I was determined to remain strong and composed, to comfort them as best I could in an unthinkable tragedy.

Lucius had said nothing since Quintus found him on the battlefield. He remained silent as they gathered up the bodies around him. He only watched as the priests finally took Aius from his arms and prepared him for his departure.

Quintus rejoined us on the other side of Lucius.

Like lightning bugs sparking across the valley, the pyres began to burn. Flames crackled as they reached the kindling base of each pyre. Dried pine and olive branches burned with an eager hunger, but it would take hours for the flames to consume these fallen warriors.

Smoke hung low, like the ghosts of the fallen gathering about and enveloping us. It shrouded the faces of Lucius and Quintus beside me, making shadows where their eyes and cheeks should have been.

But I knew the look on my husband's face then. I'd seen it before, when we buried his comrades in Gaul and, sadly, many times since.

Then Lucius moved.

He stepped forward, not fast or with urgency, but with purpose.

At first I thought he meant to say goodbye. A final touch, one last look, or one last word that might follow his brother to the afterlife.

But I noticed something unsteady in his gait, something broken behind his gaze. Something told me he wanted to join his brother in the flames rather than pull him out.

Without thinking, I reached and took him by the arm.

I saw then that Quintus was holding him up by the other.

Lucius stopped. His tears fell freely then, streaking down the dried blood and mud on his cheeks.

The three of us stood like this, linked and silent, as the fires crackled and roared.

We said nothing. I'd lost enough in my own life to know words could bring no comfort. Only grief could speak loud enough to be heard now.

We maintained watch until most of the others had retired. My husband and his legions had much to do, but still he waited with Lucius, and I waited with them.

When at last the flames burned low and only embers glowed beneath the collapsing wood, I approached my husband and placed a hand on his arm.

"He needs a moment alone," I said.

Quintus nodded and allowed me to lead him away, but only after he placed his forehead against his friend's and kissed his cheek.

Lucius sank to his knees as we departed.

Our tent was quiet save for the soft pop of the brazier and the occasional whisper of wind outside. Rhea sat in the corner with Toria tucked to her chest. Our daughter was fast asleep, totally and mercifully unaware of the world around her.

When Rhea spotted us, she quickly dried the last of her tears.

If the stories were true, she'd been there when Aius was born. Held his mother's hand as she gave birth. She helped Aius take his first breath and then cared for his mother as the labor took her life.

I could see in her eyes she felt this loss in her bones.

But she summoned a warrior's composure. She stood and walked to her son with a straight back.

Quintus reached down and took Toria gently from Rhea's

arms and cradled her like something too precious for a world so cruel.

Finally, he broke.

He sank to the ground with Toria pressed delicately to his chest. This was the depth of sorrow that can't find words, that doesn't care for pride, position, or honor. But more than sorrow, love. And this was what made me adore my husband.

I knelt beside him and wrapped my arms around his strong shoulders.

He tried to speak but couldn't. His tears ran through Toria's soft hair.

"Say nothing," I whispered. "Just hurt now."

We wept together.

I ached for Lucius and the loss of his brother. I ached for Quintus and the loss of his friend and so many of his men. And yet, I ached just as deeply for all the grief to come.

This was war. Civil war. And I feared the worst of it was only beginning.

SCROLL XXVII

Gavius Sertorius—Seven days before the Kalends of March, 667 Ab Urbe Condita

Athens no longer burned. Not with fire at least.

But even now, weeks after we took Athens, and days after we choked out the last resistance on the Acropolis, Athens still smoldered—in spirit, in silence, in the ways its survivors shuffled through the rubble like ghosts.

We spent the last several days hunting down Pontic loyalists and making examples of them. Sulla made it a priority to find those emissaries who came to us, so haughty and bold, and fulfill his promise. He vowed to have them crucified, and Sulla was a man of his word. They died after a few days, and by now the birds had pecked out their eyes and tore at their flesh, but still their bodies remained on crosses just outside the city walls.

Athens belonged to us now, and so did the Acropolis. Images of Roman victory—laurels and legionary standards—dressed all the Greek temples, all the old marble bones. Even the statues wore wreaths and red paint, the marks of occupation.

To commemorate our victory, Sulla promised a celebration like nothing we'd seen before.

And every grand spectacle required a venue to host it.

The Parthenon, once sacred, was now theatrical. As soon as our legionaries collected the bodies of the dead and put out the fires, they transformed Athena's temple to a banquet hall. Long, soft couches lined the peristyle. Torches burned and illuminated the hastily strung banners.

Exotic spices and roasted meats filled the air, their smells overpowering after so many months of rationed grain, dried figs, and stale bread.

I marveled at the spread laid out before us. I'd never seen anything like it in Rome. This wasn't simply food, it was luxury, the sort of feast even most patricians wouldn't see in their lifetime. Wine from Massilia. Flamingos from Egypt. Citrus from Hispania. Even the performers—scantily clad dancing girls, flute players, acrobats, fire breathers, and masked comedians—were too fine for the rubble of broken Athens.

I couldn't believe Sulla accomplished this. Somehow, while conducting the final assault on the Acropolis, he discovered Athens's hidden wealth, the secret reserves hoarded by the elites while their people starved. Perhaps this is how the emissaries lived while pleading for mercy outside their own gates.

I found an open seat on a couch, surrounded by fellow officers already well into their cups. I'd developed little taste for these delicacies in my life, so I ate little. But I drank much. I wasn't feeling particularly festive that evening, for whatever reason, and I hoped strong wine would correct that.

Across the room, I spotted the two Greek informants, seated stiffly beside their wives and children on couches of honor. A mountain of uneaten food lay before them. They huddled like prisoners, not guests, their eyes downcast and arms linked protectively around their little ones.

A cup clinked against mine.

Lucullus, red-cheeked and perfectly at ease, plopped down beside me.

"We've done it, Gavius, my old friend. We've taken the jewel of Greece."

"History will remember what we achieved here," I said.

He reclined on the couch and studied me. "You don't seem overly pleased. One of those dancers would certainly change that." He nodded to the Greek performers.

I blushed when I noticed one of her breasts was exposed.

"I was just thinking . . . my father served in Greece for eight years, quashing a rebellion. Eight years. And from what I understand, not a single Athenian stone was burned. How long have we been here? Three months?"

Lucullus burped. "Three and a half, technically."

I gave a small, mirthless laugh. "Less than four months and we've reduced the entire city to ash."

Lucullus sobered. "It's a shame your father hasn't shown Rome the respect he showed Athens then."

My flesh burned. I concealed my face with my cup and drank deeply.

He knew me well enough by now to know his words cut deeply. He sat up on the couch and placed a hand on my shoulder.

"I'm sorry, Gavius. Truly. I can only imagine how your heart is torn. But the truth is . . ." He leaned closer. "You have two families now. The one you were born into, and the one you're surrounded by now. The one you fought and bled beside." He gestured around to the celebrating officers around us. "You can decide which family is due your loyalty, your love."

"Thank you, Lucullus," I said. I appreciated his concern, but I wanted to change the subject.

I watched as his gaze drifted to a cluster of Greek beauties laughing near the musicians.

He cleared his throat. "I am going to make some new friends. The wine will give you enough courage to join me soon."

Lucullus clapped my back and left me.

I continued drinking, but instead of courage, I found only a hollow in my gut and more intrusive thoughts.

Before long, Sulla rose and swaggered to the center of the Parthenon banquet hall. Even if he wasn't the commander, his appearance would likely have captured everyone's attention. He was dressed as Bacchus, god of wine, with a purple toga draped over his shoulder and a rich red paint covering his face. In addition to his attire, he wore the expression of a triumphant god.

He raised his cup and the room hushed.

"Romans," he began, "my kinsman. Look around you! This is not a feast but a monument. A monument to victory. To power. To a restored Republic."

I gestured for a Greek slave to refill my cup and sat on the edge of my seat to listen intently.

"We have taken this city not with diplomacy, not with words. No, we took Athens by steel. Resolve. And what was it I said . . . something about Roman balls?"

The officers roared with approval and laughter. I joined in just as loud, for fear the others would see restraint as a lack of loyalty.

Sulla's words rose above the ruckus. "But our work is not finished. No—once our fleet is prepared, we sail east. We will chase Mithridates to wherever he skulks off to next, to Pontus even, where he dares to crown himself an equal to Rome. And when we land on his shores, he too shall witness what Athens has: the full fury of the Republic."

I roared now. I stomped my feet and raised my fist with the rest.

Sulla turned and motioned to a legionary behind him.

"Bring him," Sulla said.

The legionary obeyed, disappeared, and returned with a prisoner.

This must have been Aristion, the Athenian leader who

defied us from the Acropolis, who swore his allegiance to Mithridates and bound the Greek people to his dreadful cause.

Now he was shackled, bloody, and naked.

His face was swollen and his eyes puffy. I expected a man like that to radiate pride and resistance in his final moments, but instead Aristion displayed only the frightened look of an abandoned child.

Sulla grabbed Aristion by his arm and yanked him forward. The Greek noble did all he could to conceal his manhood and preserve the last of his dignity, which my fellow officers found quite humorous.

"This man thought himself above Rome. He knelt and kissed the ring of a foreign king. He welcomed this invader's army into lands fought for and earned with the blood of Roman legionaries. And then, craven until the end, he gorged on these delicacies you now see before you while his people starved, and he had the audacity to speak to them about liberty!"

We made our disgust known. A few drunker officers were brave enough to throw bits of food at the captive, careful not to strike our commander.

"Aristion of Athens will die for his crimes—but not yet. He has taken much from us, and now we will take something from him in return. Every Roman here will have his opportunity to exact vengeance. A mark. A tooth. A finger. A debt repaid."

The officers stood, laughing or growling, and one by one they hurried to line up.

Aristion cowered and wept.

I rose as well, but not to join them. I tasted bile in my throat and wished to depart.

The crowd was thick around me, but I pushed my way toward the exit until I heard my name.

"Gavius." It was Sulla. "You're not leaving, are you?" he said.

I could barely hear myself over the cheering officers. "I—" I hesitated. "I believe I've drunk too much wine. I thought to take a moment—"

"Nonsense!" Sulla threw his arm over my shoulder and led me deeper into the Parthenon. "You've sacrificed as much as anyone to take Athens. None deserve a share of the reward more than you do."

I would gladly accept a reward for my service, and had many times over in the distribution of loot since we took the city.

I'd killed countless scores of men in battle, and I was proud of each one. But this . . . this was no reward for me.

Still, I could not defy him. I could not disappoint him. I couldn't allow him to think my vigor for his cause was in any way diminished.

So I followed him back to the cowering Aristion, who was already a blubbering mess.

Perhaps it was the wine, but I don't recall much of what I did. Even if I remembered more clearly, I wouldn't recollect it here.

But I do remember my fellow officers cheering as I took hold of the knife. And I recall the pride in Sulla's eyes when I passed it to the next man in line and returned to him.

"Aristion is one man who represents all those who defy us. He represents all who defy Rome."

I nodded, smiled, and accepted a fresh cup of wine, and many more after.

I drank until I felt nothing and reminded myself this was victory.

The air inside the command quarters was thick with the smell of sweat, vomit, and regrets. Officers sat around the long table like wounded pups—eyelids drooping, heads cradled, mouths drawn into tight lines from the sour taste of last night's wine lingering on their tongues.

Sulla slouched in his chair. He usually recovered quickly from a night of heavy drinking, but not this time. Bacchus had truly animated him, Sulla said, but today he woke as just a mortal with all the intrinsic ramifications.

His skin was a shade paler than usual, with a few flakes of decorative red paint stubbornly clinging to his chin. A shallow bowl of figs and nuts sat untouched before him.

"Two hundred and thirty-seven by my count," said Crassus, the only officer among us who restrained himself the evening prior.

Sulla winced and pressed two fingers against his temple.

We were tallying inventory.

Not the exciting sort of inventory either: the gold, the jewels, the valuables. These had already been seized, sorted, and allocated appropriately. Now came the slow, life-sapping business of counting iron nails, mule yokes, dry grain, and the distribution of *servi*.

Lucullus widened his eyes to look at the scroll before him. "Eighty-seven others, all male, all adult, will be transferred to Delos for sale on next market day." His voice was flat as he turned to Sulla and said, "Commander, one quaestor suggested we allocate fifty *servi* as personal rewards for the bravest men of each cohort. Do you agree?"

Sulla covered his eyes. "Yes, yes. Have it done."

"We can ask the centurions for recommendations," I said. My voice was hoarse and my throat was dry.

I heard the thudding of hammers, the braying of mules, and the rhythmic shouting of our legionaries as they endured an equipment inspection outside the tent.

I fought to stay awake. My head pounded like a war drum. My vision was blurry. I could scarcely make out the writing on the scroll in my lap.

The tent flap opened and a bright beam of light poured in, followed by a moan from all the officers but Crassus.

A centurion stepped in, helmet tucked beneath one arm while he saluted with the other.

"Apologies for the interruption, Imperator," he said. "I have two captives I believe you'll want to see."

Sulla didn't even look up. "Kill them. Sell them. Whatever you like. It's too early to worry about peasants or pickpockets."

The centurion hesitated. "These two were caught trying to escape from the postern gate. When we took them, one gave a name. I don't know it, but a few of the men suggest it means something to you."

Sulla groaned and straightened in his chair. "By all the gods would—fine. Fine. Bring them in."

Legionaries led two captives into Sulla's praetorium. Fortunately for them, neither was naked or covered in wounds like the prisoner from last night's spectacle. Fortunately for me too. More of that would have caused me to regurgitate on our inventory documents.

These two were no luckier than Aristion, though. It was clear the first was disheveled, unkempt, and hungry. The other . . .

My eyes glanced back to the first man and I studied his face. It was aged and gaunt from the siege, but I could never forget those eyes.

My stomach twisted into knots as the realization dawned on me.

Despite his haggard appearance, I knew at once this was Apollonius.

My father's dearest friend, his old comrade. The same man who once taught me my letters and numbers, who guided my hands when I scribbled my first words. It'd been years since I'd seen him, but now he stood before me.

Sulla leaned forward, eyes flicking between the two captives while mine remained on Apollonius.

"Names," Sulla said bluntly.

My old tutor stepped forward, holding his shoulders as straight as he could in this condition.

"My name is Apollonius Sertorius, freedman of Quintus Sertorius."

Every man in the tent stirred and looked to me.

My limbs felt numb; they tingled like all the blood left them.

Sulla raised an eyebrow. "Well, well," he said. "This is interesting."

Everyone waited for me to say something but I averted my gaze. I pretended to study the grain provision scroll in my hand. What was I supposed to say? What could I say?

Sulla stood slowly, reminding everyone in the room of his size and strength. "You're a long way from Nursia, Apollonius. Tell me—have you corresponded with your former master recently?"

Apollonius answered calmly, "No."

Crassus questioned him next, "And are you aware of what he is doing?"

"I've heard only whispers from others."

Sulla walked around the table and faced him. "So you're aware Quintus Sertorius is a named enemy of Rome. A traitor. And by all accounts you've remained a close friend and confidant of the traitor since he granted your freedom. You should know what this means for your fate. Yet you do not appear afraid. Why? Have you lived so long in shackles that you forgot what they meant?"

I looked up, and to my shock and shame, Apollonius was looking directly at me. He actually smiled. Softly. Sadly. But with warmth.

He gave me the same look when I'd scraped my knee as a child or when I asked questions too complicated for my little mind to comprehend.

Apollonius turned back to Sulla and met his gaze. "I am a free man, Lucius Cornelius. Not because Quintus freed me but because I choose to be one. I discovered long ago that if someone cannot steal my capacity to act with courage, kindness, and virtue, they cannot take my liberty."

The tent swelled with the low laughter of the officers.

Someone muttered, "The old man thinks he's Socrates."

"Why are you here, freedman?" Crassus asked.

Apollonius kept his eyes on Sulla. "When the war with the Italian tribes broke out, I came here on holiday. I wasn't planning to return until the events were over, but war found me here first."

"The real question is how you survived the Roman purge." Crassus glowered at him.

"I have friends here in Athens. They concealed and protected me. More recently, I returned the favor. They've escaped the city, in poor spirits, but good health." He shifted his gaze in my direction. I didn't look up, but I could feel it. "Unfortunately, Sertorius' faithful hound, Pollux, died defending us."

Sulla said, "The faithfulness of dogs is incredible, isn't it? They'll remain loyal unto death . . . even when their loyalty is misplaced."

I doubt my father knew, but I ached for him regardless. To some men, horses and dogs are nothing more than protections, or a tool to be used. But they were more to Quintus Sertorius.

Sulla tapped his finger for my attention. "Gavius, do you know this man?"

My tongue felt like it had swollen in my mouth. My heartbeat drummed so loud in my ears I feared everyone could hear it.

I could not speak so I simply nodded.

"He says he hasn't spoken with your father and that he isn't privy to his plans. And yet, serendipitously, he finds himself here of all places, where your father's enemies are waging a war. Do you believe him?"

"He's a liar," someone said in a hushed voice behind me.

I found the courage to stand.

I could already hear the mockery I'd endure for this, but I ceased to care.

"If he says he hasn't spoken to my father, I believe him."

Sulla studied me with an unreadable expression.

"Apollonius is a man of honor," I said, louder. "I knew him well in my childhood, and I've never heard him tell a single lie.

If he says he was here on holiday, I believe he was here on holiday." I looked at Sulla now. "And you are correct. Apollonius and my father are close as brothers. If he was going to send someone to spy on someone as perceptive and mighty as you, it would not be his gentle-spirited friend."

Silence followed until Sulla broke it. He placed a hand on Apollonius's shoulder and squeezed it.

"Touching," he said. "I'm honored to meet a man so honorable." He turned and gestured to me. "You should thank him. For the sake of Gavius' heartfelt testimony, I will grant you a swift death."

My knees threatened to buckle. I couldn't breathe. I was naïve enough to believe my words might spare him.

But Apollonius didn't falter. He bowed his head to Sulla, as if grateful. Then he looked to me again and gave me the slightest nod, as if to say *be strong*. It was *he* who offered *me* comfort.

Sulla turned to the other captive now, and for the first time I did as well.

Every muscle of his exposed flesh rippled beneath dark skin. The jagged scar across his shaven head intensified the rage in his eyes.

The man stepped forward and squared himself with Sulla.

His voice was deep, guttural, haunting. "I am called Barca by the Romans, but that is not my name. I was born Masensen. I am a warrior. I am a free man. And I will not grovel for your mercy."

Sulla's eyes lit up with delight, as if the revelation cured him of his hangover instantly.

"So you are Barca! The famed *lanista* turned outlaw. I placed a hefty bounty on your head; you should be honored."

The shackles around Barca's clenched fists shook.

Sulla looked past him to the centurion. "You've just earned a year's salary. Well done."

I realized now that Sulla wouldn't ask me for my opinion again. And even if he did, it wouldn't matter. I returned to my seat and hung my head.

Sulla smiled at Barca. "I might ask why you are here, but it no longer matters. Your companion here will die clean. You . . . you'll die screaming.

Barca did not flinch. He only stared back, daring Sulla to try.

"Take them away," Sulla ordered.

As the legionaries forced them outside again, I remained frozen in my chair. Staring at the document I couldn't read.

I didn't know whether it was my hands shaking or everything around me.

I felt Lucullus drawing closer. "Sounds like he was kin to you," he said. "I'm sorry for your loss, but there is no other way. We can't allow him to take information back to your father."

"My only family now is this legion," I said and felt a few officers clap me on the back.

SCROLL XXVIII

Quintus Sertorius—Four days before the Kalends of March, 667
Ab Urbe Condita

The night was still—eerily so.

A light snowfall began as the sun set the night before, and a strong wind sent it swirling around our camp, but now all was quiet.

The soft, rhythmic breath of Arrea beside me helped me fall into a light sleep, though never much deeper. Between us lay little Toria, who'd reached an age where she refused her crib, preferring the warmth and comfort of her parents. Her tiny fist rested on my chest. Even as I slept, I measured the rise and fall of her breath, grateful for each.

I was in the halfway realm between sleep and oblivion when someone shook my shoulder.

I reached beneath my pillow and closed my grasp around the cold handle of my *pugio*, the natural reflex of any lifelong fighter. I nearly drew it but found only my mother there beside my bed.

In the corner of our tent, where my mother liked to read father's letters, a small candle burned.

"What is it? Are we under attack?" I asked.

I listened for any sound of trouble outside our tent but heard nothing, not even the snoring of legionaries.

She shook her head. Her eyes, usually sharp and focused, were wide with panic and strained from lack of sleep.

"Mother?" I whispered hoarsely. "What is it?"

Fortunately, Toria slept deeply. She gave a soft whimper and rolled over. Arrea stirred awake beside me.

She raised a trembling hand, and in it was a scroll—old and discolored, the ink on it beginning to fade with the sands of time, its edges frayed like a retired battlefield standard.

"I've been reading your father's scrolls," she said.

The tension in my shoulders eased. I released the grip on my *pugio*. I didn't know why something in thirty-year-old letters would concern her so deeply, but at least my family was safe in the present.

"I've discovered something. Something awful . . ."

I pushed back the covers and sat on the corner of the bed and took her hand.

As mother tried to collect her thoughts, I considered what could cause this disturbance. It would have been out of character, but perhaps my father had taken a campaign wife when he served in the Balearic Isles. Perhaps I had a half-brother or sister out there somewhere?

The candlelight shimmered in her sad eyes.

"It's Fabius," she said.

My vision narrowed. I could hear only my mother's words.

"He betrayed them, Quintus. He sold out their position to the enemy, and it led to an ambush. That's how . . ."

"That's how what, mother?" I said.

"That's how Lucius's father died. In this ambush."

My flesh burned hot but my blood ran cold as the snow outside our tent.

She slipped the scroll into my hand before I could say another word.

I scanned my father's neat, careful penmanship in the faded ink. There it was, again and again throughout the scroll.

Fabius. Fabius. Fabius.

It was a common name among the nobility. But for a common legionary? It had to be him, the very man I'd entrusted with our safety for so many months.

As if she felt my broken heart, Toria began to cry. Arrea took her up and wrapped the wool blanket tighter around her, as much for warmth as a small way of protecting her from this treacherous world.

I remembered hearing about the ambush now. It was the one part of my father's service in the legion he refused to speak about. The one moment we were told not to ask about. And it was clear now Fabius was the perpetrator.

Unfurling the letter further, I read how my father was tasked with hunting down Fabius but failed in his pursuit. Fabius escaped. My father ends this sad story by saying that his former companion was exiled, and some believed him dead.

"What will you do?" Arrea asked the question haunting me.

Toria continued to cry. She was reaching for me. Sometimes she needed the comfort of her father's strength, but perhaps this time she wanted to comfort me.

I let the scroll fall and took Toria into my arms and held her to my chest. Her tears dried.

"I can't lose the mercenaries," I said, almost to myself. "Without them, I risk a terrible imbalance. If I sever ties with Fabius, I may lose the ability to keep Cinna and Marius in check."

Lucius Cornelius Cinna was an elected consul, and Marius was the most famous Roman who'd ever lived. I had only warriors to justify my claim. The size of my army would directly correlate to the amount of influence I'd have after victory.

Rhea placed a hand on my knee. "Maybe they were never yours to begin with."

I looked at her.

"They provide value, yes, but only if they can be counted on. If their loyalty is in question, Fabius's army is not an asset, but a liability."

I ran my fingers through Toria's curly hair.

"I never trusted him completely," I said. "But now . . . his loyalties clearly lie with the highest bidder, and Sulla's allies will always outbid me."

They nodded but said nothing else.

Our tent was silent save the slow crackle of tallow candles.

"I will look him in the eye," I said. "I will get the measure of it and I'll deal with it."

"I think you must," mother agreed. "Take an armed guard with you. Some of your most trusted men."

I rarely disagreed with my mother, but this time I shook my head. "No," I said with conviction. "I cannot allow turning my camp into a battlefield."

Arrea rubbed my back. "Then take Lucius at least," she said.

"Lucius is still in mourning. I cannot trouble him with this now. He's lost too much already."

"Quintus, a treacherous man is a dangerous one. You cannot walk into the lion's den alone," mother pled.

"And yet I must," I said softly.

Neither argued further.

I would have left then and there if I could. It was all I could do to remain on the edge of my bed.

"Get some rest," I said. "Worry not about all this." I gently kissed Toria between the eyes. "Tata will take care of everything. You two just worry about our little one."

Mother extinguished the candle.

I laid back down but kept Toria nestled to my chest with one hand while I held Arrea's with the other.

Sleep wouldn't return, I knew.

I listened to Toria's breathing and my own heartbeat. The pinprick of starlight poked through the roof of our tent, cold and distant.

And I awaited the sun.

I rose instantly when the sun crested above the Latium hills.

As I expected, Somnus did not visit me again in those hours since my mother's revelation. Those terrible words—my father's written words and my mother's stricken voice—echoed in my mind relentlessly.

Fabius. Traitor. Liar. Killer.

I slid my *pugio* into my belt without a sound. I fastened my breastplate and buckled my helmet as quietly as I could manage.

Toria was nestled up beside her mother now. I leaned forward and kissed my daughter on the head, my wife on the cheek.

Outside, the morning cold enveloped our camp in a mist. More of the night snow stuck than I expected, and the chill in the air indicated it wouldn't melt soon.

Campfires crackled to life, and sleepy voices murmured low as men crawled out from their tents. I walked with purpose across our fortifications to the eastern wing, where our mercenaries camped. Frosted snow crunched beneath my boots.

I followed the sound of Fabius's practiced voice until I found him seated by a low fire, a half-dozen mercenaries perched on rocks and empty crates around him.

The eastern sky bloomed pink behind them, casting their silhouettes toward me as I approached.

The men tore at bread and dipped it in porridge between fits of laughter. Fabius's voice rose above the rest, animated and confident.

When I stepped into the circle, they hushed.

"Commander!" Fabius said, his arms open in welcome. "Would you honor us? Sit and eat. Have you heard the tale of when I nearly married a Vestal? It was purely by accident, mind you. I was about to tell."

My stomach twisted when I looked at him, that easy grin on his face, but I kept my voice even. "I need to speak with you. Alone."

He cocked his head to the side. "Is this military business or private?"

I considered it. "Personal matters."

"Ah." He nodded his head. "Well then, we can talk here. We are alone when only my mercenaries are with us. I am them; they are me. What troubles you, my friend?"

I considered pressing the issue. I contemplated dragging him away from his followers and forcing him to talk with me man-to-man.

"What's that in your hand?" he said.

I unfurled the scroll, but it rolled back up the moment I moved my thumb. Instead of reading from it, I tossed it to his feet.

"One of my father's letters. He wrote them while you served together on campaign."

He wore a nostalgic smile. "I remember him scribbling away at these whenever the tribunes spared us a moment."

I offered him a moment to pour over the contents of the letter. His smile didn't falter, but something in his eyes changed.

"I've been wondering when you would read this," he said. "Seems like a fair and accurate account, as far as I can tell." He rolled up the scroll.

"You said you decided not to reenlist, Fabius. You failed to mention you were exiled. You said you were my father's friend, leaving out that you betrayed him."

He shrugged. "Those are the parts I'd be inclined to conceal, nay?"

I gestured to his men. "Do your followers know you're a traitor? Do they know you were exiled for selling out your brothers for coin?"

He shrugged, lackadaisically. "Don't know," he said. He extended the letter to the mercenaries around him, offering it to anyone interested.

They declined and continued chewing on their bread.

"This family of warriors doesn't care about who we were before. About what we've done. That's in my past."

Fabius gestured like he would flick my father's letter into the fire between us but threw it to me instead.

"Your actions made my closest friend an orphan. He grew up without a father because of you."

He winced. "An unintentional side effect of my rash decisions," he said. "I assume you're talking about Faustus Hirtuleius? I was nearly as close with him as your father. I never meant for harm to come to him."

His ignorance stunned me.

"What did you expect would happen when you gave legionary intelligence to Rome's enemies? Did you not expect your brothers to die in the ambush?"

He looked up and considered it. "Battle was coming sooner or later, regardless of my efforts. But you ask what I expected . . ." He pointed back to my camp. "I expected Rome to conquer them, like she always does. Like she *did*, I remind you. We won the battle."

"They. They won the battle," I said.

For the first time he frowned. He crossed his arms and leaned back on his stump. "I fought beside them. I fought just as hard as they did."

"It must have been difficult to fight, so weighed down by the coin you earned with Roman blood."

He took a deep breath and met my gaze. "I'm not proud of what I did," he said. "Nor am I ashamed. I was young and foolish. My pater familias disowned me by the time I grew hair on my chin, probably for the egregious debts I'd accrued." He looked at his men. "Even then, I wasn't very good at dice."

They chuckled.

"I only joined the legion to escape my debtors. But as the campaign continued, I knew I'd have to return home soon enough. I needed coin, and a lot of it. The legion paid me but a fraction of what I owed."

"Instead of facing the just consequences of your actions, you allowed your brothers to suffer for you."

He nodded sadly. "I did." He stood now and pointed my direction. "And believe you me, I have paid for it a hundred times over."

"You're still alive when many others are not because of you. You haven't paid for it yet."

"Are you here to pass judgement then?" He craned his head.

The time came for me to make a decision. Fabius not only admitted his fault but rationalized it. I could not kill him, not here, not with so many of his devoted around him. Could I ask him to put the past behind him, to swear a new oath that his loyalty to me would be stronger than his loyalty to the legion? No. It didn't matter what he did or said now. The veil was torn.

"Your past suffering bears no weight on the present," I said. "I cannot trust you. I need you to leave immediately. If your men will honor their oaths and continue to fight beside me, I will pay them what is owed and they can return to you after we're victorious."

The mercenaries continued to watch me, only half-interested, enjoying their breakfast.

"If they will not fight without you, then I order all of you to break camp and depart by nightfall. The quaestors will ensure everyone is compensated for time served and then our time together will be over."

Fabius warmed his hands over the fire. He exhaled deeply and shook his head. He made his deep disappointment known.

His voice was hardly more than a whisper when he said, "It's earlier than I planned . . . but I suppose it's time."

He whistled once and the mercenaries sprung to their feet.

I took a single step back and reached for my dagger, but some of Fabius's loyalists had come up behind me while we talked.

They seized my arms before I could draw my weapon.

I could shout an order to arms, and my legionaries would come running to my defense. With some fortune, Rome's true soldiers could defeat Fabius's mercenaries. But at what cost?

Instead, I kept my mouth shut. I would find another way out of this. I had to.

As more and more hands clamped down against me, I stopped resisting. Instead, I just stared at Fabius, and he stared back.

"Bind and gag him," Fabius said. "Keep him in my tent until we're ready. Antipater, send word to Consul Octavius. Tell him we'll meet at dusk."

One grabbed my eye patch and covered my good eye with it. They laughed.

Another jerked back my arms and coiled a leather belt around my wrists.

"You are making a mistake, Fabius," I said.

And it was the last thing I said before a dirty strip of cloth was shoved into my mouth and tied around my head.

"Perhaps," he said. "But I made an oath, and this time I plan to honor it. And I also intend to be paid."

SCROLL XXIX

Gavius Sertorius—Three days before the Kalends of March

The torches burned low along the outer courtyard wall, casting long, shifting shadows across the stones. The Athenians called it the *desmoterion*, but it was no more than a burial pit with a door now. Once it had held thieves, beggars, drunkards—men who'd broken civil codes and offended the gods. Now it housed the enemies of Rome.

I wasn't supposed to be here.

The two guards posted outside the main chamber warmed themselves beside a brazier. They looked up sharply as I approached, one gripping his spear, the other brushing crumbs from his beard.

"Tribune," said the older one, bowing stiffly.

"I need to speak to the two prisoners brought in last evening," I said. "Sulla's orders."

The bearded one frowned. "Should we summon the interrogation detachment?"

"No," I said, a little too quickly. "He asked me to handle this personally."

The younger one smirked, thinking he understood. "Ah. One of those kinds of talks."

I didn't correct him. Instead, I took the offered torch and descended the narrow steps into the darkness.

The air grew heavier with each step, rank with filth and fear. The flame guttered as I walked past cell after cell—men chained, curled into corners, their bodies little more than bone. Some stared at me, blank and defeated. Others reached out weakly through the bars, muttering prayers or curses.

Most of them wouldn't live to see another moon.

Finally, I saw them.

Apollonius was kneeling, head bowed, lips moving in silent prayer. Barca sat upright against the wall, half-asleep, his broad frame making the tiny space seem even smaller. His arms were bound in iron, but his posture was one of defiance, not submission.

"Apollonius," I whispered.

He looked up at once, and the weariness in his eyes fell away, replaced by a gentle warmth.

"Gavius," he said, stepping toward the bars. "By the gods, look at you. You've grown." He smiled faintly. "How are you, my boy?"

"I'm not sure," I said honestly. "I wish... I wish things were different."

Apollonius nodded solemnly. "I know."

"I don't understand any of this," I said. "My father. Why did he join traitors? Why would he destroy everything we've sacrificed to build?"

Apollonius didn't speak at first. He simply watched me, those eyes of his as calm and deep as a forest spring.

"I don't have that answer," he said. "But I've known Sertorius for twenty years. One thing I can say with certainty is this: he doesn't act out of vanity. Or selfishness. He acts out of conviction. Even when it costs him everything."

He leaned forward, wrapping his fingers around the rusted

iron bars. "If your father's choices break your heart, know they broke his too—and yet he still believed they were just. He wouldn't have made those choices otherwise."

I swallowed. The knot in my chest made it difficult to breathe.

Barca grunted, raising his head. "I've known a lot of Romans. More than I would've liked. They wear honor like a mask— eager to display it, quick to discard it. But not your father. Honor is carved into his bones."

"Honor? What is honor?" I spoke with more vitriol than I intended.

Apollonius answered softly. "It doesn't mean following orders, not when they change at the whim of whoever currently holds power. It isn't just following the laws dead men scribbled on scrolls. Honor means acting by the highest law inside you. Refusing to yield to fear, to selfishness. *Virtus*. Even when it hurts."

Even when it kills you.

"Is that why you are here?" I asked Barca. "Following *the highest law inside you*?"

He stood, chains clinking. "Your father cares for this man. He was in danger. I came to bring him home."

If I understood correctly, this man—who my father had known less than a year—sacrificed his life to save someone he didn't even know. For my father. That upset me. It almost angered me, though I didn't know why.

"Is that why you helped Gaius Marius escape justice? Is that why you worked with traitors?"

The confusion on his face was apparent, even in the shadows. Then a bitter, unpleasant laugh echoed throughout the *demoterion*.

"Is that what Sulla told you? I never met this Gaius Marius and wouldn't pluck a harp to save him. I have been with your father, mother, grandmother . . . and sister," he said. "Your commander spread this lie to justify hunting us down like dogs. Did Sulla tell you that? Did you know your ancestral home is ash because of him?"

I didn't know. Of course I didn't know. But now that I did, my skin singed with heat—as if I, too, had turned to ash.

I stepped back from the iron bars, as if distance would protect me from the truth or conceal my dismay.

Apollonius and Barca exchanged a look. I didn't know him well enough to interpret the imperceivable changes to his stone-like face. Apollonius, though, loosened his shoulders and exhaled.

"It isn't your fault, Gavius," he said.

"You're mistaken. Sulla told me my father was not a target. Sulla said . . ." The tremor in my voice angered me. "And even if Sulla sent men after you, he had cause. Maybe he received false reports."

But I didn't believe that. My ability to lie—to conceal—impressed me. Perhaps I developed the skill watching my commander.

A thrashing rage fought in my chest, behind my eyes, against restraints, like the chains around Barca's ankles. I contained it, somehow, but it refused to leave despite my words.

"I know you believe that, young Gavius," Apollonius said.

The sagacious old man was wrong for once.

The piercing clatter of Barca's chains flooded the *demoterion*. "Your sister is not a year old and yet she's less gullible than you," he raised his voice. "Wake yourself. If you believe every-thing powerful Romans tell you, you'll not survive long in this world."

I hadn't been spoken to this way since I joined the legion. Yet I wasn't angry with Barca.

Sulla lied to me. After all I'd sacrificed for him, all I'd accom-plished on his behalf. He met my gaze and lied.

Barca was right about trusting others. I knew that now. But

perhaps Barca was the liar. Or was my father, the man I grew up idealizing like a god, the true deceiver?

I couldn't make sense of it now. I wasn't able to distill all this to a simple, indelible truth.

And yet, I still knew what I had to do.

I stepped closer. My voice dropped to a whisper. "What if I could free you before the execution?"

Apollonius stepped back. "No," he said. "Gavius, no. I will not see you throw away your life for ours. We've made our peace."

Barca's expression turned hard. "I sailed an ocean to save your father's friend. Not to watch his son hang in my place."

Apollonius said, "Instead, take the boat waiting for us. Return to Rome and join your father. Return to your family."

I met his gaze. "I'm not leaving. The legion is my family now." I'd said this enough I spoke without indication of remorse or doubt. "I'm not asking your permission," I said. "I'll come back in three nights. You can tell my father I am grateful for all he's done for me. Consider this my parting gift. Unless he alters his course and ends the siege of Rome, we will be enemies."

Apollonius ignored my words and focused instead on my intended actions. "Please reconsider," he said. "Don't let your heart drive you into a grave. Not for two old men."

"I'm not old," Barca muttered, deadpan. "You are old."

Apollonius looked at me again, and there was light in his eyes.

"You're more like your father than you realize," he said. "And he would be proud of the man you're becoming."

I turned and walked back into the darkness, past the other moaning prisoners, past the stink and rot and despair, until I reached the upper stair.

The guards looked up as I returned the torch.

"Learn anything?" the bearded one asked.

I rubbed at my knuckles like they were sore and offered a tired smile. "Some things," I said. "But not enough."

He nodded. "Come back when you want another go."

I didn't answer.

I stepped back into the cool air of the Athenian night, heart racing, mind clear. For the first time in weeks, I knew exactly what I had to do.

SCROLL XXX

Quintus Sertorius—Three days before the Kalends of March, 667 Ab Urbe Condita

The ropes around my wrists bit deep, and the blood in my hands had long since grown cold. But my binds didn't weigh as heavily as my thoughts in the silence.

Fabius and his mercenaries forced me to my feet after sundown. My legionaries had already eaten, shaved, and lain down in their cots for rest, probably wondering why their commander hadn't issued any orders for them.

Word of my absence must have spread. Legionaries came searching, no doubt at Arrea's request. But Fabius, ever the trickster, played the part well. He joked easily, calmed their nerves, and soon I heard their boots crunching away across the dirt.

I lay motionless in a tent—mere feet from where they searched—unable to call out, unable to move.

Come morning, my camp would sound the alarm and search teams would divide to hunt for me. Eventually, Arrea would have no choice but to tell them everything, and they wouldn't be deceived by Fabius another time. But it would be too late.

As Fabius and his mercenaries led me out of our postern gate, I turned back toward camp. The flicker of campfires managed to pierce through my misplaced eye patch. I knew somewhere in that haze my wife was panicking. I could almost hear her panicked heartbeat. And Toria—my precious daughter —might already be reaching for the empty space on our bed where her father should have been.

I stumbled, but Fabius's mercenaries steadied me and pushed me onward.

Once we were far enough from camp no one would hear my shouts, Fabius pulled the cloth from my mouth and returned my eyepatch to its proper place.

I prepared myself for an assault, but none came.

My captors hadn't bound me any harsher than necessity demanded, and they had yet to strike me. No, my betrayer was colder than that, his visage wrapped in a grim, comfortable calm.

We continued to walk in silence under flickering torchlight for a moment.

"You're quiet this evening," Fabius said. "I assumed you would have much to say, much to ask."

We passed beneath a canopy of olive trees along the Via Sacra.

"You've given me a lot to think about."

He clasped his hands behind his back and eased our pace.

"I suppose I have," he said. "Is there any messages you'd like me to relay to your family?"

I almost lost my anger. I wanted to curse him and demand he never speak to my wife, daughter, or mother again, but I resisted the impulse.

"Was this always your plan, Fabius? From the very beginning?"

He didn't answer right away.

He rubbed at the stubble of his jaw and exhaled. "No. No, I don't believe so. I didn't know what would happen in the end," he said. "Sulla hired me to hunt you down but not to kill you.

His request wasn't even for me to capture you. I lied about that too."

"He asked you to report to him," I said.

He nodded. "Sulla wanted you tracked. Those others he sent, the ones we fought in Nursia? He never expected those urchins to capture mighty Sertorius. Sulla wanted you to know you're alone, hunted, and lacking options. He knew your desperation and the desire to protect your family would make you rash. He expected you to raise an army. He anticipated your march on Rome."

I clenched my cold, numb fists. "Sulla has always excelled in the art of deception."

Fabius continued. "He offered me good coin to plant the seeds. But you didn't require encouragement, did you? You would've marched on Rome with or without me. You can't help yourself," he said. "This was perfect for me, for my men. Paid by both sides and earning trust in the process. But I always knew things would escalate to a decision, eventually."

"A decision?" I said. "You weren't certain who you'd side with in the end?"

More than simply betraying me, Fabius expected me to believe he might as well have remained loyal, as likely as flipping a denarius.

"I *could* have been loyal to both." He clenched his jaw. "We could've taken Rome together. You both would've been happy, and I would be rich. But you escalated the timeline."

"Why, by all the gods, would Sulla want us to take Rome?"

"He'd love nothing more than to see your reputation destroyed, to hear the people mock you as they mock him," he said. "He never said anything more, but I can see beneath the surface. He wants you and your allies to take Rome, sow havoc and spill blood, so that when he returns from the East, the people will beg him to slaughter you all. Beg him to conquer Rome and rule it as a king if it only means their loved ones stop dying."

"The Republic will never tolerate Sulla as a king."

He shook his head. "The people don't care who sits on the damn curule chair or what title they use. The plebs want to go about their lives: working, sleeping, eating, and fornicating until they die."

"They may not care now," I said. "But they will care when they perceive all they've lost. Marius is dangerous, but Sulla is capable of far worse depravity."

"We see the world differently, Quintus," he said. "You see cause and effect. You see right and wrong. You seek patterns and meaning. Purpose. You think the world can be whole and clean, ordered properly if you just draw the lines well enough. I see only the probabilities of survival, probabilities of profit, and probabilities of death."

"I believe Rome is worth fighting for," I said.

"Rome?" He spat into the dust, uncharacteristic vitriol in his voice. "Rome is a name we call a long-dead thing. The Republic. The Senate. The people. Gods help us, none of it is *real*. You're not even living in a dream, Sertorius. You're living in the skeleton—the decayed *bones*—of a dream."

I looked at him. "Enlighten me then, Fabius. Tell me what is real to you if this isn't."

The torchlight ahead danced shadows across his face. "Gold. Power. Survival. I stopped pretending anything else matters a long time ago."

"And yet you admired my father," I said. "Your love for him was real, even if nothing else was; I could see it."

He didn't answer.

I spoke to whatever goodness still dwelled inside him. "You fought beside me. You broke bread with my family. You swore loyalty to our cause."

"Aye, I swore to you and to Sulla as well. You'll find, Sertorius, once you break one oath, it's quite easy to break others. People are obsessed with the comfort vows bring them, but they mean nothing. If only you'd realized that, you wouldn't be here.

Instead, you remain willfully blind to the truth, to the nature of man."

We reached a ridge overlooking the city. Even in darkness, Rome glimmered—lanterns flickered in the hands of guards on patrol, oil lamps burned in the upper-story windows of modest insulae.

Fabius seemed uncomfortable with the silence. "You trusted me," he said. "That made it easier. Who do you think our anonymous benefactor was?" He shook his head at my naivety.

Was he suggesting Sulla himself funded my efforts? Why would he do such a thing?

"Your allies will take Rome and then muck everything up. They'll leave it worse than they found it, and Sulla will win in the end. I don't even believe in the Fates and I know this. With or without you. Regardless of my loyalty or betrayal. Probabilities, Sertorius," he said. "You aren't equipped to defeat men like Sulla."

"Because I don't see the world as you do?" I asked.

He nodded. "Precisely."

I said, "Rome is broken, but she isn't dead. If your friends don't have me executed, I'll find a way to restore her."

He sighed. "I used to believe Rome needed men like you. Men like your father," he said. "Now I think you're what destroys it. You're so rigid in your virtue you're unable to bend."

I kept my tone even. "And men like you bend until you snap."

He didn't respond.

We spent the remainder of our walk in silence save boots trodding cobblestone and the clinking of chain mail.

The gates opened, slow and steady, to allow our entry. I watched our movements in the darkness, trying to anticipate where they meant to lead me.

My gods, Fabius and his colleagues were bold. They led me straight to the Forum.

Rounding into Rome's heart, a bloom of torchlight cut

through the dark, casting long shadows before revealing the white robes of the senate. They came flanked by a silent wall of armored guards, the metal of their chain mail catching every flicker of flame like distant lightning on still water.

Consul Octavius stood before them with his arms folded and lips thin as a dagger's edge. Lanterns lined the marble arches, but otherwise all was dark and silent. This isn't how I imagined the Forum when I dreamed of my return. It reminded me more of the night I fought on the steps of the rostra, before our flight.

The flames caught the whites of too many eyes—watching. Waiting. For me.

"My capture changes nothing," I said. "Octavius may execute me if he likes. But our forces will still take Rome. Only now, Marius and Cinna have no one to hold them accountable to their oaths."

"I don't care," Fabius said. "I don't care what comes next so long as I'm paid."

The two parties stopped about one hundred feet apart.

"Well, go on then," I said. "Finish what you started."

He tightened his grip on my arm and led me into the lion's den.

The stone beneath me was slick with ice, gleaming like glass in the pale light. Still, I held my head up and fixed my gaze on the looming statues above as they watched us—mute, judgmental, unconcerned.

The only sound was the measured footfall of Fabius and his men as we neared Consul Octavius and the semicircle of senators behind him. The torchlight flickered over faces both proud and wary. They looked like hunters face-to-face with a wounded —but dangerous—boar.

"That's him. That is Quintus Sertorius." Octavius spoke in the practiced patterns of a patrician. "You've done well, mercenary. For a moment, I doubted your loyalty."

Fabius stopped us a few feet away from the consul and his

party. "Your doubts confirm my skill. I'm thorough in my deception, consul," he said.

Octavius smiled. "As is the creature you've brought me." He eyed me from head to toe. "This is the man who's brought us so much hardship?"

I studied their faces, recalling previous exchanges in the shadows of the Curia and laughter once shared over wine in the *comitium*—before politics became war.

Their eyes reflected no empathy, and mine asked for none.

"I've seen enough from the other two commanders," Fabius said. "Cinna is a dullard, and Marius has half his wits. This is the one you should be worried about. Without him, you can crush the others."

He lied so easily. I knew, and he did, too, they couldn't resist much longer. Our superior forces would take Rome eventually, regardless of who commanded them. The question wasn't whether they would yield but how many citizens would bleed for their pride beforehand.

But Fabius's honeyed words had their desired effect.

"Bring the coin," Octavius said.

A legionary dragged a sack toward us, struggling against its weight. He untied a knot and pulled back the folds to reveal the shimmering gold coins contained inside.

Fabius's grip tightened. He couldn't contain himself.

"May I weigh it?"

Octavius snarled. "I'm the consul of Rome," he said. "Not some lowly thief. Your payment is the amount promised."

"Very well." Fabius shrugged. He led me to within a few steps of Octavius. "Go on, consul," he said. "Take him."

Octavius folded his arms. "Senator or not, he's a commoner. I'll not touch him. Savages like this are as likely to bite your hands as shake them. Guards!" He snapped. "Take him to the carcer."

Fabius released me and I prepared myself.

Remarkably, I felt calm. I had no impulse to curse them or plead my case.

I knew what awaited me—public disgrace, my name dragged through the mud, my accomplishments distorted. They'd beat me, starve me, parade me to trial, and then march me toward the Tarpeian Rock.

And still, I did not resist.

Two guardsmen neared, cautiously reaching out to see what I would do.

Fabius looked up from the sack of coin. "Oh, Consul, I almost forgot."

His blade rang out before he thrust it into a guard.

"Now, now!" Fabius shouted.

I kicked the other guard back and retreated.

Everything blurred around me. Within moments, the binds around my wrists fell.

Octavius and the senators shrieked and scattered like birds from a dropped cage.

Fabius thrust a sword—my sword—into my tingling hands.

"Fight," he said.

The contingent of Roman guards charged. Fabius's mercenaries rushed around us in looser formation, but one no less disciplined, as if they'd prepared for this reversal.

A few of the Roman guards rushed toward me, eager to claim the prize meant for Fabius if they were successful.

Their haste was to be their undoing.

My sword found the first man's ribs, and I twisted it free in a spray of blood.

A mercenary pounced on the other like a wolf unleashed.

The paved stones of the Forum came alive with steel and screams.

Saturn must have watched from his temple on the hill above as the melee of a hundred men fought to the death.

The guard outnumbered us, but they were young. Inexperienced. This wasn't a real battle, but clearly, they'd never seen one. This was the sort of brawl Fabius and his men lived for.

Another guard rushed me. He drove his shield into my body and the breath from my lungs. But this didn't stop me from slashing his leg.

The wound severed his limb above the knee. He collapsed.

The third guard was more fortunate, as he died the moment my sword reached his throat.

As the bulk of the remaining guardsman fled, I heard a cry, one familiar and unfamiliar.

A few mercenaries bolted past me in pursuit, but I turned to find Fabius with a spearhead buried in his gut.

Fabius stumbled back and collapsed. The spearmen above him panicked. He tried to run, but didn't make it far before two mercenaries pounced on his back with blades of their own.

The rest of the guards scattered.

I dropped to a knee beside Fabius.

"Damn it," he said. He took one look at his wound before lying back against the stone. "How's that for a surprise?" He coughed. Blood sputtered up and poured down his cheek.

"You might yet live," I said.

Fabius's mercenaries gathered around, each reaching forward and placing a hand on him.

He clutched the wood of the spear piercing him and tested it.

"No, I'm done," he said. "If there are any gods, they're celebrating."

Seeing the placement of his wound, I knew he was right. The blood pooled up beneath him and ran through the cracks in the Forum's stone.

"If that was your plan all along, you might have let me know," I said.

He tried to answer but coughed up more blood. He grimaced and gritted his teeth before saying, "I'd like to claim it was. It wasn't." He wheezed now, each breath rattling.

"What changed your mind then?"

His gaze moved past me to the stars above Rome. "Not sure, to be honest. Though, I did . . . I did recall your father's maxim."

The mercenaries wept.

"What was the ending?"

His limbs trembled, and he labored for breath between each word. "Fight bravely, serve faithfully, sacrifice everything . . . and die with honor."

"Don't leave us, Fabius," one mercenary said.

"I wasn't quite ready to die." Fabius rolled his head to the side and spit. "But who is? Decided if I was . . . to die . . . better to die well."

"You did," I whispered.

"Someone fetch a healer!" a Thracian mercenary with bloody teeth shouted. "It's not too late."

Fabius chuckled, which caused another fit of coughing.

"*Oi*, it's over. Sound like . . . women. I made you tougher than . . . this, didn't I?" he said. "I have . . . one last . . . order. Go . . . camp. Tell them . . . the Capena Gate open . . . now."

"More fighters will come, but we can open the gates and hold out until reinforcements arrive," a man said behind me.

Two mercenaries sprinted off into the night to deliver his message.

"You broke your vow to Rome and to my father. But you kept your word to me," I said. "If we can open the gates, we can take the city without bloodshed. Without starving the Roman people any longer."

"Just don't . . . don't muck it up. Like . . . like Sulla thinks you will." He took a deep, wheezing breath. "You have what you wanted. If my men don't starve, I . . . do too."

"I'll take care of them," I said.

Fabius didn't require further explanation. He knew I would.

We held his limbs still when he started shaking too much to control.

His men told him goodbye, some sharing a few stories. He

would have laughed if he could, but at least he took his last breath with the hint of a smile on his lips.

Some might say it was more than he deserved, but I was glad of it.

I closed his eyes.

I stood and gave the mercenaries a few moments with their commander. The Palatine was dark, but starlight silhouetted the temples. Most of Rome slept, unaware of what just took place, unaware that Rome itself just changed hands—not by fire and battle but by shadows and sacrifice.

Soon, we opened the gates, and our armies marched in the darkness to join us.

Fabius's last lie saved the city.

SCROLL XXXI

GAVIUS SERTORIUS—THE Kalends of March, 667 Ab Urbe Condita

The moon hung low and yellow over Athens's rooftops, like a god's judgmental, half-shut eye. I crouched in shadows, as I had the past three nights, across from the prison's side entrance. I drew my hood close to my face, to protect me from the chill but also to conceal. I'd left behind any emblem of my rank.

I'd managed so little sleep my mind was starting to escape me, but I forced myself to remain alert. My heartbeat thudded in rhythm with the steady footfall of the changing guard.

The third shift always handled the changing of the guard more lazily than the others. They met near a pavilion across the street from the prison entrance, shared a quick cup of wine, and exchanged the same half-witted gossip about Greek maidens, dice games, and how much they hated the lot they'd drawn for guard shift.

They had little of note to say but seemed to take comfort in their shared plight. Under different circumstances, I'd have addressed them as Tribune Gavius Sertorius and set them straight, but tonight their lack of military bearing was to my favor.

The two guards on third shift began making their way across the dim street, the orange glow of torchlight illuminating only what was just before them. Unlike the other guard shifts who handed the cell keys directly to their successors, these two left the keys dangling from a nail beside the entrance.

"Prepare yourself, lads; the cells are stinking worse every hour," one departing guard said as they met the others.

Now was my only opportunity. Was I fully prepared for this? Unlikely. But the execution was scheduled for the following morning. If I allowed this moment to pass me by, Apollonius and Barca would die within hours.

The departing guardsmen took off their helmets, scratched at their scalps, and grabbed a wineskin.

"I can't imagine it's any worse than last night," another guard said.

"Just wait, you'll have the stench in your nostrils until tomorrow night's shift."

Now. I kept low and moved fast.

I reached the door while the guards continued their errant chatter. My hand nearly held the keys when I heard a voice call out behind me.

"Oi! Who goes there?"

I turned to find the commander of the watch. For three nights I'd watched this exchange take place, and the commander had never been present. He likely appeared unannounced to ensure his guards behaved properly in his absence.

Fortuna spit on me.

I released the keys and faced him, careful to keep my eyes downcast lest he recognize my face.

"Rat catcher," I said quickly. "Imperator's orders."

He placed one hand on the hilt of his gladius and took a step forward.

"Since when do Romans do filthy work like that? We've chattel for that, don't we?"

"Since the last few locals sent in never came out. Imperator says only Romans go in now."

The guard blinked. My lie bounced around his skull like a loose marble. Eventually, it stuck.

"Huh. As you say. On your way then." He waved me on. "Try not to stir them up. Everyone's had enough of their wailing."

I waited for him to turn toward his guard, which immediately stole his attention.

"You four. Position of attention, now!"

That would hold his focus for a moment. I snatched the keys from the wall and hurried inside.

The darkness was even thicker inside than without, the air heavy with mold, rot, and the sour stench of old blood and waste. I took the one hissing torch from the wall and used it to light my way through the damp stone hallways.

Few of the prisoners looked up as I passed, though the moans of those who'd yet to accept death echoed down the corridor like a ghostly song.

I found them.

Barca stirred first, his back still straight despite his days in chains. Apollonius, even thinner than before, rose from where he knelt in prayer.

"Gavius, we hoped you—"

"We need to hurry," I said.

They gathered near the bars of their cage as I fumbled through the keys. My hands trembled; the keys fell through them. The piercing ring against stone sounded like an explosion.

"Here." I held out the torch, which Barca reached through his cage to hold.

I was able to consider the keys more carefully now, but couldn't help but steal a few glances over my shoulder.

I tried the first key. Not a fit. Then the second. Not correct.

The watch commander's scolding would be ending soon, and then the fourth shift would arrive at their posts. If they were observant enough to notice the missing keys, they'd be down here soon.

Fortunately the third key was a match. The heavy iron key found its place and turned with a metal thud.

"Gavius, I must protest one final—" Apollonius started.

"Now." I pulled back the cell door and gestured for them to follow.

The poor captives around us stirred to life and moaned for us to save them.

I took the torch back from Barca and led them through the narrow passageways.

I stopped at the door to steal a glance outside but realized there was no point. Either we would escape or we wouldn't.

Instead, I picked up the pace and began running, expecting the two of them to follow.

From the corner of my eye, I caught the fourth shift guardsmen heading our way.

"Stop! Who's there?" they shouted.

We did not answer but ran harder still.

Steel hissed from scabbards.

"Our ship awaits in Piraeus. Take us there," Barca said, his voice steady despite the speed of our flight.

Soon, a trumpet blared three times. A hundred legionaries would be descending upon us any moment, and my rank would do nothing to protect me against them.

"Here," I shouted.

They followed me into an alleyway, and then onto a street cramped on either side by meager dwellings. We ducked under the tunics hung out on cords to dry and dashed around empty market stalls to break sight.

I'd prepared a route of escape while I watched and waited the past few nights, but we were already completely off course. Now, I could only look up at the moon and hope my sense of direction would lead us west toward the Piraeus Gate.

"Gavius—" Apollonius gasped. He was flagging, huffing, each step labored.

I grabbed him under the arm and half-carried him onward.

"They went this way!"

"I see them."

Barca turned over a stack of crates behind us.

"We're nearly to the gate," I said.

We broke away from the maze of tiny, winding paths into the open. To my immense relief, the gate was open. If I'd attempted the escape even a night prior, we would have found it shut. But Sulla was a man of his word, and he'd promised to open the Piraeus Gate once more as an act of goodwill to the Athenians who lived through our victory.

If we could only reach that gate, Apollonius and Barca would have their freedom. I would figure out my next steps later.

"They are gaining on us!" Barca shouted.

"No, just a bit farther," I said.

But Apollonius, thin as he was, began to weigh down more heavily. He'd eaten nothing for days and little for months. There was no strength left in his limbs.

"Come, Apollonius, we're so close," I said.

I heard the sound of Barca's measured footfall cease. He stopped in his tracks and turned.

"Keep going," he said.

"No," I snapped. "We'll make it. Once we pass through that gate, shadows will conceal us until we reach the port."

"I gave your father my word, and I will not fail him," Barca said. "Go."

Apollonius and I stood frozen for a breath too long.

"Now, damn you!" he barked.

I tightened my hold around Apollonius and set off.

"Come and take me, Roman dogs!" Barca's voice reverberated through the sleeping Greek city.

As we reached the threshold of the gate, I stole one last look over my shoulder.

Barca stood in the middle of the street, facing his assailants, his silhouette framed by torchlight and the glint of Roman steel around him.

He was unarmed and outnumbered fifty to one, but one wouldn't know it to see how the guards hesitated before him.

And then we escaped into the shadow.

The sea breeze stank of blood and rot.

It carried the scent of death down Athens's road, the old path now flanked by crucifixes. They rose like rows of jagged, broken teeth, each one bearing a body in various stages of dying or decomposition.

I stood beside Sulla as if nothing happened the night prior, as if I hadn't led his prisoner to the docks and watched him sail away. I kept my eyes forward, refusing to look at the wretches around me. Sulla, however, looked at each one, his gaze lingering on twitching feet and gaping mouths.

Beside us, a hammer struck a nail. Again. Then again.

I tried to avoid flinching. I refused to let my eyes water, as it would give me away more than a direct admission.

I clenched my jaw and swallowed, ignoring the taste of bile in my throat. The hammer struck again.

"Go in, damn you," a legionary grunted.

"Straight up and down. Your angle is wrong," another replied.

Once they were satisfied, they began the arduous task of raising the cross. It slammed into the pre-dug hole with a bone-jarring thud.

Unlike all the others before him, this man did not cry out. He did not weep or so much as moan.

I felt Sulla's gaze fall on me. Somehow, I knew he was watching. He wanted me to look up.

I obeyed Sulla's unspoken command and looked up at the cross before us where Barca's mangled body hung.

The Numidian warrior's head drooped to his chest, his eyes half closed. Perhaps he'd finally lost consciousness or died. It would have been a mercy. He'd fought off the guards for as long as he could, long enough to allow our escape. But eventually he sustained too many wounds and he fell. But even then, as they bound him, he shouted that death could not have him until it earned him.

Blood ran freely down Barca's dark, weathered arms, but his face remained still.

Until it came to life.

He found Sulla standing there beneath him and snarled with all the rage and power a man can contain in such conditions.

His voice rose like thunder over the moans of the dying men around him.

"You can wait here until the ends of the earth, you coward, but you'll never hear me scream," Barca roared, pulling forward so much I thought he might free himself from the cross and attack.

"You can take my life, but you cannot beat me." He glared at Sulla through swollen eyes. "I win."

The legionary executioners stepped back as if the power of Barca's words might cut them.

Everyone fell silent, even the other prisoners. The sea breeze seemed to slow.

Bloody spittle flew from his split lips as he shouted, "I am Barca, scourge of Sulla, and let all men know that—"

Sulla drew his sword and pierced Barca's ribs in one swift motion. The Numidian warrior's body jerked once and finally stilled.

This was a mercy for Barca. Better to die swiftly than to suffocate over the course of days. But Sulla didn't do this out of kindness. He had promised Barca a slow death, but in the end, Sulla couldn't tolerate the weight of the insults.

Sulla approached me and dried the blood from his gladius on the sleeve of my tunic.

"Look at me," he said.

I met his gaze.

"I'll not ask about your part in this." His voice was calm, soft even. "Because you would either need to lie to my face or tell the truth. Either way, I'd have no choice but to put you on a cross there beside him."

I could not look away, but neither could I stop blinking. I couldn't breathe. I could only remain still as a statue and listen.

"I will forget this betrayal, which did not happen, but only if you swear anew your loyalty to me."

I didn't hesitate. Even a moment's pause could cause doubt.

I knelt and brandished my dagger. I placed it to my palm and dug its edge into my flesh.

"Swear your unending, undying loyalty. . . . Not to your father. Not to your family, your ideals, nor your naïve, youthful notions of justice. Swear an oath of loyalty to the Republic. To Rome. To me."

My heart felt like a stone dropped into a bottomless well, but I didn't delay my reply.

"I swear fealty to you, Imperator Lucius Cornelius Sulla," I said. "Above all else. I will serve you, even unto death."

Sulla smiled. "Rise," he said.

He placed an arm around my shoulders and led me away from the crosses, telling me about all we would accomplish when spring soon arrived.

I pretended to listen. I did not wipe the blood from my palm.

I let it drip.

Like a wound that would never close.

SCROLL XXXII

QUINTUS SERTORIUS—TWO days after the Kalends of March

We took the city, but it didn't yet belong to us.

Fabius's blood had barely dried on the Forum's stone when our legions marched in.

I stood on the rostra and watched our entry. Marius stood to my left, his scant gray hair wild, his cloak damp from the morning mist. His eyes gleamed—not with relief but hunger. Cinna stood on the other side, arms folded, lips pursed tight with the same political caution he always wore like a helmet.

The legionaries sang songs of triumph as they entered, and the centurions allowed it. Some knelt and kissed the stones of the Via Sacra like they'd crossed a desert to find it.

We had taken Rome, and without unnecessary bloodshed. I should have felt triumph but all I felt was . . . weight.

I turned to my colleagues. "I would ask again that you reaffirm your oaths to do no harm to the people of Rome. We cannot use this moment to exact vengeance on our enemies."

Cinna gave a half nod. "I vow to not willingly cause the death of anyone."

I did not like his phrasing. It felt like the practiced words of a lawyer who dances around the use of language.

Marius, however, was more direct.

He spit. "I'll make no more promises. To you or anyone else," he said. "The time for mercy ended when Sulla set our city on fire. He turned Rome into a battlefield. Not Gaius Marius."

I looked away from them. I wouldn't allow them to destroy Rome after I fought so hard to take it. But I also couldn't talk them out of it. I would remain wary, watchful. And stop them by any means necessary if it came to that.

More soldiers entered. Some were mine, veterans from Gaul, Greece, or the war against the Italian allies. Others served Marius, easy to identify by the roughness of their appearance and their ravenous eyes. And then there were Fabius's mercenaries, who celebrated with wine and song as they always did but perhaps a touch more somber now without their commander.

After the columns found their place in the Forum, the rest of the camp began to flow in. Trains of civilians—wives, children, slaves, craftsman.

I saw Lucius among them.

He moved slowly, pushed along by the crowd, as though half carved in stone. Usually he shaved slick every morning, but now his face was concealed by a scraggly beard. He wore no armor— just a black tunic, plain and threadbare, the color of mourning.

Octavius and his loyalists had retreated to the Janiculum at the announcement of our entry. At least for now, they still maintained the guise of legitimacy.

And I did not trust the men beside me.

Our fight was not over, and the path before me was fraught with terror—but I worried about Lucius the most.

Not far behind him, I spotted my family.

Rhea. My mother. My conscience. My guiding light, who never failed to lead me even in her silence.

Arrea. My wife. My anchor. The flag I fought for. The home

that I could return to no matter how much burned down around me.

And in Arrea's arms, my daughter. Little Toria. Half asleep and half curious about the clamor of the conquering army around her.

The sight of them, knowing they were in Rome again and safe for now, cut through the fog inside me like the first warm day of spring, which was almost upon us. I reminded myself I fought for them. They were why I risked everything. Not to sit on marble chairs in the Curia or to have my name carved into stone beside other dead men.

I fought to build a Rome they deserved. A Rome that deserved them.

Marius would seek vengeance.

Cinna would seek power.

And the Senate would scheme in shadow until Sulla's inevitable return at the head of his legions.

But, as I watched our celebration begin, I renewed the unspoken vow to myself. The vow I made long ago: to hold the line against Rome's enemies at all cost.

To stand between tyranny and silence, no matter the cost.

We had taken Rome, but the harder victory—the one that mattered most—remained before me.

I would not rest until the Republic was reborn, not as it was before Sulla marched his troops to our gates. No, until the Republic was born as it could be. As it ought to be.

For my daughter.

For my people.

For Rome.

To receive Vincent's spinoff series "The Marius Scrolls" for FREE just scan the QR code below!

YEARS

- Ab Urbe Condita - Literally translates to "from the founding of the City".
- The traditional date given to Rome's founding is 753 B.C.
- Therefore: 88 B.C. = 666 Ab Urbe Condita.

MONTHS

- July and August hadn't yet been renamed for Julius Caesar and August.
- In *The Sertorius Scrolls*, Quintilis and Sextilis are used instead, respectively.
- All other months are recognizable in their modern translation.

DAYS

- Instead of counting days in a straight sequence, the Romans counted from three fixed points:
    - Kalends - the first day of the month
    - Nones - Varied by month, usually the 5th or the 7th
    - Ides - Varied by month, usually 13th or 15th
- Days were expressed in relation to these markers. For example:
    - May 3rd = Two days after the Kalends of May
    - March 14th = The day before the Ides of March

DRAMATIS PERSONAE

Apollonius—freed *servus* of Quintus Sertorius, close friend, and mentor

Arrea—wife of Quintus Sertorius, freed slave

Barca—former gladiator, *lanista* of a successful gladiator school

Caecilia (Metella)—sister of Metellus Pius and daughter of Metellus Numidicus. Betrothed to Lucius Cornelius Sulla

Caesar, Gaius Julius—a child at the time of the Civil War, nephew by marriage of Gaius Marius. Son of man by same name. Future dictator

Catalina, Lucius Sergius—brother-in-law of Marcus Marius Gratidianus, a military tribune under Gnaeus Pompeius Strabo

Catulus, Quintus Lutatius—elderly statesman and former consul of the Roman Republic. Serving as the father of the senate (*princeps senatus*) during the Social War

Cicero, Marcus Tullius—serving as a junior tribune under Gnaeus Pompeius Strabo. A friend of Gavius Sertorius. Later becomes famous as an orator, writer, and statesman

Cinna, Lucius Cornelius—former ally of Gaius Marius, a political nonentity with ties to both senatorial parties during the Social War.

Crassus, Marcus Licinius—the son of a wealthy patrician family with growing ambitions. An ally of Lucius Cornelius Sulla

Fabius—mercenary captain with a small army under his command. Served with Quintus Sertorius's father decades previously.

Gratidianus, Marcus Marius—nephew of Gaius Marius, cousin of Marcus Tullius Cicero, brother-in-law of Lucius Sergius Catalina. Serving as a tribune under Gnaeus Pompeius Strabo

Hirtuleius, Lucius—childhood friend of Quintus Sertorius. Served alongside Quintus in the war against the Cimbri and Teutones, and in Greece

Insteius, Aulus—childhood friend of Quintus Sertorius. Served in Greece alongside Quintus. Twin brother of Spurius

Insteius, Spurius—childhood friend of Quintus Sertorius. Served in Greece alongside Quintus. Twin brother of Aulus

Juba—prince of Numidia, who has been held captive by the Romans since his youth. Captured by Gaius Papius Mutilus during the Social War

Lucullus, Lucius Licinius—*tribunus laticlavius* (senior tribune)

under the command of Lucius Cornelius Sulla during the time of the Social War. Friend of Gavius Sertorius

Marius, Gaius—former consul (six times previously) who was considered the "Third Founder of Rome" for his success in defeating the Cimbri and Teutones. Uncle of Gaius Julius Caesar. Bitter rival of Lucius Cornelius Sulla

Marius the Young, Gaius—son of the former consul

Mithridates—King of Pontus, a powerful kingdom in northern Anatolia. He is mounting a war against the Roman Republic which is expected to begin soon. Mithridates' riches make command of the war against him desirable to many Roman generals

Mutilus, Gaius Papius—a Samnite noble who was elected "consul" by the rebelling Italic League during the Social War. He leads the main Samnite army in southern and central Italy

Pius, Quintus Caecilius Metellus—a Roman statesman from an important family, serving under Gnaeus Pompey Strabo. Son of Metellus Numidicus, the enemy of Gaius Marius

Pollux—dog of Quintus Sertorius, brought back with him from Greece. Named after the twin gods Castor and Pollux as a reference to a friend, Castor, who served with Sertorius in Greece

Pompey, Gnaeus—son of Gnaeus Pompeius Strabo, and important officer under his father's command

Rhea—mother of Quintus Sertorius, grandmother of Gavius Sertorius

Rufus, Publius Rutilius—former consul, exiled on false charges for extorting the provinces

Rufus, Quintus Pompeius—cousin of Gnaeus Pompeius Strabo, political ally and friend of Lucius Cornelius Sulla

Sertorius, Gavius—a son of Titus Sertorius by birth. After his father's death in battle and his mother's suicide, he was adopted by his uncle Quintus Sertorius. Raised by Arrea, wife of Quintus Sertorius, while his adoptive father was away at war

Sertorius, Proculus—deceased father of Quintus and Titus Sertorius, husband of Rhea. An influential local magistrate in the village of Nursia

Sertorius, Quintus—protagonist of The Sertorius Scrolls. Son of Proculus Sertorius and Rhea, brother of Titus Sertorius. Husband of Arrea and adoptive father of Gavius Sertorius. Former officer of the legions with over a dozen years of military service

Sertorius, Titus—deceased brother of Quintus Sertorius. Son of Proculus Sertorius and Rhea. Birth father of Gavius Sertorius

Spartacus—a young gladiator of Thracian decent. Fighting in Barca's ludus

Strabo, Gnaeus Pompeius—a prominent member from a noble family in Picenum. Despite being a "new man," he levied a large army from those local to Picenum and fought against rebel tribes there. Elected Consul during the Social War

Sulla, Lucius Cornelius—a rising politician and military commander. Born to a tarnished but patrician family. A legatus at the time of the Social War. A bitter rival of Gaius Marius

Sura—Quintus Sertorius's faithful warhorse since the Cimbrian War. Named after the late mother of Lucius Hirtuleius

Sulpicius, Publius (Rufus)—an ambitious young man from a patrician family who seeks a political revolution and the alleviation of his many debts. Ally of Gaius Marius

Toria—daughter of Quintus Sertorius and Arrea, short for "Sertoria"

GLOSSARY

GENERAL

Ab Urbe Condita—Roman phrase and dating system "from the founding of the city." The Ancient Romans believed Rome was founded in 753 BC, and therefore this year is AUC 1. As such, 107–106 BC would correspond to 647–648 AUC.

Acropolis—The ancient citadel of Athens.

Agnomen—A form of nickname given to men for traits or accomplishments unique to them. Many conquering generals received agnomen to designate the nation they had conquered, such as Africanus, Macedonicus, and Numidicus.

Amicus (f. Amica)—Latin for "friend." The vocative form (when addressing someone) would be amice.

Arausio—the location of a battle in which Rome suffered a great loss. Numbers were reported as high as ninety thousand Roman casualties. Sertorius and Lucius Hirtuleius barely escaped with their lives, and Sertorius's brother Titus died upon the battlefield.

Ave—Latin for "hail" or "hello."

Balatrones—"jesters," an insult.

Boni—Literally "good men." They were a political party prevalent in the Late Roman Republic. They desired to restrict the power of the popular assembly and the tribune of the plebs while extending the power of the Senate. The title "Optimates" was more common at the time, but these aristocrats often referred to themselves favorably as the boni. They were natural enemies of the populares.

Buccina (pl. Buccinae)—A C-shaped Roman military trumpet.

Cac—Latin for "shit."

Caldarium—hot baths.

Carcer—a small prison, the only one in Rome. It typically held war captives awaiting execution or held those deemed as threats by those in political power.

Carnifex—Latin for "executioner."

Carthage—an ancient city that struggled against Rome for supremacy of the Mediterranean Sea until it was completely destroyed in 146 BC.

Carthago delenda est—"Carthage must be destroyed," a saying made famous by Cato the Censor.

Centuriate Assembly—one of the three Roman assemblies. It met on the Field of Mars and elected the Consuls and Praetors. It could also pass laws and acted as a court of appeals in certain capital cases. It was based initially on 198 centuries, and was structured in a way that favored the rich over the poor, and the aged over the young.

Century—Roman tactical unit made of eighty to one hundred men.

Cimbri—a tribe of northern invaders with uncertain origins that fought Rome for over a decade. Sertorius began his career by fighting them.

Client—A man who pledged himself to a patron (*see also* **patron**) in return for protection or favors.

Cocina—Latin for "kitchen."

Cognomen—the third personal name given to an ancient Roman, typically passed down from father to son. Examples are Caepio, Caesar, and Cicero.

Cohort—Roman tactical unit made of six centuries (*see also* **century**), or 480–600 men. The introduction of the cohort as the standard tactical unit of the legion is attributed to Marius's reforms.

Collegium (pl. Collegia)—Any association or body of men with something in common. Some functioned as guilds or social clubs, others were criminal in nature.

Comitiatus (pl. Comitia)—a public assembly that made decisions, held elections, and passed legislation or judicial verdicts.

Conium Maculatum—hemlock, used as a poison.

Contiones (pl. Contio)—a public assembly that did not handle official matters. Discussions could be held on almost anything, and debates were a regular cause for a contiones to be called, but they did not pass legislation or pass down verdicts.

Contubernalis (pl. Contubernales)—A military cadet assigned to the commander specifically. They were generally considered officers but held little authority.

Contubernium—The smallest unit in the Roman legion. It was led by the decanus (*see also* **decanus under Ranks and Positions**).

Cum Ordine Seque—lit. "follow in good order."

Denarius (pl. Denarii)—standard Roman coin introduced during the Second Punic War.

Dignitas—a word that represents a Roman man's reputation and his entitlement to respect. Dignitas correlated with personal achievements and honor.

Dominus (f. Domina)—Latin for "master." A term most often used by slaves when interacting with their owner, but it could also be used to convey reverence or submission by others. The vocative form would be domine.

Domus—the type of home owned by the upper class and the wealthy in Ancient Rome.

Ede Faecum—lit., "eat shit."

Elysium—concept of the afterlife, oftentimes known as the Elysium Fields or Elysium Plains.

Equestrian—Sometimes considered the lesser of the two aristocratic classes (*see also* **patrician**) and other times considered the higher of the two lower-class citizens (*see also* **plebeian**). Those in the equestrian order had to maintain a certain amount of wealth or property to remain in the class.

Es mundus excrementi—lit. "you are a pile of shit."

Faex—Latin for "shit."

Falernian wine—The most renowned and sought-after wine in Rome at this time. The grapes were harvested from the foothills of Vesuvius.

Filii Remi—lit. "Sons of Remus," a name used by Roman citizens who opposed Roman rule during the Social War.

Filius Canis—lit. "Son of a bitch."

Garum—fish sauced beloved by the Romans.

Gerrae—"Nonsense!" An exclamation.

Gladius (pl. Gladii)—The standard short-sword used in the Roman legion.

Gracchi—Tiberius and Gaius Gracchus were brothers who held the rank of tribune of the plebs at various times throughout the second century BC. They were political revolutionaries whose attempts at reforms eventually led to their murder (or in one case, forced suicide). Tiberius and Gaius were still fresh in the minds of Romans in Sertorius's day. The boni feared that another politician might rise in their image, and the populares were searching for Gracchi to rally around.

Ides—the 15th day of "full months" and the 13th day of hollow ones, one day earlier than the middle of each month.

Impluvium—A cistern or tank in the atrium of the domus that collects rainwater from a hole in the ceiling above.

Instate Hostibus—lit. "Chase the enemy!"

Insula (pl. Insulae)—Apartment complexes. They varied in size and accommodations but generally became less desirable the higher up the insula one went.

Jupiter's Stone—A stone on which oaths were sworn.

Kalends—The first day of the Ancient Roman month.

Latrina—Latin for "bathroom."

Latrunculi—lit. "Game of Brigands," a popular board game of sorts played by the Romans. It shares similarities with games like chess or checkers.

Lorica Hamata—chainmail armor worn by Roman legionaries

Lorica Musculata—anatomical cuirass (breastplate) worn by Romans made to fit the wearer's male human physique.

Mos Maiorum—lit. "the way of the ancestors," this is the unwritten code of social norms used by the Romans.

Murum Aries Attigit—lit. "the ram has touched the wall." This expression was used to indicate that it is time to strike, or that it is too late to turn back.

Nomen—the hereditary or family name of the Romans. Examples are Sertorius, Julius (as in Julius Caesar), or Cornelius (as in Lucius Cornelius Sulla).

Nones—the 7th day of "full months" and 5th day of hollow ones, 8 days—9 by Roman reckoning—before the Ides in every month.

October Horse—A festival that took place on October 15th. An animal was sacrificed to Mars, which designated the end of the agricultural and military campaigning season.

Optimates—*see* **boni**.

Oscan—a language spoken by several Italian tribes.

Passum—a raisin based wine, originally developed in ancient Carthage.

Pasteli—honey cakes with sesame seeds, a beloved Greek pastry.

Paterfamilias—the male head of the family or household.

Patrician—a social class made up of Rome's oldest families.

Patron—A person who offers protection and favors to his clients (*see also* **clients**), in favor of services of varying degrees.

Perduellis—lit. "public enemy", or "enemy of the state". Closely associated with the crime of *perduellio,* Rome's earliest form of treason.

Peristylum—An open courtyard containing a garden within the Roman domus.

Pilum (pl. Pila)—The throwing javelin used by the Roman legion. Gaius Marius changed the design of the pilum in his reforms. Each legionary carried two and typically launched them at the enemy to begin a conflict.

Plebeian—Lower-born Roman citizens, commoners. Plebeians were born into their social class, so the term designated both wealth and ancestry. They typically had fewer assets and less land than equestrians, but more than the proletariat. Some, like the Metelli, were able to ascend to nobility and wealth despite their plebeian roots. These were known as "noble plebeians" and were not restricted from any power in the Roman political system.

Popular assembly—A legislative assembly that allowed plebeians to elect magistrates, try judicial cases, and pass laws.

Posca—vinegar wine, typically consumed by the lower class and considered to be of poor quality.

Praenomen—the first name given to Roman males, generally eight days after their birth. Examples are Gaius, Quintus, and Lucius.

Proletariat—one of the lowest social and economic classes, comprised of the poor and landless.

Res Publica—"Republic," the sacred word that encompassed everything Rome was at the time. More than just a political system, res publica represented Rome's authority and power. The Republic was founded in 509 BC, when Lucius Brutus and his fellow patriots overthrew the kings.

Roma Invicta—lit. "unconquered Rome," an inspirational motto used by the Romans.

Salve—Latin for "hail," or "hello."

Salvete—a casual, familiar greeting.

Sancrosanctitas—a level of religious protection offered to certain political figures and religious officials.

Saturnalia—A festival held on December 17 in honor the Roman deity Saturn.

Scutum (pl. Scuta)—Standard shield issued to Roman legionaries.

Servus (pl. Servi)—Slave or servant.

Sesterces—an ancient Roman coin, roughly $.50 in today's value.

Sibylline Books—a collection of oracular texts the Romans considered to be prophetic.

Sinite Milites Exsultare—lit. "Allow soldiers to rejoice."

Stola (pl. Stolae)—the traditional garment of Roman women, similar to the toga worn by men.

Taberna (pl. Tabernae)—Could be translated as "tavern," but tabernae served several different functions in Ancient Rome. They served as hostels for travelers, occasionally operated as brothels, and offered a place for people to congregate and enjoy food and wine.

Tablinum—A form of study or office for the head of a household. This is where he would generally greet his clients at his morning levy.

Tata—Latin term for "father," closer to the modern "daddy."

Tecombre—The military order to break from the testudo formation and revert to their previous formation.

Tesserae—a common game of dice. Rolling three sixes was called a "Venus" and was considered the highest score one could achieve.

Testudo—In military terms, the "tortoise" formation. The command was used to provide additional protection by linking scuta together.

Teutones—a tribe of northern invaders with uncertain origins that fought Rome for over a decade. Along with the Cimbri, they nearly defeated Rome. Sertorius began his career by fighting these tribes.

Toga virilis—Lit. "toga of manhood." It was a plain white toga worn by adult male citizens who were not magistrates. The donning of the toga virilis represented the coming of age of a young Roman male.

Torna Mina—lit. "Turn and charge!"

Tribe—Political grouping of Roman citizens. By Sertorius's time, there were thirty-six tribes, thirty-two of which were rural, four of which were urban. This term is also used to describe the various Italian tribes, some of which were Roman citizens, others were allied with Rome but not citizens, and others still were hostile toward Rome.

Triclinium—The dining room, which often had three couches set up in the shape of a U.

Triumph—A parade and festival given to celebrate a victorious general and his accomplishments. He must first be hailed as imperator by his legions and then petition the Senate to grant him the Triumph.

Vale—Latin for "farewell," or "be well."

Valetudinarium (pl. Valetudinaria)—a hospital, typically present in Roman military camps.

Via (pl. Viae)—Latin for "Road," typically a major path large enough to travel on horseback or by carriage.

Zeno—The founder of Stoic philosophy. Sertorius was a devoted reader of Zeno's works.

DEITIES

Apollo—Roman god adopted from Greek mythology. Twin brother of Diana. He has been connected with archery, music and dance, and the sun.

Asclepius—The Greek god of medicine. There was a temple to Asclepius overlooking the Tiber River, and this is where Rabirius and many other wounded veterans congregated.

Bacchus—The Roman god of wine, orchards, and fruit. Sometimes connected with madness, ecstasy, and fertility. His Greek equivalent is Dionysus.

Bellona—The Roman goddess of war and the consort of Mars (*see also* **Mars**). She was also a favored patron goddess of the Roman legion.

Bona Dea—the "Good Goddess," she was connected with chastity and fertility among married women. The term was occasionally used as an exclamation.

Castor—Along with Pollux, twin half-brothers in both Greek and Roman mythology. Sometimes both are referred to as mortal, other times they are both considered divine. Most often, one is considered to be born mortal and the other divine, with the latter asking Jupiter to make them both divine so they could stay together forever. They were eventually transformed into the constellation Gemini (meaning "twins"). Their temple in Rome's forum was extremely important and sometimes facilitated meetings of the senate and elections.

Cybele—*see* **Magna Mater**

Diana—The Roman goddess of hunters, the forest, and the moon. Twin sister of Apollo. Quintus Sertorius gives her credit for saving him in a previous battle, and therefore he considers her his patron goddess. Her Greek equivalents are Artemis and Hecate.

Dis Pater—The Roman god of death. He was often associated with fertility, wealth, and prosperity. His name was often shortened to Dis. He was nearly synonymous with the Roman god Pluto or the Greek god Hades.

Fortuna—Roman goddess considered to be the personification of luck, chance, and fate. Lucius Cornelius Sulla believes he is beloved by Fortuna.

Gaia—Greek Goddess considered to be the personification of the earth.

Hermes—The Greek god of messengers, travelers, orators, and occasionally thieves. His Roman equivalent would be Mercury.

Janus—the Roman god of beginnings, gates, duality. He is depicted with two faces, one looking back and the other forward. The month of January was named after him, which represented an opportunity to reflect on the previous year and look forward to the next.

Jupiter—The Roman king of the gods. He was the god of the sky and thunder. All political and military activity was sanctioned by Jupiter. He was often referred to as Jupiter Capitolinus for his role in leading the Roman state, or Jupiter Optimus Maximus (lit. "the best and greatest"). His "black stone" was something to be sworn on.

Magna Mater—"Great Mother," she was adopted by the Romans in the late third century BC from the Anatolians. She was connected with and sometimes assimilated with aspects of Gaia and Ceres.

Mars—The Roman god of war. He was the favored patron of many legionaries and commanders. Unlike his Greek equivalent, Ares, he was respected and considered a "pater" of all Romans.

Mercury—*see* **Hermes**

Pluto—the Roman god of the underworld and the afterlife. His Greek equivalent was Hades, but Pluto often represented a more positive concept of the god.

Pollux—*see* **Castor**

Proserpina—the Roman goddess of the underworld. Her Greek equivalent was Persephone. She was connected with female and agricultural fertility, as well as the springtime.

Saturn—God of the Roman Capitol, time, wealth, and agriculture. He was the father of many Roman gods, including Jupiter. His Greek equivalent was Cronus. His temple in Rome's forum at the base of the Capitoline Hill was extremely important throughout Roman history.

Somnus—Roman god who was the personification of sleep. His Greek counterpart would be Hypnos.

Tiberinus—the god of the Tiber river.

Venus—The Roman goddess of love, beauty, desire, sex, and fertility. Her Greek equivalent was Aphrodite.

Vulcan—The Roman god of fire, metalworking, and the forge. He was often depicted with a blacksmith's hammer and a lame leg due to a childhood injury. He was considered to be the ugliest of the gods but was at times a consort of **Venus**, the goddess of beauty.

Zephyrus—Greek god of the West Wind. He was associated with flowers, springtime, favorable winds, and speed. His Roman equivalent was Favonius.

BUILDINGS, ROADS, AND LANDMARKS

Appian Way (Via Appia)—the oldest and most important of Rome's roads, linking Rome with farther areas of Italy.

Aqua Marcia—the most important of Rome's aqueducts at this time. Built in 144–140 BC.

Argiletum—a route leading to the Roman forum.

Basilica Aemilia—located at the juncture of the Via Sacra and the Argiletum, this was one of the most celebrated buildings in Rome.

Basilica Porcia—the first named basilica in Rome, built by Cato the Censor in 184 BC, it was the home of the ten tribunes of the plebs.

Basilica Sempronia—built in 170 BC by the father of Tiberius and Gaius Gracchus. It was a place often used for commerce.

Circus Maximus—a massive public stadium that hosted chariot races and other forms of entertainment. It's speculated that the stadium could have held as many as 150,000 spectators.

Cloaca Maxima—the massive sewer system beneath Rome.

Comitium—a meeting area outside of the Curia Hostilia. The rostrum stood at its helm.

Curia Hostilia—The Senate House. The Curia was built in the seventh century BC and held most of the senatorial meetings throughout the Republic, even in Sertorius's day.

Forum—The teeming heart of Ancient Rome. There were many different forums, in various cities, but most commonly the Forum refers to the center of the city itself, where most political, public, and religious dealings took place.

Field of Mars—"Campus martius" in Latin. This was where armies trained and waited to deploy or to enter the city limits for a Triumph.

Fucine Lake—known as Fucinus Lacus to the Romans, this was a large lake in central Italy.

Liris River—one of the primary rivers of central Italy.

Mare Nostrum—the Roman name for the Mediterranean Sea. This means "our sea" in Latin.

Ostia—Rome's port city, it lay at the mouth of the river Tiber.

Pillar of Hercules—a phrase used to describe the promontories that flank the Strait of Gibraltar, which connects Spain to Africa.

Porta Triumphalis—the triumphal gate. Triumphing armies would ceremoniously enter here.

Regia—a building just off the Via Sacra, the Regia was originally the main headquarters for the kings of Rome. By the late Republic, the Regia was used as the residence for the Pontifex Maximus, the highest religious official in Rome.

River Reno—a river in northern Italy, near Mutina.

Rostrum (pl. Rostra)—A speaking platform in the Forum made of the ships of conquered foes.

Senaculum—a meeting area for senators outside of the senate house, where they would gather before a meeting began.

Servian wall—the defensive barrier around the city of Rome, constructed in the 4th century BC.

Subura—a rough neighborhood near the Viminal and Quirinal hills. It was known for violence and thievery, as well as for the fires that spread because of the close proximity of its insulae.

Tarpeian Rock—a place where executions were held. Criminals of the highest degree and political threats were thrown from this cliff to their inevitable deaths.

Temple of Asclepius—located on the Tiber Island, it was a temple of healing. The sick and ailing made pilgrimages here in hope of healing.

Temple of Bellona—dedicated to the consort of Mars and goddess of war, this was a temple often used for meetings of the Senate when they needed to host foreign emissaries or meet with returning generals awaiting a triumph. It lay outside the city limits but close to the Servian wall.

Temple of Castor and Pollux—oftentimes referred to simply as "Temple of Castor," it remained at the entrance of the Forum by the Via Sacra. It was often used for meetings of the senate, as it was actually larger than the Curia. Speeches were often given from the temple steps as well.

Temple of Concordia (Concord)—a temple devoted to peace and reunification in the Roman Forum. It often held meetings of the senate.

Temple of Jupiter Capitolinus (Optimus Maximus)—a temple devoted to Rome's patron God, which resided on the Capitoline hill. It was sometimes referred to as the "Capitol."

Temple of Saturn—a temple of deep religious significance that lay at the foot of the Capitoline hill in the Roman Forum. Sacrifices were often held here following a triumph, if the generals didn't surpass it to sacrifice at the aforementioned Temple of Jupiter.

Tiber River—a body of water that connected to the Tyrrhenian Sea and flowed along the western border of Rome. The victims of political assassinations were unceremoniously dumped here rather than receive proper burial.

Tullianum—a prison for captives awaiting death. (*See* **Carcer under General Glossary**.)

Via Appia—*see* **Appian Way**.

Via Cassia—the northern road from Rome, this road passed through Etruria and was one of the main routes for travelers heading north.

Via Latina—"Latin road," led from Rome southeast.

Via Sacra—the main road within in the city of Rome, leading from the Capitoline hill through the forum, with all of the major religious and political buildings on either side.

Via Salaria—"Salt Road" led northeast from Rome. This was the path Sertorius would have taken to and from his home in Nursia.

Via Triumphalis—the "triumphal way" leading from the Field of Mars to the Capitoline hill. Roman generals awarded a triumph would take this road during their triumphal ceremony.

RANKS AND POSITIONS

Aedile—Magistrates who were tasked with maintaining and improving the city's infrastructure. There were four, elected annually: two plebeian aediles and two curule aediles.

Aquilifer—the eagle bearer of each Roman legion.

Augur—A priest and official who interpreted the will of the gods by studying the flight of birds.

Auxiliary—Legionaries without citizenship. At this time, most auxiliaries were of Italian origin but later encompassed many different cultures.

Centurion—An officer in the Roman legion. By the time Marius's reforms were ushered in, there were six in every cohort, one for every century. They typically led eighty to one hundred men. The most senior centurion in the legion was the "primus pilus," or first-spear centurion.

Consul—The highest magistrate in the Roman Republic. Two were elected annually to a one-year term. The required age for entry was forty, although exceptions were occasionally (and hesitantly) made.

Decanus (pl. Decani)—"Chief of ten," he was in a position of authority over his contubernium, a group of eight to ten men who shared his tent.

Evocati—An honorary term given to soldiers who served out their terms and volunteered to serve again. Evocati were generally spared a large portion of common military duties.

Flamen Dialis—Priest of Jupiter Optimus Maximus.

Hastati—Common front line soldiers in the Roman legion. As a result of the Marian Reforms, by Sertorius's time, the term *hastati* was being phased out and would soon be obsolete.

Imperator—A Roman commander with imperium (*see also* **imperium**). Typically, the commander would have to be given imperium by his men.

Immunes—those who were exempt from physical labor within the Roman legion.

Legatus (pl. Legati)—The senior-most officer in the Roman legion. A legatus generally was in command of one legion and answered only to the general. The vocative form would be legate.

Legion—the largest military unit of the Roman military. A legion was comprised of roughly 4,800 men at the time of Sertorius.

Legionary (pl. Legionarii)—soldiers which made up the Roman legion.

Medici Optimi—the senior most medicus.

Medicus (pl. Medici)—The field doctor for injured legionaries.

Military Tribune—officer of the Roman legions. They were, in theory, elected by the popular assembly, and there were six assigned to every legion. By late second century BC, however, it was not uncommon to see military tribunes appointed directly by the commander.

Optio (pl. Optiones)—second in command of a legionary century, they served directly under a centurion and were generally considered next in line if the centurion was to fall.

Pontifex Maximus—The highest priest in the College of Pontiffs. By Sertorius's time, the position had been highly politicized.

Pontiff—A priest and member of the College of Pontiffs.

Praetor—The second-most senior magistrate in the Roman Republic. There were typically six elected annually, but some have speculated that there were eight elected annually by this time.

Prefect—A high-ranking military official in the Roman legion.

Princeps Senatus—"Father of the Senate," or the first among fellow senators. It was an informal position but came with immense respect and prestige.

Proconsul—A Roman magistrate who had previously been a consul. Often, when a consul was in the midst of a military campaign at the end of his term, the Senate would appoint him as proconsul for the remainder of the war.

Publicani—Those responsible for collective public revenue. They made their fortunes through this process. By Sertorius's time, the Senate and censors carefully scrutinized their activities, making it difficult for them to amass the wealth they intended.

Quaestor—An elected public official and the junior-most member of the political course of offices. They served various purposes but often supervised the state treasury and performed audits. Quaestors were also used in the military and managed the finances of the legions on campaign.

Rex Sacrorum—A senatorial priesthood, the "king of the sacred." Unlike the Pontifex Maximus, the rex sacrorum was barred from military and political life. In theory, he held the religious responsibility that was once reserved for the kings, while the consuls performed the military and political functions.

Tribune of Plebs—Elected magistrates who were designated to represent the interests of the people. Sometimes called the Plebeian Tribune or People's Tribune.

Tribunus Laticlavius—lit. "the broad-stripped tribune" the senior of the six tribunes assigned to each legion.

CITIES AND NATIONS

Acerrae—A Roman colony in Campania. Acerrae would serve as a base of operations for the Romans throughout the war. Samnite general Papius Mutilus besieged the city early in the war.

Aesernia—An important Roman colony in Samnite territory, it remained loyal to Rome despite being surrounded by rebels. It was quickly besieged by Samnite armies, and those within were faced with starvation and disease.

Alba Fucensis—sometimes called Alba Fucens and othertimes referred to simply as Alba, this city was located near the Fucine Lake and Marsi territory. The city remained loyal to Rome but was swiftly attacked by the rebels.

Asculum—The city situated in Picenum was the first to rebel against Rome. They rounded up and butchered all Roman citizens, which sparked the Social War. This city was a target for both sides throughout the duration of the war.

Capua—the primary city of the Campania region and therefore an important stronghold for Rome during the war. The city was specifically known for its gladiator spectacles.

Cisalpine Gaul—The portion of Gaul on the Italian side of the Alps. Sometimes referred to as "Nearer Gaul." It was conquered in the third century BC. Although it comprised much of what is today northern Italy, it continued to be administered as its own province.

Corduba—A city in Hispania, it was originally conquered by the Romans in 206 BC. A Roman colony was established there roughly fifty years later.

Corfinium—A city situated within the tribal territory of the Paeligni (and close to the Marsi), it was chosen as the new "capital" for the Italic League when they rebelled against Rome. It's military positioning was the cause of this distinction. It was renamed **Italica** at the onset of the war.

Firmum—An important city within Picenum. It was sometimes called "Firmum by the sea" as it was a coastal city. Several battles took place near Firmum during the Social War.

Genua—The capital city of Roman Liguria. It was originally destroyed by the Carthaginians during the Second Punic War but was rebuilt and received municipal rights from the Romans following the destruction of Carthage.

Herculaneum—a city in Campania, near Pompeii. It was either taken quickly by the rebels or joined willingly after the onset of the war.

Italic League—The name for the fledgling nation of Italian tribes who were united against Rome. Their aims were likely on achieving the citizenship, at least originally, but after the onset of the war, the Italic League likely sought to destroy Rome and replace her entirely.

Italica—*see* **Corfinium**

Lusitani—The Lusitanians were a collection of tribes native to Hispania that fought many wars against Rome. Although the most notable Lusitanian general, Viriathus, was betrayed and assassinated in the mid-second century BC, the Lusitani continued to oppose Rome.

Mutina—A city in northern Italy, which was made a Roman colony in 183 BC. It served as a citadel throughout several wars, as its high walls were difficult to penetrate.

Numidia—An ancient kingdom comprising much of northern Africa. Gaius Marius and Lucius Cornelius Sulla both earned a great deal of prestige for their parts in defeating the Numidian king Jugurtha. The notorious cavalry of Numidia thereafter served Rome in battle.

Nursia—Sertorius's home, located in the Apennine Mountains and within the Sabine tribes. It was famous for turnips and little else until Sertorius came along.

Pompeii—A city located in Campania, Pompeii joined the rebellion soon after the Social War began. Pompeii had a large port that was very important during the war.

Salernum—A city located in Campania, Salernum fell to the Samnite armies under the command of Papius Mutilus soon after the onset of the Social War.

Stabiae—A city located in Campania, Stabiae was quickly captured by the Samnite armies under the command of Papius Mutilus soon after the onset of the Social War. Like Pompeii, it was a port city and therefore of strategic value to both the Romans and the Italic League throughout the war.

ACKNOWLEDGMENTS

First, I must thank my wife. Life has thrown a lot our way during the time I wrote *Wolf at the Gates*, and without her, this book wouldn't have been completed. Your advice, encouragement, and support mean more to me than you'll ever know. In Quintus' love for Arrea, I try to reflect a fraction of the love I have for you, sweetheart—but I could never truly articulate it. Thank you for everything.

My children have been a constant source of joy throughout this time. Even on the hardest days, they are my *why*. And when I desperately need something to pull me back from Ancient Rome, they are there to bring me home. Mila, this book is for you. I am so proud of you, and I'm so proud to be your 'B'. When I was your age, I dreamed of being an author, and through hard work and the grace of God, I'm now able to write books like this. Always follow your dreams. You're going to accomplish amazing things in this world, and I'll be here to support you every step of the way.

I'd also like to thank the many historians who've made this work possible. There are too many to name, but specifically the works of Plutarch, Philip O. Spann, Philip Matyszak, G.P. Baker, Arthur Keaveney, and Adrienne Mayor have helped illuminate the world of Sertorius, Sulla, and Mithridates. Without the work of these great historians—both ancient and modern—my stories would lack substance and depth. I'm devoted to honoring the past by remaining as true to history as possible.

Next, my team of editors deserves a special thank you. Without them, this book wouldn't exist. Your passion for these stories rivals my own, and I can't tell you how much that means to me.

Susan Cornell, you're my front line of defense. Without you, I shudder to think about the 1-star reviews that would've flown in for those pesky errors.

Rebecca Henderson, thank you for going above and beyond—and for working so diligently to help me meet my deadlines.

And finally, thank you, Jayme Davis. I suppose giving me life and raising me deserves its own acknowledgement, but I want to specifically thank you for your work on this book. How have I *not* asked you to proofread before?! You are so gifted, Mom. Several mistakes would've been published without your help, and I can't thank you enough. Oh, and also—I love you.

Now I must thank the Legion. You are my tribe. Thank you for joining up, for your interest in hearing about my writing, for reading, and for all your encouragement over the past eight years. I may offer free eBooks, maps, glossaries, family trees, and more... but I can never truly reciprocate how much you've given me. On my toughest days—when the blinking cursor on a blank screen stares back at me menacingly—I think about you. Your support gives me the courage to push on.

For those of you who haven't joined the Legion, we'd love to have you. Just head over to my website. We're building an awesome community of readers who love history and great stories.

Finally, I'd like to thank you—the reader. I know life demands so much from you. I'm sure you're busy. I'm sure there are other ways you could spend eight hours of your time. I can't thank you enough for giving my books a chance. I hope you found this time well spent, and that you enjoyed the journey. I'll continue working as diligently as I can to write stories you'll love.

 If you have questions, criticisms, or suggestions, please feel free to email me. If not for your support, I wouldn't be able to live out my childhood dream of telling stories.

Keep Fighting,
Vincent B. Davis II
09/23/2025

ABOUT VINCENT

Vincent B. Davis II writes historical fiction books to keep the past alive through the power of storytelling. He is also an entrepreneur, speaker, and veteran who is a proud graduate of East Tennessee State University and was honorably discharged from the US Army in 2022. Armed with a pen and an entrepreneurial spirit, Vincent quit his day job and decided it was as good a time as any to follow his dream. He's since published several historical fiction novels, most of which have become Amazon International Best Sellers.

When Vincent isn't writing stories and traveling back through history, he enjoys the present with his wife and their three little legionaries, their two rescued pups, and two kittens. Vincent is also a devoted and depressed Carolina Panthers fan.

Join Vincent in celebrating the past through the pages of his books. His newsletter, The Legion, is more than just another author email list. It's a community of readers who enjoy free additional content to enhance their reading experience—Maps, family trees, free eBooks, and more. You can join the community and snag your freebies at vincentbdavisii.com.

www.ingramcontent.com/pod-product-compliance
Lightning Source LLC
Chambersburg PA
CBHW060223030726
47499CB00004B/1163

9781965288016